*The Potter's Lady*

# Books by Judith Miller

*The Carousel Painter*

BELLS OF LOWELL*
*Daughter of the Loom* • *A Fragile Design*
*These Tangled Threads*

LIGHTS OF LOWELL*
*A Tapestry of Hope* • *A Love Woven True*
*The Pattern of Her Heart*

POSTCARDS FROM PULLMAN
*In the Company of Secrets*
*Whispers Along the Rails* • *An Uncertain Dream*

THE BROADMOOR LEGACY*
*A Daughter's Inheritance*
*An Unexpected Love* • *A Surrendered Heart*

DAUGHTERS OF AMANA
*Somewhere to Belong* • *More Than Words*
*A Bond Never Broken*

BRIDAL VEIL ISLAND*
*To Have and To Hold* • *To Love and Cherish*
*To Honor and Trust*

HOME TO AMANA
*A Hidden Truth* • *A Simple Change* • *A Shining Light*

REFINED BY LOVE
*The Brickmaker's Bride*
*The Potter's Lady*

*www.judithmccoymiller.com*

*with Tracie Peterson

· · · REFINED BY LOVE · · ·

# The Potter's Lady

# JUDITH MILLER

## BETHANYHOUSE

a division of Baker Publishing Group
Minneapolis, Minnesota

Published by Bethany House Publishers
11400 Hampshire Avenue South
Bloomington, Minnesota 55438
www.bethanyhouse.com

Bethany House Publishers is a division of
Baker Publishing Group, Grand Rapids, Michigan

Printed in the United States of America

Library of Congress Cataloging-in-Publication Data
Miller, Judith.
        The potter's lady / Judith Miller.
            pages ; cm
        Summary: "Rose McKay has just graduated from the Philadelphia School
    of Design for Women and is now making every effort to succeed in the pottery
    business in post-Civil War West Virginia, including taking advice from her
    handsome competitor—but has she put her trust in the wrong man?"—Pro-
    vided by publisher.
        ISBN 978-0-7642-1256-7 (softcover)
        1. Young women—West Virginia—Fiction. 2. Pottery, American—West
    Virginia—19th century—Fiction. 3. West Virginia—Social life and cus-
    toms—1865-1918—Fiction. I. Title.
    PS3613.C3858P68  2015
    813'.6—dc23                                                          2014047435

Scripture quotations are taken from the King James Version of the Bible.

Cover design by LOOK Design Studio
Cover photography by Aimee Christenson

Author is represented by Books & Such Literary Agency

15   16   17   18   19   20   21         7   6   5   4   3   2   1

To Rosie Curran-Benger,
my dear friend Down Under.

*But now, O Lord, thou art our father;*
*we are the clay, and thou our potter;*
*and we all are the work of thy hand.*

*Isaiah 64:8*

# Chapter 1

*Philadelphia, Pennsylvania*
*May 1872*

Rose McKay stared out the narrow window of the Philadelphia School of Design for Women. Her gaze darted between passing buggies and wagons before perusing the pedestrians traversing Broad Street. Where was Ewan? Her brother said he'd be here by two o'clock. If he didn't hurry, they'd miss their train.

"Why don't you sit down, Rose? Staring out the window isn't going to make your brother appear any sooner." Mrs. Fisk, director of the school, nodded toward one of the perfectly arranged chairs in the sitting room.

Inimitable paintings and sculptures, all of them fashioned by students who had attended the school, adorned the entry hall and sitting room where visitors were received. To have a creation displayed in either place was considered the most prestigious award any student could achieve. Each year, one student received the Excellence in Design Award. Along with the plaque came the honor of having one piece of work on display. Rose's heart warmed at the thought of her own work joining those of the previous students. This year, she had been the award recipient. Though Rose had been honored by the announcement, her fellow students had resented the choice and had been quick to make their feelings known to her.

Rose had never been truly accepted into their ranks. She was, after all, an Irish immigrant who never would have gained entry into the prestigious school had it not been for the influence and money of Frances Woodfield, Ewan McKay's mother-in-law. Still, the harsh comments of the other students when she'd received the commendation, as well as during the remainder of the year, had been painful.

"I do wish the upholstery had been completed prior to your departure, Rose. You must return so that you can see the divan when it is completed." Mrs. Fisk motioned to the west side of the room. "We'll place it over there in front of the fireplace, where it can be seen to full advantage."

The hours Rose had devoted to designing the divan's upholstery had been innumerable, and seeing the completed project would have given her great joy. Yet not enough to remain any longer than required. Although she'd done her best to remain cheerful and kind during her two years at the school, she no longer wished to endure the pranks and unkind remarks of the young women here who considered themselves to be above her. Returning home would relieve her of future ridicule.

She rubbed her arms and shuddered as she recalled the spring dance. Rose had never had an escort for any of the parties or dances at the school, a matter Melissa Bonsart insisted upon resolving by arranging an escort for Rose. When Rose didn't immediately accept the secondhand invitation, Melissa had resorted to an angry diatribe, stating the young man, Matthew Skilling, was from a fine Philadelphia family. When Rose could listen to no more, she'd relented and fallen headfirst into Melissa's trap. A trap that had served to undermine any remaining trust she'd had in these false friends.

Raucous laughter and unkind remarks had followed the arrival of an Irish lad dressed in tattered clothing. When Rose discovered the girls had convinced the young Irishman he would be welcomed at their party, Rose's anger swelled. There had been no "Matthew Skilling." Not only had they embarrassed her, they'd also humiliated the young man who, like Rose, had done nothing to deserve their callous treatment.

Truth be told, the conniving behavior of those girls reminded Rose of her Aunt Margaret. Their meanspirited actions had awakened Rose to a sad understanding: There were far too many scheming people willing to abuse others for their own pleasure, power, or greed.

"Did you hear me, Rose?" Mrs. Fisk nodded toward the fireplace.

"Yes. I think you've chosen a perfect space. If I ever return to Philadelphia, I'll be sure to stop here first." Rose, however, secretly doubted she'd ever return to Philadelphia. Though she'd received an excellent education at the design school, the young women she'd encountered during the past two years had imbued Rose with a distinct distaste for Philadelphia and its social mores.

"I'm saddened to see my very best student returning to the hills of West Virginia, where I doubt you'll ever use your education. I want you to write to me if you're unable to find employment that satisfies your creativity."

Rose strained forward for a glimpse outside. "Thank you, Mrs. Fisk. I'll keep your offer in mind, but . . . Ewan's arrived!" She jumped up from her chair and rushed toward the front door. Before he had an opportunity to knock, Rose yanked open the door. "I thought you would never get here. What kept you? We'll have to hurry, or we'll miss our train."

Ewan arched his brows and chuckled. "Good afternoon to you, too, Rose." The scent of blooming lilacs wafted through the open door. Had it not been for the long, cold winter, the two flowering bushes outside the front entrance would have bloomed six weeks ago.

Rose grinned and took a backward step to allow her brother entry. "I'm sorry. I didn't mean to assail you the moment you arrived, but I've been worried, and I missed you so." She turned to look at the grandfather clock that stood sentry in the hallway. "We could miss the train if we don't hurry."

"We have plenty of time, Rose." Ewan stepped inside and wrapped her in a warm embrace. "I didn't realize you were so eager to leave."

"Mr. McKay. It's good to see you. Your sister has been quite worried about you." Mrs. Fisk stepped closer. "I've tried my best to convince Rose she should remain in Philadelphia, but she seems to think a return to West Virginia is best." A frown creased the older woman's forehead. "I truly do not believe she'll be able to find employment that will lend her an opportunity to use the skills she's acquired." She shook her head and *tsked*. "Such a shame to have talent waste away, don't you agree, Mr. McKay?"

"Aye, 'tis not good to squander a God-given talent, but I think Rose will discover a way to use her abilities." His lips tilted in a grin. "Civilization does not begin and end in Philadelphia, Mrs. Fisk."

"Of course not. I didn't mean to imply . . ."

Ewan held up his hand. "No offense taken, Mrs. Fisk. Just like the rest of the family, I know Rose intends to find a way to use her talents. Should she have any trouble, I'm sure she'll set pen to paper and let you know."

Rose tugged on Ewan's arm. "We shouldn't keep the carriage waiting, Ewan. I had my baggage delivered to the train station, but we'll need to make certain it arrived safely and purchase our tickets."

Ewan patted the pocket of his jacket. "I've already purchased the tickets." He glanced toward the stairs. "Do you have no friends you wish to offer a final good-bye?"

Rose shook her head. "No. I'm ready to be on my way."

Gray skies loomed overhead as Rose looped arms with her brother and descended the front steps of the three-storied brick building. She was thankful for the education she'd received inside the large second-floor classrooms but glad she would no longer inhabit one of the third-floor sleeping rooms.

Rose lifted her gaze to the third floor. Several of her former classmates stood at one of the bedroom windows. They were laughing and pointing toward the carriage. She hoped their laughter wasn't a signal they'd played some final trick she hadn't yet discovered.

As her brother assisted her into the carriage, Rose glanced over her shoulder. "How are Laura and the girls? I'm eager to see all of them." Rose had been determined to pursue further education, but being away from her younger twin sisters, Ainslee and Adaira, had proven more difficult than she'd anticipated. And she'd sorely missed Tessa, Ewan and Laura's young daughter. She was eager to reunite with all of them.

"They are doing quite well and are every bit as impatient to see you." Her brother maintained a close gaze on her as they rode to the train station. His brow creased with concern as he reached for her hand. "You don't seem yourself, Rose. You've said no more than a few words since we left the school. Is there something bothering you that you have not told me about?"

"Nay. I'm pleased to be going home, but I am a little worried about locating employment." She tipped her head to the side and peeked from beneath her bonnet. "And before you tell me to leave my cares at the Lord's footstool, I've already tried. I'm not as successful as you when it comes to turning loose of my worries."

"I'll not be finding fault with you, for I've had a wee bit of trouble putting my own advice into practice these past weeks."

Rose turned to face her brother. "What kind of trouble? Nothing with Laura or the girls, is it?"

"Nay. As I said, they're all fine. I'll tell you later. We'll have more than enough time to talk on the train." He glanced out the carriage window. "I was hoping to have a bit of time to visit Fairmount Park before we boarded the train. Mrs. Woodfield said it would be quite lovely this time of year. Have you been there?"

"Aye. She's right. The park is beautiful. I visited last spring but haven't been there since then."

Her thoughts rushed back to the visit that had proved to be an opportunity for her classmates to inflict another of their many pranks. They had completed their tour of the zoological gardens, and Mrs. Fisk agreed they could go to the small bridge that crossed the brook and then meet her at the pavilion for lunch. Rose still didn't know who had pushed her into the brook, but the visit had been cut short because of the incident. Mrs. Fisk had been unhappy. After all, she'd reminded them they shouldn't go near the water. Rose didn't reveal she'd been pushed. She knew it would only cause retribution.

"Then I'm doubly sorry we do not have time. I'm sure you would have enjoyed another visit."

Rose shook her head. "I've had my fill of city life, Ewan. I'm eager to return to Bartlett."

They had been on the train for more than an hour, yet Ewan hadn't decided how to tell Rose about the troubles at home. This should be a happy time for her. She'd finished school and was returning to her family. At least that's what she believed. Before they stopped in Grafton to tour at least two businesses, he'd be forced to tell her the truth.

When she glanced at him, he offered her a weak smile. It was the most he could muster right now.

"Tell me what has happened at home these past weeks, Ewan."

He massaged his forehead and pretended to concentrate. "Let me think. What has been happening?" He inhaled a deep breath. "Laura, her mother, and the twins have been busy planning a party to celebrate all your accomplishments. From what I've been told, it is going to be the best party of the season, maybe the entire year. The invitations have gone out, and the response has been superb. Those are Laura's words, not mine." He forced a smile. "Laura and her mother have been busy planning the decorations and creating menus."

Rose sighed. "You know it isn't the party I'm asking about. I'm not a child. There's something more that's causing the worry I see in your eyes."

Ewan leaned against the hard wooden seat, wishing he'd paid the extra price to ride in one of the expensive coaches with padded seating. When they arrived at their next stop, he'd see if tickets were available for one of those more comfortable coaches. Perhaps he shouldn't spend the money right now, but if he was going to be alert when they arrived in Grafton, he'd need some rest.

After inhaling a deep breath, Ewan grasped his sister's hand. "Aunt Margaret has become more difficult to deal with now that

Uncle Hugh has died." Ewan rubbed his jaw. "She has forced me out of the brickyard."

Rose's mouth dropped open. "What? How? You're a partner."

Ewan shook his head. "I'm not a partner. Uncle Hugh promised to draw up the agreement after Laura and I married, but since his mind was gone after he suffered the high fever and apoplexy, the papers were never signed."

The hard wood seemed to poke Ewan's bones, and he shifted sideways as the train chugged onward. Rose's eyes shone with fear, or was it anger? Back when Hugh's illness had rendered him helpless as a bairn, Ewan decided the girls should not be drawn into the problems regarding the brickyard. Laura and her mother had agreed. But now, with Aunt Margaret's recent decision looming over him, he had no choice.

"Why didn't I know all of this before now?" Rose's lips tightened into a hard line.

Ewan offered a brief account of how he'd come to his decision, but her shoulders stiffened when he said he hadn't wanted to burden her or the twins.

When Rose didn't respond, he sighed. "Can't ya see, Rose? 'Twould have served no purpose."

"I'm not a child. You lump me together with the twins and act as though I'm too young to understand anything."

"That's not true, Rose. You were busy with schoolwork, and we didn't want to distract you." He hesitated a moment. "I think that's the word Laura used." He nodded. "Aye. We should not distract you from your studies." Deciding it might be best to take the offensive, he folded his arms across his chest. "Had you known about this, what would you have done?"

She was silent for a moment. "I would have come home."

"That is exactly what we thought you would do. We agreed

you were too close to finishing at the design school, and we did not want you to quit."

Rose appeared sullen for several minutes, and Ewan decided it was best to let her absorb the news. If he'd only been more observant, Margaret's motives would have been clear months ago. Why had he been so unmindful when, on her own, she'd hired Andrew Culligan? Never before had she hired any worker for the brickyard. She said he'd been hired because of his knowledge and as a favor to a friend, but what friend? Margaret's friends were far and few between, and Ewan had never before heard any mention of a Culligan family. But he'd simply accepted her word and put the man to work operating the pug mill, the horse-drawn machine where they tempered the clay.

Before long, Margaret had reassigned Culligan to work the VerValen machinery. She'd insisted he was far too experienced to be working the pug mill. And she'd been correct. The man knew as much about brickmaking as Ewan, although the two men disagreed about quality. Ewan insisted upon proper mixing, drying, and firing to ensure the finest bricks Crothers & McKay could produce, while Mr. Culligan was prone to taking shortcuts to increase profits. The idea of those extra earnings pleased Aunt Margaret more than the production of first-rate bricks.

When Aunt Margaret had brought Mr. Culligan to the office a few weeks ago and instructed Ewan to explain all of the contracts, bookkeeping, and time records, he'd advised against the idea. "You don't know this man well at all. You shouldn't give him access to all of our financial records, Aunt Margaret. It isn't wise."

She had vehemently argued that someone else should understand the business aspects of the C&M Brickyard. After all, what if Ewan should suffer the same fate as Hugh? What would she do then? There would be no one to help her through the muddle. Ewan had considered telling her that Laura could help.

They had purchased the brickyard from Laura's mother, and it had been Laura who had taught Ewan how to keep the books and read contracts. And it had been Laura and Mrs. Woodfield who had introduced Ewan to the men who eventually placed large orders for C&M bricks. However, any mention of Laura's name to his aunt would only create further hostility.

Since Uncle Hugh's illness, Laura had refrained from visiting the brickyard. Aunt Margaret continued to regard Laura as an interloper who'd married Ewan with the idea of one day having the brickyard returned to the Woodfield name. Of course, this assumption was without merit, yet convincing Aunt Margaret had proved impossible.

"I suppose you were right not to tell me right away. There's nothing I could have done, but I wish there was some way I could help." Rose offered him a meager smile, but the usual shimmer had disappeared from her blue eyes.

He reached for her hand and gave it a slight squeeze. "Before this journey ends, you may be able to help me a great deal. Laura's mother is going to loan me money to purchase a new business, so there are some serious decisions to be made. But right now, we must disembark and catch our train to Grafton to tour one of them."

# Chapter 2

*Grafton, West Virginia*

Rylan Campbell bent his head low against the beating wind. A flash of lightning and a rumble overhead signaled a spring storm would soon arrive in Grafton, West Virginia. Several fat raindrops splattered the brim of his cap as he crossed the railroad tracks that fronted the Bancock Pottery Works. Once inside, he pulled off his cap and slapped it against his pant leg. As he continued toward the office, he greeted several of the jiggermen, turners, and handlers who'd arrived only moments earlier.

Over the years, Rylan had worked with most of them, at least for short periods of time. There had been longer training periods in some areas, but once he'd turned sixteen, his stints had been primarily to learn the intricacies of properly performing each task. He'd been assigned to some areas more than once, mostly when they ran short of help, but once a new worker was hired, he'd be transferred to learn another phase of the business.

The owner, Mr. Bancock, had taken a liking to Rylan, and

because the young man was eager to learn, promotions had been swift and frequent. Though none of the other workers had exhibited any resentment toward him, there were some who thought he lacked the experience to become Mr. Bancock's assistant.

He'd begun work at the pottery when he was only twelve years old and had never opened his lunch pail anywhere else. But even Rylan understood that most anyone would consider a man of twenty and four too young to oversee a pottery works. However, he'd done so when Mr. Bancock had fallen ill last year, and he'd won the respect of his fellow workers. When Mr. Bancock returned, he'd educated Rylan in the business aspects of the pottery. He'd encouraged the young man to learn about contracts, shipping schedules, wages, and hiring employees. And when he'd completed his training, the older man declared him talented enough to own his own pottery works one day.

Rylan had nodded and smiled at the adulation, but he knew a poor Irishman would never have enough money to own a pottery works, and so did Mr. Bancock. Still, the two of them pretended that maybe one day it would happen. Maybe one day Rylan would come into enough money to purchase a pottery of his own. And maybe one day pigs would fly.

Robert Wilson, one of the talented jiggermen and foreman in the clay shop, hastened to meet Rylan's stride. "I hear we're to have some visitors today."

Rylan nodded. "That's my understanding." No use denying the truth, though he wondered who had disclosed the information. Other than the overseers of each work area, Mr. Bancock and Rylan hadn't informed anyone else of the impending visit. It seemed one of the overseers had loose lips, and the news had spread through the pottery like wildfire on a hot summer day.

"Terrible shame Mr. Bancock's illness is gonna cause him

to sell the business. What's that gonna mean for all of us?" He arched his bushy eyebrows. "Think we should be looking for jobs at one of the other potteries? I'm not eager to move, but I hear tell there's always openings at the potteries in East Liverpool."

"Now why would ya even be considering such a thing, Robert? 'Twould be foolish to head off to Ohio when there's no reason. Having someone come to take a look around means nothing more than that. Who's to say if he even has the money to buy the place?" Neither Rylan nor Mr. Bancock wanted any of the employees to quit their jobs. They needed every one of them to keep the place operating. Giving Robert a friendly slap on the shoulder, Rylan gave a wink. "Besides, any owner, whether Mr. Bancock or someone new, would count his blessings to have a jiggerman fine as yerself working for him."

"That may be true, but who's to say for certain what any new owner might do?" Rylan's compliment hadn't satisfied Robert in the least. He'd heard his abilities touted by many through the years, so Rylan's words hadn't eased the man's concern. "I need to put food on the table for my family, so it would be good to know if Mr. Bancock plans to be fair and honest with those of us who have been loyal to him."

The moment they stepped inside, the gathering clouds burst forth. Sheets of rain pummeled the expanse between the railroad tracks and the front door and pounded on the windows. The rain would be welcomed by the steamer captains who traversed the Tygart River. With less snow than usual last winter, the thaw hadn't provided enough runoff to raise the Tygart to the navigable levels they preferred. The rain would also be appreciated by Mr. Bancock and all the other businesses that shipped their goods by steamer.

Bancock Pottery was situated on acreage between the railroad tracks and the Tygart River. The location was one of the pottery works' greatest assets. If the river wasn't navigable due to winter's freeze or summer's lack of rain, Bancock Pottery could still ship pottery by rail.

"Mr. Bancock has never been anything but forthright with his workers. I don't think you need to be doubting him now, Robert."

Rylan had spoken the truth, but he didn't add the fact that there had been few contracts signed over the past months, a happenstance that made both Mr. Bancock and Rylan nervous. This was the month when most of their buyers either sent word or arrived at the pottery to negotiate what they would purchase throughout the coming year. On several occasions, Mr. Bancock had voiced concern that some of their customers had learned of his illness and were contracting with other potteries. While Rylan shared that concern, he also feared their most experienced workers would soon locate other jobs. If that should happen, Bancock Pottery would quickly revert from a valuable asset to a worthless liability. Such a catastrophe would place all of them in dire straits.

"What time are these folks coming to see the place?"

Robert's question forced Rylan back to the present. "I don't know for sure. Last I heard, they were to arrive on the train last evening and come here sometime today. I don't know if they've yet arrived in town."

"What do ya know about them?" Robert leaned close and nudged Rylan. "I know Mr. Bancock's told ya a thing or two. Wouldn't hurt none to share it with those of us that's doing the actual work. Might relieve some of the worry most of us been feeling."

"Mr. Bancock's the one you should be asking, not me." Rylan stepped toward the office. Robert had a way of bantering until he managed to wheedle whatever information he wanted.

Rylan exhaled a sigh when the office door opened and Mr. Bancock strode toward them. He nodded at the two of them and offered a cheery greeting before resting his hand on Rylan's shoulder. "I need you in the office to help me prepare for my meeting with Mr. McKay."

Robert shifted his lunch pail to his left hand. "McKay? Is that the name of the fellow who's going to buy the pottery, Mr. Bancock?"

Mr. Bancock's shoulders stiffened. "I don't know who told you Mr. McKay is going to purchase the business." The owner directed a sideways glance at Rylan. "Mr. McKay is merely coming to look around and see if Bancock Pottery is a business that might interest him." Mr. Bancock's lips drooped into a frown. "I've learned word has spread from the slip house to the warehouse that the pottery is up for sale. However, the business has not yet sold, so I would consider it a favor if you would try to put a stop to the rumors circulating among the workers."

"I'll do what I can." Obviously embarrassed by Mr. Bancock's comments, Robert shifted his gaze toward the clay shop. "I should get to my work."

Before he could depart, Mr. Bancock stilled him with a touch of his hand. "When a contract has been signed, I will person-ally announce the change of ownership to all of the employees and answer any questions that may arise. Please pass along that message, Robert."

Robert nodded and, with his lunch pail swinging from one hand, rushed toward the clay shop. Mr. Bancock turned to Rylan. "I don't know when Mr. McKay plans to arrive, and I don't know what he may ask to review, so we must have all of our paper work arranged so that it will be easily retrieved if need be."

Rylan walked alongside the owner. "Are you thinkin' I'm the

one who told about the visit today? Because if you are, I want ya to know it wasn't me. I didn't say a word, Mr. Bancock."

The older man glanced at him and gave a slight nod. "I figured it was one of the overseers. Just the same, I'm glad to know it wasn't you. I suppose it's just as well the employees know a prospective buyer is visiting today. Mr. McKay will expect to tour the entire pottery, and it wouldn't take long before the workers put two and two together."

Once inside the office, Rylan set to work arranging the contracts by year. The stack for the current year looked mighty slim compared to those for previous years. Rylan stood back and glanced at the mounds. There had been a steady decline over the past three years, but this year was downright meager. Any additional contracts would be for small, unexpected orders, but maybe they could land an unforeseen contract that would provide a windfall of sorts.

When Mr. Bancock turned to examine his work, Rylan nodded toward the end of the row. "This may not be the best way to arrange the contracts. If he's any kind of a businessman, it won't take but one glance to realize the business has been falling off over the past few years."

"Leave them as they are, Rylan. I won't hoodwink Mr. McKay or any other man who may consider the purchase of this business. I've always been upright in my dealings, and I don't intend to change that now."

The decision didn't surprise Rylan. Mr. Bancock was a man who did his best to live by the teachings of the Bible. He wasn't one to preach at folks, but whenever he had a chance to reveal his faith to others, he didn't hesitate. It was Mr. Bancock who'd convinced Rylan to attend church with him on Sunday mornings, and it was Mr. Bancock who'd given him a Bible with lots of underlined passages. He'd said those passages would help

Rylan deal with the difficulties of life. And they had. Lately, Rylan had been clinging to many of those passages, but fear still ran deep.

What if the new owner decided to dismiss him? Would he be able to find employment in another pottery? He possessed a variety of skills and had trained for a time in each area of the pottery, but he wasn't a talented jiggerman like Robert, who could find work in most any pottery.

Locating an opening for an owner's assistant wouldn't be easy, especially for a man his age. Rylan surveyed the stacks one final time and quietly reminded himself of some verses he'd read in Luke. If God cared for the fowl of the air and the lilies of the field, wouldn't He care enough to provide Rylan with a job? The thought offered a modicum of comfort as he turned away from the table and removed the ledgers from the office safe.

At noon Mr. Bancock decided to skip his usual lunch at the restaurant near the train station. Worried that Mr. McKay might appear while he was away, the owner asked Rylan to fetch him a sandwich. By two o'clock, Mr. Bancock had walked to the front door more times than Rylan could count.

Mr. Bancock dropped into his chair and rested his chin in his palm. "Maybe there was some confusion about what day he was scheduled to arrive. Or maybe he missed his train." He murmured several other possibilities, but his mutterings were mere speculation. "Don't know why I'm worrying so much when I know the future of this pottery is in God's hands. Just seems hard to always keep that thought clear in my head."

"I could go over to the hotel and see if Mr. McKay has registered." Rylan wanted to do something to help ease the older man's anxiety, something tangible that might give Mr. Bancock a little much-needed information.

The older man massaged his forehead and stared toward the

door. "I think that is a good idea, Rylan. Don't tell the hotel clerk your name or where you work. I wouldn't want him to tell Mr. McKay I was inquiring about him. Wouldn't want him to think I'm too eager."

Rylan nodded. He doubted Mr. McKay would jump to such a hasty conclusion, but he would heed his employer's admonition. Grabbing his cap, Rylan headed for the door and walked outside. After depositing a half-inch of rain, the thunderstorm had passed. Stepping off the boardwalk, Rylan lifted his nose and inhaled the fresh scent of spring. The earlier gloom had departed, and cerulean skies now framed the jagged mountains. Careful to avoid the muddy roadway, he walked the short distance to the railroad tracks.

The pottery sat across the tracks and about a half mile south of the hotel on a triangular plot of ground along the western edge of the Grafton rail yard. The B&O Railroad owned the hotel, so the hotel lobby also served as a depot station. Rylan stopped outside the hotel and cleaned the mud from his shoes on the cast-iron boot scraper. The hotel clerk made certain the lobby's decorative tile floor remained spotless, and he looked askew at those who failed to clean their boots before entering.

Stepping inside, Rylan gazed around the expansive room. A train had arrived not long ago, and the lobby hummed with activity. Along the east side of the combination lobby and depot, there were several wooden benches, which were occupied by passengers awaiting the arrival or departure of a train.

Printed signs advising gentlemen that they should not expectorate on the floor hung above metal spittoons that had been strategically placed throughout the room. A small ticket office was situated to the rear of the benches. On the west side of the room, a glass-enclosed cabinet displayed boxes of cigars and sundry items that might interest travelers or hotel guests.

Beyond the display of goods was a walnut registration desk in the shape of a half moon that wrapped around the clerk like a protective shield.

With his gaze set upon the hotel clerk, Rylan strode past the wooden benches and stopped at the desk. The clerk was a tall man with a neatly trimmed mustache and balding pate. He lifted his long narrow nose high in the air and pinned Rylan with a hard stare. "Train tickets are purchased at the desk across the lobby."

"Aye, but I'm not here for a train ticket. I'm wonderin' if you'd be so kind as to check your book and tell me if a Mr. McKay has registered." Rylan forced an amiable smile. "If all went as planned, Mr. McKay should have arrived last evening."

The clerk shook his head. "We aren't in the habit of giving out the names of guests registered in our hotel, young man." He hiked his nose an inch higher. "Whether Mr. McKay has registered with us or not is not a matter we would discuss with—"

"Did I hear someone asking for Mr. McKay?"

Rylan spun on his heel. "Aye, that you did. Are you Mr. McKay?"

"I am. And who might I be talking to?"

Rylan's gaze traveled between a man with chestnut brown hair and a young woman with deep blue eyes and a beautiful smile who stood at his side. Was the lovely young lady his wife?

He tore his gaze away and faced Mr. McKay. "My name is Rylan Campbell, sir." He hesitated a moment, uncertain what he should do. At this point, there was no way he could heed Mr. Bancock's order. Mr. McKay was staring at him with arched brows, obviously expecting to know more than his name. Rylan cleared his throat. "I work at Bancock Pottery."

A flash of recognition shone in Mr. McKay's eyes, and he gave a quick nod. "And you've come to see what time I plan to visit the pottery, am I right?"

"Aye. Right you are."

Mr. McKay rested a hand on Rylan's shoulder. "I'm glad you appeared, Rylan. My sister and I were planning to leave for our visit with Mr. Bancock right now. 'Twould be appreciated if you'd show us the way."

The young woman nudged her brother's arm. "And may I present my sister, Rose McKay. She's quite eager to see the pottery."

"Nice to meet you, miss." Rylan tried to keep from staring, but her eyes lured him in like a magnet. His sister. Not his wife. Relief washed over him, but he'd better focus on the job at hand and not the girl in front of him.

He turned toward Mr. McKay. "I hope you won't be disappointed. It's a fine pottery. I've worked there since I was a young lad. And you won't find a more honest man or better employer than Mr. Bancock." He needed to quit rambling. Mr. Bancock wouldn't approve.

"That's good to know. I hope our late arrival hasn't caused undue concern for Mr. Bancock, but we'd also scheduled a visit to the brickyard, and the rain caused a delay of our tour of the yard."

They stepped outside, and Rylan directed them down the wood sidewalk, looking for the best place for Miss McKay to cross the railroad tracks without stepping in too much mud. All the while, his mind was racing. Why had they been at the brickyard? Rylan had heard Mr. Trent was hoping to sell the place.

He sucked in a gulp of air. "Were you looking to buy Mr. Trent's brickyard, Mr. McKay?"

Rylan held his breath as he awaited the answer. Surely if Mr. Bancock knew Mr. McKay was visiting other companies in the area, he would have told Rylan. No doubt Mr. Bancock would find the news distressing.

"I'm giving it some consideration. My family and I currently live in Bartlett where I operated a brickyard. Before that I worked in many a brickyard in Northern Ireland." He offered his arm to his sister as they started across the railroad tracks. "What about you, Mr. Campbell? Is it Ireland you call home, as well?"

Rylan shook his head. "Nay. I consider this country my home, though my parents came here from Ireland. They crossed the ocean when I was a wee babe. From what they tell me, I nearly died on the ship, but I don't remember any of it."

"Well, glad I am that you arrived safely. Too many of our countrymen perished on those ships."

As they continued toward the pottery, Rylan's thoughts remained fixed on the knowledge that the acquisition of the Bancock Pottery was much more tenuous than he had imagined.

# Chapter 3

Upon Rylan's return, Mr. Bancock's lips formed a deep frown. The pottery owner hadn't wanted Mr. McKay to know he was eager to sell. Seeing the visitor alongside Rylan meant only one thing to Mr. Bancock: He'd lost his ability to bargain from a position of power. Rylan couldn't dispute the fact that Mr. Bancock might have more difficulty negotiating now. But that difficulty would arise more from Mr. McKay's interest in the Trent Brick Works than Rylan's chance meeting with Ewan and Rose McKay.

As Rylan and the McKays stepped inside, Mr. Bancock forced a smile. Rylan made brief introductions, and his employer extended his hand to Mr. McKay and nodded at Rose. "Pleased to meet both of you and welcome to Bancock Pottery Works."

Rylan sighed with relief when Mr. McKay explained to Mr. Bancock how they'd met in the hotel lobby. "A fortunate coincidence that we would walk up just as young Mr. Campbell arrived."

"I'm pleased he was able to escort you." Mr. Bancock glanced toward the street. "This morning's rain left us with a great deal of mud." With his brows arched ever so slightly, Mr. Bancock directed a forgiving look at Rylan before returning his attention to Mr. McKay and his sister. "Would the two of you like to begin by reviewing the ledgers and contracts before touring the pottery, or is the opposite your preference?"

Ewan turned to his sister. "What do you say, Rose? A tour of the pottery or an examination of the books?"

Both Rylan and Mr. Bancock followed suit and directed their attention to the young woman. Rylan was pleased to see the sparkle of excitement in her eyes. He was certain they perfectly matched the deep blue glaze of their finest pottery.

Yet her excitement pleased him for other reasons, as well. He remembered his first visit to the pottery so many years ago when he'd been hired to help one of the turners, the journeymen who turned the cups and bowls on a horizontal lathe in the clay shop. He had been struck with unexpected exhilaration on that day.

Almost a third of the workers in the clay shop had been journeymen, but the rest were helpers—mostly young boys or women, anyone unskilled and willing to work for the meager wages paid by the journeymen so they could complete more pieces in a day. Many of the men had their wives and children work for them so they didn't have to pay a non-family member wages.

The turner, Joseph Priety, had hired and trained Rylan as a handler. The training had been brief, but once he'd gotten the knack of things, he'd been able to attach handles to hundreds of cups each day. Mr. Priety paid him forty cents a day, a sum Rylan had thought quite magnificent until he learned the other handlers were being paid ten cents more each day. That had been his first lesson in business, and he'd been learning ever since.

Rose looked up at her brother and grinned. "I'd prefer to see the pottery rather than the books, of course." She glanced at Mr.

Bancock. "I just completed my education at the Philadelphia School of Design for Women, and I had the opportunity to visit two potteries during my studies. I'm eager to see if your pottery is much the same." She let her gaze drift toward Rylan. "I believe those potteries were a bit larger than yours, Mr. Bancock."

The owner nodded. "What is most important is not the size of the business but the quality of the product."

"That's true, Mr. Bancock." She flashed him a smile. "I hope your artists create some of the same gilding and lovely hand-painted designs we examined in those potteries."

He motioned toward the door. "Follow me. We should begin at the slip house, since that is where the process begins."

Mr. McKay matched the older man's stride, leaving Rose to walk alongside Rylan. He hadn't expected her to come along to the slip house, but she appeared determined to be included. Snatches of Mr. McKay's conversation drifted on the afternoon breeze, and it didn't take long before Rylan realized Mr. McKay was explaining the reason for their delay.

When they stepped inside the slip house, Mr. Bancock waved to the supervisor. "These folks are here to tour the pottery. Why don't you explain the process?" Mr. Bancock stepped closer to Rylan while the supervisor detailed how the dry clay, flint, feldspar, and water were mixed together in a blunger to form liquid clay known as slip.

Rylan's employer leaned close to his ear. "Did you know Mr. McKay already visited the brickyard earlier today?"

Rylan nodded his head. "He told me at the hotel." A look of defeat shone in the old man's eyes. "He hasn't purchased the brickyard yet, so don't give up hope. I think his sister is more interested in the pottery."

Before Mr. Bancock could ask anything further, Mr. McKay looked in their direction. "Your process is somewhat different from the process we use for making bricks, but there are some similarities. I see you use a pug mill to work the clay."

Mr. Bancock nodded. "We do, but before we place the clay in the pug mill for kneading, the excess water must be strained in the filter press."

Rose wrapped her shawl tighter around her shoulders. No doubt she hoped to ward off the dampness that permeated the slip house. Her gaze darted around the room and settled on several burly men hefting huge rectangular blocks of clay across the room. When they thrust the large hunks of clay onto the wedging table, the crashing thud was so powerful, she took a backward step and bumped into Rylan.

Rylan grasped her shoulders as she struggled to gain her footing. He dropped his hold the moment she'd steadied herself. From the heightened color in her cheeks, he was certain of her embarrassment.

"I'm still startled when I come in here and the men make that first toss of the clay onto the wedging board." He hoped his words would ease the awkward moment.

The hint of a smile curved the corners of her mouth as she continued to watch the men work their clay. "Wedging reminds me of kneading bread." Her smile intensified. "Of course, the clay is much more difficult to work."

Rylan nodded and returned her smile. "I hope your bread would not be so heavy as those wedges of clay."

"I must admit that it has been a long time since I've made any bread. If I tried to knead and bake a loaf, it might turn out even heavier."

Her brother glanced over his shoulder when she chuckled. "Was there a joke I missed, Rose?"

She shook her head. "No, Ewan. I merely mentioned that kneading clay reminded me of making bread."

Although Mr. McKay's brows dipped and his eyes registered confusion, he didn't ask for further explanation. Instead, he returned his attention to the pottery owner. "Where next, Mr. Bancock?"

"The clay shop." Mr. Bancock directed them toward the brick building. Once inside, he opened his arms in a sweeping gesture. "This is the largest department of the pottery. You will see about a quarter of the pottery workers in here." He motioned Mr. McKay to one of the work stations, where the jiggermen and their helpers worked in harmonious movement. "About one-third of these workers are skilled."

Ewan moved beside one of the jiggermen and watched for a moment. Without looking up, the man nodded toward his machine. "I make seven-inch plates."

"And how many plates do you make in a day?" Ewan asked.

"On good days when my helpers are here, I can make fifty dozen a day." He pulled down the mold lever and swiped away the excess clay before dipping his hand in a pot of water. "There are jiggermen who may be faster, but no one can make a finer plate. We all take pride in our work, whether we're making cups, plates, or special orders for urns and vases." He spoke with a hint of bravado, almost as if he expected Ewan to challenge his worth.

Rose moved a bit closer to the owner. "Do you have difficulty maintaining workers, Mr. Bancock?" When he shook his head, she continued. "I heard this man say something about not being able to work at full capacity because his helpers aren't always here." Without waiting for his answer, Rose turned toward her brother. "We need to be certain we won't experience a shortage of workers."

Mr. Bancock cleared his throat. "To answer your question, Miss McKay, I have no greater difficulty maintaining employees than any other pottery. Or brickyard. As I mentioned before, the skilled workers hire and pay for their own helpers."

The jiggerman lifted the lever of his mold and, with both hands, removed the plate and placed it alongside several others on a board. "We hire young fellows to work in the batter-out and mold-runner jobs. They need to be strong and fast. But even with their youth, they tire out and take days off. Then we run behind. I can't fault them too much. I figure the mold-runners travel about fifteen miles a day, carrying wet or dry molds that can weigh between six and twelve pounds. And being a batter-out requires just as much vigor."

The jiggerman pointed to one of the young workers who placed a chunk of clay on the table and lifted a thick circular piece of plaster referred to as a bat. "That bat weighs near twenty pounds."

The muscles in the youthful worker's arms bulged beneath the rolled-up sleeves of his chambray shirt as he raised the bat over-head and slammed it onto the mound of clay. When the clay was properly prepared, the batter-out lifted the bat onto the mold.

Mr. Bancock nodded toward the boards where the jigger-man placed the wet plates. "During the course of the day, the batter-out also carries boards that weigh about fifty pounds to the finisher. He lifts at least a couple thousand pounds a day."

The jiggerman bobbed his head. "This here is brutal work. And well I should know. I did both of those jobs before finally becoming a jiggerman."

As they continued through the clay shop, Mr. Bancock stopped long enough to give them a brief description of the work. Rylan came alongside Rose when they neared the section where cups and bowls were produced. He folded his arms across his chest and tipped his head close to hers. "When I became a handler, I believed I had the most important job in the pottery."

He grinned down at her. "When I turned thirteen years old, I changed my mind."

Rose gave a slight shake of her head. "These children should be in school, not working alongside their parents or hired to help the skilled workers."

"That may be true, but any of these children will tell you they prefer food and a warm bed rather than school. And I'm guessing not every child in Ireland receives a grand education. When I started to work in the pottery, my mam and da told me schooling was the same in Ireland as it is in this country—for those with money."

Rose acknowledged there was some truth to his comment, but she didn't totally agree. "Even if children must work, they should still have an opportunity to learn how to read and write." She gave him a sidelong glance. "Do you know how to read and write, Mr. Campbell?"

Rylan greeted one of the workers before giving Rose an affirmative answer. "I can even keep books, Miss McKay. I went to school until I began working in the pottery. The rest I learned at home or from Mr. Bancock. If the desire is strong enough, these things can be learned."

"Aye, but there must be opportunity, as well. How many children who worked in this pottery received the opportunity to learn from Mr. Bancock?"

There was a gleam of satisfaction in her eyes when Rylan admitted he was the only one who'd been given that opportunity. "To have one child learn is better than none, isn't it?" He was enjoying this exchange with her and didn't want it to stop. Miss McKay was the most interesting young woman he'd ever met, and she was quite pretty, as well.

"Indeed, one is better than none, but how much better if all children had that same opportunity."

There wasn't any further time to discuss children or education. Mr. Bancock waved Miss McKay and her brother into the greenware room so they could glimpse the numerous shelves of pottery. "We allow all of the greenware to dry in this room and then it's placed in the saggers." He nodded toward the oblong fireclay saggers being filled with the pieces of dried greenware.

"The kiln crew loads the saggers into the kilns for the bisque firing. After the bisque firing, the kiln drawers remove the ware from the saggers and transfer it to ware baskets that are then taken to the bisque warehouse. No need to go to the kilns. I doubt your sister would appreciate the excessive heat." He turned to look at Ewan. "Would you like to visit the warehouses or continue to the glazing and decorating rooms?"

"'Tis getting a wee bit late in the afternoon. I'm thinking it might be best if we return tomorrow to complete the tour and go over the books. I know Rose is quite interested in the decorating, and I don't want to rush through the remainder of our visit." Ewan arched his brows. "Unless it is inconvenient for you, Mr. Bancock."

Mr. Bancock straightened his shoulders. "Whatever you prefer, Mr. McKay. I want to make sure you have time to see everything before you make any decision. I believe this to be the finest pottery in the entire state, but you must decide whether it is where you wish to invest your money. If it's God's plan for you to be here, I know it will happen."

Ewan extended his hand to the older man. "What you say is true. I, too, am a man who believes God directs my path."

After Ewan had assured Mr. Bancock they would return at nine the following morning, Rose grasped her brother's arm.

The two of them picked their way through the drying mud and crossed the railroad tracks before Rose looked up at her brother.

She wasn't certain if he was merely tired or if he'd been disappointed with their visit to the pottery. Years ago it would take only a glance, and she'd know Ewan's mood, but she'd been away from him too long, and there had been many changes in both of their lives. The frequent teasing and pranks at school had trained Rose to hide her emotions. She imagined that Ewan had learned to hide his, as well. Maintaining his temper while coping with Aunt Margaret and the operation of the brickyard had likely honed Ewan's ability.

They'd walked the short distance to the hotel and were entering the front door when she squeezed his arm. "You're very quiet. I'm eager to hear your impressions of the pottery."

"I do na think it's fair to compare the brickyard and pottery until our visit is complete and I examine the books." A hint of Ewan's brogue laced his comment. "I have a feeling Mr. Bancock is keen to sell." Rose arched her brows as Ewan directed her toward the dining room. "Let's have our supper before we go to our rooms. The weight of this decision is heavy on my soul. Once I go upstairs, I want to spend time in prayer before I go to bed."

She would have preferred a late supper but didn't complain. While Ewan had gone to call on Mr. Trent and visit his brickyard earlier in the day, Rose had remained at the hotel and relaxed. She waited to speak until they were seated and had both ordered the evening special of lamb chops and roasted potatoes.

After giving her linen napkin a quick shake and spreading it across her lap, she leaned forward. "Did you find Mr. Trent indifferent?"

"Nay. Why do you ask?"

"You said Mr. Bancock appeared eager to sell, so I wondered

if Mr. Trent had been uninterested when you were at the brick-yard." She swallowed a sip of water. "I didn't find Mr. Bancock particularly forceful."

A waiter stepped forward and poured their coffee before moving to the next table. Ewan poured cream into his cup and stirred. "He was not forceful, but I sensed urgency in his be-havior. Did you not notice how he looked at Rylan when we arrived? There was something that passed between them. Mr. Bancock was doing his best to hide his disapproval, and Rylan acted apologetic, yet I'm not sure why." He lifted his coffee cup.

"You saw all of that? No wonder you're weary." She gig-gled. "I merely thought Mr. Bancock was worried because we were late for our appointment. Perhaps I need to become more vigilant."

"When one conducts business, watching others is as impor-tant as reviewing their books. That's a wee bit of brotherly advice for you." He grinned and saluted her with his cup be-fore returning it to the saucer. "I think he's a man eager to sell because of his poor health."

Rose slumped back in her chair. "Did he speak to you of his illness?"

"Nay, but I overheard a couple of the workers talking when we were in the slip house. One of them said he didn't think Mr. Bancock would be alive this time next year."

Rose exhaled a small gasp. "How very sad. I'm sure the work-ers have deep concerns if they know of Mr. Bancock's illness."

"Aye. All of the workers appeared worried. Did ya not notice?"

Rose scrunched her forehead as she attempted to recall any-thing unusual. She shook her head. "I didn't observe anything of that sort, but I did notice Mr. Bancock hurrying Rylan inside as we were crossing the railroad tracks."

"Is that so? And how did you happen to see that event? Were

you looking over your shoulder so as to get one more look at Rylan Campbell?" He grinned and gave her a wink. "I have to admit he's a fine-looking young lad and appears to be a hard worker. I'm thinking a girl looking for a husband could do much worse." When Rose grimaced at the mention of a husband, her brother chuckled. "But we both know that since you're not interested in marriage, you did na even notice his good looks."

Rose gave a firm nod. "Mr. Campbell was very nice and he does know the pottery business well, but his appearance is of little interest to me."

"Ah, so now that I mention his good looks, he's *Mr. Campbell*." Ewan's eyes sparkled. "Only a minute ago, he was Rylan. I think you noticed more about Mr. Campbell than you care to mention, dear Rose."

Ewan was enjoying his bit of teasing, so she tamped down her urge to offer a prickly answer. She didn't want to appear easily hurt, but the taunting at school had increased her sensitivity. Telling her brother she'd grown weary of the ongoing references to her unwedded state would serve no good purpose.

Choosing her words carefully, Rose first offered her brother a warm smile. "What I noticed about Mr. Campbell—or Rylan, if you prefer—was his knowledge regarding Mr. Bancock's pottery and Mr. Bancock's actions toward Rylan. Almost as if he was a son or the heir-apparent to the business. Yet how could either of them believe such a transfer of ownership could ever take place?"

Ewan shrugged. "Stranger things have happened. Who would think a poor Irish immigrant like me would be looking to purchase a brickyard or a pottery? Much is dependent upon prayer, hard work, and the circumstances God weaves into our lives. Were it not for Laura's mother, I'd be much like young Rylan.

Longing to own my own business, but without the means to do so."

The waiter arrived with their dinner, and Rose touched her palm to her midriff as she eyed the plate of food. "I doubt I can eat all of this, but it does smell delicious."

"Aye, that it does. And I'll be happy to help with whatever you're unable to eat." He forked one of the roasted potatoes and grinned. "That's what brothers are for."

"That—and teasing their sisters." She cut into the lamb chop and took a moment to enjoy the first bite. "Tell me more about your visit to the brickyard. You've said little, so I'm guessing you found it unappealing." She wanted to say she *hoped* he'd found it a disagreeable place and was not giving it further consideration, but she withheld her position for the moment.

Ewan touched his napkin to his lips. "These lamb chops are delicious." He cut another piece of the lamb before he met Rose's gaze. "I thought the brickyard could be a sound investment for us, but I told Mr. Trent I would not make any quick decision because I need to be flexible. Much depends on seeing the books at the pottery and deciding which business will yield the better profit. Of course, it would be much easier for me to step back into a brickyard. I know the business well, but Mr. Trent's yard is smaller than what I hoped for, and he has no VerValen machine. They still make all their bricks by hand. In order to meet large orders like we did at C&M Brickyard, I would need to purchase a VerValen."

Rose's heartbeat quickened at the response. "Then you're going to purchase the pottery."

Ewan stopped eating and stared at her. She'd spoken the words with more determination and authority than she'd intended.

"That is not what I said, Rose. An examination of Mr. Bancock's books will tell me more. But I will tell you, I'm not finding comfort in the idea of learning a new trade. Making bricks is what I have always done, and where I can probably best succeed."

"But don't you see, Ewan?" She reached across the table and touched his hand. "I can help with the pottery business. With your business experience and the design and creative skills I learned at school, we can own the best pottery in West Virginia."

"This is not a decision we'll be makin' this evening or even tomorrow. Before I give Mr. Trent or Mr. Bancock an offer, I'll be spending time in prayer and seeking the opinion of both Laura and her mother."

The idea of waiting so long worried her. If Mr. Bancock feared they might not return tomorrow, what might he think if Ewan left town without giving the man an answer?

She pushed a piece of potato around the edge of her plate. "But what if one or both of them should be unwilling to wait for your decision?"

Ewan hiked a shoulder. "Then I suppose I won't be doing business with them."

Rose inwardly sighed. She was certain the pottery would be the better choice—at least for her.

# Chapter 4

When Rylan arrived at work the next morning, Mr. Bancock was once again rearranging the contracts and ledger books. His hair stood in tiny gray peaks, and his shirt, the same one he'd worn yesterday, was rumpled and stained with ink. After Ewan McKay's departure, Rylan had talked with Mr. Bancock for several hours in an effort to assure him the visit had gone well. He had even stayed and prayed with the older man well into the evening hours.

Rylan sighed. By Mr. Bancock's appearance this morning, it was obvious he hadn't slept well. Rylan wondered if he'd even gone to bed. Rylan understood his employer's desire to make a good impression. The older man's health and finances both made the sale necessary. And though he'd placed ads in several newspapers, only two bids had been forthcoming. Both were from rival pottery owners who wanted to put a competitor out of business. Both offers had been abysmal. Both had been rejected by Mr. Bancock.

Mr. McKay's request to tour the operation had been the first viable possibility he'd received, and the letter had buoyed Mr. Bancock's spirits to new heights. As they had prepared for the

41

visit, he'd become overconfident, certain Mr. McKay would purchase the business and certain he'd receive an excellent price. As soon as he learned of Mr. McKay's interest in the Trent Brick Works, Mr. Bancock's bold stance had taken flight, and his thoughts of driving a hard bargain had dissolved like salt in water.

When Rylan stepped closer, Mr. Bancock pointed to the worktable. "I think this arrangement is better, don't you?" Rather than looking at Rylan, his attention was fixed on the window. "I thought they would be here by now. Mr. McKay said nine o'clock, didn't he?"

The morning work bells clanged in the workshops. "He did, but it is only seven." Rylan feared his employer's disheveled appearance would not make much of an impression on the prospective buyers. "Did you remain here all night?"

The older man nodded and pressed his hands down the front of his shirt. "Yes, I wanted to make certain everything was in order, and when I couldn't sleep I stayed up and prayed."

Pity seeped through Rylan's bones as he traced a hand over the stacks of paper work and ledgers. "Everything is in fine order, Mr. Bancock. I think it would serve you well to go home for a while. Maybe coffee and some breakfast will help to settle your nerves before Mr. McKay arrives. And a fresh shirt would be good, as well."

Mr. Bancock's eyes flitted about the office as though taking stock of the room for his very first time. "I suppose you're right. I won't make much of an impression in this soiled shirt." He tugged at one of the stained cuffs.

"Either way, you'll feel better after some breakfast."

Mr. Bancock examined the worktable one final time before lifting his hat from a metal hook near the door. "I'll be back by eight thirty. If Mr. McKay should arrive early, send one of the boys from the glazing shop to fetch me."

A sharp pain pierced Rylan's heart as he watched Mr. Bancock trudge across the railroad tracks, his shoulders hunched and his head thrust forward. The older man had been like a father to him all these years and had promised to protect Rylan's job when the business sold. Of course, how he'd be able to accomplish that feat remained a mystery. Besides, selling the business—not saving Rylan's job—remained the greatest necessity. If need be, he would leave Grafton and locate work, hopefully in another pottery. He might have to accept a lesser position somewhere else, but he would rely on God and see where the future might lead.

After a glance at the clock, Rylan strode out of the office and headed for the slip house. Every morning he stopped in each department to retrieve time sheets for the previous day. Each foreman was charged with maintaining a daily record, and though Rylan thought it would be more productive to enter the records each Friday before preparing the payroll, Mr. Bancock disagreed. He wanted a daily report of absent employees and recorded each day's production against the number of employees in the various departments. Production decreased when employees were not in attendance, so those who made a habit of absenteeism were soon seeking other employment.

Along the way Rylan greeted many of the workers and then stopped in the decorating room, where he paused to admire the work of Mr. Wheeler as he applied a hand-painted design to an urn. Because skilled artists were the highest-paid employees in a pottery, Mr. Bancock had steadily decreased production of specialty pieces over the past five years and concentrated on ware that could be produced at a lower cost. Mr. Wheeler was the only decorator who remained an employee of Bancock Pottery.

Rylan had disagreed with the decision to eliminate the other artists. He'd said as much to Mr. Bancock, but to no avail. The owner wanted to keep costs down and had decided the decorating section should be entirely eliminated by the end of the year.

"Good morning, Mr. Wheeler." Rylan nodded toward the urn. "That's a beautiful design you've painted. I'm sure it will sell quickly."

The decorator's bushy brows lifted. "I'm pleased that you can appreciate my workmanship, Rylan. Seems Mr. Bancock has lost all interest in having beautiful pieces created in his pottery." Mr. Wheeler dipped his brush into a tin of paint and wiped the excess along the edge of the can. "Between you and me, I'm going to go ahead and look for work at one of the potteries in Fairmont or Wheeling. May even go up to East Liverpool, though I'm not eager to leave West Virginia. My wife's been after me to locate another job ever since Mr. Bancock let most of the decorators go." He traced his brush along the edge of a leaf to create the perfect shading. "I reckon she's right, but I kept hoping things would change around here."

Rylan liked Mr. Wheeler. The decorator had encouraged Rylan to remain in the decorating shop back when Mr. Bancock first offered to take him into the office and teach him about ledgers and contracts. Mr. Wheeler had argued that working in the office was a waste of Rylan's artistic talents, but Rylan had ignored the decorator's suggestion and taken Mr. Bancock's offer. Though Rylan possessed a good eye for design, he never believed his future would lie in the decorating shop.

As if Mr. Wheeler had been reading his thoughts, he pointed the tip of his brush in Rylan's direction. "Bet you're glad you didn't listen to me when I tried to persuade you to stay here and apprentice with me."

Rylan didn't miss the sadness in Mr. Wheeler's eyes. He'd been working at the pottery for more than twenty years. Moving to another pottery would be a difficult adjustment. "Don't do anything just yet, Mr. Wheeler. There's a possible buyer for the pottery. His sister is with him, and they'll be coming through later this morning. She's interested in design, so I'm thinking they may want to expand the decorating section."

Mr. Wheeler gave a slight nod. "I'll offer up a prayer or two that it all works out, Rylan. Nothing I'd like better."

When Rylan returned to the office, he discovered Mr. Bancock peering out the front windows. The older man had changed his shirt and combed his hair, but his shoulders remained slumped from pain. "It's half past eight and there's no sign of them, but I suppose there will be time enough for concern if they haven't appeared by nine o'clock." He glanced at Rylan. "Did you collect the time sheets?"

Rylan handed the paper work to the older man. "This should keep you busy until they arrive."

Mr. Bancock grasped the papers in his right hand and moved away from the window. "You're right. I might as well accomplish something this morning."

Moments later, Rylan patted the gentleman's shoulder. "They're coming, Mr. Bancock."

He pushed up from his desk. "I'm hopeful the Lord will reveal this to be the business Mr. McKay should purchase. Let's do what we can to help Him, Rylan."

Rylan wasn't sure how one did such a thing, but he would try. He owed that much and more to Mr. Bancock.

The greetings were brief, but Rylan was certain Miss McKay appeared even lovelier today. She was wearing a shirtwaist that was a close match for her deep blue eyes, and Rylan was drawn by her passion for the business as she inquired about the decorating shop. When Mr. Bancock answered they would soon see the area, she smiled and stars dimpled her cheeks. How could he have missed that charming feature yesterday? What would it be like to be around someone so talented and lovely each day? Following behind Mr. McKay and Mr. Bancock, Rylan escorted Rose toward one of the warehouses, his imagination taking flight as he began to consider working for Miss McKay and her brother.

"This is the warehouse where dust and dirt are brushed from the ware before it is sent to be glazed. Mostly women and a few children work in this area." Mr. Bancock waved his hand toward the door but didn't step inside.

Rather than passing by, Rose stepped into the warehouse and looked around the vast area. "How can they breathe with all this dust flying about?" Rose wrinkled her nose and removed a handkerchief from her pocket. She lifted the linen square to her face and covered her nose and mouth.

Rylan grasped her arm and directed her toward the door. "Those who work in this warehouse are used to it. There's no way to avoid dust when you're cleaning the ware. If it becomes too bad, they wet down the floor, but this task cannot be overlooked. The ware has to be free of dirt and dust before it can be glazed." He shot her a grin. "You'll not find it terribly bothersome after you've been working at the pottery for a while."

Rose arched her brows. "If we purchase this pottery, there will be some definite changes, especially regarding cleanliness."

Remembering Mr. Bancock's earlier appeal, Rylan nodded his head. "I'm sure that any changes you make will please the employees, Miss McKay. We all look forward to helping you in any way we can."

"That's good to hear, Mr. Campbell, though my brother has yet to make a final decision about the business."

Mr. McKay turned around and waved to them. "Come on, Rose. You're lagging behind."

After hurrying forward, Mr. Bancock led them into the next section. "This is the glazing room. Glazing is what makes the ware impervious to liquids. The workers who glaze the ware are called dippers. Most of the dippers hire women and children to work for them. That way they don't have to take time to remove the excess glaze from the pieces or transport the ware." He nodded toward several of the children. "All of those are Harry Perdue's young'uns, and that's his wife over there." He lowered his voice a notch. "The men with families have an advantage because they can put their wives and young'uns to work and don't have to pay outsiders to help."

Rylan saw the look of disapproval that crossed Rose's face. Didn't her brother have any children working in his brickyard? She could visit most any coal mine, pottery, brickyard, or other industry in the state, and she'd see children working. He wanted to ask her about her visit to Trent Brick Works and if she'd not seen children working alongside their fathers, but he kept his lips sealed. Any such talk might lead to trouble, and he didn't want to be the cause of any problems for Mr. Bancock.

Rylan gestured toward the kilns. "This is where the ware is fired after it's glazed. The second firing is known as the glost firing." As they entered a small section of another brick building, several women sat side by side wielding rubber stamps. "Each piece is stamped with the Bancock pottery mark."

Rose clasped a hand to her bodice. "These women stamp every piece of ware made in this pottery?" Rylan nodded, and she released a small gasp. "I can't imagine performing such a monotonous task day after day."

"I'm sure if your children needed food on the table, you'd be willing to stamp pottery, Miss McKay." He took note of the pity that shone in her eyes before he hurried her toward her brother and Mr. Bancock. "You'll be pleased to know that the decorating shop is straight ahead. You'll be able to watch our artist at work."

When Rose's mood lightened, Rylan smiled, pleased his comment had gained the desired effect. While Mr. Bancock and Mr. McKay continued to talk, Rylan escorted Rose inside the decorating shop and urged her forward. The artist glanced up from his work, and Rylan nodded. "Mr. Wheeler, this is Miss Rose McKay. She's been eager to see your work."

"Not much to see around here anymore, Miss McKay, but you're welcome to sit on one of the empty stools and stay as long as you like." Mr. Wheeler's apron bore splashes of various colors, and a hint of gold gilding decorated his bow tie. Rylan wondered if he realized the mishap.

Rose leaned forward and carefully examined Mr. Wheeler's painting. "Your work is beautiful. If all of your artists possess as much talent, my brother will be fortunate to own this pottery."

"Then your brother best look elsewhere. There are no other decorators in this shop, Miss McKay."

Rose's face crimped in a frown as she looked up one row of workbenches and down another. Unoccupied wooden stools sat empty at the work spaces. "Well, it certainly appears there are a great number of work spaces available for decorators. Where are they?"

Mr. Wheeler looked at Rylan from beneath hooded eyes and gave a quiet *harrumph*. "Those who could find work have gone to other potteries." He nodded toward the doorway. "If you've any more questions about the lack of decorators, you best ask Mr. Bancock. He's the one who gave 'em their walking papers."

The words had barely been uttered when Mr. McKay and the owner walked inside. Deep furrows wrinkled Mr. Bancock's forehead, and his bushy brows dropped low. He glowered at Mr. Wheeler. "Did I hear you speaking my name, Frank?"

The decorator picked up his brush and continued with his work. "Indeed, but you need not worry. I spoke nothing but the truth."

Moments later, Rose peppered Mr. Bancock with myriad questions regarding the pottery's lack of artists and decorators. She was firm in her final request: She wanted to review the ledgers regarding all specialty ware. Mr. Bancock agreed but was quick to add that a brief glance at the books would tell her he'd made the proper decision.

"Skilled decorators like Mr. Wheeler, the ones who can apply beautiful hand-painted designs and gilding, are the highest-paid employees in a pottery." Mr. Bancock turned his attention away from Rose and back toward Ewan. "Unless you can sell those items as quickly as the cheaper ware, your profits will quickly disappear. If you don't have to worry about turning a profit, you need not worry. You can hire as many decorators as you like and make hundreds of hand-painted vases that will sit in your warehouse."

Before taking a brief tour of the packing house, Mr. Bancock mentioned the pottery's advantageous location near the river as well as the railroad. He was quick to point out that products created in his pottery bore an excellent reputation, and he'd be willing to have the pottery works continue to bear his name. There was eagerness in Mr. Bancock's tone as they returned to the office, and Mr. McKay and his sister sat down to begin their examination of the books.

When they had finished their review of the contracts and ledgers, Mr. McKay shook Mr. Bancock's hand. "I won't be making a decision today, Mr. Bancock. I'm returning to my home in Bartlett, where I'll discuss our opportunities with my wife and her mother, who is investing in our new endeavor. But should we decide upon purchasing your pottery, we'll have an offer to you within ten days." Mr. McKay hesitated a moment. "Is there anything else you think I should know before we make our decision?"

Mr. Bancock's eyes shone with both sorrow and weariness. "Only what I told you about Rylan. Keep him as your second in charge, and you'll do fine. He's talented and knows the business. I'd be beholden if you'd do that for me."

Embarrassment seized Rylan. He appreciated Mr. Bancock's endorsement, but being present during the plea for his job was uncomfortable. Besides, he didn't want his employment to be a part of Mr. McKay's decision.

He forced himself to look at Mr. McKay. "Please don't make your decision based on keeping me, Mr. McKay. If you have another plan in mind, I can find work elsewhere."

Ewan nodded and extended his hand. "Thank you, Rylan. I do not know what the future holds, but I count it a pleasure to have met you."

After bidding the McKays farewell, Rylan picked up the time sheets and handed them to Mr. Bancock. "Do you think their answer will be favorable?"

"Who can say? One thing is certain: It's going to be a very long ten days."

# Chapter 5

*Bartlett, West Virginia*

Though it was difficult, Rose withheld her thoughts regarding the purchase of the pottery works on the train ride home. Ewan had said enough to let her know he was leaning toward the brickyard. And she truly could understand his desire to remain in a business he knew and understood. Still, she couldn't help but think he would change his mind once he considered all of the ramifications.

As the train chugged into the Bartlett station, Ewan mentioned the celebratory party that lay ahead. Rose did her best to appear excited, but being the center of attention didn't appeal, especially after her unfortunate experiences at the galas hosted at the design school. She wished her sister-in-law would have consulted her before planning the party and sending invitations.

Even if Laura had protested, Mrs. Woodfield would have insisted upon a celebration, and she wouldn't want to offend Laura's mother. The woman had been like a grandmother to the twins and her, even before Ewan and Laura married. She'd even insisted they address her as Grandmother Woodfield.

The entire family had moved into Woodfield Manor when Laura's mother suffered a terrible bout of pleurisy last winter. Laura wanted to help with her mother's care, and Mrs. Woodfield longed to have the family with her.

Rose leaned forward and looked out the window. Flanked by Mrs. Woodfield and Laura, Rose's twin sisters, Ainslee and Adaira, stood on the platform just outside the depot door. "I was hoping they would have Tessa with them."

Ewan peered out the window. "I'm sure you'll have more than enough time to get reacquainted with her once we arrive home. According to her nanny, our sweet little daughter has become quite a little handful."

"I would think that Beatrice could handle most any child. After caring for her seven sisters and brothers, it's hard to believe one baby would cause her any problem."

"I believe she's discovered there's quite a difference between being a nanny and looking after your sisters and brothers."

Ewan and Laura had hired Beatrice Murphy, a distant relative, to act as nanny to the infant daughter they had adopted shortly after they wed. The child had been born out of wedlock to Kathleen Roark, Margaret Crothers's sister. Unfortunately, the adoption had deepened an already simmering rift among family members, a disagreement that began when Uncle Hugh would not honor his word and make Ewan a partner in the brickyard.

Hugh had been far more forgiving toward Kathleen's mistake, but Margaret still blamed her sister for ruining the Crotherses' reputation in Bartlett. This was a belief Rose thought quite silly, since Kathleen's lying-in and Tessa's birth had received less attention from the wagging tongues than had Margaret's unforgiving behavior toward her own sister.

A sure-footed conductor stepped down the aisle and announced the train had arrived at Bartlett station and would depart for Fairmont in fifteen minutes. Rose pinned her hat in place while Ewan gathered a newspaper and his hat.

The moment Rose stepped down from the train, the twins rushed forward and nearly knocked her to the platform. She chuckled and wrapped her arms around them. "What happened to those etiquette classes the two of you were taking from Miss Pfingstel? I doubt she'd approve of such a rowdy greeting."

Ainslee giggled. "Miss Pfingstel isn't anywhere near the train station, so we don't need to worry about being scolded."

Rose leaned back and looked down at her sisters. "Is that how it works? You behave and use proper manners only when your instructor is present?" She shook her head, but her attempt to give the girls a reproving frown fell short, and she giggled along with them.

After receiving a welcoming hug from both Laura and Mrs. Woodfield, they walked to the carriage while Ewan made arrangements to have the trunks delivered by wagon.

The moment they'd settled in the carriage, Adaira turned to Rose. "Wait until you hear all the plans Laura has made for your party. We can hardly wait for tomorrow night to arrive." She inhaled a gulp of air. "Laura said both of us are allowed to remain downstairs for the dancing if we'd like." She glanced at her twin. "Ainslee said she doesn't want to, but I'm going to stay up and enjoy the midnight supper."

Rose forced a feeble smile and glanced at her sister-in-law. "You really shouldn't have gone to such trouble and expense. You know I'm not particularly fond of parties, especially when I'm guest of honor."

Mrs. Woodfield patted Rose's hand. "Now that you've completed your schooling, it's time to locate the young man with whom you want to share the rest of your life. Laura and I have made certain that invitations went out to a number of eligible young men who have moved to the area since you went away to school." There was a lilt to her voice that set off Rose's internal alarm. Though she knew Mrs. Woodfield wasn't planning any sort of prank, the remark created the same wary feelings Rose had experienced when the girls at school had plotted against her.

While the twins covered their mouths and tittered, Rose groaned inwardly. She didn't want Mrs. Woodfield, or anyone else, seeking out beaus for her. Truth be told, a husband, or even a beau, was the last thing she wanted. She'd observed the reaction of the girls at school when a beau decided to move on to another girl. Most were unable to attend to their schoolwork for weeks on end. She didn't want her future determined by finding the proper man. Instead, she wanted to help Ewan make a success of the Bancock Pottery Works.

Of course, that would happen only if Ewan set aside his idea to purchase the brickworks. If she could win Laura and Mrs. Woodfield to her side, Ewan would surely change his mind. But first she would need to have the women give up their plans to find her a husband. That might prove more difficult than convincing Ewan to purchase the pottery.

"With a move from Bartlett, I don't think this is a proper time for me to seek a husband." Rose allowed her gaze to travel between the two older women. "There may be some perfect fellow living in Grafton."

Ewan chuckled. "I believe our Rose took a liking to the young man who is Mr. Bancock's assistant at the pottery works." He scrunched his right eye together in an exaggerated wink.

"Oh, tell us about him," Adaira cooed. "Is he quite handsome?"

"What's his name, Rose? Did he call on you while you were in Grafton?" Ainslee scooted to the edge of the leather carriage seat.

Rose wrinkled her nose and glared at her brother. "I am not interested in Rylan Campbell except as an employee of the pottery works, should you decide it would be a good investment for the family." She met Ainslee's inquisitive stare. "No, Mr. Campbell did not call on me while we were in Grafton. And if he'd asked Ewan's permission to do so, I would have given my regrets." She inhaled a deep breath. "I do hope we've now come to an end of all questions regarding Rylan Campbell."

Her comment terminated any further questions about Rylan, as they'd arrived at Woodfield Manor. The twins clambered up the front steps of the house while the adults followed behind at a slower pace.

Once inside the front door, Rose turned to Ewan. "Have you decided when we'll tell Laura and Grandmother Woodfield about the pottery?"

Ewan gestured to the two women. "Ladies, when would you like to hear our report about the pottery and the brickyard?"

Rose didn't miss the special emphasis he placed on the brickyard, but she didn't comment. Instead, she waited for Laura or her mother to reply. She hoped they wouldn't want to wait until after tomorrow's party.

When they hesitated, Rose inched closer to Laura. "Ewan promised to send word within ten days, so we shouldn't wait long. Perhaps we could sit down after supper this evening?"

Mrs. Woodfield smiled at her. "My, you are eager, Rose. I'm beginning to think Ewan may be correct in his assumptions about that young man at the pottery." Before Rose could offer further objection, Mrs. Woodfield continued. "I think there should be plenty of time after supper, don't you, Laura? We've done all we can toward preparations for Rose's party until tomorrow."

Laura nodded and looked at her husband. "After supper is fine with me if Ewan doesn't have any objection."

"I know better than to object when I'm outnumbered three to one." He turned toward Rose, his lips curved in a half smile. "I'll save my objections for when we actually begin our discussion."

Rose sighed. Had Ewan already made up his mind to purchase the brickyard? She didn't want to believe her brother would come to a decision before listening to his wife and Mrs. Woodfield. Then again, maybe he believed it would be a simple matter to convince them the brickyard was a better choice. If so, she needed to be prepared. But a visit to the nursery would come first.

Since their trunks hadn't yet arrived from the depot, Rose set aside all thoughts of unpacking and hurried upstairs to the nursery. The sound of Tessa's chatter tugged at her heart as she stood in the doorway and watched her creating a small arrangement with her wooden blocks. Pleased by her accomplishment, Tessa clapped her hands before glancing over her shoulder toward her nanny for affirmation. Rather than acknowledging the child's accomplishment, Beatrice continued with her mending.

"You've made a lovely structure with your blocks, Tessa." Rose strode into the room and dropped to her knees beside the child. "You're becoming such a big girl."

Upon hearing "big girl," Tessa gave a firm nod. "I am big."

While she continued to interact with Tessa, Rose looked at Beatrice. "Our little Tessa is growing like a weed, isn't she?"

"I s'pose she is. Nothing surprising 'bout that. They all grow up and cause even more trouble." She shook her head and jabbed her needle into the torn chemise. "I wish my own mam and da would have stopped at one instead of creating that brood of theirs that runs wild. Glad I am to be away from that noise and ruckus day after day. I've had me fill of crying babes, fightin' boys who think they're men, and lazy girls who don't lift a hand to help with the housework."

Beatrice's seeming lack of interest in Tessa and her comments regarding children surprised Rose. If she had no interest in caring for a child, why had she begged Ewan for the position? Was it simply to get away from home? Then again, perhaps Beatrice was merely having a bad day. On Rose's previous visits home, Beatrice had doted on Tessa. No doubt being alone with a small child proved to be taxing day after day. Now that Rose was home, perhaps she could step in to help with Tessa and allow Beatrice some free time, but she'd first gain Laura's approval. She didn't want to overstep the minute she arrived home.

"Lots of goings-on downstairs for the past few weeks. Quite a party the missus is planning for you." Beatrice held up the chemise and sighed when she located another ripped seam. "I've stitched this chemise enough times to make a new one." She looked up at Rose. "Hard to believe we both come over to this country from the same poor conditions." Her gaze traveled the length of Rose's figure. "Just look at you—all dressed in finery and educated, whilst here I sit mending the same chemise I've been wearing for the last five years and wiping slobber from a babe's mouth."

Beatrice's summation didn't come as a complete surprise. Most of the relatives Uncle Hugh had brought over from Ireland hadn't fared well. Mostly because Uncle Hugh had paid them meager wages and insisted they work for him until they'd reimbursed him for their passage to America. Ewan's attempts to raise their wages had been futile. By putting off signing a partnership agreement with Ewan, Uncle Hugh continued to maintain full control of the money. And, upon his failing health, Aunt Margaret stepped into his position. A few of the relatives had managed to reimburse Uncle Hugh. They moved out of his housing and went to work at the coal mines. The rest continued to live in the company-provided housing and work at the brickyard.

Beatrice knotted and cut her thread. "If your brother hadn't married into wealth, I'm thinking you'd be wiping snotty noses and washing dirty diapers, just like me."

In spite of Beatrice's sharp words, Rose was touched with compassion for the young woman. Beatrice's assessment was correct: If Ewan hadn't married Laura Woodfield, he would be drawing paltry wages working at the brickyard, and Aunt Margaret would be controlling their lives. The fact that Laura and Ewan had fallen in love and Laura's mother had approved of the marriage had changed all of their lives for the better, especially since Uncle Hugh's illness and death.

"How would you like to attend the party tomorrow evening, Beatrice?" One evening of diversion wouldn't change the young woman's station in life, but it would permit her some time to mingle with adults and perhaps enjoy a few dances.

"And what would you think I'd be wearing to your fine party, Miss Rose? My mended skirt and shirtwaist?"

The sarcastic emphasis Beatrice had placed on *Miss* when she addressed her didn't escape Rose's attention, but she forced a smile and pressed on. Though she hoped it wasn't true, Rose knew she might have had some of those same jealous feelings if she were in Beatrice's position.

"When Tessa takes her nap, come down to my room. We're almost the same size. I'm sure there are several gowns in my wardrobe that would fit you perfectly. You could choose the one you like best, but there's one of yellow silk that would be lovely with your red hair and blue eyes." Rose held her breath, uncertain how her offer would be received.

The tight lines around Beatrice's lips relaxed, and her eyes softened. "You think the missus would agree? And if she did approve and if your dress fit me, who would look after Tessa while I was at the party?" She shook her head. "Nay. I'm not destined to ever enjoy fancy parties and such."

"Of course you are. I'm certain one of the twins would be willing to come to the nursery and sit with Tessa. Ainslee has already said she's not interested in attending the dance. So long as there's someone here in case Tessa wakes up, I'm certain Laura won't object." Rose's excitement mounted as her idea took shape. Though it was a celebration in her honor, Rose had never been keen on parties. Seeing Beatrice attend would give her pleasure and make the evening more bearable.

Beatrice gave her a slight nod. "So long as you make sure the missus doesn't think I put you up to this. I can't be losing my position here."

The wariness in her tone wasn't new to Rose. Most of her fellow countrymen possessed a suspicious nature, especially when someone offered something unexpected. Like most immigrants, they'd been let down and betrayed often enough that they were slow to trust. Sadly, many were guilty of the same bad conduct themselves—sometimes directed toward outsiders, but sometimes aimed at their own relatives and neighbors. Rose had seen the behavior enough to understand Beatrice's fear.

"You can be present when I speak to Laura, if you like." As soon as she'd made the offer, Rose wanted to pull back the words.

While she wanted to ease Beatrice's doubts, she now realized that having Beatrice present would place Laura in a difficult position. She silently chastised herself for extending an invitation to Beatrice without first speaking to Laura. Rose's intentions had been good, but she'd been too impulsive. She could only hope Laura wouldn't object.

"Nay. You go and ask her and bring me word. I don't want to be looking her in the eye if she says she doesn't want the likes of me at her fine party."

Rose stooped down and gave Tessa a quick kiss on the cheek before she hurried from the room. Guilt knotted in her stomach as she hastened downstairs to the second floor. She should have taken time to defend Laura, should have told Beatrice that Laura would never look down upon her. Instead, she'd hurried down the stairs fearful Beatrice might change her mind and ask to come along while she spoke to Laura.

As Rose approached her bedroom door, Mrs. Woodfield came upstairs. "Did you see Tessa? Hasn't she grown?"

"She has, indeed." Rose inhaled a deep breath.

Mrs. Woodfield hesitated a moment. "Don't forget that we're going to have our meeting after supper tonight."

The meeting. If she was going to wage a meaningful argument against the brickyard, she needed to be prepared. Before she took time to speak to Laura about Beatrice, she'd write out her reasons why the pottery would be a better investment for the family. Beatrice would have to wait.

# Chapter 6

Conversation during supper consisted of a barrage of questions regarding school and the award Rose had received. Ewan appeared lost in thought while she detailed several different events in which she'd participated, careful to leave out the unhappy incidents. She hoped that the twins would decide to further their education, so she didn't want to say or do anything to discourage them. Besides, they'd likely attend school together and have each other for encouragement or help. Though the twins disagreed, Rose thought the advantage of having a twin far outweighed any disadvantage.

Mrs. Woodfield dabbed her napkin to her lips. "I believe we should plan a trip to Philadelphia in the future so that we can all see the fabrics you designed, Rose. Wouldn't it be fun?" She glanced around the table, then gave a slight shake of her head. "I do think it was a terrible oversight they didn't have the divan upholstered prior to your departure." She tapped her index finger on the edge of the table. "Perhaps I should write a letter to Muriel Fisk."

Ainslee leaned forward. "Who's Muriel Fisk?"

"She's the director of the school, and I've known her for

years. I do believe their lack of attention to your winning entry in the contest was a terrible oversight." Mrs. Woodfield glanced down the table toward Rose. "They should have allowed enough time to display your work prior to the end of the school term."

The last thing Rose wanted was anyone making a fuss over the award. School was now behind her, and nothing would be solved by causing problems for Mrs. Fisk. Besides, the woman had been very kind to Rose, and she wouldn't want the director reprimanded due to a letter of complaint from Mrs. Woodfield.

"I have a lovely framed certificate acknowledging my first-place award, Grandmother. I saw the fabric after it had been woven, and that was enough of a prize for me. Please don't write a letter. I consider Mrs. Fisk a fine director who does everything she can to help the girls attending design school."

"Not quite everything, or she would have—"

"Mother, I believe Rose is quite satisfied. She's been clear about her wishes, and I'm sure you won't override her decision." Laura looked at her mother and arched her brows.

Mrs. Woodfield inhaled a deep breath and sighed. "I'll abide by your decision, Rose, but changes don't take place unless we let our voices be heard."

Rose thanked the older woman for her kind understanding, but from her look of defeat, Rose was certain she'd disappointed the woman. No doubt Mrs. Woodfield had planned to sway Rose's decision. The quietude that followed was deafening.

Wanting to end the silence, Rose searched for something to fill the void. "I was thinking it would be lovely if Beatrice could attend the party tomorrow evening." She looked directly at Laura. "I know I should have discussed it with you first, but I was caught up while visiting with her and blurted out an invitation. She declined, saying she had nothing to wear, but I assured her one of my gowns would fit." They were all staring at her as though she'd lost her senses. She'd even captured Ewan's attention. Swallowing hard, she continued on before Laura could refuse the suggestion. "Of course, Beatrice said she still could not attend because she needed to be upstairs to care for Tessa, but I told her Ainslee might be willing to sit in for her." Rose gestured toward her sister. "Ainslee's already said she didn't want to remain downstairs for the dance, so I thought it would all work perfectly. Don't you agree?" She heaved a sigh and forced a smile.

"The idea is a bit unique, but I suppose if you've already extended an invitation, we can hardly tell her she isn't welcome." Laura glanced at her husband. "After all, she is extended family."

Ewan's brows knitted together. "Aye. Far removed but still family, I suppose." He turned toward Rose. "In the future, you should speak to Laura before you extend invitations. I realize this is your party, but adding extra guests without permission is not proper."

Rose mumbled her apologies and thanked Laura for her kindness before turning toward Ainslee. "Are you willing to look after Tessa during the dance? I'm sure she'll be asleep, so you can read a book. I've brought home several you might enjoy."

Her sister agreed to the arrangement as the maid entered the room with a layered peach cake for dessert. Rose clasped a hand to her midsection. "Oh, my favorite."

Once they'd all been served, Rose dipped her fork into the moist confection and was thankful the delicious dessert created enough excitement to dispel further mention of her inappropriate invitation to Beatrice. When they'd all finished their cake, Ewan leaned back in his chair.

"I believe we have a meeting to attend, ladies." He winked at the twins. "I'm sure the two of you can find something to occupy your time while we discuss some business matters."

The girls were pleased to make their escape to the backyard garden. The scent of lilacs drifted through the French doors as the two of them departed. While Rose inhaled the familiar fragrance, she glanced across the table at Laura and realized her timing during supper had been ill conceived. After discouraging Mrs. Woodfield from writing a letter to Mrs. Fisk and extending an improper invitation to Beatrice, Rose wondered if she'd be able to win the two ladies to her side regarding the pottery. For sure, she hadn't done anything to align herself with them during supper.

After they'd all taken their seats in the library, Ewan gave the ladies his impressions of the brickyard. "Since Rose didn't accompany me, she'll not have an opinion about the yard, but from what I've told you, I think you'll agree that it would be an excellent investment. Mr. Trent is eager to sell, and I think I could get him to lower the price a little."

Rose perked to attention. "But you told me on the train that Mr. Trent has no VerValen Machine and he's never had any sizeable orders. If that's the case, his operation would be too small to support the family or to secure contracts as you've managed in the past."

Mrs. Woodfield arched her brows. "Rose is correct. You'd be able to contract only small orders that wouldn't bring in sufficient income." She lifted her shoulders in a slight shrug. "Then again, there's no reason we couldn't purchase a VerValen, is there?"

"My hope would be that if Mr. Trent would lower the price, we could purchase the brickyard and a VerValen for no more than the price originally set."

"Do you truly believe he'd lower his price that much?" Mrs.

Woodfield pursed her lips. "I can't imagine a man so anxious to sell that he'd take a loss. If that's the case, I wonder if there's something he's hiding. Did you have a look at his books, Ewan? What level of profit has he been making these past few years? Did he say why he's selling?"

Rose's shoulders finally relaxed. Until Mrs. Woodfield had asked her pointed questions about Mr. Trent's profits and his reason for selling the brickyard, Rose was certain Ewan had gained the older woman's allegiance. Now it appeared she wasn't completely convinced.

After answering Mrs. Woodfield's many questions, the older woman glanced toward the door and sighed. "I thought Catherine was going to bring tea." She gestured to Rose. "Do see if she's forgotten, dear."

Rose scurried down the hallway and into the kitchen. Catherine was leaning against the worktable visiting with Sally, Mrs. Woodfield's personal maid. They startled and turned as Rose clattered into the kitchen.

Catherine's eyes widened and she clasped a hand to her mouth. "I forgot tea for the missus. Tell her the kettle's boilin', and I'll have it to her in a jiffy."

Rose offered a hurried thank-you and rushed back to the library. She hoped nothing of importance had been discussed during her absence. "Catherine was delayed, but she'll bring tea in a few minutes. The kettle is boiling." Rose glanced at the others. "Did I miss anything while I was gone?"

"We're still discussing the advantages of the brickyard." Ewan leaned forward and rested his arms across his thighs. "After so many years working in a brickyard, I'm thinking we'd be better to invest in what I know. If it will ease your worries, I'll get answers to all of your questions, and then we can move ahead."

Rose frowned. Ewan had turned away from her and was speaking directly to his wife and mother-in-law. She'd been excluded—as though she didn't matter. She cleared her throat. "I understand Ewan's concern about investing in an unfamiliar business, but I did want to mention something that has come to mind since I've returned home."

Catherine tapped on the door, entered the room, and placed the tea tray near Mrs. Woodfield. The older woman thanked the maid and dismissed her before she looked at Rose. "Exactly what is it that has come to your attention, Rose?" Mrs. Woodfield arched her brows.

"There are already many problems among our relatives who live here and work at C&M Brickyard. If you purchase Mr. Trent's brickyard, I think Aunt Margaret will believe you plan to compete against her for contracts. And she'll make certain every member of the family believes the same thing. It will not matter that you've left Bartlett and gone to Grafton. You'll still be able to vie for the same large contracts she hopes to keep."

"Dear me, Rose makes an excellent point, Ewan." Mrs. Woodfield poured a cup of tea. "I'm sure any of your previous business contacts would much prefer doing business with you rather than Margaret Crothers, but we all know that would stir up more than one nest of hornets. How had you planned to convince Margaret you're not competing against her?"

"I had not used my time thinking about Aunt Margaret. Instead, I was looking for a business I could operate to support our family. 'Tis true Margaret would likely believe I'm trying to put her out of business or at least cripple C&M, but I know in my heart that is not my intent. Am I to be controlled by what she thinks or by what I believe is best for our family?"

"First and foremost, we should be seeking God's guidance when we make our final decision, but I do believe we should

honestly discuss any problems that are already evident to us."
The older woman sipped her tea and looked at her daughter.
"Don't you agree, Laura?"

"I do, but I don't think we can let Margaret control our future. She could have done right by Ewan and honored Hugh's word to make him a partner. If she weren't greedy and vengeful, there would be no need for Ewan to seek another business venture. Should we purchase the Grafton brickyard, Margaret should place the blame on herself, not on Ewan." Laura smiled at her husband and patted his arm.

Rose appreciated the show of support and love between the couple, but if she was going to win, she needed Laura on her side. If she didn't turn the tide now, they'd agree to the brickyard without ever considering the pottery.

"I agree Margaret has brought this upon herself, but those who work at C&M do not deserve what will surely become a battle for contracts. If Ewan wins the contracts and Margaret decreases wages or men lose their jobs, she'll point the finger at Ewan. Wouldn't it be the right thing to simply avoid competition with her? If we had no other choice but a brickyard, it might be understandable. If we choose the pottery, the family cannot hold any of us responsible if C&M fails. Is that not worth the risk, Ewan?"

He rested his forehead in his palm, his features now twisted with apprehension. "I know what you say is likely true, Rose, but I feel no confidence in anything other than a brickyard."

"But I've said I'll do whatever it takes to help you. If Rylan and the other workers remain, I don't understand your fear. You know how to operate a business, and I'm sure you'll quickly discover the process for winning contracts, just as you did when you took over C&M."

He shook his head. "I had Laura's help in order to make the

proper contacts when Uncle Hugh purchased the brickyard. There is nobody who—"

Mrs. Woodfield picked up her cup. "I don't think you need worry in that regard, Ewan. A word here and there among our friends will connect us with the proper contacts, but until you are confident and eager to try something new, I feel conflicted about the proper path. Perhaps we should all give the matter further thought and prayer."

Rose scooted to the edge of her chair. "When do you propose we meet again? There isn't much time. Ewan promised he'd send word within ten days."

The sun had gone down, and the twins had gone upstairs at least an hour ago. Concern shone in Laura's eyes. "With the party tomorrow night, there will be a great deal to accomplish before our guests arrive." She looked at Ewan. "Perhaps if the four of us ate breakfast here in the library, we could finish our discussion and come to an agreement."

Ewan nodded. "We can meet for breakfast, but if we need more time, I'll wire Mr. Trent and Mr. Bancock. I don't want to be rushed into a decision."

Rose's emotions ascended and fell as swiftly as a fiddler's bow. Even if she won a battle or two, she feared she was going to lose the war. Now that Ewan said he wouldn't be rushed into a decision, she doubted the wisdom of insisting upon tomorrow's meeting. She'd need to spend a great deal of time in prayer, but she'd first go up to the nursery and tell Beatrice she'd been allowed to attend the party.

When Rose arrived in the library the following morning, Mrs. Woodfield was already seated and finishing a cup of coffee. The older woman nodded toward the windows. "I do believe we're going to have a beautiful day for your party, Rose. The sunrise has been lovely."

Rose glanced at the clock. "When I saw you drinking coffee, I thought I might be late."

"As a matter of fact, you're early. I doubt Ewan and Laura will be down for at least another fifteen minutes. I'm glad for this time alone with you. I had hoped we would have an opportunity for a private chat." She placed her cup in the saucer. "Would you like coffee, or should I have Catherine bring a pot of tea?"

Why would Mrs. Woodfield want to speak with her alone? Rose wasn't certain, but she didn't want their time alone interrupted by the delivery of a tea tray. "Coffee will be fine." She'd never acquired a taste for coffee, but with enough sugar and cream, she could force down a swallow or two. "What would you like to discuss, Grandmother?"

The older woman pressed her fingers along the folds of her silk-taffeta day dress. "I'm impressed by your enthusiasm for the pottery, and I know you're eager to use the skills you've learned in school." She hesitated a moment. "However, if we purchase Bancock Pottery Works, I will expect a great deal from you. Ewan has expressed his discomfort with a new venture, which has made me hesitant, but after much prayer, I do feel purchasing a brickworks would create a permanent breach within the Crothers and McKay families. A matter I find extremely distasteful, for it's my hope that one day Margaret will mend her relationship with her sister." She sighed. "The day will come when Tessa will be told the truth about her adoption. When that time arrives, it would be wonderful if Kathleen could return and meet her child and reunite with her sister, as well. At least that's been my prayer."

After hearing Mrs. Woodfield's explanation, Rose was uncertain whether the older woman's reasoning constituted a sound business decision, but that didn't concern Rose. All that mattered right now was the knowledge that Mrs. Woodfield was on her side. Once Mrs. Woodfield mentioned her concerns regarding Tessa, she was certain both Laura and Ewan would agree to the decision. Excitement raced through her like a bolt of lightning. Soon, she'd begin her new adventure.

At the sound of footsteps in the hallway, Mrs. Woodfield touched Rose's hand. "Let me explain my concerns to Ewan and Laura, but remember, if we purchase the pottery, I expect great things from you. I have no doubt Ewan can invigorate a failing brickyard into a prosperous business that can support the family, but I'm not as certain he can do the same with the pottery. That will rest on your shoulders, Rose. So tell me now if you have any uncertainty about your ability to make this pottery works into a thriving business."

Though a dart of fear shot through her, Rose straightened her shoulders and avowed their pottery would become the finest and most prosperous in all of West Virginia.

## Chapter 7

A gnawing guilt followed Rose from room to room as Laura revealed the menu and the elaborate decorations she had planned for the party. Laura stopped and pointed to an area in the parlor just beyond the dining room where four upholstered chairs had been discreetly arranged behind potted plants and a flowing drape.

"During dinner, a string quartet will provide music. They'll be out of sight while we eat. After supper, the palms and draping will be removed, and additional musicians will join them to provide music for the dance." She smiled at Rose. "I hope you approve. I know it would have been much more fun if you could have helped with the plans, especially the guest list."

Rose shook her head. "The décor is beautiful and the guest list is perfect, Laura. Had I been here, I couldn't have even imagined such perfection, much less accomplished the task." She grasped Laura's hand. "I'm overwhelmed you've gone to such expense."

"Your graduation is an important event and should be marked by a celebration you'll never forget." Laura squeezed her hand. "And you need not worry about the expense. It's my mother's

71

gift to you. She's very proud of all you accomplished at school. She loves you and the twins. When Ewan and I married and she asked you and your sisters to address her as Grandmother Woodfield, she assumed that role."

Knowing Grandmother Woodfield would bear the expense of the party eased Rose's earlier guilt. The fact that the older woman had refrained from telling Rose made the gift even sweeter. Laura was right. This would be a celebration Rose would never forget. "'Tis truly kind of Grandmother. She is so generous to all of us."

Laura smiled and nodded. "You're right. She is wonderful— even if she can be a bit prickly at times." She turned and stared out the window, her gaze focused on the spring blooms that dotted the flower garden with splashes of color. "I have such fond memories of the party my mother and father hosted for me when I finished my education at Elmira Female College in New York. This is a milestone in your life, and it should be marked with an extraordinary gathering of friends and family." Laura inhaled a deep breath. "I need to quit reminiscing and get back to our party arrangements."

Taking the lead, Laura moved through the rooms and checked off the items that had been completed. When they neared the library, she gestured for Rose to follow her. "I want you to have a look at the guest list." She smiled. "One name in particular. A young man."

Rose startled to attention. Was Laura attempting to play matchmaker? Surely she understood that there would be no time for gentlemen callers, especially after the discussion in the library this morning. Before they'd made their decision to purchase the pottery, Mrs. Woodfield had been clear with Ewan and Laura. She was voting for the pottery and expected Rose to contribute greatly to the success of the business. Knowing she was eager to succeed at their new venture, why would Laura believe she'd be pleased to see any single men on the guest list?

"Do you think Mr. Bancock will accept the offer Ewan has prepared?" If she reminded Laura of their recent decision, perhaps she'd reconsider any discussion of possible suitors.

"Although we offered less than he asked, Ewan doesn't believe Mr. Bancock has any other offers. There's a possibility he'll refuse. If so, I imagine he'll at least send us a counteroffer. We prayed about our decision, and I believe we'll eventually own the pottery." Undeterred, Laura withdrew a sheet of paper from her writing desk and traced her finger down the list. "Ah, here it is. Mr. and Mrs. Jeremiah Harkness and their son, Joshua Harkness."

Rose let her gaze drift across the page as Laura pointed to the names. She'd met Joshua Harkness before. His father had conducted business with Ewan on several occasions and owned numerous businesses in Pennsylvania and West Virginia. Joshua had traveled to Bartlett on several occasions and had even attended church with them one Sunday.

Rose hadn't seen him for several years, but she had never considered Joshua as a possible suitor. She was quite certain he would have little interest in her. If memory correctly served her, Rose recalled him as quite handsome and rather aloof. Whether he had changed was irrelevant to her, for once their bid was accepted, she planned to fill all of her time at the pottery.

"Why do you think I'd be interested in Joshua Harkness?" Rose remained nearby while Laura returned the guest list to her writing desk.

Laura's lips curved in a shrewd smile. "I believe Mother mentioned you and Ewan should visit nearby potteries and learn all you can before we take control of our new business."

"She did, and I hope that will be possible. I'm willing to travel by myself if Ewan believes the business owners will provide access and meet with an unaccompanied woman." Rose wrinkled her nose. "You know there are very few forward-thinking businessmen. Most still believe we should have one apron string tied to the cookstove and the other tied to the bedpost. And if women are employed, it's at a pitiful rate of pay."

"Rose McKay!" A look of surprise crossed Laura's face as the desk drawer closed with a click. "I can only imagine what would be said if anyone overheard your remark. Your reputation could be ruined by such an unladylike comment. You need to be careful as you begin your new position at the pottery. Even though you may not agree with the attitudes of some businessmen, you'll not accomplish your goals with a fractious approach."

Rose looked away as shame swept over her. Laura was correct. To be successful, she couldn't let her personal beliefs about such matters influence her attitude. But that didn't mean changes couldn't happen within the workplace. She hoped she could at least make a wee difference for the people they would employ at the pottery, especially the women and children. However, this wasn't the time for such thoughts.

"I'm sorry, Laura. Why did you mention Joshua Harkness?"

Laura's shoulders relaxed. "Among the many businesses owned by Jeremiah Harkness, one is a pottery in Fairmont. Joshua recently moved to Fairmont to become the head of Harkness Pottery Works. I thought he might possess some helpful information and perhaps offer a tour of their pottery. He might even tell you some of the obstacles he's had to overcome since taking over." She hesitated a moment. "When I prepared the seating list for supper, I placed you next to him, but I can change the arrangement if you'd prefer something else."

"No. Oh, Laura, that's absolutely perfect." Rose rushed forward and wrapped her sister-in-law in a crushing hug. "You think of everything." A slight groan caused Rose to release her hold. She stepped back and looked into Laura's eyes. "I'm sorry. Did I hurt you?"

Laura massaged her side. "Only a few broken ribs." She chuckled when Rose clasped a hand to her lips. "Don't worry. I'm fine. I'm truly delighted you're pleased by my choice of your dinner partner." She gestured toward the kitchen. "I do need to check on preparations, but no doubt you'd rather be off doing something else." She arched her brows. "Perhaps trying on your gown one last time?"

Rose smiled and nodded. While there might be time for a final fitting of her own dress, she was more intent upon finalizing her plans with Beatrice, who had taken Rose's advice and selected the yellow silk. Though Rose was certain it would be a perfect fit, Beatrice had worried the bodice might be too tight. Rose once again thanked Laura before she hurried upstairs. She'd take the dress to the nursery and care for Tessa while Beatrice tried it on. If it didn't fit, there wouldn't be time for alterations. They'd have to change their selection.

Careful to avoid stepping on the hem, Rose trundled upstairs to the nursery. Tessa sat at a small table and chairs with a book. Craning her neck around the billowing dress, Rose smiled at the little girl. "Good morning, Tessa."

The little girl waved, then pointed to her book. "Want to read?"

"Let me help Beatrice and then we'll read." Rose turned toward the nanny. "Is this a good time for a fitting?"

Beatrice beamed at her. "Aye." Her eyes shone with delight, and she traced her fingers down the yellow silk. "'Tis like setting me eyes upon a field of sunflowers." Rose placed the dress across Beatrice's extended arms.

While Beatrice stepped into the adjoining room that served as her bedchamber, Rose sat down beside Tessa, but the girl quickly picked up the book and moved to Rose's lap. Tessa snuggled against Rose as she opened the book and began to read.

A short time later, Beatrice reappeared. Though her hair remained in an unfashionable knot and there was no jewelry to accent the neckline of the gown, she made a striking appearance. The gown fit as though it had been made for her.

She grasped a handful of fabric in each hand and performed a mock curtsy. "Thank you, Rose. It's truly beautiful, and the fit is good, don't you agree?"

Rose nodded. "Perfect. I have a necklace that is ideal with the gown. You can wear it this evening. Every young man at the dance will take notice of you. They'll be begging to write their name on your dance card."

Beatrice's smile faded. "I did not think about the dancin'. I don't know any of the fancy steps." She grimaced. "I'll be makin' a fool of myself if I try to fit in with the fancy folks. You know what they say, Rose. You can't make a silk purse out of a sow's ear."

Rose lifted Tessa onto her chair and then stood. "Don't say such a thing. You'll fit in just fine. I can show you a few basic steps, and when someone asks you to dance, tell him the truth: You'd be pleased to accept, but you've not mastered the art of dancing just yet. You're so lovely, the fellows won't mind if you step on their feet."

When she finally departed the nursery, Rose was sure Beatrice would be the most sought after young woman at the dance. The thought pleased her. It would be great fun seeing someone else enjoy the party.

Rose had barely completed her toilette when the guests who had been invited to attend the early supper started arriving. She was descending the stairs when she saw the Harkness family entering the foyer. Several years had passed since she'd last seen Joshua. He'd always been attractive, but he was now more muscular. His shoulders had broadened, and he appeared at least four inches taller. A slight smile played at her lips as she thought of the girls at school who would have swooned to be seated next to Joshua Harkness at a dinner party.

Laura motioned her forward. "Do you remember Joshua Harkness, Rose?"

Rose gave a slight nod. "Of course. I believe you attended church services with us when you last visited Bartlett several years ago."

He smiled. "I don't recall attending church, but I do remember you." He grinned. "You became angry when I asked if you had as many thorns as the roses in my mother's garden."

"I had forgotten you were one of the many who teased me about my name." Rose chuckled. "You need not tremble in fear. I no longer lose my temper when jokes are made about thorns and roses."

He pretended to wipe perspiration from his forehead. "I'm relieved to hear that. I was preparing to run for the door."

They entered the large parlor and continued to visit while the remainder of the guests arrived. When dinner was announced, Joshua expressed pleasure that they would be seated side by side. "I must admit I didn't want to come to this party, but my parents insisted. I confess that I'm glad I gave in to their wishes."

Rose was unaccustomed to the flattery of men, and her cheeks warmed in embarrassment as Joshua complimented her eyes, her dress, and her sense of humor. How had she ever thought him aloof? While they dined, Rose suddenly understood how the girls at school had become captivated by the attention of young men. During the soup, salad, and main course, Joshua remained responsive, his interest in her never waning. He agreed to have her visit the pottery, but quickly added he'd much prefer to take her to a social gathering in Fairmont or Wheeling. Never before had she experienced the giddy feelings that now swirled through her midsection. Though she disliked acting like the girls at school, there was no denying the fact that Joshua Harkness would be quite a catch.

He leaned closer as fluted dishes of snowball custard were served to each of the guests. "Perhaps I should write my name on all the lines of your dance card before we finish dessert."

At his mention of the dance, Rose was struck by an idea. Even though she'd given Beatrice a few lessons, the nanny remained fearful she'd appear foolish on the dance floor. She took a sip of water and turned toward Joshua. "I wonder if I could ask another favor of you."

"Two favors in one evening?" He grinned. "For you, I may be able to manage two. Other than visiting my pottery, how else may I be of service to you?"

Rose quickly explained that she'd invited Beatrice to the dance, and the nanny's fear of making a mistake on the dance floor. "I would be so grateful if you would dance with her several times throughout the evening. She's a distant relative, and since she's had few opportunities to attend formal parties, I want her to enjoy the evening."

"Few opportunities or none at all?" Joshua gave her a sidelong glance. "Is this her *first* time at a formal dance?"

"Yes, but I did practice with her a wee bit, and she's really quite agile. You need not—"

He held up his hand to stay her. "I only inquired so that I might know exactly what to expect. I had hoped to have the first dance with you, but if you think it would be more helpful to . . ." he hesitated. "What is her name?"

"Beatrice Murphy."

He nodded and continued. "If you think it would be more helpful to Miss Murphy, I'll sign her card for the first dance. And others if you'd like."

"Oh, would you, Joshua?" Rose's excitement mounted. "Your offer is truly generous." She couldn't believe her good fortune. Not only had Joshua agreed to have her tour his pottery, he was also going to dance with Beatrice. He was a kind gentleman, and she owed Laura a debt of gratitude for inviting him to her party. "Perhaps you could sign her card for the first two dances so she will feel comfortable if others don't immediately ask her to dance."

His brows dipped into a frown. "Why wouldn't they? Is she unappealing?"

"Quite the opposite. When you see her, I think you'll agree that she is lovely. But since she isn't known to anyone other than our family, I worried the young men wouldn't approach her."

He tilted his head back and grinned. "If I didn't know better, I'd think you hadn't attended many parties, Rose."

His question set off her internal alarm. What had she said or done that made him think she was still a novice at social events? Doing her best to appear coy, she fluttered her eyelashes, a technique the girls at school often practiced. "Why would you say such a thing, Joshua? You attended a private school and know there are parties and dances every month."

"True. But some of the fellows who weren't particularly good-looking or lacked personality never attended a social function while at school. I imagine that would be true for some of the girls, as well." His lips curved in a generous smile. "My earlier comment was rather obtuse. I should have said that if Beatrice is attractive, the men will flock to her, and you need not worry."

When dinner came to an end and they made their way into

the other room, Rose excused herself to fetch Beatrice. While ascending the stairs, she contemplated what Joshua had meant by his earlier remarks. Did he believe she hadn't attended many parties because he thought her unattractive or dull? He'd been attentive throughout dinner, but his words struck a chord that took her back to humiliating events at school. Events she longed to forget.

Making her way to the third-floor nursery, Rose pushed the unpleasant thoughts from her mind. She didn't want to ruin the evening with thoughts of school. Those days were behind her.

Ainslee sat in an overstuffed chair with Tessa snuggled beside her. "We're having a bedtime story." Ainslee motioned Rose closer. "Wait until you see Beatrice."

Before she could say anything more, Beatrice stepped into the nursery. Rose's breath caught as Beatrice turned in a circle, the yellow gown spilling at her feet like dazzling sunlight.

As she followed the nanny downstairs, Joshua's words rang in Rose's ears. She need not worry about Beatrice. Men would flock to her.

Instead of taking Joshua's hand for the first dance, Rose was escorted by her brother onto the dance floor. The stringed instruments and flickering candlelight provided a pleasing ambiance that revealed Laura's close attention to every detail of the party. While circling the room in her brother's arms, Rose's gaze drifted to the vision in yellow silk, who was smiling at Joshua. He returned her smile as they navigated the fringes of the room. A strange twinge of jealousy caught Rose by surprise. How silly. She barely knew Joshua and she'd asked him to dance with Beatrice. Why should she feel anything other than delight?

Joshua had done exactly as she'd requested, and from all appearances, he was acting the perfect gentleman.

As the final strains of music resonated throughout Woodfield Manor, Ewan squeezed Rose's hand. "Has someone claimed the next dance, or shall we continue?"

"Laura might desire the next dance with you." Just because she'd asked Joshua to dance the first two dances with Beatrice was no reason Laura should give up dancing with her husband.

"I doubt I'll manage even one dance with her tonight. Her dance card was full before I ever attempted to sign it." He grinned. "If I know my wife, she's gathering names of contacts who can possibly help us with the pottery business."

Rose glanced toward her sister-in-law and observed her deep in conversation with a businessman from Pittsburgh. "I know I could never influence many folks, but I did manage an invitation to visit the Harkness Pottery Works in Fairmont."

As they began the next dance, Ewan gave a slight nod. "I noticed you two talking all through supper. I was surprised he didn't claim the first or second dance with you."

Rose smiled as she detailed the arrangement she'd made with Joshua. "He's signed my card for the next dance, but I was grateful for his help."

Ewan turned his attention toward the couple. "From what I can see, I don't think you unduly burdened the lad. Both he and Beatrice appear to be having a fine time." As they continued to circle the floor, Ewan nodded in Beatrice's direction. "What you did for Beatrice was a kind gesture, but I hope you've told her she won't be attending parties in the future. She's been employed to care for Tessa, and I'm sure this could cause some jealousy among others who work in the house."

Rose's cheeks flamed. "I'm sorry. I hadn't given thought to Beatrice's appearance at the party creating additional problems.

I'm sure Beatrice understands, but I'll talk to her in the morning just to be clear."

Moments later the dance ended, and Ewan took Rose's hand and escorted her to Joshua's side. "I've delivered my sister, Joshua. I believe you have the next dance with her."

Several young men now surrounded Beatrice, all of them vying to sign her dance card. One of them nudged Joshua's arm. "You've certainly taken more than your share of dances with Miss Murphy."

He leaned close to Rose's ear. "Only as a favor to you."

"In that case, I'm sure you can resolve the frustration of these young men and cross your name from her dance card."

"Absolutely." Joshua cleared his throat. "Since I've already had the pleasure of two dances with Miss Murphy, you gentlemen may remove my name from further dances on her card. That should give most of you an opportunity to become acquainted with her."

Beatrice appeared to wilt when Joshua offered to relinquish his dances, but she soon regained her confidence. "All but the last dance. I refuse to have any of you write over his name for that one. My first dance was with Mr. Harkness, and I would like to end the evening with him, as well." Her lips curved in a demure smile as she turned toward Rose. "You don't mind, do you, Rose?"

"No, of course not." Her heart thudded in her chest with such force, she was certain anyone nearby could hear the hammering beat. She clenched her hands into tight fists. Her heart cried out against Beatrice's request, but with a group of onlookers surrounding Beatrice, there was no choice. Besides, a proper hostess would never deny such an appeal.

When the music began, Joshua extended his hand. "I do hope you aren't displeased that I signed for several of Beatrice's dances. When I looked at her card and saw all those empty lines, I couldn't help but feel a surge of pity for her."

"Thank you for your kindness to her." Rose forced a smile. "I was surprised that you'd signed for the last dance with her."

He loosened his hold a modicum and looked down at her. "I do apologize. This is your graduation party, and I should have asked to be your partner for the last dance, but I assumed you had already given that dance to another." The lights in the room glistened as he attempted to soothe her. "Beatrice worried she wouldn't have a partner when the evening ended, so I signed her card."

Rose wanted to tell him she'd expected to enjoy the last dance with him, but she was being foolish. She hadn't seen Joshua for several years, and they'd never been well acquainted. Just because he was attentive at supper didn't mean he wanted to share every moment with her.

Besides, her future would be at the pottery in Grafton, not with Joshua Harkness in Fairmont.

# Chapter 8

*Grafton, West Virginia*

Rylan's breath caught as he sorted through the mail at the post office. The return address on the envelope revealed the letter was from Ewan McKay. Clutching the letter in his hand, he sprinted toward the pottery with his mind racing faster than his feet. What if Mr. McKay had decided to purchase the brickyard rather than the pottery? What would Mr. Bancock do? What would the employees do? He squeezed the mail a little tighter as his thoughts skittered like grease in a hot skillet. Mr. Bancock must sell the business, but a new owner would likely mean changes.

There had been no other offers before or after Mr. McKay's visit, and Mr. Bancock's newspaper advertisements hadn't yielded any further prospective buyers. Rylan offered a silent prayer that this letter would bear good news for all of them. He wanted the best for Mr. Bancock, but he longed to have things stay the same. A few minutes later, he crossed the steel railroad tracks that divided the pottery from the main section of town.

Waving the letter overhead as he entered the office, he stepped alongside Mr. Bancock's desk and came to a halt. "The letter arrived." He dropped the mail on the owner's desk and inhaled several gulps of air. Still fighting to catch his breath, he tapped his finger on the envelope. "From Mr. McKay."

Mr. Bancock nodded but made no move to retrieve the letter from atop his desk. "I can see it is from Mr. McKay."

The suspense of the moment was almost more than Rylan could withstand. He pranced from foot to foot, like a child awaiting a peppermint stick. "Would ya like me to open it?"

The old man's weathered features folded into a frown. "I am not so frail I cannot rip open an envelope."

Just when Rylan thought he could bear it no longer, Mr. Bancock slid the envelope toward the edge of the desk and traced his fingers across his name. With slowness that set Rylan further on edge, Mr. Bancock turned over the envelope and ran his finger beneath the seal. With the same unhurried movement, the owner withdrew and unfolded the letter.

"What does it say? Is he going to be the new owner?" Rylan grasped the spindles of a nearby straight-backed chair and pulled it close to the desk. He dropped into the chair and fixed his gaze on the pottery owner. "Well?"

Mr. Bancock removed his wire-rimmed glasses and placed them on the desk. "Mr. McKay has made an offer to purchase my business but for less than I had asked."

Rylan watched his employer for some sign of either elation or displeasure. Mr. Bancock wouldn't be pleased to sell for less than his asking price, but with his diminishing health, surely he would view any respectable offer as a godsend.

"Is it a price you are willing to accept?"

If Mr. Bancock didn't do something soon, all of their skilled workers were going to quit and find work elsewhere, which would make the business even more difficult to sell.

Mr. McKay's visit had troubled any number of employees, and Rylan had heard rumors that some of them had been discussing a move to East Liverpool. Rylan had approached the workers and attempted to ease their concerns, but to no avail.

"First I must pray. I believe Mr. McKay is an honest man, but that doesn't mean he's offered me the value of my business."

Rylan tipped his head to the side. "I do not want to offend you, but the price you placed on the business may not be the proper value. Over the years you've cared for this pottery as if it was yar own wee child. Have you thought that the price you set for the place might be includin' some of that love you hold in yar heart?" Rylan arched his brows. "Much as ya love this place, ya know what the doctor has said."

Mr. Bancock folded the piece of paper and returned it to the envelope before tucking it into the pocket of his jacket. "I know there's not much choice but to accept his offer, but I'll not be doing anything until I spend some time in prayer. Best you not say anything to anyone else. When the business is sold, I want to be the one to tell the workers. And if it's to Mr. McKay, I'll ask him to be present when I do." Though it was only two o'clock, Mr. Bancock pushed to his feet. "I'm going home for the remainder of the day. Please see to closing up, Rylan."

Rylan wasn't surprised to hear that Mr. Bancock would pray about his decision, nor was he surprised to hear the owner wanted to be the one to tell his workers when the business sold. However, he had expected Mr. Bancock to be more forthcoming about the amount Mr. McKay had offered. Though the owner had no obligation to tell Rylan, he had been included in all of the business conducted in the office for more than two years. Truth be told, he knew as much about the assets and liabilities of the business as Mr. Bancock, for it was Rylan who balanced the ledgers, completed the payroll sheets, and placed the weekly wages in each employee's pay envelope.

Rylan stepped to the door and stared at Mr. Bancock's departing figure. Shoulders slumped, the old man trudged across the railroad tracks, a picture of defeat. Rylan longed to do something that would help save the business. Both for Mr. Bancock's sake, as well as his own. For years, the pottery owner had provided Rylan more than a place to work. He'd been a teacher, a friend, and a substitute father. Mr. Bancock had helped Rylan turn loose of long-held resentments toward his father and stepmother. *"You're hurting yourself more than you'll ever hurt them. With that root of bitterness growing in your heart, you'll soon become mean and unlovable, a man others will avoid."* Rylan had listened to the older man's counsel, and after many weeks of Mr. Bancock's patient Bible teaching, Rylan had accepted the undeserved gift of God's forgiveness. Eventually he'd forgiven his parents: his stepmother for the harsh changes she'd forced upon him, and his father for giving her the freedom to create a house filled with misery. Rylan had continued to forge his future and forget his wretched childhood, but now his nightmares had returned.

During working hours he'd set aside his own worries and encouraged his fellow employees, but when he went home at night, the past haunted him. Would the new employer be like his stepmother? Would he be degraded and humiliated? Would a new owner come into the pottery and force changes Rylan couldn't accept?

During the week that followed, it took every ounce of strength Rylan could muster to avoid asking Mr. Bancock if he'd made a decision. Rylan had promised himself he would not inquire.

Mr. Bancock would talk when he was ready. But Rylan didn't know if he could stay his questions much longer.

He glanced at the clock and then looked out the front window, worried that his employer hadn't yet appeared. When he'd finished posting the invoices and payments to the ledger, the clock chimed nine times. Mr. Bancock was late only on mornings when he had an appointment or when he was ill. He hadn't mentioned an appointment when they departed last night. Fear prickled Rylan's skin. What if Mr. Bancock's condition had worsened and he needed help? In the past a neighbor boy would deliver a note to Rylan if the man needed him. But there had been no sign of the youngster today. Maybe Mr. Bancock was too ill to get out of bed and send a message.

Rylan grabbed his hat, then quickly closed and locked the office door. Before heading off, he stopped in the decorator shop and told Mr. Wheeler he'd be back shortly. As he spoke to the decorator, the rumble of an oncoming train sounded, and he chided himself for waiting so long. At least five minutes would pass before he could cross the tracks. If the train had extra cars, it could be even longer.

Rylan fixed his attention on the tracks, hoping to see the caboose come into sight. With each passing coach and boxcar, his fear mounted. His thoughts raced from one horrible event to another, each one worse than the last, until he finally glanced heavenward and realized he needed to pray, not worry. For what seemed an eternity, he asked God to protect Mr. Bancock until he could get to him. He asked God to hurry the train, and he asked God to make him fleet of foot once the train passed by.

When he opened his eyes, the caboose had flown by, and Rylan found himself staring across the tracks at Mr. Bancock and Mr. McKay. Filled with a surge of gratitude, Rylan uttered a quick prayer of thanks as he waved to the two men and waited for them to cross.

Mr. Bancock's bushy brows knit together above his deep-set eyes. He was only halfway across the tracks when he shouted to Rylan, "Where are you going? Did you leave the office unlocked?"

His voice was tinged with a harshness that surprised Rylan. "You are never late, and I thought you might need help. I was going to your house to see if you'd suffered some unexpected sickness during the night."

As the two men came alongside Rylan, Mr. McKay nodded. "How kind of you to worry about your employer, Rylan." His lips curved in a bright smile. "Good it is to see you again."

"Good to see you, as well, Mr. McKay." Rylan turned toward Mr. Bancock. "I didn't know Mr. McKay was paying a visit today, or I wouldn't have worried about you."

Mr. Bancock ducked his head and avoided Rylan's eyes. "I thought it might be best to keep the news to myself. Never know when the train will be late or something might happen to change circumstances. I didn't want things getting all stirred up among the workers."

When they arrived at the office, Rylan withdrew his key and unlocked the door. He hesitated as the two men stepped inside. "Do you want me to go and pick up the time sheets, Mr. Bancock?"

The owner's face tightened with confusion. "Of course not. I want you here in the office so you can learn about the future of the pottery." He waved toward the exit. "Close the door. I don't want anyone able to listen in on our discussion."

Rylan closed the door and sat down in the remaining chair, pleased Mr. Bancock chose to include him.

"I asked Mr. McKay to return because I want the workers

to meet him and know he will be the new owner of the pottery. Today we will sign the papers to make everything official." Mr. Bancock looked at Mr. McKay. "I know this trip was inconvenient for you, so I thank you for making this extra effort. To tell the workers together will be much better for both of us, I think."

"Aye. For sure, I want your workers to stay on after I take over. Making pottery is a new business for me, so their experience will be needed. I told my family Mr. Trent's brickworks would be a safer choice for me, but they were thinking it was time to try something new." Ewan glanced around the office as though he still wasn't at ease with the decision. "I will be pleased to join you when you tell the workers I've bought the business. You should be clear when you tell them their jobs are secure."

Mr. Bancock gave a slight shake of his head. "I think you should tell them that part, Mr. McKay. They'll have no doubt if they hear those words from your lips."

Ewan nodded. "You're right. I want to be certain there's no doubt in their minds."

Rylan inched forward on his chair. "Sounds like you're not planning on changing things here at the pottery, Mr. McKay."

Ewan leaned forward and rested his arms on his knees. "I'm thinking there will be some changes, Rylan, but we won't know what will be working best for us until we've been here a wee bit. Once I study things for a time, I'll know more about what might need changing. Even so, I plan to make certain those who worked for Mr. Bancock will have a job with me if they want one." He reached out and patted Rylan on the shoulder. "Truth is, I think we'll need even more workers. My hope is that we can expand and become competitors with some of the larger potteries in the area. I'll likely need some help from you when we begin the bidding process."

Mr. Bancock had talked of expanding some time ago, but

that had never happened. He'd possessed neither the money nor the desire to go into debt. Eventually, the business had diminished in size. For now, Rylan hoped the only thing Mr. McKay wanted to change was the decorating shop. The pottery needed to offer a greater variety of hand-painted and gilded pieces, but they would need more artists if they were to accomplish that goal.

Most of the artists who'd previously worked for Mr. Bancock had located work over the past few months. Still, a few might be convinced to return for a higher wage. And there had been talk of Miss McKay's talents in design during their visit. Maybe she was planning to pick up a brush and ask Mr. Wheeler for instruction. With her skills, she'd likely master the craft in no time.

"I'll be pleased to help you prepare bidding proposals or help anywhere else you need my assistance, but I think you're wise to move slowly with any changes."

Rylan had hoped the comment would elicit more information about any possible changes, but Ewan merely nodded and thanked him.

This likely was not the time to pursue the matter, but Rylan needed more reassurance Mr. McKay wasn't going to turn his world upside down. "So you'd be waiting quite some time before you do anything to change the place?"

Ewan smiled and shook his head. "I wouldn't say quite a while. If I'm going to turn this operation into a successful business, I need to gain contracts for large orders, and securing large orders means we'll need more workers. Since the business has diminished and there are fewer workers than in years past, there isn't a need to add more kilns or increase work areas right now." His smile broadened. "But if things go as I plan, that day will arrive sooner rather than later."

Rylan's anxiety heightened as he digested the new owner's words. He told himself he should remain silent, but he couldn't hold back. He didn't want Mr. McKay to walk in and create major changes in this place that he considered his home.

"There's much to be said for not biting off more than you can chew. Big contracts mean more money, but if we can't meet the demand on schedule, it will hurt the pottery's reputation."

"Rylan!" Mr. Bancock glared at him. "Mr. McKay does not need you telling him how to conduct business. He operated a large brickyard for many years. I think he knows how to make sound decisions."

Rylan bobbed his head. "Aye. I'm sure he does, Mr. Bancock. I was just trying to point out—"

"'Tis quite all right. No need to worry about Rylan adding his ideas, Mr. Bancock. I'm a man who likes to hear from his workers. Nothing Rylan says is going to displease me. I may not always take the advice of those who work for me, but I'm always willing to listen. Having three sisters caused me to become a good listener early in life." Ewan chuckled. "You have any sisters, Rylan?"

"Nay."

"Then I'm guessin' your mother taught you that listening is important in life, aye?"

Rylan shrugged slightly. "Mam died when I was ten, but the woman my da married made sure I listened." His thoughts raced back to the many times his stepmother had cuffed him for not giving her the attention she demanded.

Mr. McKay winked. "I've learned it takes soft reminders from our womenfolk to turn us into proper gentlemen."

Rylan didn't reply. The reminders Rylan received from his stepmother had never been kind or soft. And she'd cared not at all about making him into a proper gentleman. Instead, she'd expected him to bring home a full pay envelope each week and complete his daily chores.

After a fleeting grin, Ewan turned to Mr. Bancock and tapped the papers atop the owner's desk. "Time is wasting, and I'm eager to make this pottery my own, Mr. Bancock. Once we've signed the contract, let's speak with the workers."

Pen in hand, Mr. Bancock hunched over the desk and placed his signature on the last page of the contract. Moments later, Mr. McKay did the same. Rylan didn't notice an exchange of money but guessed the men had gone to the bank before coming to the pottery.

Mr. Bancock looked up from the desk and gestured to Rylan. "Why don't you go and gather the men who can leave their work areas for a short time. Tell them I have important news and want to speak to them near the packing house."

Rylan nodded and pushed up from his chair. He walked outside and turned toward the clay pit. One by one, he carried the message to the various divisions of the pottery. Questions flew in his direction, but he answered each one the same. "Mr. Bancock says he has important news. You need to come to the meeting and find out for yourself."

From young to old, all of the workers appeared anxious as they gathered near the packing house. An air of anticipation hung heavy in the air, as if they knew today marked a new beginning for all of them.

93

# Chapter 9

*Fairmont, West Virginia*
*Early Summer 1872*

After placing a small bag on the rack mounted above their coach seat, Rose sat down beside Mrs. Woodfield. Soon after they'd made themselves as comfortable as possible on the hard wooden seat, the conductor looked at his watch, then signaled the engineer.

Mrs. Woodfield blew a sigh as the train chugged away from the Bartlett station. "I do wish we could have taken a train that had a first-class car." The older woman scanned her surroundings and curled her lip. "It doesn't seem it would be too difficult for the railroad to put a bit of padding on these seats."

Rose eyed several male passengers in dirty work clothes wearing mud-caked boots. "I doubt the cushions would remain clean for very long. I am truly sorry Ewan insisted you or Laura accompany me. He doesn't realize I'm quite capable of traveling by myself."

If all had gone according to plan, it should have been Ewan accompanying her to tour the Harkness Pottery Works in Fairmont. Instead, he had already taken over the leadership of their recently acquired pottery works in Grafton.

The contract to purchase had contained a clause stating Ewan would not take possession of the pottery for two months, as both Mr. Bancock and Ewan had agreed they both would need adequate time to make necessary arrangements: Ewan to purchase a comfortable house and move his family, and Mr. Bancock to notify his customers and fulfill any outstanding contracts.

The plan had been a good one, but only a week after signing the contract, the pottery owner's health had taken a downward turn, and the doctor predicted that Mr. Bancock would never again return to work at the pottery. The news had caught all of them by surprise. An immediate takeover of the business wasn't to Ewan's liking, but there had been no other option.

Mr. Bancock's departure left much resting on the shoulders of the family, Laura in particular. During the days that followed, Laura had compiled a long list of items that needed to be accomplished prior to their move. In the process, she'd managed to delegate several tasks to others. The particular responsibility of escorting Rose to Fairmont had been assigned to her mother.

Mrs. Woodfield *tsked* and shook her head. "It isn't proper, my dear. Just take a look around you. Who knows what advances some of these men might make toward a young woman traveling alone. Ewan believes women need protection, and he's correct."

Rose wrinkled her nose. "I traveled by myself while I was away at school, and I was fine. Nobody ever accosted me."

Mrs. Woodfield's brows furrowed, and her lips drooped into a frown. "Did Mrs. Fisk know you were traveling unaccompanied? She has an obligation to protect the young women who—"

Rose touched Mrs. Woodfield's arm and interrupted. "Mrs. Fisk did not know. She would not have approved, but most of the girls traveled unaccompanied from time to time. As for me, if I had waited for an escort, I doubt I would have ever been outside the school."

"I think you're exaggerating, but I'm willing to overlook your indiscretion while you were at school. However, now that you're back home, you must follow social mores. For you to travel alone is simply unacceptable." She directed a stern look at Rose. "Do I make myself clear?"

"Yes, I understand, but I'll not say I agree." She gave the older woman a sidelong glance. "Since I must follow the rules, I want you to know I do appreciate your willingness to come along. I'm sure a tour of Harkness Pottery isn't of great interest to you."

Mrs. Woodfield chuckled. "Truthfully, it is not, but I'll escort you at least as far as the office. I doubt Joshua will mind if I forego accompanying the two of you for the full tour." Her lips curved in a sly smile. "He appeared quite taken with you at your party, and I'm sure the two of you would like a little time alone. Not that you'll be off by yourselves in a pottery filled with workers. Still, it will give you two an opportunity to visit by yourselves before I join you both for supper this evening."

Joshua's note inviting Rose to tour the pottery last week had also included an invitation for Rose and her chaperone to join him for supper at the restaurant located in the Grand Hotel. Laura and Mrs. Woodfield were certain the invitation indicated an interest far beyond a tour of the pottery, but Rose wasn't so sure. She'd not voiced her thoughts about Joshua or the invitation, as she'd not change the opinion of either Laura or her mother.

Instead, Rose decided she'd bide her time and see if Joshua was simply fulfilling the promise he'd made during the party. Of course, there had been no need to include an invitation to supper. The offer could simply be a courtesy extended to visitors from out of town.

Though she thought Joshua quite handsome and kind, Rose expected nothing more than what had been included in his invitation: a tour of the pottery followed by supper at the hotel. Her years at school had taught Rose not to raise her expectations, especially where men were involved.

She didn't intend to change her attitude at this juncture, not when Ewan was depending on her assistance with the pottery. Right now, she wouldn't consider Joshua anything more than a friend. She silently repeated that caveat when she stepped off the train a short time later and looked into Joshua's coppery-brown eyes.

Her memory had betrayed her. He was even more handsome than she recalled. He greeted her with unexpected enthusiasm and warmth that both surprised and pleased her. Lightly grasping her elbow, he led Rose and Mrs. Woodfield past the baggage carts and toward the station door.

"You ladies can wait in here while I see to your luggage." He nodded toward the small case Rose held in her hand. "Let me take that for you." A surprising chill raced up her arm as his hand lingered on hers for several moments. When she looked up and met his gaze, his eyes twinkled with pleasure.

She silently chided herself, but she was unable to look away from his muscular frame as he strode out the door.

"He's quite handsome, don't you agree?"

Mrs. Woodfield's question pulled Rose from her private thoughts. "I hadn't noticed."

The older woman chuckled and shook her head. "I don't believe that's the whole truth, Rose. My eyesight isn't perfect, but I didn't miss the glimmer in your eyes when Joshua greeted you. And I didn't miss the look of admiration in his, either."

Heat raced up Rose's neck and settled in her cheeks. She wanted to deny Mrs. Woodfield's comment, but to do so would only lead to further remarks and more embarrassment.

"I arranged for your baggage to be delivered to the hotel. Would you ladies like to go directly to the pottery, or do you prefer to go to the hotel first?" Joshua's forehead wrinkled into deep ridges when he turned toward Rose. "Are you not feeling well? Your cheeks are bright red."

"I'm fine. Just a little warm." She gestured to the older woman. "Which would you prefer, Grandmother?"

"I generally suffer from headaches when I travel, but I'm feeling quite well right now. Why don't we go to the pottery, and you can complete your tour. There should be time to rest afterward, don't you think, Joshua?"

"Of course. We don't have to tour all of the pottery today. We can do as much or as little as you'd like. There will be time to return tomorrow if you'd prefer."

Mrs. Woodfield sighed. "I suppose so, but we planned to leave on the two o'clock train tomorrow."

Joshua escorted the two of them out of the train station and into an awaiting carriage. Before stepping inside, he signaled the driver. "Take us back to the pottery, Henry."

"Your pottery must be quite successful, Joshua." Mrs. Woodfield settled against the leather-cushioned upholstery.

He rubbed his chin and gave a slight shake of his head. "What would make you assume the pottery is profitable, Mrs. Woodfield?"

"Why, the fact that you have an expensive coach and driver." She gestured toward the interior of the carriage. "I can't imagine that anyone struggling to make ends meet would have such luxuries."

"The carriage belongs to my father, and Henry has been a

driver for the family for many years. He agreed to move when Father sent me to Fairmont. At least that's what I was told. In truth, I think Father sent him along to keep an eye on me and report any problems."

"And have you had any?" The silence that followed caused Rose to hastily rephrase her question. "What I meant was, have you had any problems at the pottery?"

Joshua's lips curved in a lopsided grin. "The pottery has been nothing but problems. My father believes I should have it operating at a profit within a year. His expectations are unrealistic, and I've told him as much." He shifted on his seat. "The way things are going, I doubt this pottery will ever make a profit."

Rose scooted forward on the carriage seat. "Then you must develop something special that will help the business change course." The idea of receiving such a challenge excited her. It was the same feeling she'd experienced when Mrs. Fisk had described the Excellence in Design contest. "I'm sure you're capable of meeting the challenge your father has issued."

"You may be right, but working in a pottery isn't where I planned to make a name for myself."

Mrs. Woodfield arched her brows. "And exactly where did you hope to achieve fame and fortune, Joshua?"

"I thought my father would want to have me work alongside him in his office so I could learn about all of his businesses. If I'm going to take over one day, I need to know about more than operating a pottery."

Mrs. Woodfield folded her hands in her lap. "Your father is a successful businessman, so I'm certain he gave your placement a great deal of thought. He likely believes it's best to learn about his companies by dealing with the difficulties of each business firsthand."

Joshua offered a lackluster smile and appeared relieved when the carriage came to a halt. "Ah, here we are." He exited the carriage and held out his hand to assist Rose. As she stepped down, he swooped his hat across in front of him and gave a mock bow. "Harkness Pottery awaits you, my lady."

Rose giggled. His performance inspired her to play along, and she dipped into a slight curtsy. "Thank you, kind sir." She stepped aside so Joshua could assist Mrs. Woodfield.

"No need to bow for me. My bones would creak too much if I attempted a curtsy." Mrs. Woodfield gestured toward the front door of the pottery. "Just show me to a chair in the office where I can sit and listen to you explain the workings of the business. Once you've finished, you and Rose can take your walking tour while I remain behind and read my book."

Rose quickly surveyed the area before Joshua led them inside. From her observation, the pottery was situated in a good location. There was river access, and though it would have been better to have been situated a little closer to the railroad, it wasn't terribly far. Still, it did mean that any goods being shipped by rail had to first be loaded onto wagons and transported several miles to the depot.

Rose had taken note of several businesses located close to both the river and the railroad tracks located a short distance to the north. Once they'd entered the office and been seated, Rose motioned over her shoulder in the direction of the distant railroad tracks. "I wonder why the original owner didn't locate the pottery with better access to both the railroad and the river."

Joshua shrugged. "I've wondered the same thing. I checked some of the land records and discovered that he could have purchased the land where the lumber mill is situated. One of the men working in the clay pit says it's because the clay deposits were better here, but there are large clay deposits on much of the nearby land." He leaned back in his chair. "I think he was trying to save money. In the end, it didn't work out that way."

He cast a look at the ledger books, and Rose wondered if the pottery was suffering greater financial woes than Joshua cared to admit. If so, he'd truly need to discover some innovative way to either increase profits or decrease his losses.

Mrs. Woodfield cleared her throat. "You may begin, Joshua. I'm eager to hear about Harkness Pottery."

Rose thought that might be a bit of an exaggeration, but at least the older woman listened and asked questions as Joshua gave a brief overview of the company. He carefully avoided financial details and information regarding contracts, but Rose hadn't expected him to reveal such private information. She gave him her full attention, though her real interest was in discovering what lay beyond the office door. How many employees worked for the company, what products were created, what sold best, what were the working conditions like, and were there any different methods used that would improve their own pottery in Grafton?

"I think I've covered most aspects of the business, but if you have questions, I'd be glad to try to answer them, though I may have to pass them along to some of the employees if they're difficult."

He chuckled, but Rose thought there was likely some truth in his remark. Joshua had been at the pottery for some time now, but his lack of interest in the business was obvious. Instead of being hidden away in a pottery, he wanted to be sitting at an oversized desk in Wheeling or Pittsburgh.

Mrs. Woodfield shook her head. "No questions. You and Rose go on with your tour, but don't be gone more than a few hours. I'll be ready for a rest by then."

"Unless Rose is extremely interested in some area of the

pottery, we shouldn't be gone long at all. I doubt she'll want to go to the clay pits or kilns." He turned toward Rose. "Am I right?"

"You're correct that I don't want to see those areas, but if you have a large decorating shop, I may want to spend some extra time there." She stood and glanced at Mrs. Woodfield. "Are you certain you'll be all right here? Joshua's driver could take you to the hotel if you'd be more comfortable there."

"Since I really don't need to act as your chaperone on the tour, perhaps it wouldn't be unseemly for me to return to the hotel." She pinned Joshua with a stern look. "I'll expect you to be the perfect gentleman and return Rose to the hotel as soon as she's completed the tour."

"You can trust me to deliver her back to you safe and sound. Just let me speak to Henry, and you can be on your way."

Once Mrs. Woodfield departed, Joshua escorted Rose to the clay shop. "This is where the clay is prepared and molded into a variety of different products. I think you'll discover it's much like the place Ewan has purchased."

Rose nodded as they passed the perspiring, muscular men heaving large wedges of clay; the skilled jiggermen creating plates, cups, and vases; and the youthful, unskilled mold-runners and batters-out. She surveyed her current surroundings with the same critical eye she'd used at Bancock Pottery and was surprised to discover that Harkness Pottery came up short.

While she'd thought the situation at Bancock Pottery quite dirty and unsanitary, Mr. Bancock did employ two women who cleaned the shops each night. Here at Harkness Pottery, layers of clay dust coated all of the work areas. The dust on the floors was so thick it quickly coated her shoes and the hem of her skirt.

When they entered the area where the warehouse women were dusting dirt from the ware, Rose looked in on women and children cleaning the ware while breathing the clay dust that filled the air. The whisking of brushes on bisqueware accompanied the labored breathing, coughing, and wheezing at each workbench.

"I thought the work areas at our pottery were terrible, but I believe your pottery is far worse, Joshua. Do you hire any janitors to clean?"

He leaned against the doorjamb, careful to keep his nose turned toward the fresh air. "My father wants me to turn this into a profitable business. I've cut expenses wherever I can. I've told the workers in each shop to clean up after themselves before they leave for the day. Seems they'd rather work in the dust and dirt than stay and clean the place." He shrugged. "It's their choice."

Rose didn't concur, but she remained silent. She wanted to see the remainder of the pottery. If she criticized too much, Joshua might curtail their tour. "I'm told that most of the potteries have difficulty keeping all but the skilled workers for long periods of time. Is that true for you, as well?"

"I don't keep up with the comings and goings of those who work for the skilled workers. They hire their own unskilled workers and pay their wages, so I never see their names on my payroll. I do employ the rest of the unskilled workers, and they quit more often than I'd like. They don't give a reason for why they're leaving, but I think they find the work more tedious than they expected."

Rose agreed that stamping the company trademark onto the bottom of the ware for ten hours a day would be tedious, but she suspected many of the unskilled workers became sick from breathing the clay dust or dipping the ware into glaze that contained lead. After touring Bancock Pottery, she'd spoken to Dr. Balch, their physician in Bartlett, and discovered there were already existing medical studies detailing the dangers of lead.

As they entered the decorating shop, Rose scanned and silently counted the number of workers. Unlike Bancock Pottery, the worktables in the Harkness Pottery employed more than twenty decorators, who were hand-painting intricate designs onto plates and serving pieces while several other employees gilded large urns and vases. She approached one of the worktables for a closer examination. Though she'd been impressed to see so many decorators, none of them possessed Mr. Wheeler's creativity and skill.

"You have a lot of decorators. I believe there's a good profit to be made selling high-quality items that are hand-painted by skilled artists." She glanced over her shoulder. "Do you agree?"

He grasped her elbow and led her from the area. "I never express such ideas in front of the workers. If they believe I have a great need for their skills, they'll want more money, and the decorators are already the highest-paid workers in the pottery."

"That's what Mr. Bancock said. I was disappointed to learn he'd dismissed all of his decorators but one. I'm hopeful we may be able to hire some of them back. And I plan to work on ideas in the decorating shop, as well. I believe we can create a market for unique patterns."

"I'm not sure I agree with your concept. I dismissed most of my artists and replaced them with decorators willing to take lower wages. These decorators aren't quite as talented, but they get the work out faster. I've decided producing in greater quantity is the answer to making money."

Rose arched her brows. "So you believe quantity is more important than quality?"

Joshua tipped his head to one side. "I believe I'll make more money by paying lower wages and producing more ware. I've set quotas that must be met each day. Simple as that."

She smiled and shook her head. "I disagree. I believe quality will win."

"I suppose only time will tell who is correct, but I intend to make a profit with this pottery as quickly as possible."

She matched his stride as they returned to the office. "So you can move into an office in Wheeling or Pittsburgh?"

"Exactly. I don't want this to be the final stop in my career. I know you and your brother have big dreams for your pottery, but my dreams take me far beyond Harkness Pottery."

Rose wasn't offended by his reply. She thought he would probably achieve his goal. Not because of his hard work and dedication, but because his father and grandfather before him had been willing to labor long hours and make the necessary sacrifices to gain success.

They were a short distance from the hotel when Joshua mentioned her graduation party and then inquired about their pending move to Grafton.

"Ewan's recent letter stated he was negotiating to purchase a house he believed we would all enjoy. There's some question about whether the owner will agree to Ewan's offer. We're all eager to be together again, so I'm hopeful they'll come to an agreement."

"And will Beatrice be moving to Grafton with the family?"

"As far as I know she will. Why do you ask?"

He fumbled with his jacket and finally withdrew his watch. Instead of snapping open the clasp to check the time, he rubbed the gold case back and forth between his thumb and fingertips. "I merely wondered. When our family has made moves in the past, some members of the staff didn't care to leave the area. When we danced, Beatrice mentioned she has family in Bartlett. I thought she might want to remain close to them."

Joshua's question followed her as she climbed the hotel

staircase and entered the rooms she shared with Mrs. Wood-field. He'd not inquired about any member of her family, yet he'd asked about Beatrice. Why he would care if Tessa's nanny remained in Bartlett or came with them to Grafton mystified her.

# Chapter 10

*Bartlett, West Virginia*

When Rose and Mrs. Woodfield arrived home, Laura met them at the front door. She held a letter in her hand. "Good news from Ewan. The house is ours. The owner finally agreed to the price he offered." Laura tapped the envelope. "They haven't yet moved out, but he wants us to prepare for our move."

Mrs. Woodfield gave her daughter a firm nod. "I'm glad we had the servants begin packing as soon as Ewan departed for Grafton. I think we should make a trip to see the house for ourselves before we begin arranging for furniture shipment. What if our furniture doesn't fit in the new house?" She looked around the parlor. "Since I don't plan to sell Woodfield Manor just yet, I think we should leave most of the furnishings here. You and Ewan may grow weary of having me around, and I wouldn't want to return to an unfurnished house. Besides, I think it would be lovely if you and Ewan purchased new furnishings for your home."

"As long as there is a bed to sleep in and a dining table and chairs where we can take our meals, I doubt Ewan will care about furnishings. And I'm doubly certain he won't want to spend precious hours choosing draperies and carpet." Laura brightened and looked back and forth between Rose and her mother. "I do think a trip to Grafton is in order so we'll know what we must purchase, but I'll want to be frugal, Mother."

Mrs. Woodfield gave a slight nod and stepped into the hallway as Joseph and Zeke carried in their baggage. "Don't take those upstairs. We're going to depart again."

Zeke's forehead creased, and his eyes shone with confusion. "You want me to lug these back out to the wagon and take you back to the train station, Mrs. Woodfield?"

"No, we won't leave until tomorrow. Sally can unpack any of the personal items I'll need and carry them upstairs." She turned to Laura and Rose. "I best go upstairs and rest, or I'll have a headache and have to stay home."

Laura grasped Rose's hand as the older woman marched upstairs. "Come sit down and tell me about your visit to the pottery. Did you discover anything that might be helpful with our pottery? Was Joshua attentive? Did he escort you and Mother to supper? Did the two of you have any time alone?"

Rose followed her into the parlor and sat down next to her on the divan. "Let me see if I can remember all of your questions. No, I don't think visiting Joshua's pottery was helpful. Yes, Joshua was attentive, and yes, he escorted us to supper, and yes we did have some time alone." Rose giggled. "Was that everything?"

"Your memory is quite good, but I would enjoy some additional details. I'm surprised your visit didn't yield any helpful ideas for the pottery. From what Joshua told Ewan during your graduation party, I expected to hear news of exciting innovations being made at their pottery."

The comment caught Rose by surprise. Had she missed something during her tour of the pottery? Had Joshua intentionally withheld information? "I didn't see anything I would consider new or original. He didn't divulge any of his contracts or let me review his books."

Laura tapped her index finger to her lips and stared into the distance. "No. I don't think it was a contract. He said something about making changes at the pottery. Both Ewan and I wondered if he'd come upon some new piece of equipment or a unique process for making the ware."

Rose shook her head. "Joshua wouldn't spend money to purchase equipment for the pottery. He wants only to turn a profit so he can convince his father he can take over for him one day soon. The changes he's making aren't ones that Ewan would ever consider."

Laura gasped as if shocked that Rose would make such a sweeping statement. "What do you mean? Ewan has never objected to trying new ideas."

"Joshua's ideas aren't new. He's decided the best way to make a profit is to lower costs, mostly on the backs of his workers." Rose straightened her shoulders. "I disagree with him, but he believes his way will make him successful."

"I've always known his father to be a good businessman, not overly sentimental but fair in his business dealings. My father conducted business with him for many years before the war." Laura tucked a stray wisp of hair back in place. "And what about the social time you had with Joshua? Did you find him to be a gallant escort?"

Heat spread across Rose's cheeks. "I did. He's a true gentleman, and I do like him, even if I don't agree with how he conducts his business and treats his workers."

Laura leaned a bit closer. "Did you and Joshua make plans to see each other again?"

"He did say that he would come and visit once we've moved to Grafton. He said I could show him through our pottery."

"Nothing more? Did he mention taking you to dinner?"

"Yes, but I said it wasn't necessary."

"Rose McKay! How do you intend to be courted when you tell a man his invitation is unnecessary?"

Rose shrugged. "I like Joshua, but if he merely wishes to visit the pottery, I don't want him to feel obligated to see me socially."

Laura sighed and massaged her forehead. "Dear, dear Rose. I fear your knowledge of men is quite limited. Men must gather their courage in order to ask a lady to accompany them on an outing." She arched her brows. "Don't you see?"

Rose wasn't sure she did. It all sounded rather silly. Like a game of cat and mouse. "I have a bit of a better understanding. Thank you for taking time to explain, Laura. I promise to be more careful in the future." Rose glanced toward the pounding of shoes on the staircase.

Ainslee soon appeared, her hair flying behind her. Though the twins would soon turn sixteen, they seldom took time to fashion their hair, both of them preferring no more than a loose ribbon tied around their locks. Both Ainslee and Adaira teetered between immaturity and adulthood, their behavior as unpredictable as the weather.

"Rose, you're back! Did you have fun? Grandmother Woodfield says we're going to Grafton. I can hardly wait." Before allowing time for an answer, she turned to Laura. "Are we all going?"

"Yes, we're all going. Even Tessa," Laura said.

Ainslee turned to her older sister. "Well, did you have fun?" There was a trace of jealousy in her tone.

Rose decided she wouldn't reference the hotel and fine meals she'd enjoyed. No need to say anything that could create envy.

"It was nice to tour the pottery and learn more about how Joshua operates his business."

"Visiting a pottery doesn't sound like fun." Ainslee wrinkled her nose. "I'm going upstairs to lay out my clothes to wear tomorrow."

Laura's gaze followed after Ainslee for a moment before she turned back toward Rose. "Would you ask Beatrice if she would pack a small bag for Tessa before you go to your room?"

Rose pushed up from the divan. "I'll be happy to stop at the nursery. I missed Tessa." She glanced over her shoulder as she strode toward the stairway. "Is Beatrice traveling with us to Grafton?"

Laura shook her head. "No. I think we can manage without her. I'm sure she'd enjoy an extra day off to visit with her family."

Rose's thoughts rushed back to Joshua's recent inquiry. Resting her hand on the newel post, she stopped before ascending the steps. "Has Beatrice said if she plans to move to Grafton with us?"

"Yes. Why do you ask?"

"I thought she might want to remain close to her family. 'Tis only a half-hour walk to her house now, but once we move, she'd need to ride the train to visit her relatives." Rose continued up the stairs before Laura quizzed her further. It would be awkward to explain that it had been Joshua who'd asked about the nanny's future plans.

As she topped the stairs leading to the nursery, Rose spied the small sampler hanging on the nursery door handle. Ignoring the *Visitors, Please Knock* message the nanny had embroidered on the sampler, Rose opened the door and stepped inside the nursery.

Beatrice's features creased into a tight frown. "Did ya not see the sampler hanging on the door, Rose?"

Had the two of them not been distant relatives, Rose doubted Beatrice would have taken such a tone with her. The two young women had never met while living in Ireland, and they'd met only a time or two after Beatrice and her immediate family arrived in West Virginia. Yet Beatrice assumed a lack of formality toward Rose and the twins that she would never take with Laura or Mrs. Woodfield.

"Aye, but I've told you in the past, I do not consider myself a visitor. Besides, I think the message a bit of nonsense."

Rose didn't understand why anyone would need to knock. The doorway led directly into Tessa's play area. The room where the toddler took her daily naps was separated by yet another door.

She continued across the room with her attention focused upon the child. The little girl lifted a rag doll in one hand and swung it around. The doll hit a stack of blocks that topped to the floor. Rose smiled as she knelt down beside Tessa. "I hope you haven't hurt your baby. Maybe she needs a hug." Rose lifted Tessa's arms to surround the doll. "There. Give your baby a big hug."

Tessa squeezed the doll and giggled.

"'Tis time for her nap. If you're wantin' to play with her, you'll need to come back later." Beatrice strode toward them and grasped the child's hand.

Tessa cried in protest, and Rose pushed to her feet. "Why don't you let me put her down for her nap? We're going to be leaving for Grafton in the morning, and Laura asked that you pack a change of clothing for Tessa and a few small toys."

Beatrice's eyebrows dipped low on her forehead. "Is the missus expectin' me to come along?"

"Nay. You're to have the day off. We'll leave on the early morning train and won't return until evening."

Beatrice brightened and immediately released her hold on Tessa's hand. "Fine it is, then. I'll see to packin' a bag while you put her to bed."

Rose held Tessa's chubby hand as she stepped into the child's sleeping room. Though it was an adequate size for a small bed, rocking chair, and table, there was space for little else. While she quietly read a fairy tale to the child, Rose could hear Beatrice shuffling about in the other room. Soon, Tessa's eyelids drooped closed, and her soft snores signaled she was fast asleep.

She quietly tiptoed out of the room and pulled the door behind her, leaving it slightly ajar so Beatrice could hear the child when she wakened. As Rose entered the playroom, Beatrice closed the small bag and glanced up at Rose. "She asleep?"

Rose nodded. "I'll stop by later after she's awakened from her nap."

"Would ya have a few minutes to sit here and listen for Tessa? I'd like to fetch myself a bite of food. I'm guessin' that what with fussin' over the old missus, Catherine forgot to bring me my tray."

Rose nodded her agreement, but Beatrice's reference to Mrs. Woodfield as the "old missus" annoyed her. No matter what privileges Beatrice received, she continued to remain sullen and unappreciative. And though Rose hadn't expected special thanks for having extended an invitation to her graduation party, Beatrice's behavior toward her sometimes reminded Rose of the insufferable behavior she'd received from her classmates. For a moment, she thought of speaking to Beatrice about her conduct but doubted anything she said would be taken well. After all, she didn't pay the nanny's wages.

As she opened the door leading into the hallway, Beatrice looked over her shoulder. "How was Joshua?"

The hairs on the back of Rose's neck prickled. Was Beatrice

determined to offend? First the remark about Mrs. Woodfield and now her question regarding Joshua. Beatrice flashed a fleeting smirk.

Determined to avoid conflict, Rose forced a smile. "He was quite well. We enjoyed dinner on several occasions, and I toured his pottery. The visit proved most helpful."

"All under the watchful eye of the old missus, I'm guessin'."

Rose bristled. "Both of us were pleased to have Grandmother Woodfield join us on our outings."

"Sure, and I'm believin' that." Beatrice flung the remark at Rose and then yanked the door closed behind her with a thud.

Rose stared at the door for several moments and attempted to sort through the last half hour. What had begun as a simple request to pack Tessa's clothing had turned into something much different. Something Rose didn't understand.

While Rose leaned down to pick up Tessa's toys, pieces of the recent conversation with Beatrice popped into her thoughts. After gathering the child's scattered belongings into her arms, Rose placed them in the hand-carved toy box. She'd never owned a beautiful toy box, but then again she'd had few toys—none of them worthy of such a beautiful container. She traced her fingers over the intricate design, thankful that Tessa would grow up without the scars caused by poverty and hardship. Advantages enjoyed by those living in Woodfield Manor had caused Beatrice to become jealous and bitter.

She sat down near the small bookcase filled with books. Some had belonged to Laura, but others had been purchased since Tessa's birth. Most were far beyond the understanding of a two-year-old, but Mrs. Woodfield said a child was never too young to learn. "You can never know what is captured in a young child's mind. That's why the books we read to her must be of excellent quality."

Rose thought the little girl would rather play peekaboo than hear one of Shakespeare's sonnets, so whenever she visited, she read a sonnet before playing. Beatrice's ability to read was limited, so Rose doubted she would ever choose anything written by Shakespeare. After tracing her fingers along the spines of several books, her fingers stilled and she removed a leather-bound volume. As she lifted the book from the shelf, she turned toward the window and noticed an envelope on the windowsill.

She stretched forward until her fingers touched the envelope. With a claw-like motion, she inched the missive into her grasp and turned it over. Her breath caught at the sight. The envelope bore the return address of Harkness Pottery Works and was addressed to Beatrice at the address of her family's home rather than Woodfield Manor. She stared at the envelope, her disbelief increasing by the second. The pounding of her heart sounded like a thousand drums, each one keeping time to a different beat.

The envelope had already been opened and left in plain sight. After only a brief moment, Rose convinced herself it wouldn't be so terrible to examine the contents. She slipped one finger beneath the flap, but before she could remove the pages from their hiding place, the door opened.

Beatrice gaped at the letter in Rose's hand before releasing a blood-curdling screech. "What are you doing reading my personal mail?" Her features twisted in an angry contortion as she dashed across the room and snatched the letter from Rose's hand. "You may be related to the Woodfields, but it don't give ya no right to read my mail."

Rose blanched. "I didn't read it. All I saw was the outside of the envelope, but I'll not deny that I'm more than a little interested in why Joshua Harkness would be writing to you."

"Are ya thinkin' I'm not worthy of a letter from him? Is that why you're asking? Or is it because you think he took more than a passing interest in me the night of your party?" Beatrice's questions were spewed with a huge dose of venom.

Granted, the nanny had a right to be angry, but Rose was shocked by her rancor. She hadn't read the letter, but surely her curiosity as to why Joshua was writing to Beatrice was understandable.

Rose inhaled a cleansing breath. "I apologize for touching your letter, Beatrice, but it was lying out in the open, and I did not read it. You may recall that I introduced you to Joshua and insisted he dance with you. I am not jealous, merely curious why he was writing to you."

"The only reason you didn't read it is because I walked in on you." Beatrice tipped her nose toward the ceiling as though she'd suddenly become the lady of the house rather than a servant. "How can I forget you *insisted* Joshua dance with me when I have you around to remind me?" She shoved the letter into her apron pocket. "Ya need not be worried. The letter was to tell me my brother might find work at the Harkness Lumber Mill. When we talked at your party, I told him my brother, Liam, was looking for work."

Though she'd told Beatrice she wasn't jealous, Rose experienced an unexpected sense of relief upon hearing why Joshua had written. "Then it's good that you have the day off tomorrow. I'm sure your brother will be pleased you heard from Joshua."

Beatrice's lips tipped up on one side. "Not near as pleased as me."

The nanny's words replayed in Rose's mind as she strode down the hallway. Her fingers tightened around the glass doorknob leading into her room as she recalled Joshua's inquiry regarding Beatrice's plans to move to Grafton. With a deep sigh, Rose turned the knob and pushed open the door. She was making a mountain out of a molehill.

# Chapter 11

*Grafton, West Virginia*
*Mid-July 1872*

The move to Grafton had gone more easily than anticipated because several relatives who had worked for
Ewan at the brickyard agreed to help pack and load the
families' belongings. Since Laura and Mrs. Woodfield agreed
they would leave most of the furniture at Woodfield Manor, the
task proved more manageable than originally planned.

Now that they were settled and Rose had begun her position
at the McKay Pottery Works, she could barely contain her enthusiasm. Since his arrival, Ewan hadn't changed the operation, but
now the two of them were going to sit down with Rylan and the
various foremen to discuss modifications and additions to the
business. Over the past few days, she'd taken time to introduce
herself and visit with the workers in each of the departments.
The women and children had been welcoming and open during
her visits with them. The men had answered her questions but
offered nothing more. Though she'd been dismayed by their
unwillingness to communicate with her, Ewan said she expected

too much. Men weren't accustomed to having a woman as their superior, and it would take time for them to accept her. Only Rylan seemed to welcome her without question.

This morning, she hoped the men's reluctance to accept her could be set aside and there could be open discussion among all of them. If so, she believed the foremen could help alleviate any concerns the other men might have about her.

From the narrow windows in Ewan's office, Rose watched as the foremen slowly gathered in the entrance hall shortly before ten o'clock. They watched the large clock that hung near the entrance. None of them appeared pleased. None of them seemed eager to step inside the office before ten o'clock. Not even Rylan Campbell, who had taken up a position beside Mr. Wheeler. The two of them were deep in conversation when the clock struck ten and the circle of men disbanded and trudged toward the office door. Rose thought they looked like men preparing to ascend to the gallows.

She glanced at her brother. "They certainly are a gloomy-looking group. I hope this isn't a forecast of how the meeting is going to proceed." The door opened before Ewan could respond, and Rose turned to greet the men with a welcoming smile. She was somewhat disappointed when only one of the foremen and Rylan smiled in return.

Ewan had already explained it would be best for him to take the lead during this first meeting, and she agreed. While Ewan told the men there would need to be changes made in the pottery in order to return it to a profitable operation, he didn't touch upon several of the ideas they'd privately discussed. And though he said they had plans to make things better for all of the workers, he didn't mention how that would be done.

Robert, their finest jiggerman and the foreman in the clay shop, leaned his muscular arms on the long wooden table where they'd gathered. "So can I tell my men they can be expecting more money come payday?"

"Nay, you cannot tell them any such thing, Robert. It's my hope that one day every man, woman, and child working in this pottery will have more money in their pockets, but right now we're barely making ends meet. 'Twould not be wise to make promises about pay when I have no way of knowing what's going to happen in the future. Until the day comes when I'm sure we're making enough money to pay better wages, you should say nothing about an increase in wages."

Robert leaned back in his chair and folded his thick arms across his chest. "You may not know that the potteries in East Liverpool offer better wages for experienced workers, Mr. McKay, but I'm giving you fair warning that all the men out there know it, and they're not happy." He lifted his arms from his chest and pointed his thumb over his shoulder toward the workshops. "If you're not going to give us more money, then why all this talk about making things better for the workers? The thing that's gonna make life more bearable for them is money."

Ewan traced his fingers through his hair. "I understand money is important, but if I pay out more than I have coming in, the company will go under, and I don't think any of us want to see that happen. As for the wages being paid in East Liverpool, I cannot stop any man from doing what is best for his family, but it's my hope they'll remain and work with me to see this pottery become the finest in West Virginia."

"In the entire United States." Rose beamed at the group of men. "That is our goal."

Robert guffawed and gave her a look of utter disdain. "You best go and visit some other potteries in Ohio before you go thinking you're gonna be the best in the country, Miss McKay.

Once you've bested the potteries in East Liverpool, then you can think about the rest of the country."

Rose placed her folded hands on the table and met Robert's scornful stare. "Thank you for your suggestion, Mr. Wilson. I have already visited one pottery located here in West Virginia, but I intend to visit others as time permits."

Rylan frowned at Robert and gave a slight shake of his head. "No need to be bad-mannered, Robert. I don't think Miss McKay asked for your opinion."

Rose turned toward her brother. "Perhaps Ewan will reveal some of our plans to make the pottery more competitive, which will, in turn, permit us to gain more contracts and eventually lead to higher wages. If time permits, I'd be pleased to speak to all of you about some other ways we intend to provide meaningful changes to the pottery."

Ewan gave a brief summation of their plans to bring back additional decorators and offer new designs that would draw interest from their previous buyers. When the men appeared unmoved, he inhaled a deep breath and continued. "We need to lure old customers back to this pottery. One way we can do that will be to offer something that will appeal to those customers. Once we have their interest, we can regain their confidence by meeting orders on time and producing the best product on the market. I hope that we will be able to expand all areas of the pottery very quickly, but I believe the quickest and most economical method will be through producing several unique designs to capture their interest. In the end, we must always deliver an excellent product. That was my goal in my brickyard, and it will be my goal in this pottery. We will always strive to please the customer."

Mr. Wheeler, the only remaining decorator in the pottery, cleared his throat. "I do my best to create beautiful pieces, but

I don't think your idea is going to be successful unless you can offer more than what one man can produce, Mr. McKay."

Ewan nodded his agreement and spoke of his desire to re-hire some of the former decorators. "In addition, my sister is a talented designer who will work closely with the decorating shop. I think you'll find her ideas original and inspiring."

Robert drummed his fingers on the table. "How is it the pottery is making enough money to hire more decorators but not enough to pay better wages to the rest of us?"

Ewan sighed. "In truth, the pottery is not making enough to pay extra decorators, but I set aside a portion of money for this purpose when I purchased the business. You do not have to agree with my decision, Robert, but I must do what I believe will restore this pottery to a profitable company. I hope you and the rest of the workers will give me an opportunity to prove I'm a man of my word. I'll be here working as hard as the rest of you."

The other foremen watched Robert's every move. There was little doubt he held sway over much that happened in the pottery and winning his allegiance could prove difficult.

"In addition, Rylan is going to be working with me to submit bids that will recapture some of the larger contracts that were once filled by this pottery."

The jiggerman grunted and gave a slight nod before frowning in Rose's direction. "What are the other big changes you're planning to make—the ones that don't include any money, Miss McKay?"

Rose rubbed her hands together, pleased Mr. Wilson had addressed her. After observing Ewan's dour look, she was sure he wanted to call an end to the meeting, but she decided to press on. Once the men saw how her ideas would improve the quality of life for their family members, she was certain she'd garner their support.

After gracing the men with a sweeping smile, she removed a folded sheet of paper from her skirt pocket. She unfolded the paper and pressed it flat while the men strained forward for a glimpse of her notes.

They were silent as church mice while she set forth her idea to impose new regulations in regard to cleanliness, but they shifted in their chairs when she set forth her idea that any worker under the age of fourteen must attend school for a half day at least four days a week. Before she had time to explain the details, the men who employed children expelled a hue and cry that could be heard far beyond the doors of Ewan's office.

Rose jumped to her feet and waved for the men to remain calm. "If you'll give me a chance to explain, this shouldn't be a problem for any of you, and it will provide the children with a better life as they grow older." She frowned at the men. "For those of you who are fathers, I would think you'd be applauding my suggestion. For those of you who are not, I suggest you consider someone other than yourselves for a moment."

Robert slapped his palm on the table. "I figured this would be the kind of thing we could expect with a woman helping to run things. I don't know about the rest of you, but I like things just the way they are. We don't need to use our work time cleaning the place, and we sure don't want to be paying wages to kids who are sitting in a classroom." He pushed away from the table. "I refuse to do any such thing."

Rylan pointed a finger at Robert. "Careful with your tongue, Robert. You're not in the workroom shoutin' orders to your workers."

The reprimand from Rylan had no effect, and Robert continued his tirade. Moments later, Rose glowered at him. If only he'd be quiet for a moment, she could explain that he wouldn't be paying the children while they were in school. There was no way she could gain the men's attention while Robert had the floor. Soon the other men were murmuring their agreement.

After a few more minutes passed, Rylan banged on the table. "That will be enough!" Silence reigned as the men gaped at him. "Nothing will be accomplished with all of this shouting and anger."

"Rylan is correct." Ewan pushed his chair back from the table. "The matter of schooling for the children can wait until a later date. The issue of cleanliness, however, will not wait. I have gone through the ledgers and I believe some of the absenteeism is due to illness that can be reduced if we maintain better sanitation. I expect you to abide by my sister's instructions in this matter."

Robert shook his head. "Shoulda known a woman coming in here would mean we'd be dealing with this kind of nonsense." He stood up, his attention fixed on Ewan. "I'll follow whatever rules you put in place, but it don't mean I'll like 'em or that I'll not be looking for work elsewhere."

Rose smiled at him. "Thank you for your comments, Mr. Wilson. I'll be praying that we'll soon have your cooperation. Our plans are for the good of every worker in this pottery, and that includes you."

Murmurs buzzed among the men—all but Robert, who glowered at Rose. "It's not prayers but good business decisions that will bring about my cooperation, Miss McKay."

Ewan stood and dismissed everyone except Robert. "I'd like to speak with you alone."

Robert jerked his shoulder toward Rose and Rylan as he returned to his chair. "Are the two of them going to be here while we talk?"

"No." Turning toward his sister, Ewan pointed to his desk. "While I meet with Robert, why don't you and Rylan gather the designs we discussed? Take them to the decorator shop and see if Mr. Wheeler has any suggestions for improvement."

Rose gaped at her brother. "Improvement? I thought we'd agreed the designs were—"

"Aye." Ewan narrowed his eyes and tightened his lips into a thin line. "Mr. Wheeler will be able to give you important details about the actual production of the pieces and whether they will be profitable."

Upon hearing Ewan's response, Robert looked at Rose and grinned like a Cheshire cat. She clenched her hands until her fingernails bit into the flesh of her palms. She'd seen that same look at school when the girls played their pranks and embarrassed her, but she hadn't expected to see it in the pottery. Her stomach churned, and she longed to remain and address Robert's smug smile, but Ewan's tone had been enough to signal her that he was unhappy with her behavior during the meeting.

She collected the designs from atop Ewan's desk and marched out of the office without further comment. The sound of Rylan's steady footfalls thudding alongside her added to her annoyance. She didn't need him at her side in order to talk to Mr. Wheeler.

"There's a shorter route if you cut through—"

"I'm not interested in a shorter route. Right now, the longer walk will do me good." She inhaled a deep breath. "Do you agree with Ewan? That I shouldn't have brought up the subject of schooling the children?"

"Change is hard on these men."

She blew out a huff of exasperation. "So you agree with him?"

"Most folks like to eat their food one bite at a time. You gave them a mouthful."

"But they didn't show me enough respect to let me explain."

"Respect?" He chuckled. "With these men, you have to earn that, Miss McKay, and they don't give it easily."

Irritation burned deep beneath her skin, but there was no need to vent her frustration on Rylan. He hadn't asked to escort her. No doubt, he would rather be doing something else. Probably anything else. "If you have other work, I can speak with Mr. Wheeler by myself."

"Thank you, but I'd best do what your brother asked. Besides, I like Mr. Wheeler and enjoy talking to him."

Rose gave a slight nod. "I hope he's in a better mood than Mr. Wilson. I could not believe my ears when he voiced his objections to schooling the children. Even a man without children should understand the value of education."

They turned to the right and circled around the slip house. The pungent smell of freshly turned dirt filled Rose's nostrils as they continued on past one of the warehouses and the kilns. A crew of several men was loading saggers filled with dried ware into one of the kilns for the bisque firing. Rose stopped for a moment to observe their skill as one of the men climbed several steps and entered the large kiln with a loaded fireclay container on his head while he carried another in his arms. What strength it must take to accomplish such a feat. Several young boys were loading the saggers, and she wondered if they aspired to follow in the footsteps of these men or if they longed for a better life. One that could be gained through education.

She turned and voiced her thoughts to Rylan.

Rylan didn't look at her. "Like I said, it takes some folks time to get used to the idea of change. Most of us aren't keen on new ideas, and it sounds like you got a pocketful."

Rose stopped short. "We all must change and adapt, or we'll never improve. Why, we'd still be without Singer sewing machines or Pullman sleeping cars or the Morse code if there hadn't been inventors who wanted to change our lives for the better."

"I never had use for a sewing machine or a sleeping car, and that's a fact. I do see the value of the Morse code for sending telegraphs, but what you want to do here at the pottery isn't the same as men inventing newfangled machines. Forcing young'uns into a schoolroom or telling workers their shops are dirty 'twill not endear ya to anyone."

A group of young boys raced by, their shirttails flying behind them. "Those children will never invent anything if they don't have an opportunity to learn. Can't you understand that?"

The muscles in Rylan's jaw tightened. "Maybe not, but they'll be helpin' to put food on the table. For most of them, a bowl of stew is more important than learning how to do sums."

Rose turned and continued toward the decorating shop. "They didn't give me a chance to explain that they can do both. I can create a schedule so they'll be able to continue working at their jobs. The children don't work continuously during the day, so they can come to class when they're not working." When Rylan didn't reply, she pushed for a response. "How can they object to something that will be good for the children?"

"I can't speak for others, but I don't think many will agree to the change."

Rose sighed. Perhaps the men wouldn't immediately consent, but she was sure the mothers would find in her favor. She'd begin with them. What woman didn't want her child educated? She'd appeal to the women regarding the cleanliness, as well. Women didn't want to work surrounded by layers of dust and dirt. Yes, that was her answer. She would win favor with the ladies, and the men would follow.

# Chapter 12

*August 1872*

While Rose had believed it would be easy to convince the women their children needed schooling, Rylan understood it would take far more effort than she anticipated. He advised Rose that the mothers wouldn't be easily convinced, but she disagreed. He still wasn't certain if she ignored him because she thought she was right, or if her efforts to win the women to her side had been exacted to prove him wrong. Though he took no pleasure in being right, his advice had been sound. Despite Rose's impassioned pleas, the women refused the offer of schooling for their children unless the journeymen who hired them agreed.

Rylan admired her determination, even if her efforts at change chafed, so he'd met with the skilled workers who employed children as their helpers. Without Rose's knowledge, he'd asked them to give the idea of school a try. If it didn't work, they could always voice their complaints and have it shut down, but he suggested they cooperate with Miss McKay on this issue. He ended each talk with the same question. "We owe it to the young'uns to give them a better chance than we ever had, don't we?"

Although they'd been less than enthusiastic, the men had agreed, except for Robert Wilson, who had been the lone holdout.

After a grueling day working on bids and preparing proposals for Ewan's review, Rylan trekked through the pottery. All the other workers had departed, and in the quietude of the pottery, he recalled the look on Rose's face the day the school had opened. She'd taken precious time away from decorating to welcome each of the children by name and promised them that education would open a world of possibilities for them. Though he still wasn't sure Rose should get their hopes up, he had no doubt her intent was pure.

A light coming from beneath the door of the decorating room caught his eye. Concern creased his brow. Had someone not extinguished their lamp?

He paused at the door when he heard singing—a lone female voice. Though Ewan was still in the office, what was Rose doing here so late in the evening?

He nudged the door and, finding it unlatched, pushed it open until he could see her. She was seated on a high stool with a large vase in front of her. After a few minutes, she tucked the wooden end of the paintbrush between her lips and tilted the vase to the side and examined her work. She smiled and her dimples appeared.

He'd not seen them much lately. Probably because they'd not been able to see eye to eye on much of anything. Maybe this was the opportunity he'd been praying for to ease the tension between them.

He gave the door a soft knock.

She jumped and nearly toppled the vase. "Rylan, you almost caused me to ruin a half-day's work!"

His gaze swept the shop and saw stacks of other bisque pieces waiting to be decorated. Had she truly spent half a day on this one piece?

"I apologize. I didn't mean to startle you. I saw the lamp and feared someone forgot it." He stepped close enough to get a good look at her vase. He sucked in his breath. What talent she had. A mass of autumn-colored roses trailed down its length and rested on the moss green base color. When this piece was fired, the glazes she'd chosen would make the flowers spring to life. "It's beautiful, Rose."

"Thank you, but it's not quite done." She closed her eyes, then added a swirl of amber.

"Do you see the completed design in your mind?"

"*Hmm.*" She tapped the end of the paintbrush against her lips. "I guess I do. Don't you?"

He chuckled. "No. When it comes to decorating, I prefer working with the whiteware."

"Why?"

"Knowing I've successfully re-created the same design gives me satisfaction. I enjoy the sameness."

She set down her brush. "The repetitive work would be tedious to me."

"Maybe, but I enjoyed it. There was a lot of satisfaction in completing all of the pieces alike."

She swiveled on the chair toward him and seemed to bite back a comment. "I'm glad you're here. I wanted to ask you to speak with Robert about giving his young workers permission to attend school."

"Me?"

"You know Robert well, and he doesn't like me. I don't want the children he's hired to suffer because of it."

"I'll talk to him, but I don't know if it will do any good."

Little did she know that he'd already met with the man every day for the last two weeks. All to no avail.

"I'd truly appreciate it." She scooted off the stool and picked up the vase. When she took a step, her heel caught on a loose floorboard. Clutching the vase, she stumbled forward.

Rylan caught her about the waist. "Are you all right? Did you twist your ankle?"

Her cheeks bloomed with color. "No, I'm fine. I should have remembered about that board."

"I'll take care of that."

"You can let go of me now."

"Yes, you can," Ewan barked as he stepped into the room. "Rylan, would you care to tell me what is going on in here? When you gave me the proposals to review and left the office, I thought you said you were going home."

Rylan yanked his hands away from Rose and turned to see a glowering Ewan.

Rose moved between them. "Ewan, stop frowning. Rylan saw a light on and came to check to see if someone left a lamp burning. Instead, he found me still working. When I stood up, I tripped. Thank goodness he caught me, or I'd have dropped this vase."

"I seem to owe you an apology, Rylan." He grinned. "Thank you for saving my sister, and more importantly, the vase."

She swatted her brother's arm. "Now, are you here to take me home or not? I skipped lunch to work on the vase, so I'm famished."

"You skipped lunch? You shouldn't do that. You might get ill." Rylan frowned, then cleared his throat when he saw Ewan hike an eyebrow in his direction. "You're needed here."

"Indeed, she is." Ewan offered her his arm. "As are you, Rylan."

As the trio left the pottery, Rose turned to Rylan with expectant blue eyes. "You won't forget what I asked you to do, will you?"

"No. I'll do it first thing in the morning." He rubbed his chin. "But don't get your hopes up."

"Why not? Sometimes hope is all we have."

Robert glanced up from his mold as Rylan drew near. "What brings you out here, Rylan? Same thing as yesterday?" He bent his head and swiped the perspiration from his forehead on his shirt.

"You can keep working. If you don't make fifty dozen today, I don't want you saying my visit with you was the cause."

The workman guffawed as he lifted the handle of his mold and removed a plate. "I wouldn't do that."

Rylan arched his eyebrows. He wasn't so sure the blame wouldn't land on his doorstep if Robert fell behind. "All the same, go ahead and keep working. You're right about why I'm here. I'm hoping you've had a change of heart about letting these young fellows attend school over in the shed."

Robert sighed. "They're all three wantin' to go, but I got my doubts about how it's gonna work out. You know I need my helpers." He cocked an eyebrow. "How come you're pushing so hard about this? You always said you liked keeping things they way they was. Now you're all for this school. You trying to catch that gal's eye by getting all of us to agree?"

The comment caught Rylan off guard. "This is about the helpers getting some schooling, nothing else."

Robert squinted his left eye in an exaggerated wink. "If you say so, but just 'cause you say it, don't mean I believe ya. You was always the first one dragging your feet whenever anything got changed around this place. Course maybe this particular change don't matter 'cause it won't make a difference to you over in that office of yours."

The words stung, and Rylan wanted to fling them back in Robert's face. He wished he could tell Robert he was wrong. But he couldn't. All of it was true. He did long for Rose to think of him as someone other than her brother's assistant, as more than an employee who would do her bidding when she met with defeat among the workers, but that wouldn't happen. Rose had a beau. One who had money and owned a business, a man willing to travel from Fairmont to Grafton to court her. Rylan could never compete with the likes of Joshua Harkness.

Though Rylan disliked admitting it, Robert was right about the school, too. Having the helpers attend classes didn't change anything for him, so he'd willingly taken up Rose's cause. She wanted more changes, and he was saving his objections for the ones he didn't want to accept—the ones that would affect him. Humiliation settled in his belly like a lead weight, but it wasn't heavy enough for him to admit the truth to Robert.

"Robert." He drew in a long breath. "This isn't about what's best for me or Miss McKay. It's about what's best for your boys."

"I guess if you can tell me how I'm gonna keep my numbers up with my helpers over in the shed learning how to read, I might give 'em my go-ahead to attend."

"Thank you, Robert. I'll tell Miss McKay, and she'll come down and give you a schedule you can use. I think she planned for the boys to come to one of their classes while you're at lunch, and they'll trade off for the other class. She'll let them eat their lunch in the classroom."

"Don't know how much they'll learn during lunchtime, and I'm telling you now that if one of the boys is out sick, then none of them can go to the classes. I got to have at least two of 'em here working all through my stint. Understood?"

Rylan nodded. "Like I said, I'll have Miss McKay come down and go over the schedule. Make sure you tell her about your need to always have two helpers working—and tell the boys, too. Don't want them being disappointed."

"Back when I was a kid, I was glad I didn't have to go to school. I don't understand how these young'uns think nowadays." Robert shook his head. "If this slows down how many plates I make each day, I'll yank them boys out of Miss McKay's school faster than she can swish her petticoats."

"Talk to me first, Robert. Don't want you to do anything you'll regret." Rylan waved his hand and strode off before Robert could question him about his final remark. The man might be a fine jiggerman, but Rose McKay had made up her mind. Every child in this pottery would be enrolled in classes, or they wouldn't be permitted to work.

Robert had no idea Rose had set a deadline for enrollment at the end of the week. She believed Robert's helpers had already missed important lessons, and they'd become discouraged if they fell too far behind. Rylan had been careful not to mention the deadline. He knew Robert. The man would have met her challenge and quit his own job to prove a point. And whether Rose agreed or not, they needed Robert Wilson.

Rylan shoved his hands into his pockets as he strode out of the clay shop. Miss McKay had won this battle, but she'd had her share of help, both from him and from her family. While she continued working with Frank Wheeler and the other decorators Ewan had recently hired, Rose's twin sisters had cleaned the shed and set up the classroom.

He'd discovered Rose's sisters hard at work when he walked past the old building last month. The two of them had chattered at him like two magpies, each one more eager than the other to tell everything they'd accomplished. He'd sat down on one of the wooden benches, enthralled as Adaira told him how Rose had enlisted their help. Their older sister had recruited their support, and they'd accepted the challenge. In turn, they'd enlisted the help of Ewan's mother-in-law, who had secured donations from a charitable group as well as from some of her wealthy friends. With the funds, the girls had purchased books, pencils, paper, slates, a portable chalkboard, ink, and pens. They'd also been pleased to announce they had sufficient funds to pay the teacher for the year and a promise of additional funds if the school proved successful. He was amazed by their tenacity. The trait seemed to run in the family.

Though he'd not spoken to either of the twins since that day, one of the helpers told him both girls were providing tutoring to students who needed extra help. No doubt the twins would be assigned all three of the fellows working for Robert.

They were a little older than the youngsters working as spongers and handlers or those working alongside their mothers in one of the warehouses brushing dirt and dust from the ware or in the glazing rooms. Rylan hoped they wouldn't give the girls any trouble. Maybe he'd stop by the classroom later and tell the teacher the boys would begin tomorrow and mention she should send word if there were any problems.

Right now, he wanted to tell Rose he'd met with success. Truth be told, he felt as though he'd accomplished the impossible. As he entered the workroom, the strong odor from the gilding the decorators brushed onto specialty pieces hit him afresh. The smell was one he neither liked nor disliked, but each time he left the shop, his eyes watered and his nose burned, though Mr. Wheeler said it was merely his imagination at work.

Mr. Stinson, one of the decorators who'd been rehired, waved his brush in the air. "What can we do for you this fine day?"

Rylan glanced around the room. "I was hoping to speak with Miss McKay."

The decorator ran the tip of his brush around the edge of a pale blue decorative urn. "She had a gentleman come looking for her earlier, and she went back to the office." He winked and lowered his voice. "Mr. Wheeler says he's Miss McKay's beau."

Rylan's chest tightened, but he forced a smile. "Thank you. I'll look for her at the office."

Since the minute he'd gained Robert's approval, Rylan had anticipated Rose's reaction to the news. He'd been eager to see the look in her eyes when she learned all the children were now enrolled in school, but upon hearing Joshua was in town, the news didn't seem as important.

Instead of returning to the office, he stopped at the makeshift school to inform the twins and Miss Spangler, the teacher, that they'd have three more students come tomorrow.

He stood in the classroom doorway for a moment. Along with several other workers, he'd helped carry and arrange long wooden tables and benches in the room, but he'd not visited since classes had begun. Several young girls and boys sat at one table and a group of older children at another. Miss Spangler stood beside a portable blackboard instructing the older children, while Ainslee and Adaira helped the younger students.

He gestured when Adaira looked up. She smiled and hurried toward him. "Welcome to our classroom, Rylan. I'm glad you've come to pay a visit."

"I won't stay long. I know you're busy, but I wanted to let you know that Robert Wilson has agreed to send his three helpers to classes. That means all of the children are now enrolled."

"That's wonderful news." She beamed and waved to the

teacher. "We will have full enrollment beginning tomorrow, Miss Spangler. The three remaining students in the clay shop will attend."

"Excellent. Perhaps you could go and obtain their names and discuss their schedules with their supervisor so we can be prepared for them."

Adaira nodded her agreement as Rylan motioned toward the front of the classroom. "I expected to see more students than these few. Are they not appearing as promised?"

"They're all attending, but we must adapt to their work schedules. That means they appear at different times on different days throughout the week. We've become used to it. They're all eager to learn, so it makes helping them a pleasure." She looked toward the blackboard and gave a slight nod toward the teacher. "I don't know what Miss Spangler will do once Ainslee and I return to school, but we're doing fine for now."

"I'm glad to hear it. Perhaps one of the ladies who does volunteer work for the charity groups would be interested in helping. Mrs. Woodfield has joined several societies here in Grafton, and she may be able to give you some names by the end of the summer."

Adaira nodded. "I do hope so, but most of the women in those groups are more interested in doing handwork or raising funds than in donating their time, especially if it means they must actually associate with the folks they're raising money to help."

"You may be right, but I think some of those ladies don't know where help is needed, and you or Rose can point them in the right direction."

"Maybe I am being too harsh." She giggled and nodded toward the door. "I'll do my best, but Rose won't be much help. The school was her idea, but she hasn't had time to help. She's worried about gaining new customers with her designs, so she's either working on those at home or over at the decorator shop."

"Then you may need to rely upon Grandmother Woodfield and the good Lord to send another helper once you return to school." As they prepared to part ways, he nodded toward the clay shop. "The new boys are older than most of the others. I don't think they've had much schooling. All three of them said they want to attend classes, but if there's any trouble, let me know."

"I don't think we'll have any problems with them, but thank you for the offer." She glanced over her shoulder as she walked away. "If they become rowdy, one of us will send word to you."

Rylan remained outside the shed for a few moments, then headed back toward the office. Surely by now Rose and Joshua would be gone. Adaira might believe her sister didn't have time for anything other than the decorator's shop and creating designs at home, but it seemed that every time Joshua arrived in town, she was able to make time for him.

He inhaled a deep breath and held it as he approached the office door. Once inside, he blew out the air. Neither Rose nor Joshua was in the office. Relief washed over him as he dropped into his chair.

# Chapter 13

"Rylan! Glad I am that you're here." Ewan held several large envelopes in his hand. "I want to make certain these bids get mailed today. Could you take them to the post office for me? I'd not be asking you to take care of such a simple task, but I know I can trust you to be sure they get there before the afternoon mail goes out on the train."

While rising from his chair, Rylan extended his hand and took the parcels. "I'll go right now. I can mail them and then go have my lunch before I return." He hesitated a moment and glanced around the office. "I heard Mr. Harkness was here for another visit, but it appears he's already departed."

Ewan nodded. "Aye. He's in town to visit Rose. The two of them were here for a short time before she returned to the decorators' shop. Joshua visited with me for a little while and then went to the hotel to get settled." He reached into his pocket and withdrew several coins. "For the life of me I cannot understand why he continues to arrive so early in the day. Rose has told him she's not free until evening, but still he arrives before noon." He handed the coins to Rylan. "This should be more than enough for the postage."

"Maybe he thinks she'll leave work when he gets here." Rylan shrugged. "I keep wondering how he can be away from his own pottery so often."

"I've wondered the same thing. I work here at the pottery all day as well as working on bids and other paper work during my evenings at home. I'm thinking he has some understanding of the business that I've not yet discovered. Over the past few months, he's won several of the contracts I had hoped would be ours." Ewan traced his fingers through his hair. "I can't quite figure him out."

"Neither can I." Rylan tucked the envelopes under one arm and waved with the other. "I'll be back after lunch."

As he crossed the railroad tracks and walked into town, Rylan's thoughts didn't stray far from Ewan's comments regarding Joshua Harkness. The man's visits didn't make much sense. When he could leave Fairmont on the late-afternoon train and arrive before dinnertime, why would he continue to arrive so early in the day? If Rose weren't busy at the pottery or if he came to call on Sundays, it might make sense. Maybe he had other business that required his attention in Grafton, but Rylan had never heard of the Harkness family having any business interests in town. Yet it was possible.

"Got some mail that needs to get on the afternoon train, Clyde." The postmaster adjusted his spectacles and then examined and weighed the envelopes. "Cost ya four cents each for these. They're over the half-ounce weight."

Rylan dug the change from his pocket and pushed it across the marble counter. "You'll be sure they get on the afternoon train?"

He chuckled. "You're as insistent as that fellow from Fairmont. He wanted to make sure his mail got on the afternoon train, too. Asked me three or four times."

"Wouldn't have been Joshua Harkness, would it?"

Clyde scratched his head and stared at the counter for a moment. "Yep. That's it. Harkness. Said he owns a pottery in Fairmont and needed to get some bids sent out. You know him?"

"Not very well, but we've met." Odd that Joshua would wait until he was in Grafton to mail out bids, but maybe that's why he arrived early each week. Perhaps he needed a bit of peace and quiet to concentrate on his work.

"I'll tell you the same thing I told him. Unless I drop dead, the mail will make it to the train on time." He guffawed and slapped his palm on the counter. "Course I ain't planning on dying anytime soon, but you never know what the good Lord might have in mind. If you're staying in town for lunch, there's a good special at the hotel today. Chicken and gravy on them fluffy biscuits Flora makes. That woman can sure mix a fine biscuit. If she didn't already have a husband, I'd snatch her up for myself."

Rylan grinned and strode toward the door. "Take care of yourself, Clyde. Thanks for the suggestion about lunch. Guess I'll go to the hotel instead of McGregor's."

Most days Rylan carried his lunch to work, but at least one day a week he treated himself to lunch at McGregor's, where he could hear if anything new was happening in town. He knew the owner, Mac, and most of the folks who ate there were local. The place had a nice feel to it—warm and friendly, unlike the home where he'd grown up. But today he'd take Clyde's advice and try the hotel restaurant.

He took a dirt path, a shortcut that led from the post office to the rear of the hotel. It would save him several minutes, and he could circle around to the front entrance once he got there. As he neared the hotel, he caught sight of Joshua Harkness standing beside the rear entrance leaning close to a woman. His breath caught. Had Rose told Ewan she was going back to work and then left with Joshua?

He stepped into the sprawling overgrowth of bushes and weeds that lined the path. Certain he couldn't be seen, he continued to watch. Joshua had turned his head and now stood closely facing the girl, his back toward Rylan. He appeared to be kissing her, but from his vantage point, he could see only the back of Rylan's head, the girl's red hair, and the fullness of a striped skirt.

Not a lot of details, but the auburn hair was enough to confirm the girl with Joshua wasn't Rose. He blew out a sigh, but his sense of relief was soon replaced by an unremitting curiosity. If it wasn't Rose with Joshua, who was it? As he struggled to gain a better view, Rylan carefully maneuvered through the thigh-high undergrowth that lined the path.

If he moved any closer, they would surely hear the snapping branches and rustling of brush and weeds. Now that he'd moved so near, he'd boxed himself in. He couldn't return to the path without drawing their attention, and he didn't want to pop out of the brush and reveal he'd been spying. He'd need to do something soon, or there would be no time for lunch, and he'd be late making his return. Ewan would worry.

A mosquito circled overhead before taking aim and alighting on Rylan's forehead. Without thinking, he swatted the insect, then shuddered when Joshua jerked and looked over his shoulder. Holding his breath, Rylan watched as Joshua grabbed the girl's arm, and the two of them hurried inside. Once they were out of sight, Rylan exhaled and dropped to the ground. Afraid Joshua might be watching from inside the rear door, Rylan remained in his hiding place long after the couple disappeared from sight.

Today, he'd probably have to go hungry. But given what he'd seen and how it could affect Rose, he didn't have much appetite anyway.

Joshua yanked Beatrice inside the lower hallway of the hotel and pushed her into a corner near the stairway. "Stay there! Don't move. Someone was watching us. I'm sure of it."

"Look what ya've done!" Her high-pitched wail echoed in the empty stairwell. A pale blue ribbon lay limp across her outstretched palm. Joshua glared in her direction. "You ripped the ribbon from me dress when you grabbed me." While lifting her fingers to her auburn locks, she glanced in the mirror at the foot of the stairway and let out a yelp. "Look at me hair! I'll never get it back in proper order."

Joshua reached for her arm and pulled her close to his face. "Be quiet and get back in the corner where you can't be seen."

"There's no one out there." Beatrice huffed and folded her arms across her chest. "You're acting the fool if you think someone would take precious time to follow the two of us."

He grasped the tip of her chin between his thumb and forefinger. "You may not be worth much, but I am. Now do as I say." He reached into his jacket and removed a key. "Go up to my room, keep your head down, and watch from the window. If I don't see any movement from down here, I'll be up in a few minutes."

She smirked and snatched the key from his hand. "You think y'er pulling the wool over me eyes, but I know what y'er doing."

Joshua wanted to push her up the stairs, but he lowered his voice and did his best to hold his temper in check. "Other than telling you to look out the window, what am I doing, Beatrice?"

"Y'er getting me up to your room without an argument." She batted her lashes.

"Not once have I had any trouble getting you into my room, so why would you take time to say something so foolish? It's getting you to do what I've told you that causes our arguments." He stopped himself before he said something that would cause her Irish temper to flare and send her into a screeching tirade. "Please, just do as I'm asking, Beatrice. I'll give you a little extra to pay for your ribbon. I'll even give you enough to pay for a new dress if you'll get upstairs and do as I've asked. If you see anyone out there, come to the top of the stairs and let me know."

She turned toward the stairs, her auburn hair cascading around her shoulders like a waterfall. How he loved drawing his fingers through her mass of thick red curls. With each step, her hips swayed a little further to the left and then to the right. She knew he was watching, that she could captivate him with her movements, and he wouldn't be able to look away.

When she reached the top of the stairway, she turned and looked down at him. "I thought you was supposed to be watching for some stranger in the bushes." Her lips curved in a suggestive smile. "A wee bit more fun watching me, wasn't it?"

Joshua gestured for her to go to his room, and he returned to the doorway. He peered around the doorjamb, determined to locate the culprit who'd been following them. He strained to see something, anything that would indicate someone was hiding, but there wasn't any sign of movement. Maybe Beatrice was right. Maybe he'd let his imagination get away from him.

He waited a few more minutes before turning toward the stairway. What awaited him in his room was far more interesting than staring at a dirt path lined with overgrown bushes and weeds.

Beatrice was dutifully holding aside an edge of the lace curtain and peering out the window. She twisted around when he entered the room and pinned him with an alluring look. "Couldn't stay away for long now, could ya?" She lifted the sheer curtain and draped it over her head. "I think I could make me a bridal veil out of one of these curtains if you've a mind to show me y'er a true gentleman."

Joshua crossed the room and chuckled. Using his thumb and forefinger, he lifted the curtain from atop her head. "I barely know you well enough to be thinking about any more than what you have to give me on this fine afternoon." He pulled her to her feet and wrapped his arms around her in a tight embrace. "Did you bring the information I asked for?"

Beatrice struggled against his hold and pushed him backward onto the bed. A breeze wafted through the open window and sent the curtains floating against the back of her dress. "I'll have nothing to give ya this afternoon or any afternoon until I see money in me hand. And extra it'll be for today. I ain't forgot you promised to pay for me dress and ribbon."

If she weren't so pretty, he would have lost patience with her the first time the two of them had secretly met in Bartlett. She'd proved a poor dance partner, but she made up for it in other ways. Rose didn't realize what a favor she'd provided when she'd asked him to dance with Beatrice at her party. She was a pretty girl who was looking for a good time and an easy way to make some extra money, and he could provide what she wanted. He enjoyed his time with her. Even more, he appreciated her ability to supply him with the figures Ewan bid on proposed contracts.

When the McKays moved to Grafton, they'd switched Beatrice's day off to Wednesdays, a change that had created a slight cessation in Joshua's visits with the nanny. Once certain that Wednesday would remain her day off each week, he'd set about revising his own schedule. None of his employees dared question his absences during the middle of the week, but when his father had paid a visit on a Wednesday and found him away from the pottery, he'd remained overnight and questioned Joshua when he returned to Fairmont.

The matter had taken some quick thinking, but Joshua had learned how to dodge the truth at a young age. He hadn't even blinked while telling his father that he'd begun paying visits to the McKay Pottery each Wednesday in order to discuss business with Ewan and also to court Rose. Knowing his father hoped to see an alliance forged between the two families made the explanation partially true and quite believable, at least to his father.

The patriarch of the Harkness family believed his son's marriage to Rose was the best and easiest way to merge the two families and their business holdings. At the moment, Joshua was more than willing to let his father believe he was interested in the same thing. Since then, the questions from his parents had been queries about Ewan, his pottery, and Joshua's outings with Rose. Realizing his father and Ewan would meet at social gatherings and perhaps some business meetings in the future, Joshua was careful to tell them only the truth about his visits with all of the McKays. During discussions with his parents, he simply omitted the fact that his Wednesday afternoons were spent in the company of the McKays' redheaded nanny and that the reason he was securing so many new contracts was due to the facts and figures she supplied him during his visits.

The girl had proved to be a good source of information and provided him with enjoyable entertainment. He wanted—no, he needed—to keep her happy for the time being. Eventually, he would break her heart. When that happened, she might create problems, but he'd take his chances. If she caused him any trouble in the future, he'd find a way to silence her. Otherwise, she might find herself on a ship to some foreign country, where she'd never be heard from again.

For now, he'd let her think she controlled him. He'd pay her what she asked, and he'd buy her trinkets from time to time to keep her happy. But in the end, she'd discover the truth, and she'd wish she had never stepped onto the dance floor with him at Rose McKay's party.

Rylan gulped a large breath of air and made a quick dash across the dirt path and skirted around the livery. Once he crossed the path, he couldn't be seen from the rear of the hotel. He hoped Joshua and the redheaded girl hadn't seen him. If he was smart, he'd go back to work, but he wanted to go inside the dining room. If he took a table where they couldn't see him, he might be able to discover exactly what was going on between them.

From what he'd seen, it appeared Joshua had more than a passing interest in the girl. But what about Rose? For sure, it appeared betrayal was afoot. How could Joshua deceive someone as beautiful and kind as Rose? Besides, wouldn't Joshua's family expect him to marry a young woman of means, someone like Rose? Wasn't that why he'd been coming here each Wednesday and escorting her to the theatre or joining her family for dinner? So why was he secretly meeting another woman?

He rushed toward the hotel, his anger rising as he gained a clear understanding of Joshua Harkness and his ungentlemanly behavior. How could he treat this young woman in such a manner? More important, how could he lie to Rose? She believed he was a kind, good-hearted man who didn't have a mean bone in his body.

Yanking his hat from atop his head, Rylan entered the

hotel and strode to the doorway leading into the restaurant. He stepped to one side and gazed around the room. When a waitress approached him, he gestured toward the room. "I'm looking for a couple, both about my age. She's wearing a dress with blue stripes and has auburn hair. His hair is light brown and he's wearing a suit."

The waitress shook her head. "I've been working since breakfast. Haven't seen any redheads or good-looking fellas, except for you." She grinned. "There's a table free in my section if you want it."

He shook his head. "Thanks for your help, but I'll take a seat at the counter since I don't have much time."

After placing his order for the special, he continued to survey the room. There were no hidden spaces in the dining room, no large ferns or columns a couple could hide behind, but where had they gone? While he downed biscuits topped with chicken and gravy, he tried to figure out how he'd missed them. Had they gone in the back door, walked down the hallway, and departed out the front door? That wasn't possible. He would have seen them as he walked toward the hotel. He lifted his gaze and stared at the ceiling.

Were they in a room upstairs? Was Joshua courting Rose and secretly meeting another woman, as well? His thoughts raced as he finished the last bite of lunch and wiped his mouth. After downing a final gulp of coffee, he walked to the hotel lobby and peered down the hall. Joshua always stayed at this hotel, so asking if he was registered would yield nothing more than the room number. Unless he planned on marching upstairs and knocking on Joshua's hotel door, knowing the room number served no purpose.

A boy who appeared to be no more than twelve appeared in the hallway carrying a tray of dirty dishes covered with a linen cloth. Rylan stepped into the boy's path and smiled at him. "You deliver food to the rooms here?"

"When they need me. The rest of the time I'm a cook's helper." The boy turned sideway in an attempt to step around Rylan. "I gotta get back to the kitchen. You need something?"

"I just wondered if you'd seen a redheaded lady upstairs with a fellow who has a room here—Mr. Harkness."

When the boy hesitated, Rylan reached in his pocket and removed a coin. "Would this help you remember?"

The boy snatched the coin out of Rylan's fingers and dipped his head. "This here tray come from their room. They always eat the noon meal in there. I deliver it and pick up the dirty dishes. They leave 'em outside the door for me, and the fella always gives me a tip. The lady always turns her head when I bring the food into their room, like she doesn't want me to see her, but I'd have to be blind to miss that red hair. I ain't s'pose to say nothing." Balancing the tray on his arm, the boy tucked the coin into his pocket. "But I got to think of my sick mama. What you give me will help pay for her medicine this week." His brows dipped low with worry. "You won't say I told you, will ya?"

Rylan shook his head. "Not a word. Thanks for your help."

The boy scurried off toward the kitchen, and Rylan walked out the front door. He'd have to hurry, or Ewan would question where he'd been all this time. Rylan wasn't sure if he should tell his employer about what he'd seen, but one thing was certain: Ewan would be concerned about those bids getting in the mail.

When Rylan returned to the office, Ewan glanced at the clock. "Any problems? I was beginning to get worried."

Rylan shook his head. "No problems. Clyde said to set your

mind at ease. He'll make sure your mail is on the afternoon train. Guess I took a little longer than usual eating lunch. Clyde mentioned the noon special at the hotel, and I decided to go there. Figured it might be busy, but the chicken and gravy on biscuits tempted me."

Ewan looked up from the pile of paper work strewn across his desk. "Aye, the hotel is always busy during the noon hour." He gestured for Rylan to sit down. "I asked Rose to come to the office. She should be here shortly. We are going to have to make some decisions about the pottery, and you need to be here."

Excitement swelled in Rylan's chest, and he straightened his shoulders. He hadn't expected to win Ewan's confidence so quickly. To be included in decisions with Ewan and his sister must mean they valued his opinion. Ewan had been poring over the books the last few days, and the figures weren't good. Perhaps they hoped to figure out some new way to increase orders.

While he waited, he tapped his foot against the wooden floor, his thoughts returning to the earlier events he'd witnessed in town. Should he tell Ewan what he suspected? If Rose was his sister, he'd be thankful for any information that would help to protect her, yet he didn't know how Ewan might receive the news.

Rylan didn't want his new employer to think him a man who stirred up trouble, especially since he didn't possess any real evidence of Joshua's wrongdoing. Rylan traced his fingers through his thatch of unruly hair. Revealing what he'd seen was too risky. He'd have to figure out another way to make Rose and Ewan think twice about Mr. Harkness.

Minutes later Rose hurried into the office, her indigo print dress protected by a stained canvas work apron. With a slight huff, she withdrew a hairpin from her apron pocket, tucked several wayward strands of hair into place, and jammed the pin into her upswept coif. That done, she dropped onto the chair beside Rylan.

He gave her a sidelong glance and wondered if she'd be devastated to learn what he'd seen only a short time ago. Did she already love Joshua, and would his unseemly behavior break her heart? She deserved a man who would cherish and love only her, not a philandering cad.

A momentary wave of guilt washed over him as he embraced thoughts of a future—a future with Rose at his side. If Joshua wasn't courting her, would she consider him as a suitor? Nay. He silently chastised himself. Rose would marry a wealthy young man, a man of importance—a man like Joshua Harkness.

He was pulled from his wandering thoughts when Rose shifted in her chair. "Sorry to keep you waiting, but I needed to finish the piece I was working on, or it would have been ruined. Aren't our weekly meetings enough to take care of any problems?"

Ewan rested his arms on the heavy wooden desk. "Some things don't need to be discussed with all of the supervisors present, and if I ask you and Rylan to remain after a regular meeting, some of the foremen would quiz Rylan about what was discussed. It puts him in a difficult position."

Rose folded her hands and leaned back in the chair. "As long as it doesn't take long. We're busy in the decorating shop."

Her tone bore a hint of impatience, and Ewan frowned. "Aye, and we're busy here in the office, as well. We're trying to decide how we're going to pay all the bills and have enough money to pay the wages to the workers each week."

She rubbed her temple. "I apologize. I didn't mean to imply what I'm working on is more important than what you and Rylan are doing."

"I know." Ewan gave her a hint of a smile. "I wanted you to

know we prepared several bids, and Rylan mailed them earlier today, but there's no guarantee we'll get the contracts. If it's like the ones I sent out earlier in the month, we'll get more rejection letters." He pushed a ledger book across the desk in her direction. "If you take a look, you'll see the numbers don't match up very well."

Rylan stared into a far corner. Being in the middle of a disagreement between family members wasn't any more comfortable than being quizzed by the foremen. Besides, he had his doubts he'd be pleased with the outcome of this conversation. He and Ewan had already discussed the pottery's finances.

Ewan was certain they needed to modify and enlarge their production in order to compete. Rylan disliked the idea of adding or removing items currently produced and believed it was too soon to consider further changes. Rose had already instituted more modifications than most of the workers wanted. Who could guess what she might suggest during this meeting?

Rose leaned forward and pushed the ledger back toward her brother. "I believe you, Ewan. I don't need to look at the figures. You may be surprised to know that I've given this matter a great deal of thought. I haven't forgotten that I'm the one who said we could make the pottery a prosperous business. I have an idea that may change this pottery forever."

Her words sent a chill sluicing through Rylan's body. Change. Rose's favorite way to resolve problems, and his greatest aversion.

She scooted to the edge of her chair, her eyes shining with excitement. "If you would have asked for my ideas a few days ago, they would have been very different from the one I'm going to give you today."

Ewan placed his hand atop the open ledger. "And why is that?"

She reached into her apron pocket, but rather than a hairpin, she withdrew an envelope. "This is a letter I received from Mrs.

Fisk." She looked at Ewan. "You'll recall she is the director at the Philadelphia School of Design for Women."

"Aye. I remember meeting her. I didn't know you'd stayed in touch with her."

"We've exchanged a few letters. She's remained interested in my future plans."

Ewan chuckled. "I do remember she didn't think you'd be able to use your skills anywhere but in a large city. Does she still hold with that belief?"

"I think she agrees I'll be able to use my talents here at the pottery."

"What does she have to say that we need to hear?" Ewan leaned back in his chair.

"She's sent me a bit of news that has changed my thinking. Before today, I was going to suggest we cease producing anything other than our specialty pieces."

"What?" Rylan jumped to his feet. "How would that help anything?" Fear and anxiety gripped him in a tight hold.

Rose startled and her mouth gaped open.

Rylan could feel the heat rise in his cheeks as he dropped to his chair. "I'm sorry. I didn't mean to shout."

Rose gave him a slight nod. "Since you asked, I thought we could develop a plan to make our pottery into an exclusive business that would create one-of-a-kind pieces that would fetch prices far above anything we currently make. News travels quickly. Once our work was sought after by the wealthy, we could begin to name our price." She leaned toward her brother. "I thought we could exhibit pieces in the homes of some of your business contacts, and soon we'd have orders pouring into the office."

Ewan shook his head. "That sounds good to you because it's the area of the pottery that holds your interest, but it isn't a practical plan. Do you realize how many people would lose their jobs if we created only specialty items? We need to think about them, too."

"Exactly." Rylan folded his arms across his chest. "We need to consider the people who have worked in this pottery for years."

"True, but the two of you need not be so disapproving." She unfolded the letter and flattened it with her hand. "Mrs. Fisk's news truly is the answer to our difficulties." She looked at Ewan. "I have been praying the Lord would send an answer to our problems in the pottery, and then this letter from Mrs. Fisk arrived."

Rylan blew out a long sigh. "Are you going to tell us what it says?"

"There's going to be a contest, and we're going to enter."

He did his best to let the words seep into his consciousness. A contest. Rose believed all of their problems would be solved by a contest? He leaned forward and covered his face with his hands. They were doomed.

# Chapter 14

Rose slapped the letter onto her brother's desk and looked at Ewan. "I hope you aren't going to be as close minded as he." The moment Rylan lifted his head, she pinned him with a glare. How could he so quickly decide her plan held no merit? "You could at least listen to the details before deciding against my suggestion. You might even like it."

"I don't see how winning a contest will do any more than add a pittance to the bank account. We need a large order for whiteware, one that will show our ability to produce good product in large quantities. That's what will get us the money we need, isn't it, Ewan?"

Rylan's defiant tone set her on edge. He was acting like a little boy who wouldn't play unless he got to choose the game. And he was looking to her brother to take his side over hers. She'd never before seen him behave with such opposition. Granted, she'd learned he wasn't a man who embraced modifications to the workplace, but she hadn't expected so much resistance to a plan that would help them succeed. While Ewan considered Rylan a genuine asset to the business, he could become a liability if he wasn't willing to accept some additional changes.

Rose nodded toward the letter. "Before you go any further telling me what we need, why don't I let the two of you read this? Better yet, I'll read it aloud, and we'll save a little time. There's no need for me to read Mrs. Fisk's pleasantries to you."

Ewan nodded. "Go ahead and read the important part."

Rose cleared her throat and held the piece of stationery by two corners.

*"The owner of the Franklin Hotels is sponsoring a contest open to potteries within a two-hundred-mile radius of Pittsburgh, Pennsylvania.*

*"The contest rules are as follows: Each pottery will submit two finished pieces. One piece should be a whiteware plate with a design that portrays the elegance of Franklin Hotels but can be produced at a reasonable price. The second piece should be a large urn of unique design and decoration, to be displayed in the lobby of our oldest and largest hotel in Pittsburgh. Both designs must be of the highest quality and from the same pottery, and the designs shall be cohesive in nature.*

*"One pottery will be chosen as the winner. A prize of one hundred dollars will be awarded for the urn, and a contract to replace all whiteware in our hotels with the new design will be awarded to the winning pottery."*

Rylan appeared dumbstruck, but Ewan reached across the desk. "Let me read that for myself. It's too good to be true."

"Mrs. Fisk wouldn't send me this information if it weren't accurate." She grinned at her brother. "For sure, we need to begin creating our designs. Mrs. Fisk believes I can win this contest. She says so right here." Rose pointed to a paragraph near the bottom of the letter.

"Aye, but I think you and Rylan should work on this together. Come up with an idea that will unite both of our projects." He turned toward Rylan. "You're the one with experience working with whiteware. You know what will function best, and Rose can create an urn that will be like nothing the judges have ever before seen." He glanced at his sister. "Is that not a fact?"

"I believe I can create a design that will impress the judges and bring us a victory, but since Rylan doesn't think the contest is a good idea, I'm not—"

Rylan twisted around to face her. "I will do whatever you and Ewan think is best for the pottery. I think I can provide help with the type of design for the whiteware portion of the contest."

Rose was taken aback by Ewan's suggestion that Rylan help her. After all, she was the one who'd graduated from design school and had already won an award for one of her designs while still attending school. She opened her mouth to voice her opinion, but before she could utter a sound, a single word pricked her conscience. *Pride.* Over and over, the word resounded in her ears. Her thoughts and behavior weren't kind or generous. In spite of his initial protestations, didn't Rylan deserve a chance to participate?

She inhaled a deep breath. "As long as we each have a measure of involvement in the design produced by the other, I think we can submit winning entries."

Though she said the words, Rose could only hope she was correct. Rylan disliked every change she'd ever suggested. How could they agree upon designs for the contest? So far the two of them hadn't discovered any common ground. She prayed that would change while working together. Even though they seldom agreed about the business, she truly liked Rylan and didn't want to be his adversary throughout the entire process.

Rylan gave a slight nod. "I agree we should both give our

opinions about the design created by the other, but I would like to have final say in the whiteware design." He glanced at Rose. "And you would have final say in your design for the urn."

Ewan cleared his throat. "That's a good idea, but the letter says the designs must be cohesive, so neither of you can become stubborn and unwilling to listen to the ideas of the other. Understood?"

"I don't think that should be a problem for me." Rylan arched his brows and looked at her. "For all my years in this pottery, I have willingly listened and learned from others."

Rose bit back the response that rushed to the forefront of her mind. She thought his assertion that he'd "willingly listened and learned" was somewhat contrary to his actual behavior. He'd objected to the school and had also sided with the workers who didn't believe cleaning their workspaces would generate better health. Although they'd already seen fewer absences from work since her cleanliness rules had been put into practice, and many of the children had begun to excel in their lessons, Rylan had yet to praise either of the changes she'd established. Granted, he'd convinced Robert to finally relent and send his youngest employees to the school, but if they were going to work together, she hoped he would truly listen to her ideas with an open mind.

Rose nodded but looked at her brother rather than Rylan. "I agree. If there is a problem, we'll first discuss it with each other. If we can't resolve the disagreement, we'll come and discuss it with you."

Ewan smiled. "It is my hope there will be no problem." He picked up the letter, and his smile disappeared. "This says all entries must be received no later than September twenty-sixth and the award will be presented two days later. That's only a little more than a month from now. If you're going to meet the entry date, you'll need to begin working on your designs. I'm sure you'll want to create a variety of pieces before you decide upon your final entries."

How foolish of her. She'd been so excited she hadn't taken note of the submission date when she read the letter. They couldn't possibly prepare for the contest within such a short time. Not do that and also keep their other work on schedule. "We're already behind in the decorating shop. I can't possibly expect the other decorators to take over my pieces and complete their own. It would be impossible."

"Then you're saying McKay Pottery shouldn't enter the contest?" Ewan pushed the letter across his desk.

Rose shook her head. She wouldn't be defeated so easily. "No. I'm saying we not only need to create the winning designs, but we also need to figure out a time when we can work on them."

"I'm free most evenings. I'd be willing to come back after supper and work." Rylan hesitated. "I believe that would allow us enough time if you think it's an acceptable idea."

"Nay." Ewan frowned. "'Twould not be proper for you and Rose to be alone here at the pottery. I'm thinking the better way would be for you to come home with us after work, eat supper, and the two of you can work on your designs in my office at the house. No need to be at the pottery until you're ready to make the pieces."

"I doubt Rylan will want to spend every evening at our house, Ewan. Perhaps the better idea would be for each of us to work independently and then meet and work on any necessary changes."

Rylan turned toward her. "If you're worried about having me around on Wednesday evenings when Joshua Harkness comes to call, ya need not worry. I'm willing to work on my own on Wednesday evenings."

She shook her head. "No, this is more important. I can forego my visits with Joshua until the contest is over."

When the meeting ended, Rose returned to the decorating shop, her mind in a whirl. Rylan's remarks about her Wednesday evenings with Joshua had caught her off guard. While she was willing to forego their weekly visits, she'd already cancelled their visit for this evening because she'd fallen behind in her work. Other than telegraphing a brief message that he should curtail his visits for another four weeks, there seemed no way she could avoid their Wednesday evening outings.

She considered sending a telegram, but Joshua deserved better. He would have questions, and she wanted time to explain her decision. The contest was important, but she was certain Joshua would make the same concession for her if he were in a similar situation.

The success of McKay Pottery rested squarely on Rose's shoulders. She'd convinced the family to purchase the pottery and had committed to make it a success. She did not intend to fail.

Conflicted feelings assaulted Rylan as he considered spending every evening at the McKay home. Polite conversation would be expected around the dining table, and he wasn't accustomed to fancy meals or polite conversation. He did recall the food served at his home before he turned ten years old. Meals that had warmed and filled his belly while boisterous laughter abounded in their small kitchen. That had been before his mam died. After that, things changed. His da remarried, and his new wife did everything in her power to make Rylan's life miserable. She cuffed him if he took more than half a serving from the stewpot, and mealtime was accompanied by rancor rather than laughter.

Even his name had changed. Instead of referring to him as Rylan, his stepmother called him "boy" or "you." The fact that his father hadn't stepped forward to protect him made Rylan's decision to leave home quite simple. Once his wages provided enough money for him to rent a room in Mrs. O'Malley's boardinghouse, he didn't look back.

His room in the boardinghouse had been a solace. A place where he could arrange everything in an orderly fashion and feel assured nothing would be changed when he returned home. The boardinghouse table had been laden with plentiful good food, and his new home had provided a safe haven for a boy of only thirteen years. He had enjoyed the stability of working in the pottery, and until Mr. Bancock sold the place, there'd been no worry about change. Of course, he'd been moved from job to job in the pottery, but that wasn't the same as the changes plucky Rose McKay had insisted upon once her family purchased the business.

Since that time, he'd accepted the idea of education for the children, but maybe Robert had been right. Maybe the only reason he'd been willing to accept that change was because it didn't affect him.

On the other hand, the cleanliness rules had been an entirely different issue. During her first week at the pottery, Rose had insisted the work areas be cleaned and had posted signs that all employees were expected to wash their hands before eating. The employees had objected, but they knew there would be no choice in the matter. For the first few weeks, Rose prowled the work areas to make certain the rules were being followed. And she'd been clear that there would be more changes in the future. Once the pottery was profitable, she wanted separate washrooms installed for the men and women to wash and change clothes before returning to their homes. Rylan was sure that she'd come up with even more newfangled ideas once she didn't have to worry about how few contracts they'd acquired.

The dwindling contracts dumbfounded Rylan. His expectations had been high when Mr. McKay started bidding on contracts. After all, the family had connections among businessmen in the big cities, and Mr. Bancock had talked as though the pottery would expand under Mr. McKay's leadership. So far, that hadn't proved to be correct, for they'd won few of their bids.

Possibly the hardest part of eating dinner each night at the McKays would be hearing Joshua Harkness's name spoken with respect. The man was a cad, of that he was certain, but it wasn't his place to point it out. However, he prayed that it would become clear before Rose's heart was broken. At least she wouldn't be seeing Joshua for a month. Perhaps she'd lose interest in him during that time.

The following week, Ewan crossed the room. "Ready for your first meal with the McKays?" Ewan smiled and squeezed his shoulder. "Glad I am to have you joining the family for the next month. I grow weary of being the only man at the table. I hope you're prepared to be the center of attention. Ainslee and Adaira, my mother-in-law, and my wife will likely all be asking ya questions."

Rylan longed to beg out of the nightly dinners, but to do so would be rude and unpleasant for him and for Ewan. "Your younger sisters and I have visited a bit at the classroom. They seem to be enjoying their time helping at the school."

"I think they may be enjoying it a wee bit too much. Both of them think they should remain here in Grafton and continue to help at the school rather than go on to boarding school and finish their own education."

Rylan followed Ewan out the front door and waited while he locked the office. "They could go to the normal school here in Grafton and help at the pottery classroom later in the day."

Ewan shook his head as the two of them crossed the railroad tracks. Rylan had been surprised when Mr. McKay appeared at the pottery on his first day of work. He'd expected the new owner to arrive in a fancy carriage with a driver. Instead, he walked to work each day. He said it helped him clear his head. Though Mr. Bancock hadn't arrived by carriage, either, Ewan McKay was different. His family had money—at least his wife's family had money. Rylan had expected Mr. McKay to flaunt his wealth like some of the other business owners in town. Instead, he worried about finances even more than Mr. Bancock had. Not that he faulted the man. If this was his business, he'd be worried, too.

"I'm going to be praying those bids you mailed last week will turn the tide for us. Not that I haven't prayed about the other bids we've submitted, but I'm worried if we don't win at least two of those bids, we're going to be in deep financial trouble."

Rylan had gone over the books with Ewan and knew his assessment was correct, but the man needed to be cheered a bit. "If we can win this contest, it will be even better than winning one or two of those bids."

"Aye, that's true, and I do na mean to appear selfish, but I would be pleased to have both. We've fallen so far behind in our orders that it's going to take a good deal of diggin' to get us back on our feet. I was foolish to think I'd be successful in keeping all of Mr. Bancock's customers."

That had surprised Rylan, as well. Mr. Bancock's contracts called for a rebidding process if the pottery changed hands. Both Ewan and Rylan assumed the bids they submitted would be accepted, as they'd matched Mr. Bancock's previous bids. But they'd been underbid, and many of the contracts had been awarded to Harkness Pottery.

Joshua had apologized to Ewan when he discovered he'd won several contracts previously held by Bancock Pottery. The young owner had even offered to withdraw his acceptance, but Ewan had rejected the suggestion. Since then, Ewan had won only two bids, both for small orders. Though he and Rylan had gone over his figures carefully with each bid and believed no other pottery would submit a lower figure, they'd been wrong. When the rejection letters came, they'd sit for hours calculating how they could submit lower bids and still make a profit. With each submission came a rejection and Ewan finally declared he'd been a fool to let Rose convince him a pottery was a better idea than a brickyard.

"I'll say a few prayers, myself, Mr. McKay. I know we need orders."

"Thank you, Rylan." Ewan glanced at him as they turned the corner. "Do you think anyone will underbid us on the proposals you mailed today?"

Rylan shrugged his shoulders. "If there's a lower bid on any of those jobs, I would be mighty surprised. I don't see how any pottery could do it for less."

Ewan smiled and gave a slight nod. "I don't know what I'd have done without you during this transition, Rylan. 'Tis easy to see why Mr. Bancock made you his assistant."

The two of them continued to walk in silence, Rylan thinking about mingling with the McKay family. He guessed Ewan was worrying about those contracts and the failing pottery.

"Here we are." Ewan gestured for Rylan to go ahead of him as they neared the walkway leading to the house.

A wooden trellis, blanketed with pink climbing roses, adorned the far end of the porch, and the scent of roses hung heavy on the late afternoon breeze. "Someone is good with flowers."

Ewan chuckled. "Both Laura and her mother have a special talent when it comes to gardening. Once we moved into the house, they couldn't wait to begin planting, but that trellis was already on the porch when we purchased the house, so we have the former owners to thank for the roses."

Mrs. McKay stepped into the foyer as they entered the house. "I thought I heard voices out there." Her lips curved in a welcoming smile. She'd met Rylan during her occasional visits to the pottery and had always been gracious. "We're delighted that you've agreed to join us for dinner while you and Rose work on your designs, Rylan." She grasped her husband's arm. "I must say that I wholeheartedly agree with Ewan that working here at the house is much more acceptable than you and Rose spending several hours alone at the pottery each evening." Her smile returned as she gestured for him to enter the parlor. "Besides, we enjoy company. Do sit down. Dinner will be served in a few minutes."

Muffled footsteps were followed by the appearance of an older lady with perfectly coifed hair and wearing a pale blue silk dress trimmed with a navy fringe. She snapped open her fan and waved it back and forth as she sat down near Rylan. "You must be Rylan Campbell, our dinner guest."

"Aye, that I am."

Ewan drew near. "Rylan, this is my wife's mother, Mrs. Woodfield."

"Pleased to meet you. I thank you for allowing me to take my meals at yar table while Rose and I work on our drawings."

He allowed his gaze to wander away from the older woman's scrutiny. While Mrs. McKay had been warm and welcoming, Mrs. Woodfield's deportment was more detached, as though she preferred to observe from a distance. Right now, Rylan shared that same feeling. Rather than be a participant in this unfolding scene, he would have preferred to peer through a window as an unobserved spectator. But he was here, and he must make the best of it. If he couldn't help the pottery survive, he'd be making the biggest change of his life—seeking a new place of employment.

# Chapter 15

Rylan had barely gathered his bearings when a maid announced dinner would be served in fifteen minutes. From a distant room, a bell rang and was soon followed by a clatter of feet in the upstairs hallway. Moments later, the twins and Rose descended the stairs and gathered with them in the parlor. They were followed by a young woman with red hair, who carried the youngest of the McKay daughters in her arms. His stomach lurched at the sight of her. Was she the woman he'd seen with Joshua?

Mrs. McKay waved the redheaded woman forward. "Rylan, this is our youngest daughter, Tessa, and her nanny, Beatrice Murphy. Beatrice agreed to come with us when we moved from Bartlett, and we're grateful for her help with our little girl." She smiled at the nanny. "Mr. Campbell assists Mr. McKay in the office at the pottery."

Beatrice gave a slight nod as she pinned him with a disparaging stare, likely wondering why the hired help was being entertained in the McKay home. Her look of disdain made him long to rush home and change into his Sunday white shirt and black trousers, but he remained glued to his chair.

The scene outside the hotel replayed in his mind as the nanny crossed the room. She presented the child to her parents, who kissed her and then returned her to Beatrice's care. Moments later, Adaira and Ainslee took up positions on either side of him. Ainslee nodded toward the little girl. "Tessa goes back upstairs with Beatrice to eat her dinner when we have guests, but Laura likes to have her come downstairs while we gather in the parlor for prayer before going into the dining room."

Rylan thought it an odd practice—not the prayer, but the fact that they gathered in the parlor rather than sitting around the table and praying before the meal. When Ewan bowed his head, Rylan and the others followed suit. Ewan's prayer was earnest. Beyond asking God to bless their food, he prayed for his family members, the staff in his home, all of the employees working for him, and then petitioned the Lord for favor regarding his recent contract bids and the contest entries. He ended by giving thanks for the Lord's protection and blessings.

Gathering the family for prayer before a meal, or at any other time, was foreign to Rylan. Thoughts of Beatrice and the hotel fled from his mind as he recalled Mam praying with him before bedtime when he was little, but that, too, had changed when his da remarried.

None of the tenants in the boardinghouse had ever offered to say a blessing over their meal, and Mrs. O'Malley had been too busy serving their food to worry if they'd prayed or not, but Rylan liked the idea of thanking God before meals. He hadn't been brave enough to pray aloud, but he'd silently prayed before his meals. If he ever had a family, he would want to pray with his children. He would want them to learn of God's love at an early age.

Not until he'd questioned Mr. Bancock had Rylan truly learned the meaning of God's love. And there'd been no doubt

Mr. Bancock believed the teachings of the Bible. Throughout the years Rylan had worked for him, Mr. Bancock had been fair to all those who worked for him and was a living example of God's love. To now work for Ewan, another man who lived his faith, was an additional blessing for Rylan. Mr. Bancock's declining health had recently required a move to a sanitarium in Wheeling, and he missed the older man's sage advice, his friendship, and his godly example.

Rose had greeted him when she and the twins entered the room, but she'd remained on the other side of the room. Unlike her twin sisters, Rose seemed to think it proper to keep distance between them. As they prepared to enter the dining room, Laura glanced over her shoulder. "You'll be seated next to Rose, Rylan."

Both twins objected, and Rose offered to give up her position, but Ewan waved a warning hand. "You girls will be sitting in your usual places. No more objections."

Rylan followed Ewan's lead and held Rose's chair before he sat down. He stared at the variety of silverware flanking his dinner plate. He was accustomed to a fork, a knife, and a spoon. After his meals at the boardinghouse, Mrs. O'Malley had collected any unused silverware and returned it to the kitchen. "Makes no sense to wash clean dishes or silverware," she'd told one of the tenants who'd objected to the practice. "But if it will make you feel better, you can wash them yourself." The fellow hadn't taken her up on the offer. After that, nothing was said when the clean silverware was collected and put away.

If he was going to complete this meal without making a fool of himself, Rylan would need to watch Ewan. When Ewan lifted his napkin and spread it across his lap, Rylan followed his lead.

Mrs. Woodfield was seated across from him, and after taking a sip of water, she leaned forward. "We're eager to hear more about this contest you and Rose are going to enter. Ewan told us the exciting news last evening."

He looked up from the bowl of creamy chicken soup that had been placed in front of him. "Rose is the one who received the letter from her school and suggested entering the contest. She can tell you far more than I can."

Rose gave him a sideways glance before turning toward the older woman. "There isn't anything further either of us can tell you. The only information we have is what was contained in Mrs. Fisk's letter."

"I must say that I'm pleased Muriel thought to send you news of the contest, even if she was a bit tardy with her communication." Mrs. Woodfield pursed her lips.

"Let's give her the benefit of the doubt, Mother. She may have only heard about the contest recently." Laura graced her mother with a charming smile.

"I suppose that's true." The older woman looked back and forth between Rylan and Rose. "Have the two of you discussed a theme or decided upon any idea that will set you apart from the other contestants?"

Rylan waited, hoping Rose would reply, but she just sat there, silent as a stone. Finally he shook his head. "Nay, we've not decided, but perhaps tonight we'll come up with a winning idea, right, Rose?"

"It's difficult to say if we'll be able to agree on anything so soon," she said, before dipping her spoon into the soup.

Mrs. Woodfield dabbed the corners of her mouth with the linen napkin and straightened her shoulders. "Well, I've given the matter some thought, and I have an idea."

Both of them stared at the older woman. This time Rose gathered her composure and addressed the woman. "I think two of us trying to agree on a design will prove difficult enough.

If the rest of you want to participate, I fear we'll never reach a decision."

Mrs. Woodfield chuckled. "Are you saying that too many cooks can spoil the broth, my dear?"

Rose smiled and gave a slight nod. "I don't mean to offend, but—"

"No offense taken. I wasn't going to offer any ideas about the design, but rather a method that might help the two of you develop a winning entry."

Mrs. Woodfield's comment aroused Rylan's interest. "What kind of method?"

A look of satisfaction spread across the older woman's face. "I think the two of you need to visit the Franklin Hotel in Pittsburgh so you have a better idea of the décor and style the owner has chosen for his primary hotel. Once you've seen the interior of the hotel, I believe you'll be better able to decide upon your design." She leaned back in her chair. Her eyes glimmered with satisfaction as she looked at her daughter. "Don't you agree, Laura?"

Laura arched her brows. "The idea is certainly promising, but I don't know how Rose and Rylan could possibly travel to—"

Mrs. Woodfield waved her daughter to silence. "I've already decided that you and I can accompany them and act as their chaperones. It's a perfect plan. We could leave as early as tomorrow morning if Ewan has no objection."

Ewan's eyes shone with concern. "While I think your idea a good one, I don't think Laura should be included in your travel plans. Even though she's been feeling better over the past two weeks, I worry she may once again become ill while traveling. I don't think it's wise."

Rylan had witnessed the strain Mrs. McKay's recent illness had caused his employer. Over the past few months, Ewan had gone home more often than usual to check on the well-being of his wife, but he'd never mentioned the cause of her illness. And she certainly didn't appear ill this evening, but he admired Ewan's concern for his wife.

"I believe Ewan is right, Mother. While I am feeling quite well at the moment, I don't think travel would be wise. You know how my health has faltered of late. I do well for a time, and then I must take to my bed." She offered her mother a sympathetic smile. "I would very much like to join you, but I'm sure the doctor would also object." She straightened her shoulders and looked at Rose. "I do think the idea holds great merit, and I see no reason why the three of you shouldn't leave tomorrow."

Mrs. Woodfield leaned sideways and patted her daughter's hand. "You and Ewan are right. I thought perhaps the trip might be a nice diversion, but it could prove too taxing." She sighed. "I do wish the doctor could discover what's been ailing you."

Rose cleared her throat. "Grandmother Woodfield's suggestion that we depart tomorrow is impossible for me. I haven't yet notified Joshua I'll be busy on Wednesdays. I had hoped to tell him in person."

"Ewan could explain, but I doubt you'd think that a good idea. I suppose we could wait until Thursday morning." The older woman gave a slight shake of her head. "I cannot understand how that young man can be away from his business for a full day every week. With such a lackadaisical attitude toward his work, I won't be surprised if I hear that Harkness Pottery has failed." She passed an oval china serving bowl heaped with green beans to Ewan. "If I know Jeremiah Harkness, he has no idea his son isn't tending to business six days a week. Has Joshua mentioned any progress with his father's pottery when the two of you visit?"

Ewan spooned green beans onto his plate and then passed

the bowl to Adaira. "You need not worry about Joshua or the Harkness Pottery. From what he's told me, they are doing much better than we are. He says their production has increased since he took over, yet he still hasn't impressed his father enough to get the office position he desires."

Laura passed the bowl of mashed potatoes to Rose. "I simply don't understand how he has increased production while you work so hard and have had little success in gaining new contracts. Somehow it doesn't seem right."

Ewan smiled at his wife. "He's obviously won some fair-sized contracts, and I've not been successful with the bids I've submitted for various jobs."

Rylan didn't miss the hint of sadness in Ewan's voice. He desperately wanted Mr. McKay to succeed. "Mr. Bancock always said that bidding required a little knowledge and a lot of God's grace. If we can win one or two of the contracts we sent off today, we will be doing much better."

"Then we shall be praying that you win those contracts. In the meantime, let's forge our plans so that McKay Pottery wins the contract being offered by the Franklin Hotels." Mrs. Woodfield directed her attention to Rylan. "Are you able to go to Pittsburgh on Thursday and be away for several days?"

He glanced at Ewan. "If Mr. McKay agrees that I can be absent from work."

Ewan forked a piece of the pork roast onto his plate. "I have no objection to the plan or to Rylan being away from work for a few days. I believe it could help if the two of you see the interior of the hotel, but Rose should be the one who decides if the time is better spent working on designs or visiting the hotel."

They all turned in Rose's direction. "I think the time will be well spent visiting the hotel. On the way home, Rylan and I can discuss our ideas."

Mrs. Woodfield beamed. "Excellent. Then we're agreed. We'll leave on the early train Thursday morning."

When they finished dinner, Rose asked to be excused. She looked at Rylan as she stood. "Since we're not going to be planning our designs until after the visit to Pittsburgh, I assume our session for tonight is cancelled."

Rylan's stomach cinched. He glanced around the table, suddenly feeling like an interloper at their dinner table. "I thank you for the fine meal, Mrs. McKay. 'Twas a pleasure joining your family, but I believe I'll bid you all good-night. As Rose mentioned, our plans are cancelled for this evening, so there's no reason for me to be here."

Rose gaped at him. "Y-you're welcome to stay, but since we aren't meeting . . ."

Rylan shook his head. "I understand. There's no need to explain."

She'd made it clear. He didn't belong.

Shame washed over Rose as she climbed the staircase and hurried down the hallway toward the nursery. Though it hadn't been her intent, her curt comment had caused Rylan to feel unwelcome. The thought that she'd sent such a message to a guest in their home created a rush of bad memories. While in school, she'd experienced the sting of rejection and had promised herself she would never exclude others. But that's what she'd done this evening. She hadn't wanted to hurt him, but she had wanted him to leave. Mostly because they seemed to disagree about almost everything.

When they'd first met, she'd thought him handsome and quite charming, but their differing views had altered her opinion. While she couldn't fault Rylan's work ethic or his desire to have the pottery succeed, she abhorred his reluctance to remain open-minded.

Joshua had at least listened to her ideas and had even concurred with her suggestions. She had hoped he would immediately begin classes for the children in his pottery and institute some of her suggestions for cleanliness, as well. A few weeks ago when she'd inquired about progress, he said his father had forbidden the changes, citing cost as the reason. Joshua's remorse, especially regarding the school, had been palpable. Though she regretted there would be no schoolroom in Harkness Pottery, Rose had appreciated Joshua's desire for change and his compassionate attitude. He'd promised that once his father loosened his oversight, there would be changes at their pottery.

Rose opened the door to the nursery and waved at Tessa. The child had finished her dinner and pointed to her dollhouse. "Let's play." Tessa jumped up and hurried across the room.

Beatrice frowned, obviously annoyed by the intrusion. "I'll need to get her ready for bed soon."

Rose ignored the remark and joined Tessa at the dollhouse. She picked up several pieces of tiny furniture and placed them in one of the rooms. "I think we need to arrange the parlor with more chairs, don't you?"

Tessa bobbed her head and gathered several of the small padded chairs and pushed them into the parlor.

"I thought you and Rylan was supposed to have some sort of meeting after supper. How come you're up here instead?" Beatrice pinned Rose with a hard stare.

"We postponed our meeting until after we make a trip to Pittsburgh." She arched her brows. "How did you know about my meeting with Rylan?"

The nanny hiked a shoulder. "Ainslee told me. She said you were doing some designs for a contest. I figured she didn't know what she was talking about until I came downstairs before dinner. I'm thinkin' that Rylan fella was feelin' like a fish out of water and things didn't go so well. That's why you're up here with Tessa and me."

Rose shook her head. "No, that's not it at all. We aren't ready to begin creating the designs yet."

"Why not? How do you know when you're ready to draw something? Do you have to wait until y'er hit with a jolt of lightning or something?"

Rose chuckled. "No, but it does help to have some ideas in mind before you sit down and try to draw a design. This project is important, so we want to be sure we submit our very best work."

Beatrice crossed the room and picked up several of Tessa's wooden blocks. "What kind of contest is it that y'er entering?" She placed the blocks inside the toy chest.

The nanny's curiosity surprised Rose. Never before had Beatrice shown any interest in the pottery or Rose's work, but perhaps this was Beatrice's attempt to establish a friendlier relationship. Though she didn't go into great detail, Rose told her the contest was being sponsored by the owner of the Franklin Hotels.

Beatrice sat down and gave Rose her undivided attention. "That sounds excitin'. What's the prize if ya win?"

As Rose revealed the prize, Beatrice rubbed her hands together and smiled. "That's a mighty good reason to make the best drawings ya can. That money would sure come in handy."

"The money would be nice, but the contracts would be even better. That's the part of the prize that will help everyone working at the pottery."

"Aye, that's true enough. How'd ya come to hear about the contest?"

Rose mentioned the letter she'd received from Mrs. Fisk.

"So can anybody enter, or is it open to only certain potteries?" Beatrice leaned forward, her eyes glimmering with excitement.

"The entries must come from potteries able to produce the dishware, since the first prize is a contract to make all of the dishware for the Franklin Hotels."

The girl nodded her head as if she understood, the glimmer still sparkling in her eyes. Did Beatrice somehow believe she could draw a design and win the cash prize?

"No one can enter simply to win the cash prize. All those who enter must verify they can produce the dishes." Rose spoke slowly, still not certain Beatrice grasped the entirety of the process.

Once again she nodded. "Sure, and I understand, Rose. I know I cannot enter, if that's what's worrying ya. Even if I could make the dishes, I couldn't draw a picture if me life depended on it. I was just dreamin' about that prize money." She leaned back in her chair. "What are you thinkin' might be a good idea for your design?"

"We're not sure. Grandmother Woodfield is going to escort Rylan and me to Pittsburgh so we can visit the main hotel and gather some ideas. We'll be leaving on Thursday morning."

Beatrice's eyes opened wide. "That Rylan fella is going to Pittsburgh with you and Mrs. Woodfield? For sure, that's quite a piece of news." Her eyes clouded with a faraway look. "I'd like to see Pittsburgh one day. Maybe when I get married, I'll go there with me husband."

The remark surprised Rose. She didn't realize Beatrice had a beau. "I didn't know you were planning a wedding."

"Not yet, but a lass needs to have her plans in mind, so when the right fella comes along, she's prepared. What about you and Joshua Harkness? I bet the two of you are making some plans for the future, what with him traveling to see you every Wednesday."

For someone who'd been eager to get Tessa ready for bed, Beatrice had certainly done a turnaround. "Right now, we're not making any plans. I have no idea what the future might hold, but I do know we won't be seeing each other on Wednesday evenings for a while."

Beatrice startled at the remark. "Why's that?"

Rose divulged her plan to curtail visits with Joshua while she worked on the designs. "I'm sure he can use the additional time to complete work at his own pottery. Though he doesn't complain, I imagine being absent every Wednesday creates a hardship for him. This will give him a much-needed break in our routine."

"You mean he won't be coming to Grafton for a whole month? That's a mistake, for sure. Not seeing a man for that long will lead to a wandering eye. You should give that idea some more thought."

Rose chuckled and patted Beatrice's hand. "No need to worry. I think our relationship will survive. If it doesn't, it wasn't meant to be."

# Chapter 16

When the train arrived at the Grafton station on Wednesday morning, Beatrice was waiting near the entrance leading into the waiting room. At first she'd considered going inside. She'd even given thought to waiting on the platform, but eventually common sense prevailed. She knew Joshua would be unhappy she was anywhere near the railroad station, but she'd convince him that no one would question an inadvertent meeting between the two of them. And if any questions arose, she'd merely say she had been expecting a visit from one of her relatives in Bartlett.

Never before had she dared to meet Joshua's train, but today was different. All night she'd worried he might not come or that he'd catch a later train. Only once had he failed to arrive on the early train, but with her luck, it would happen again today. She needed all the time she could squeeze into today's rendezvous. Unless she could convince Joshua to continue his visits to Grafton each Wednesday, she wouldn't see him for another month. She didn't think she could survive without her Wednesday meetings with him, and she wanted the extra money he furnished her. Caring for a two-year-old simply didn't provide the excitement or money she craved.

When Joshua stepped onto the brick sidewalk outside the station, Beatrice hurried toward him. His forehead creased with concern when he caught sight of her. "What are you doing here?" He scanned the area and then looked over his shoulder. "Someone could see us."

His harsh tone implied anger, but she ignored the warning and stepped closer. Once he understood the importance of her news, his attitude would change. "I wanted to make sure I got to see you today. I have something mind-bogglin' to tell ya, and since I might not see you for a month, I decided to take me chances and come to the station."

He motioned her to a small alcove at the far end of the station. "What are you talking about? Why wouldn't you see me?"

"There's far too much I have to tell ya to stand out here in the open. I'll meet you at the hotel in half an hour. Did you reserve your usual room?"

He nodded. "Come up the back stairs and knock on the door." When she turned to depart, he grasped her wrist. "You haven't found someone else to occupy your day off, have you?"

She curved her lips into a tempting smile and traced her fingers down the sleeve of his suit jacket. "How could I find anyone who could take your place?"

He shot her a warning look. "You couldn't. I'll see you in half an hour."

She remained outside the station until he was out of sight, then made her way across the railroad tracks and eventually wound through town. After a stop at the general store, she walked past the livery, the smell of hay and manure now heavy in the air. As she turned onto a path leading to the rear of the hotel, her stomach rumbled. She hoped Joshua had ordered lunch delivered to their room when he checked in.

As she rounded the corner of the hotel, she turned toward the sound of footfalls and crackling undergrowth. Her breath caught when she spotted Rylan Campbell on the path behind the livery. She ducked her head and fled inside the back door of the hotel, her heart drumming beneath the bodice of her green print dress. He didn't appear to have seen her, but she couldn't be certain.

She raced up the steps and knocked on the door with a stenciled number four on the center panel. "Joshua! Hurry and open up. It's me, Beatrice."

Moments later, the door creaked open. An old lady with white hair piled high on her head stared at Beatrice through narrowed eyes. After directing a scathing look at Beatrice, the woman glanced over her shoulder. "Henry! There's a girl here looking for someone named Joshua. What's this all about?"

Beatrice backed away from the door and waved her hand. "I have the wrong room. No need to bother your husband." She hastened away from the doorway and down the stairs before the woman could create a commotion that might draw other hotel guests into the hallway.

Once she reached the foot of the stairs, she circled around and stepped into the small alcove below the stairway and inhaled a deep breath. What was the matter with Joshua? She'd specifically asked him about his room. Did he think she'd be amused by his antics? If so, he was sorely mistaken.

After a moment to compose herself, Beatrice marched down the hallway and approached the front desk. Her frazzled condition was further aggravated when she discovered the hotel clerk absent from his post. When she could find him nowhere in sight, she continually pressed her palm up and down on the bell in rapid succession. The incessant dinging brought the clerk running to the desk.

He rushed behind the counter and grabbed the bell from beneath her hand. "How may I be of assistance, miss?" He held the bell tight against his chest and glared at her.

Beatrice didn't flinch. "If you'd been at your desk, I wouldn't have had to ring. I need the room number for Joshua Harkness. He registered a short time ago."

The clerk shook his head. "We don't give out the room numbers of our guests unless they advise us to do so."

Beatrice narrowed her eyes until they were mere slits. "Then check for his instructions, because he's expecting me."

"There's nothing written by his registration." He looked down his nose at her. "I cannot give you his room number."

Beatrice blew out a long breath. "He's a friend of mine, and either ya tell me his room number, or I'll take meself up those stairs and knock on every door until I find him."

"I can't allow you to do—"

"Beatrice! Are you here to enjoy lunch on your day off?"

She whirled around and found herself face-to-face with Rylan Campbell. *Blimey!* Now what? She stepped away from the counter and hoped the clerk would be thankful she was out of his hair for the moment.

"Aye. Sometimes I like to enjoy a bite when I come into town." The tightness in her voice alarmed her. If she didn't relax, he'd know she was up to something. "What about you? On yar lunch break from the pottery?"

He nodded. "They usually have creamed chicken on biscuits on Wednesdays, so I stop by sometimes. If you haven't eaten, you should try them."

"I'm not so sure I'm all that hungry."

"If ya change your mind, you might ask to be seated with

Joshua Harkness. I saw him enjoying the chicken and biscuits while I was in the dining room." He arched an eyebrow. "You do know Joshua, don't ya?"

She could feel the heat climb up her neck and spread across her checks. No doubt her creamy complexion was now sporting bright red splotches. "I shared a few dances with him at Rose's party when she lived in Bartlett, and I've seen him at the house when he comes callin' on Rose."

How did Rylan know she and Joshua were acquainted? She tried to recall if Joshua had ever mentioned Rylan. Her mind raced as she tried to sift through all that had happened since that first dance with Joshua, but the two of them had talked about lots of things. She simply couldn't recall, and that was enough to make her nervous.

When Rylan made no move to leave, she nodded toward the dining room. "I best get into the dining room and order me lunch." She forced her lips into a smile, gave a slight wave, and walked into the dining room.

Instead of approaching Joshua, she gave a slight nod as she walked past him and sat down at a nearby table. She ordered coffee and a sandwich rather than the special. Chicken and biscuits didn't hold any great appeal. Before her order arrived, Joshua approached her table, slipped a note atop her napkin, and left the dining room. He'd printed Room 6 on the paper.

When she'd finished her lunch, Beatrice strode past the front desk, graced the clerk with a smug smile, and ascended the staircase. Moments later she knocked on the door of room six.

The door opened and Joshua frowned. "What took you so long?"

His abrupt tone annoyed her. "Me? What about you?" She reached forward and with her palm on his chest, pushed him aside and strode across the room. She flopped down in the overstuffed chair and pointed her index finger at him. "We would've been together over an hour ago if you'd been in your proper room. When we was at the train station, I asked if you reserved your usual room, and ya told me yes. Then, when I go to room four and knock on the door, some old lady comes to the door making a ruckus. It's a wonder you didn't hear her down in the dining room."

"It's not—"

"And then I take meself to the front desk, and do ya think they'd tell me your room number? O'course not. That clerk had his nose so high in the air he woulda drowned if it started to rain."

"That's enough!" Joshua's shout caught her by surprise, and she pressed her lips together. "Are you going to spend what little time we have together barking at me?"

"Nay, but so far this day has been as sour as a cup of vinegar." She nodded toward the other chair. "Sit down. I got lots to tell ya."

For the next hour, Beatrice held Joshua captive with tales of what she'd learned from Rose the previous evening. "What's that gonna do to our Wednesday meetings? There won't be no excuse for ya to come 'round while she's gone, and you're gonna be missing your Wednesday afternoons with me. I may have to find someone else to occupy my time on me day off for the next month."

His eyes turned dark. "Don't even think about seeing someone else. I don't share."

"I could always meet ya in Bartlett. I need to go up there and see Aunt Margaret. I been neglecting my duty to her since I started meeting with you."

"What duty?"

"Nothing much. She just likes to know what's going on with

Ewan and the rest of 'em. I wrote her a couple letters instead of going to see her, but my letter writing ain't so good, and I know she's got questions for me."

"I thought there was trouble between the Crotherses and the McKays. Wasn't it Mrs. Crothers who refused to honor a partnership agreement at the brickyard when her husband died?"

"Aye, that she did. Margaret's one shrewd woman. She did Ewan out of his half of the business, and she's been doing well since Hugh died. At least that's what the rest of the family tells me, but she still bears a deep grudge against Ewan." She gave a quick wink. "Tessa was born to Margaret's sister, Kathleen. Illegitimate. Margaret was sure it would spoil her chances of being accepted by all them society folks like you and your family. She wanted Kathleen to suffer for her wrongdoing, but Ewan and Laura adopted Tessa and then helped Kathleen get a job of some sort in another state. Margaret was so furious she locked herself in her room for days. When Hugh died, she got her revenge against Ewan."

"So are you loyal to the Crotherses or the McKays?"

She snickered. "I keep me a hand in both kettles. That way I never go hungry."

Joshua folded his arms across his chest as he leaned back in the chair, extended his legs, and crossed his ankles. "If you get caught, you'll do more than go hungry—you'll starve to death. It's always better to choose your side in an argument and remain steadfast. Sounds like Margaret Crothers could be a formidable adversary."

She shrugged, uncertain what those words meant. "You do things your way, and I'll do things to suit meself. Margaret enjoys hearing the news I pass her way. And, just like you, she makes it worth my while to furnish her with a bit of gossip."

"Makes no difference to me, but I doubt you'll be working

for Ewan McKay if he ever finds out what you're doing." He rubbed his forehead. "I s'pose we could meet in Bartlett. My father owns several businesses there. If we're careful, I think it can work, especially if you keep bringing me such excellent information."

She leaned back in the chair and smiled. "Tell me all of that news ain't worth an extra bit of money in me pocket."

He stood, walked to the bed, and reached into his pocket. After peeling several bills from his money clip, he tossed them on the bed and winked. "That's for the information and your time for the rest of the afternoon."

She smiled as she jumped up from her chair and lunged toward the bed.

The next morning Rose and Mrs. Woodfield waited on the benches inside the train station. They'd been there only a short time when Rose stood and began to pace. The older woman looked up and gestured for Rose to be seated. "Do sit down. You're making me nervous, and when I get nervous, I get a headache. I don't want a headache before we even begin our journey."

"Where is he? He should already be here." Rose plopped down on the bench and folded her arms across her waist. She'd told Rylan it was best to be early when traveling by train, as they sometimes arrived before schedule. Though she'd never known the trains to depart the station early, boarding as soon as the conductor permitted would guarantee a better seat.

Mrs. Woodfield smiled and shook her head. "There's plenty of time."

She'd barely uttered the words when Rylan burst through the front door of the station, carrying a small valise in his hand.

His eyes shone with panic as he hurried toward them and came to an abrupt halt only inches in front of the bench. "Am I late?"

Mrs. Woodfield shook her head and smiled. "If you were late, we wouldn't be sitting here. Do sit down and catch your breath. The train isn't due to arrive for another ten minutes."

Rose wasn't quite as sympathetic as Mrs. Woodfield. "What kept you?"

Rylan pointed his thumb in the direction of the pottery. "I stopped by work. I wanted to prepare the time cards for Ewan since tomorrow is payday."

Rose sighed. Ewan was more than capable of locating time cards and calculating pay. However, she refrained from voicing her opinion.

"That was considerate of you, Rylan. No wonder Ewan values you." Mrs. Woodfield gave Rose a sidelong glance. "Don't you agree, Rose?"

Rose frowned at the older woman. "I agree that Rylan is a good employee, but I don't think he should have taken time to visit the pottery this morning. I'm sure Ewan could have completed the task."

"Aye." Rylan said. "There's no doubt your brother is smart and could do most anything in the office without my help, but if I can make it easier for him, then I wish to do so."

Moments later, the train chugged and hissed into the station, and the three of them boarded without further comment. Mrs. Woodfield chose seats that faced each other. Rose sat down beside the older woman, and Rylan took the seat opposite Rose.

Soon after the train departed the station, the swaying motion rocked Mrs. Woodfield to sleep. Rose retrieved a book from her bag and pretended to read so she wouldn't be forced to stare at Rylan.

A short time later, he leaned forward and gestured toward the book. "I'm guessing your book isn't very interesting."

She looked up and met his steady scrutiny. "On the contrary, I find it quite fascinating."

He chuckled. "You have yet to turn the page. I thought it might be a wee bit dry."

Heat spread across her cheeks to signal her embarrassment. "It truly is a fascinating book, but I can't seem to concentrate enough to read at the moment."

"I see. Then maybe we can talk instead."

She closed the book and set it on her lap.

"How was your visit with Joshua? Was he unhappy to learn you won't be seeing him on Wednesday evenings?"

Rylan had been amazed she would willingly cancel her weekly visits with Joshua, so his question didn't overly surprise her. Though she hadn't planned to discuss the details of her conversation with Joshua, there was no reason to withhold his reaction. "He was understanding. He did say he might visit on one or two of the Wednesdays, just in case there's a little time when he can see me." When Rylan shook his head and grinned, she continued. "I know what you're thinking, but you're wrong. I am dedicated to this project and plan to devote all of my time to winning. We've been courting only since my graduation party. When we moved to Grafton, I didn't have any expectation that he would continue to call on me. At this time, we're no more than dear friends. I've told Joshua there won't be time to see him, but—"

"'Dear friends'?" His voice crackled with disbelief. "I'm thinking a man who is willing to take a day off work each week and travel to Grafton is considering something beyond friendship." Rylan tipped his head to one side. "I'd say maybe he's got a weddin' in mind."

She withdrew a lace-edged handkerchief from her pocket and blotted her face. She couldn't be certain if it was the heat inside the railroad car or Rylan's bold remarks that had caused perspiration to dampen her forehead and palms. "I can assure you that Joshua and I have no wedding plans. I have repeatedly told him that his business should come first at this time in his life, but if he chooses to come to Grafton each week, I cannot stop him."

Rylan shrugged. "That's true enough, but does it not cause you to wonder a wee bit what he must be thinkin' and why he'd make such a choice if it's as you say and only to visit a *friend*?"

"Are you intimating that I'm not being truthful with you? Because if you are, then—"

"Nay. I believe what you've said, but it does cause a bit of wonder."

Rose frowned. "*What* causes a bit of wonder?"

Rylan glanced at Mrs. Woodfield and lowered his voice. "If there might be some other reason he comes to Grafton. Something beyond his visits with you. Have ya ever considered that?"

For the life of her, Rose couldn't imagine what Rylan was thinking and why he was so interested in Joshua and his visits to Grafton. "He comes here to call on me, but he also spends time with Ewan discussing the pottery business. I'm certain you've seen him in the office from time to time."

"Aye." A shock of hair dipped across Rylan's forehead as he bobbed his head. "When your family first purchased the business, Joshua came to the office for brief visits, but I've not seen him darken the doorway for weeks now. What does he do until he comes calling on you is what I'm wonderin'. I'd think a man would become weary of sittin' in a hotel room week after week, especially when there's a later train he could be catchin'."

Rose had contemplated the same thing from time to time. So

had other members of the family, but she'd never asked Joshua why he insisted upon the early train or why he'd constantly refused to stay at their home rather than the local hotel. He'd told her he didn't want his weekly visits to become an inconvenience. She'd accepted his decision without further question.

Before she'd digested his last remark, Rylan tapped the cover of her book to gain her attention. "Did he pay visits to you on Wednesdays when you lived in Bartlett?"

She closed her eyes. His questions were becoming somewhat annoying. "No. Unless there was a special event, his usual day to call on me was Monday."

Rylan hesitated a moment. "And was Monday the day the household staff was off work?"

Rose sighed. Why did he care about the staff and their workdays when the family was living in Bartlett? "Half of the help took their day off on Sunday and the others on Monday. Laura needed some of the staff to help if she had guests for Sunday dinner. Beatrice worked on Sundays, as well. That way she could lend a hand if Tessa became fussy during church service or if Laura entertained Sunday dinner guests."

Rylan continued to stare at her as if he expected something further. Was he waiting for her to answer his earlier question regarding Joshua's activities on his Wednesday visits?

A gnawing discomfort swept over her as she attempted to fill the silence that hung between them. "I think Joshua likely brings some of his paper work with him. His hotel room offers the peace and quiet needed to complete such tasks." She was relieved when Rylan gave a brief nod and leaned back in his seat.

In truth, she had no idea what Joshua did during the hours preceding their visits, but perhaps she should inquire when he next called upon her. Not having answers to Rylan's questions caused Rose to realize she'd been negligent, and embarrassment weighed upon her. Proper etiquette was very clear: A woman should always express interest in a man's opinions and well-being. Rather than inquiring about Joshua's welfare, she'd been too busy discussing her work at the pottery.

Once the contest was over and she and Joshua resumed their weekly visits, she wouldn't be so remiss.

# Chapter 17

*Pittsburgh, Pennsylvania*

As the train rumbled and hissed into various train stations to take on water and passengers, Rylan puzzled over Rose's naïve acceptance of Joshua's behavior. Did she truly believe he was hunched over a desk in his room tabulating figures or poring over bids and contracts every Wednesday? Undoubtedly Joshua had performed a wee bit of work from time to time. After all, there had been the bids he'd mailed while in Grafton. However, Rylan didn't believe it was work that consumed most of Joshua's time at the hotel.

Rylan had hoped his questions might spark a degree of curiosity on Rose's part, perhaps open her eyes to what he suspected was going on at the hotel, but she seemed convinced that Joshua was a decent man.

He had wrestled with the idea of being forthright and telling her what he'd observed. He'd considered telling Ewan yesterday, but since he couldn't speak with absolute certainty, he'd remained silent. If he told Rose and she confronted Joshua, he and Beatrice might offer some believable explanation as to why they were meeting. And they would surely deny the claim that he'd seen them kissing behind the hotel.

Better to remain silent. He'd planted the seed. He would now pray that the seed would take root, for Rose deserved better than Joshua Harkness. They weren't far from Pittsburgh when Mrs. Woodfield tapped the train window. "Take a look, Rylan. This is what the big city of Pittsburgh looks like." She waited until he turned to the window. "Not what you expected, I'm sure."

"Nay. Even though it's afternoon, 'tis difficult to see much of anything out there except a gloomy haze. Seems the fog should have lifted by now." He leaned closer to the window. "Unless there's a storm moving in."

"There's no storm on the horizon, Rylan. Pittsburgh is a city of industry. Unfortunately, the businesses that support the residents of the area also create this murky pall, which is heavy enough to prevent the sun from breaking through." She gave a small sigh. "In the foothills, we expect the sun to break through by midmorning, but folks who live here have no such expectation. The sun is seldom able to penetrate the shadowy layers that hover over Pittsburgh."

Rylan wondered what it must be like to never see the bright sunshine or the clear blue sky that draped the valley each day. For sure, he wouldn't like to live in such a gloomy place. As the train pulled into the station, they gathered their few belongings and shuffled through the narrow aisle to step onto the platform.

Rylan glanced about, expecting to be invigorated by the sights and sounds of the city. Instead, his spirits sagged. Even before they arrived at the hotel, the gloom encompassed and weighed him down. He prayed they would complete their business in short order, for he already longed to return to the fresh air and sunshine in West Virginia.

As they stepped down from the hansom cab, Rylan studied

the blond brick edifice that would be their home for the next few days. His gaze settled on the signage affixed to the pinnacle of the hotel. Through the bleak dreariness, he finally made out the words *Franklin Hotel* and wondered how many guests had overlooked the obscured marker.

Rylan followed the two ladies into the hotel. As they approached the front desk, he glanced toward the stairway. "I hope our rooms are on one of the lower floors."

Mrs. Woodfield chuckled. "There is an elevator, and bellboys will assist with our luggage, Rylan, so it matters little what floor we're on."

"'Tis not the baggage that concerns me, Mrs. Woodfield. I'd like to be able to look out the window and see something besides the darkness that hides this city from view. I'm thinkin' the higher I go, the worse it becomes." He turned his attention upward.

The older woman followed his look to the frieze of delicate blue and white flowers interlaced with gold ribbons that decorated the ceiling. "I believe the view of that ceiling makes up for the gloominess outside, don't you?"

"Aye, 'tis a work of beauty, for sure." He narrowed his eyes and smiled as he read the intricate Scripture reference beneath the spray of flowers. Ephesians 2, one of his favorite chapters in the Bible. He turned, hoping to point out the intricate artwork and Scripture reference to Rose, but she had wandered into the large sitting room off the lobby.

Mrs. Woodfield stepped close to the counter and leaned toward the desk clerk. "If possible, we'd like rooms on the lower floors please."

The slender man gave a slight nod that caused his spectacles to slip a notch. After tracing his finger down the ledger book, he looked up and smiled at Mrs. Woodfield. "I believe we can accommodate your request. However, your rooms will be on opposite ends of the hallway on the second floor. Is that acceptable?"

"That will be fine." She smiled at Rylan. "We're in luck. The clerk located two rooms on the second floor." With a quick nod toward the sitting room, she said, "Why don't you fetch Rose? Tell her we're going to our rooms, and ask her to join us."

While Mrs. Woodfield busied herself directing the bellboy, Rylan crossed the lobby and entered the sitting room. Rose appeared lost in thought and startled when he drew near. "Mrs. Woodfield wants you to join her. We're ready to go to our rooms."

She sighed and extended her arm. "This is one of the most gorgeous hotels I've ever seen. I've been to other hotels both here in Pittsburgh and in Philadelphia with Ewan and Laura, but we never stayed here. It's truly remarkable. I'm so glad Grandmother Woodfield decided we should come. Without seeing the hotel, it would be impossible to design pieces that are consistent with Mr. Franklin's artistic style."

"Sure, and it's helpful to see the look of things and the colors he's used in the hotel, but I'm not sure we're needin' anything that's quite so elaborate as the decorations I'm seeing in this room."

The intricately woven tapestries of unicorns and ancient warriors, the massive furniture upholstered in myriad designs, and the contrasting Minton tile floor didn't appeal to him. The only evidence of design that met Rylan's taste was the frieze on the ceiling of the lobby. "It's all a bit much, don't you think?"

Rose pinned him with a look that was as frosty as a winter morn. "Complex, elaborate décor is what will draw praise and win this contest. I learned that lesson while attending design school. Ordinary, unexciting design is not what's wanted or expected."

Rylan didn't argue, but her words chafed. Soon enough he'd say what he believed would win the contest. Rose might know what would gain a prize in design school, but he knew what would appeal to a hotel owner who would need to supply white-ware to hotel kitchens for years and years. Cost would be a factor that Rose hadn't considered. The expense of replacing plates, cups, saucers, bowls, and serving dishes in the many Franklin Hotel restaurants would become a factor in this contest, of that he was certain. Besides, he had as much to gain from winning this contest as she did.

Mrs. Woodfield reached for Rose's hand as they drew near the front desk. "You should smile, my dear. You look as though you've been eating lemons."

Rylan gave a brief nod and grinned. "Aye, ya would not want your face to freeze while y'er looking so sour, Rose."

The slight smile that had appeared after Mrs. Woodfield's cautionary remark immediately disappeared. There was no doubt he should have kept his mouth shut. His attempt at humor hadn't helped matters.

An uncomfortable silence surrounded them as they followed the bellboy to the second floor. The young man came to a halt when he approached the second door on the right. "This is the room assigned to you, Mr. Campbell. The ladies will be at the other end of the hall." He unlocked the door and handed the key to Rylan. "I'll bring your baggage to the room once the ladies are settled in their room."

Mrs. Woodfield smiled and said, "We'll meet you downstairs for dinner at seven o'clock, Rylan. Until then, we'll rest and refresh ourselves."

When the ladies departed, Rylan surveyed the room and then

dropped into one of the soft upholstered chairs. While he'd been in the company of the ladies, he'd tried to appear casual, but he'd never been in surroundings such as this. Inhabiting the realm of the wealthy could become quite intoxicating. Perhaps that was why most of them acted so snooty. They'd become accustomed to the best life had to offer.

If he ever possessed a great deal of money, he hoped he'd be kind and generous like Mrs. Woodfield. She appeared to treat everyone with the same grace and dignity, no matter their station in life.

Once inside their room, Rose hurriedly unpacked her belongings and sat down in a chair near the windows. With paper and pencil in hand, she began to sketch designs while Mrs. Woodfield napped.

Nearly two hours passed before the older woman stirred and then appeared in the doorway leading into the sitting room. "Dear me. I meant to rest my eyes only for a short time. I've been asleep far too long. I do hope I'm not going to make us late for dinner."

Rose placed her sketching pad on the nearby marble-topped table and shook her head. "We have more than enough time to get ready. As you can see, I've not begun dressing for dinner." She tapped her fingers atop the sheaf of papers. "I think I've created some exciting designs. Coming here was such a wonderful plan. Seeing how Mr. Franklin has decorated the hotel has inspired me."

The older woman crossed the room. "I'm delighted to know it's proving helpful." She extended her hand. "Let me see what you've been drawing while I slept."

Rose watched the older woman's features for any sign of

disapproval as she thumbed through the several designs. "The work is still rudimentary, but I wanted to capture my first impressions of the hotel's décor." She waited, hoping to see a nod of approval.

When Mrs. Woodfield had looked through the several pages, she handed them back to Rose. "They are lovely, my dear, but I'm surprised you've begun without Rylan. I'm sure he'll have some ideas, as well. As I recall, Ewan wanted this to be a cooperative project between the two of you." She gestured toward the bedroom. "Come along. We need to dress for dinner. We don't want to keep Rylan waiting."

Why not? Waiting was what Rylan did best. Mustn't change anything too much. Mustn't make it too ornate. He probably even dreamed in black and white.

Rylan stood outside the hotel restaurant a few minutes before seven o'clock. He didn't want to keep the ladies waiting, especially Mrs. Woodfield. He pressed his fingers down the front of his black sack coat. Before leaving his room, he'd made certain his white shirt was free of wrinkles and the knot in his wide necktie had been perfectly formed.

An oversized clock in the hotel sitting room began to chime the hour as Mrs. Woodfield and Rose descended the stairs and approached. Rose glided toward him in a gown of plum and ivory silk that enhanced her shimmering blue eyes and creamy complexion. Narrow plum and ivory ribbons had been woven into her hair, and her shoulders were draped with an intricately woven lace shawl. He wanted to look away, but his eyes betrayed him and remained fixed upon her. She was a vision of beauty that could not be ignored.

A warm smile curved Mrs. Woodfield's lips as she tapped

his arm. "Are we going to enter the restaurant, or do you plan to remain in the lobby and stare at Rose for the remainder of the evening?"

Embarrassment seized him, and he snapped to attention at the older woman's question. Hoping to hide his mortification, he forced a smile and dipped his head toward the doors leading into the restaurant. "Though Rose is truly lovely in that beautiful gown, I'm thinkin' you ladies would rather have dinner than stand in the lobby." It wasn't a jaunty reply, but it was the best he could do under the circumstances.

A waiter seated them, and once they'd ordered dinner, Rylan traced his finger over a few fine cracks in his bread-and-butter plate. The crazing on the dishes detracted from the beautiful surroundings, though he doubted most diners would take notice. "The hotel seems to be decorated with a great deal of blue, so I'm thinkin' it might be good if we thought about an underglaze in pale blue or white with maybe some small blue flowers in the center and a rim of dark blue." When Rose didn't immediately respond or reveal any enthusiasm, he arched his brows. "Or maybe the letter F in the center with a few flowers that mimic the frieze in the lobby."

Rose wrinkled her nose, as if he'd presented her with a bowl of smelly cabbage. "We don't want anything so plain. I think we need to submit designs that reflect Mr. Franklin's sense of décor. Look around you, Rylan. This hotel is appointed with a flamboyant style all its own. Trust me, we don't want something as simple as a flower or initial in the middle of the dinner plates. We need something much more complex." She took a sip of water before she continued. "While Grandmother Woodfield rested this afternoon, I worked on a number of sketches for both the dinner plates and the urn. They're not yet fully developed, but I think they'll more likely gain us a win in the contest."

While she detailed her afternoon activities, the waiter arrived bearing dinner plates filled with slices of roasted pork dressed with apples and onions, baked cauliflower, and potatoes scalloped in heavy cream and topped with a layer of cheese. Even though Rose's comments had soured his stomach, Rylan's mouth watered at the sight.

Mrs. Woodfield touched Rylan's hand. "Would you please pray before we begin our meal?"

Rylan's thoughts churned, and his stomach clenched with discomfort. He'd never prayed in front of Rose and Mrs. Woodfield. The only person who'd ever heard him pray aloud was Mr. Bancock. He didn't know how to put words together that would sound pleasing to these women, but he couldn't refuse. He bowed his head and squeezed his hands together so tight he cut off the circulation. "Dear Lord, we thank you for our safe journey and this fine food. Please bless it to our bodies." He paused and quickly added, "And please help us to be willing to listen to each other and to follow your leading, so we can combine the talents you've given to each of us."

## Chapter 18

*Bartlett, West Virginia*

Before departing for Bartlett on Saturday morning, Beatrice considered wearing the new shoes and dress she'd recently purchased, but in the end she decided upon her serviceable boots with flat heels and a faded print dress. Her choices might elicit a bit of pity from Aunt Margaret. Though she referred to Margaret Crothers as her aunt, they weren't blood relatives. Beatrice's relationship to the family was through Hugh, Margaret's deceased husband. As a sign of respect or because her parents had instructed her to do so since she was a wee child, she'd addressed them as aunt and uncle. In truth, Hugh was a third or fourth cousin, twice removed, but there was enough blood running between them that her father had somehow finagled his way onto the ship with his family in tow when one of Hugh's first cousins was stricken with the fever shortly before sailing to America.

The appearance of their family hadn't particularly pleased Uncle Hugh, and when Beatrice's father quit his job at the brickyard and went to work in the coal mines for better pay, strong words were exchanged. After that, Beatrice had given Uncle Hugh a wide berth, but Aunt Margaret was a different story. The older woman seemed a kindred spirit. She knew what she wanted and did whatever was necessary to gain victory. Aunt Margaret prided herself on being shrewd, but thus far she'd proved easy for Beatrice to manipulate.

The train fare and buggy from town would cost her, but Beatrice planned to make this journey worthwhile. At the train station she convinced a young fellow to give her a ride in his buggy for half fare, but when they arrived at Crothers Mansion, she'd offered him a kiss instead. He'd accepted, and she'd tucked her coins away for safekeeping. She stood at the edge of the driveway and waved to the fellow until he was out of sight.

"Fool!" She muttered the condemnation as she walked up the brick-lined path leading to the front porch. Her leather and canvas boots made little noise as she climbed the front steps and lifted the brass knocker attached to the massive front door.

Fia, one of the relatives from Ireland who worked as a housemaid for Margaret, pulled open the front door. "Beatrice! I didn't know you were comin' to pay the missus a visit today."

"Nor does she, Fia, but I was given an extra day off and thought to put my time to good use. It's been far too long since I've visited any of me family, and I decided to make Aunt Margaret the first stop along my way."

The maid stepped aside to allow Beatrice entry. "Sure I am that the missus will be pleased to see ya. Just have a seat in the parlor, and I'll tell her you're here." Fia hurried off as though her very life depended on how fast she could carry the news to her mistress. Knowing Aunt Margaret, it probably did.

Beatrice stepped into the parlor and surveyed the extravagantly decorated room. She was examining a porcelain figurine when Margaret appeared. "Isn't it beautiful?" She stepped to

Beatrice's side and reached for the piece, then carefully placed it back on the table. "It was very expensive. I wouldn't want it to break." She gestured toward the sofa. "This is quite a surprise. I could hardly believe my ears when Fia said you were in the parlor, but I'm truly delighted and relieved to see you."

Beatrice grinned. "You don't have to use that fancy talk with me Aunt Margaret. I'm not one of those social ladies you're keen to impress."

Margaret leaned back as though offended, but she soon recovered. "I've been hoping for another letter from you. Tell me more about Laura. Is she still feeling poorly? Have you heard what ails her?" Before Beatrice could answer, Margaret's lips screwed into a knot, and her brow creased with a frown. "Why are you here on a Saturday? Has your day off work been changed?"

Beatrice shook her head. "Nay. I told a wee lie so's to get an extra day away from the family. Writing letters is hard for me. I'd rather visit in person. Besides, I have too much news to put in a letter." She didn't add that letters were impossible to deny when they fell into the wrong hands. "I told Mrs. McKay I needed to visit home as me father is ailing. I had a letter from home last week, so she believed me. I don't think she was none too happy about the extra day away, but she can have the twins look after Tessa if she's not feeling up to it herself."

Margaret's eyes gleamed with anticipation. "So tell me all this news you've come bearing."

Beatrice folded her hands and looked about the room. "I was thinking you might offer me a cup of tea or at least a cool glass of lemonade after me traveling so far to see you."

Reaching to a small table, Margaret retrieved a small bell and gave it a hearty shake. The jangling brought Fia running to the doorway, her eyes wide and her brows arched high on her forehead. "You need something, missus?"

"I wouldn't have rung the bell if I didn't want something, Fia." She directed a look of disdain at the maid. "Bring tea and biscuits and be quick about it."

A twinge of regret swept over Beatrice. Her demand for tea had created more work for Fia. "You're lucky to have such good help, Margaret. Both Melva and Fia are trustworthy women." Perhaps a few words of praise could help set things aright. "I know they're looking for maids at the hotel in town, and I'd wager they pay a sight more than you're paying Fia and Melva." She curved her lips in a sly grin. "Best you treat them well, or they'll do like me own da and seek work elsewhere."

The cautionary comment seemed to ease the harsh lines that etched Margaret's face, and when Fia reappeared a short time later, Margaret spoke with enough kindness that the maid appeared flummoxed and nearly dropped the plate of biscuits. Beatrice smiled as Margaret praised the maid for her agility when she caught the plate.

Teacup in hand, Margaret settled in her chair. "I can bear to wait no longer. Tell me what has been happening in Grafton. I do hope it's all bad news." She cackled before taking a sip.

"Aye, 'tis mostly bad news, for sure. The doctor still hasn't decided what's ailing Laura. It's most perplexing. Some days she feels fine, and other days she takes to her bed and isn't able to do much at all."

Beatrice carefully watched Margaret's reaction. The woman loved to hear any scrap of bad news regarding the McKay family. Even more, she wanted to hear about Tessa, her sister Kathleen's child. The rift between Margaret and the McKays had begun over the brickyard, but it had deepened tenfold when the couple took in Kathleen during her confinement and then adopted the child.

"Poor little Tessa doesn't know what to think when her

mother is ailing. Sad it is to see the wee one so confused by her mother's failure to even kiss her good-night."

As planned, her final comment hit the mark, and Margaret frowned. "They told my sister they would provide a wonderful home for her child. What kind of mother doesn't kiss her baby good-night? I knew Kathleen would rue the day she turned to them for help."

Beatrice lifted her shoulders in a slight shrug. "What was Kathleen to do when you sent her packin'? Nobody in the family was brave enough to lend her a hand. They knew they'd suffer your wrath if they so much as offered her a place to lay her head. Truth is, I think Kathleen did the only thing she could to protect herself and the wee one. Can't say as I blame her for deciding to give Tessa a better home than she could ever provide. And smart she was for going to New York and learnin' a trade. Wish I could live in a big city like New York."

Margaret waved her to silence. "I don't care a whit about your opinions, Beatrice. My sister's child isn't being properly cared for, and she should know. I penned her a letter after your last visit and told her Laura was in poor health. Do you know what her first question was to me?"

Beatrice helped herself to another biscuit and shook her head. "Nay. What did she ask?"

"How I managed to get her address."

Taken aback by the answer, Beatrice inhaled a piece of her biscuit and went into a coughing spasm. Margaret pounded her on the back and pointed to her teacup. "Take a drink."

Beatrice quickly complied, and when the coughing finally abated, she withdrew her handkerchief and wiped her eyes. "You didn't tell her I gave you the address, did you?"

"I'm not foolish enough to betray my sources, Beatrice. When I replied, I said I had my ways. I did say that if she cared about the welfare of her daughter, it would behoove her to pay a visit in the near future."

"I wish you hadn't written to Kathleen. If she writes to Laura and tells her what you've said, there's going to be questions about how you learned of Laura's illness. This could all come back to haunt me." Her stomach clenched tight around the biscuits and jam she'd eaten.

"Quit your worrying. A simple answer is all that's required. I can merely say that I overheard some ladies talking at a social function, but I don't recall exactly where." Margaret flitted her hand in the air. "Easy as that. No need to get yourself in a dither. Now settle yourself and tell me what else has been happening."

Margaret's reassurance eased Beatrice's fears. The older woman knew how to sidestep questions; she would protect Beatrice. After all, Aunt Margaret didn't want to lose her ability to gain information about the McKays.

"What about the pottery? Any news on how the business is doing? I do hope Ewan is having as much difficulty as I've been having with the brickyard." She shook her head in disgust. "How he managed to keep all of those contractors in Wheeling and Pittsburgh happy is beyond me. I'm having a terrible time trying to please them, and now some of them have threatened to take their business elsewhere. They say the bricks aren't the same quality, but I think they're lying to me."

Beatrice didn't know anything about how Ewan had managed contracts for the brickyard, but she did know that, thanks to her, he was having little success in gaining contracts for the pottery. "He's not doing so well at the pottery. Most of the contracts he bids on have been going to another pottery in Fairmont. From what I've been able to hear, he's worried they may not make a go of it unless . . ." Her words faded away like a summer evening.

Margaret turned her head and positioned her ear closer. Her desire for any morsel of bad news was now exposed like the underbelly of a viper. "Unless what?"

Beatrice savored the moment. The sense of power wielded at times such as this was as warm and intoxicating as the occasional glass of whiskey she shared with Joshua. "I've been thinking that my needs continue to increase with each passing day, and you've never given me more than a few coins for the helpful information I place on your doorstep each time I visit or write to you. A bit of extra money would be helpful, what with the train fare and other expenses I suffer with each visit." She tipped her head and smiled. "A new dress would be ever so nice, but a nanny can't afford the lovely gowns owned by someone such as you."

Margaret's eyes narrowed. Though her lips stretched into a forced smile, she'd clearly found no humor in the request. Her features remained tight as she placed her teacup on the tray. "If the information you're bringing me is worth more than usual, I'd be willing to add a few extra coins to your pocket."

"I think you'll find it worth more than a few coins." After such an intriguing lure, Beatrice had expected her aunt to readily agree to any requested sum. Either Aunt Margaret wasn't as interested as Beatrice had first thought, or she was determined to hold tight to her purse strings.

Margaret picked up the teapot and tipped it over her cup. As the amber brew splashed into her teacup, she gave Beatrice a sideways glance. "I'm not foolish, Beatrice. You need to remember who it is you're dealing with. Once I hear what news you've brought, we'll decide how much it is worth." She placed the teapot onto the tray and picked up her cup. "I believe you were going to tell me about something that might save Ewan's pottery." She arched her brows and waited.

There was no use prolonging this match of wills with her aunt. If she didn't soon complete her visit, there would be no time to shop in Bartlett. "There's a contest being sponsored by a hotel in Pittsburgh." Beatrice detailed the information she'd secured from Rose. "If they win, they'll be happy as pigs in clover. That contract will set them up for years to come. Leastwise, that's my understanding. And you can be sure Rose will be entering her very best work. She's feeling responsible for the losses at the pottery since she's the one who promised Ewan all her fancy schooling would make the pottery a success." Beatrice snorted. "Guess she's finding out it takes more than some fancy school in the big city to make a business successful."

"So Ewan's laying the blame at her feet, is he?"

"I don't know as he's faulting her so much as she's taking it on herself. One of the twins told me Rose convinced both Mrs. Woodfield and Ewan that the pottery was the best idea for the family business, 'cause she could make it succeed."

Margaret rang for Fia, and once the maid appeared, she pointed to the tea tray and waved her from the room. She glanced over her shoulder to make certain Fia wasn't nearby and then leaned forward. "Do you think Rose can win this contest?"

Beatrice shrugged. "Who can say for sure, but she can certainly draw nice designs. She won some big contest while she was in school. And Mrs. Woodfield took both Rose and Rylan Campbell—he's Ewan's assistant—up to Pittsburgh so's they could see Mr. Franklin's biggest hotel and maybe get some special ideas." Beatrice fidgeted with her reticule. "I need to be getting along, and I'm lookin' for twice as many coins today."

Margaret shook her head. "I'll get your money, but I won't be paying ya double. However, if you want to earn that much, you might want to come up with some way to spoil the possibility of Rose winning that contest." The older woman's eyes shone with an undeniable vengeance. "Ewan McKay might think I've forgotten how he interfered in the problems between Kathleen and me, but he's wrong." Margaret tapped her finger to the side of her head. "I have a long memory."

"And a strong desire for revenge." Beatrice edged forward on the sofa. "I'm not sure what I can do about causing Rose to lose the contest, but I'll do me best. Of that you can be sure." She pushed to her feet. "If you have me money, I'll tuck it in me bag and be on me way."

Beatrice didn't want to be subjected to any more of Margaret's discourse regarding Ewan and his family or her miserly tricks. Each time she came calling, she was forced to hear Margaret's recollections of how Laura had wormed her way into the family by marrying Ewan for the sole purpose of regaining control of the brickyard that Laura's mother had sold to Uncle Hugh. That tirade would be followed by a lengthy rant about a friend of Mrs. Woodfield's who had supposedly convinced Uncle Hugh to donate enough bricks to construct the local widows' and orphans' home.

When she finished that tale, Aunt Margaret would once again detail how Hugh had decided to make Ewan a full partner in the brickyard shortly before his apoplexy. As she related that event, the words would spew from her mouth like venom. Once she'd completely purged herself of all dealings that had created a chasm in the family, she'd sigh and utter how thankful she'd been that her husband had become incapacitated before he could sign the papers and give away what rightfully belonged to her.

"You could stay and visit a while longer. I might be able to help you come up with a plan. Perhaps you could discover some way to destroy her designs so that they'll miss the deadline for the contest."

Beatrice cleared her throat and pulled Margaret back from her thoughts. "Don't concern yourself with a plan. Until they begin working on their designs, there's no telling what might succeed. If I see there's gonna be problems, I'll bring meself over and then we'll talk." When Margaret didn't make a move, Beatrice held her reticule in the air and gave it a slight shake.

Margaret frowned, but she stood and strode toward the door. "I'll go and get your money."

Her aunt had been gone only a few moments when Fia scuttled into the room. "How've ya been, Beatrice? Do ya still like living over in Grafton? I know you're missed at home."

"I like Grafton just fine, Fia." Beatrice glanced toward the doorway and then leaned close to the maid's ear. "If you and Melva would be brave enough to tell Margaret you're thinking to go to work at the hotel in town, I'm sure she'd raise your wages."

Fia's eyes grew wide. "I don't know. As soon as we mention money, the missus starts talking about how ungrateful we are after Hugh brought us over from Ireland."

"Pay 'er no mind, Fia. You paid back what you owed, didn't ya?"

"Aye, that we did," Fia answered, wringing her hands nervously. "The money was held out of our wages ever since we set foot on dry land."

"Then don't back down when she begins her blustering. Mark me words, she'll match what the hotel is paying if you don't go all weak-kneed when ya talk to her."

At the sound of footsteps, Fia rushed off.

Margaret stepped into the room and extended her hand. "Remember, there's more to come when you get me more information."

A smile slipped across Beatrice's lips as she accepted the trifling sum. The older woman may have outfoxed her this time, but it was going to cost her a pretty penny when Fia and Melva insisted upon an increase in wages.

Beatrice bounded down the front steps and giggled aloud.

## Chapter 19

*Grafton, West Virginia*
*September 1872*

They'd barely begun their evening meal when Mrs. Wood-field inquired about progress at the school. When the twins had originally requested waiting another year before attending boarding school, Ewan had objected. After learning Miss Spangler had been unsuccesful in her search for an additional teacher and receiving a promise from the twins that they would attend boarding school the following September, Ewan had agreed. Both Adaira and Ainslee reported the children were making great strides. Once they finished their account, Rylan nodded his agreement.

"I've spoken to a number of the mothers and some of the boys and girls, too. They're grateful for the opportunity." He glanced at Rose. "Of course, it's Rose they need to be thanking. She's the one who was determined to see the children gain an education." He smiled at the twins. "And you two young lasses deserve thanks, as well. Your hard work in the school-room is reaping benefits. Some of the older boys tell me they're beginning to understand how to do their sums, and they're proud of the wee bit of reading they've accomplished." He grinned. "I think they all realize what they learn in that school is going to help them in the future. I'm sorry I didn't support the school in the very beginning."

Mrs. Woodfield took a sip of coffee. "Why were you opposed to the school, Rylan?"

He squirmed in his chair. "Change is hard for me. With Mr. Bancock leaving, I didn't want to be forced into any other adjustments." He gave Rose a sidelong glance. "But I was wrong. Rose has good ideas. Keeping the pottery clean has helped a lot, too. All the workers agree there's been less sickness."

Ewan nodded. "For sure, that's a fact. Now if we could just win some contracts so we could keep everyone employed, I'd be happy. I want to keep everyone working, and I want the lads and lasses able to continue with their schooling. We'll have to depend on the good Lord to help us through all of this."

"There's no need to be so downcast, Ewan. The pottery isn't floundering quite yet, and I'm sure Rylan and Rose are going to do their best. With God's help, they'll have a winning entry." Mrs. Woodfield dabbed her lips with the linen napkin. "Speaking of which, now that dinner is over, shouldn't you two be working on your designs?"

Rose chuckled. "You're right." She looked at Rylan as they made the short walk down the hallway to Ewan's combination library and office. With the exception of Sunday evenings, the two of them had been working on their designs every night since their return from Pittsburgh a week earlier. On evenings when Ewan had work of his own to complete, he sat scrunched at a small desk in the fancy parlor the family used on special occasions. For a man who confessed he didn't like changes, she'd observed a great deal of change in Rylan during their time together. Though he took more time than most to fully digest suggestions and agree to change, she admired his increasing openness.

Rose glanced over her shoulder as they neared the office doorway and was met by Rylan's quick smile. "I'm hopin' we'll make some fine progress with our drawings this evening."

She nodded, but her breath caught in her throat. While she admired Rylan's newfound ability to listen and change, she'd been surprised by the sudden rush of warmth that sparked deep within when he would occasionally touch her hand or speak to her in a soft tone. She wasn't positive when she'd begun to experience these strange feelings, but her first remembrance was when they were on the train returning from Pittsburgh. Rylan was seated beside her and had leaned across to point out a herd of deer. He'd brushed her hand, and his touch had evoked pleasure.

Though they still didn't agree about everything, their collaboration had become increasingly enjoyable since their return. Now, rather than dreading the evenings with Rylan, she looked forward to this time alone when they could discuss their designs as well as the daily events at the pottery.

Yet while their relationship had progressed, the pottery continued to falter. The lack of contracts continued to create worry among the workers. Over the past month, Rylan had heard rumors that some were anxious enough to have begun looking for other employment. With each rejected bid, it became more difficult to allay their concerns.

Earlier in the day, they'd received word of yet another rejected bid, and Ewan's spirits had plummeted as the three of them had gathered around his desk to discuss the future of the pottery. The despair in her brother's voice had gnawed at Rose for the remainder of the day, and his quiet demeanor at dinner had underscored his concerns for the business.

"Ready to begin?"

Rylan's question pulled Rose from her thoughts. He spread their latest drawings across the desk and pointed to one of her designs. "I think if you put a little more deep blue right here, this urn and plate would be more connected as a set." He continued to stare at the drawings. When she didn't respond, he turned to look at her. "What's wrong? Have I upset you?"

"No." She forced a smile and shook her head. "I was thinking about our meeting earlier today. I know Ewan is despondent about the lack of success with the pottery. I feel responsible for pushing him into purchasing the pottery." She sighed and met his tender gaze. "I simply don't understand how we can be underbid on every project. It seems such an impossibility that we are losing every contract."

Rylan reached across the strewn papers on the desk and squeezed her hand. "I agree that we've hit a streak of bad luck with the bids, but I don't see how you can hold yourself responsible. You've been trying your hardest since the first day you stepped across the threshold. The rejection of the bids has nothing to do with you. Do you figure the costs and write the bids?"

She shook her head. "Nay, but . . ."

He held up his hand to silence her. "Then there's no reason to blame yourself. It's Ewan and I that do the figuring, and somehow there are potteries who can produce at a lower cost, and they get the bids. It has nothing to do with you, Rose."

She attempted to hold her tears in check, but a lone drop slipped down her cheek. Rylan cupped her chin and wiped the tear away with the pad of his thumb. "There's no need for tears."

She choked back the lump in her throat. "You don't know all of what happened, Rylan. Ewan wanted to purchase the brickyard, but I interfered and did everything in my power to convince him the pottery would be a better choice." She inhaled a deep breath. "I wanted to show off what I'd learned in school and prove that I could do something worthwhile. I let my pride take hold, and now I must live with what I've done."

Rylan's eyes shone with compassion. "You're being too hard on yourself, Rose. I don't think you made this decision on your own. 'Tis not your name on the contract with Mr. Bancock. Your brother agreed he wanted the pottery. I was there when all the meetings took place. I don't believe the choice rests on your shoulders alone. And I don't think Ewan believes that, either."

Though Rylan's words were meant to soothe her, they did little to lift the burden. She had convinced Grandmother Woodfield. In turn, the older woman had used her influence to persuade Ewan the pottery would be a better choice than the brickyard. And now the older woman's warning rang in Rose's ears. *"If we purchase the pottery, I expect great things from you. I have no doubt Ewan can invigorate a failing brickyard, but I'm not as certain he can do the same with a pottery. That will rest on your shoulders, Rose."*

"'Tis true we must all live with the consequences of our decisions, but beating yourself about the head isn't going to help. I believe Ewan suggested we all continue to pray and ask God's guidance. Am I right?"

She nodded. "He did, and I have been praying, but it seems God has turned a deaf ear."

Rylan chuckled. "God never turns a deaf ear. He may not answer the way we want or as soon as we hope, but He hears us and wants only the best for us. Ya must remember that sometimes what we want isn't what's right for us, Rose. Only God knows what we truly need."

"I know you're right, but knowing that doesn't change our situation."

"Right ya are, so what we need to do is get busy with these

drawings and create the most beautiful designs we know how to produce. If it be God's will, then we'll win that contest and have us a huge contract for the pottery."

The lilt in his voice lifted her spirits, and she nodded in agreement. "I do think you're right about the blue in this design. It will make it much better."

He chuckled. "And here I was thinkin' ya hadn't even heard me mention the idea of adding a wee bit of dark blue to that urn."

Rylan's enjoyment of his time with Rose had increased tenfold since their visit to Pittsburgh, and he reveled in the fact that she now seemed to take pleasure in his presence, as well. Evening dinners around the McKay table had become an important part of his day. The camaraderie of the family and the joy they expressed, especially the twins, had become a special highlight. Ewan's dinnertime conversation had seemed more forced of late, and Rylan remained uncertain if it was because of the pottery or because his wife was ailing again. Her absence from the dinner table had become more frequent, and he wondered about her well-being. She'd once again been absent this evening. When he offered prayers for the family, he'd begun to ask a special blessing for Mrs. McKay's health.

As they continued to discuss their designs, Rylan decided to broach the subject with Rose. Though he didn't want to pry, he didn't want to appear indifferent. "I've been meaning to ask you about Mrs. McKay. When we traveled to Pittsburgh, you mentioned she hadn't been feeling well. Since she hasn't been at dinner several times since we returned, I was wondering about her health."

Rose glanced up from her sketching. "It's kind of you to ask. She hasn't been feeling herself for about three months now, but the doctor can find no reason for her bouts of illness. I know Laura's health problems have caused Ewan a great deal of concern, and Mrs. Woodfield has been worried, as well. She's insisted Laura see a doctor in Pittsburgh, though I wonder if she'll be able to make the journey."

"'Twould be a difficult journey for someone who's not feeling well. I've been prayin' for her. She's a fine lady."

"Yes. She's been a gift to us. She's like a sister to me and a mother to the twins. I could not have asked for Ewan to marry a more wonderful woman. Family is so important, don't you agree?" Rose reached for a fresh sheet of paper.

Rylan's stomach clenched in a knot. "Aye, a good and loving family is something everyone should experience." He inhaled a deep breath and pushed aside thoughts of his childhood. He didn't want to dwell on bad memories.

At the sound of footsteps in the hallway, he shifted and caught a glimpse of Beatrice's auburn hair. He thought she was going to turn away, but she stopped short when Rose called her name.

"Did you need something, Beatrice?"

"Nay. I didn't know the two of you was still workin' in here, and I thought maybe I'd get me a book to read. I been havin' trouble sleeping."

Rose gestured toward the shelves that were lined with books of every sort. They'd moved Mr. and Mrs. Woodfield's library, as well as the books Laura had accumulated since childhood, to their new home. "Help yourself. There are quite a few to choose from."

Keeping his head bowed, Rylan watched as Beatrice meandered along one shelf. She traced her fingers along the spines of several books before she removed a thin volume. After looking at several pages, she returned it to the shelf before continuing around the room. When she'd reached a shelf near them, she sauntered across the carpeted floor and stopped by the desk.

"Are these the drawings you're making for that contest you told me about, Rose?" She turned her back toward Rylan as she leaned closer to the desk.

Rose nodded. "We're going to do a few more before we decide upon the one we like best."

"They all look quite fine to me, but then I know very little about such things."

Rylan eased his way around the desk until he could see Beatrice's face. "Did ya try the chicken and biscuits special at the hotel restaurant the day I saw you there?"

Beatrice stiffened. "Nay. I'm not much for such a heavy lunch as that, but I'm sure it was good."

He hadn't missed the wariness in her voice, nor the suspicion that shone in her eyes. Rose looked up and tipped her head to the side. "When was this?"

"'Twas on me day off some time ago. I stopped in the hotel for a bite of lunch, and Rylan was there, as well. I believe you'd been fixin' to leave about the time I arrived."

Rylan nodded. "Right you are. I'm thinkin' it was on a day when Joshua Harkness was at the hotel. I'd seen him in the dining room."

Beatrice stepped away from the desk and turned toward the door. "I best get back up to the nursery in case Tessa wakes up."

She hadn't yet reached the door when Rylan said, "I thought it was a book you were after. Did ya forget, then?"

"Nay." The braided loop of auburn hair that rested upon her nape swung back and forth when she turned toward him. "I did not forget, but I need to check on Tessa." She scurried out of the room before he could question her further.

"Strange. I didn't realize Beatrice enjoyed reading. I have some books in my room she might enjoy." Rose stood and held up the sketch she'd been working on. "What do you think?"

"I think it's almost as lovely as the woman who drew it." He shouldn't have been so bold, but it was too late to take back the words.

A bright splash of pink colored Rose's cheeks. "Thank you for the compliment, but—"

"I know what I said was improper, and I hope you'll forgive me, but I spoke the truth. You are so lovely, and I would ask your brother for permission to court you if I was a man of proper social standing—and if you weren't in love with Joshua Harkness."

Her mouth dropped open, and she backed away from him. "In love? I have never declared my love for Joshua or for any other man."

Perhaps this wasn't the right time to pursue the topic of Joshua, but there might not be another opportunity. "If you don't care for him, why do you accept him as a suitor and let him continue to call on you every week?"

"I didn't say that I don't care for him. Joshua has many admirable qualities, but I don't love him. Right now, I consider him a friend, and I think that's how he feels about me, as well." Her shoulders lifted in a tiny shrug. "Who can say what the future holds for us? Laura says that sometimes love can grow out of friendship." She hesitated a moment. "I don't know if that will happen between Joshua and me. Sometimes I think he is so determined to succeed and please his father that there is no room in his life for anything or anyone else."

"If I had the opportunity to court someone like you, I'd make room in my life and in my heart for her." His words hung in the air. After a long moment, he cleared his throat and tore his gaze from hers. "But of course, that's between you and the man who is courting you. It's certainly not any of my business."

"Isn't it?" Rose whispered.

"Not as long as you're being courted by another man."

## Chapter 20

Beatrice wasn't certain if Joshua would show up today, but she held out hope he'd be at the hotel when she arrived. She was growing tired of his taking her for granted and expecting she would appear on the Wednesdays when he might decide upon coming to Grafton. Being left to her own devices, she'd gone to his regular room last week and once again been met at the hotel door by a stranger. She had backed away, saying she couldn't remember her room number, but she wasn't certain the man believed her. Her embarrassment continued as he'd watched her walk the length of the hallway and returned downstairs. There'd been no escaping down the back stairway, and she'd silently cursed her circumstances.

That foolish pottery contest couldn't be over soon enough to suit her. Maybe then Joshua would return to his regular schedule. Better yet, once she told him about the designs she'd seen in the library, maybe he'd forget about Rose McKay and realize he needed a real woman, a woman like her. She smiled at the thought as she walked along the path behind the livery and up the back stairway.

She inhaled a deep breath before she lifted her hand and

knocked on the door of room number four. At the sound of footsteps inside, she took a backward step and glanced toward the stairs. Best to be prepared for a quick exit if someone other than Joshua appeared.

When the door opened, she sighed with relief and pushed him aside. "Glad I am it wasn't another beefy stranger opening the door to me this week."

Joshua chuckled as he closed and locked the door. "I'm pleased to hear that you missed me." He strode across the room, grasped her upper arms, and tried to pull her close.

She placed her open palms against his chest and pushed away from him. "Not so fast. We need to come to some sort of an understandin'." When he tightened his grip, she pushed back with all her strength. "I mean it, Joshua. I'm tired of playing this game of 'is he in the room or ain't he?' I'm sticking me neck out to get you the information you want, and you don't even bother to show up."

He released her with an angry grunt. The bed creaked in protest as he dropped onto the edge. "I don't want to argue, Beatrice." He crooked his index finger several times and curved his lips in a greedy smile. "Come over here, and I'll make it up to you."

"Nay." She shook her head. "The only way you'll be making it up to me is by lining me pockets with some money."

He blew out a long sigh. "You're always talking about money. I've never failed to pay for the news you bring me. Now come on over here and give me a proper welcome."

She longed to rush into his arms, but she remained steadfast. "Payment first, then I'll give ya a right and proper greetin'." She glanced over her shoulder at the chest. "Is your money in one of these drawers?"

He jumped up from the bed, shoved his hand into his pocket,

withdrew several bills, and slapped them atop the chest. "There! Take what you think I owe you and tell me your news. You can get out once we've finished our business."

"You know I prefer me payment in silver coins, not paper money."

"Your lack of trust in paper money is unfounded, Beatrice. If you want payment any other way, you'll have to wait until I go to the bank. Now tell me what's been happening. Have you managed to discover what design they're going to use in the contest?"

With a sigh, she plopped onto the lone chair across the room. Before arriving, she'd been determined to withhold everything from Joshua until she had her money and a promise he'd keep her advised of his comings and goings, but nothing was turning out as planned. For the moment, she'd have to trust him, but when they left this room, she'd tail him to the bank and wait outside for her payment.

For the next hour, she told him what she'd seen and heard while browsing through the library in the office at the McKay home. The entire matter would have gone much more quickly had Joshua not continually interrupted her with questions that caused her to forget details that she was now required to add in a haphazard manner.

"So they've created numerous designs, but they haven't made a decision on which one they'll submit just yet?"

"Aye. That's what I've said to ya. I think I saw about eight different ones, but I'm thinkin' they're gonna make all of them and see which one they like the most."

Joshua raked his fingers through his hair. "This isn't working out like I hoped. I need to see which one they're going to enter in the contest. Did you copy any of the drawings?"

"What's that y'er asking?" Beatrice snapped to attention, astonished by the foolishness of his question. "Do ya think

I could have just pranced meself over to the two of them and said, 'Hold up, Rose and Rylan. I'd like to make me a copy of these drawings for Joshua so he can best ya at the contest?'"

He pointed toward her and frowned. "I don't welcome your mockery, Beatrice." The censure in his voice and the anger flashing in his eyes instantly erased her smile. "I want those drawings. You'll need to trace them onto tissue paper and bring them to me."

"Just how do ya think I'm gonna be able to do that? The designs for the urns was real fancy with lots of squiggly lines and such. Besides, there's too many for me to copy all of 'em. I told ya there's at least eight different drawings."

"I'll have to think of something. Maybe I better go to the pottery this afternoon and see about visiting with Rose. Perhaps she'll tell me if they're close to making a decision." He gave a firm nod of his head. "That's exactly what I'll do. I'll go and see Rose. Maybe she'll invite me for dinner tonight once she sees I'm in town."

A buzz of jealousy whirred in Beatrice's head like a swarm of angry wasps. She had hoped to return to the hotel this evening and have Joshua pay for a fine meal from the restaurant. Even if she couldn't sit with him downstairs, they could share a meal in his room. Besides, it was more intimate being alone with him in his room. She needed more time to heal some of the angry words they'd exchanged.

"I thought we'd meet back here for dinner tonight, but it sounds like you'd rather be with Rose."

"You know this is important, or I wouldn't go." He traced his finger along her pouting lips. "If she doesn't invite me, I'll be right here waiting for you."

She waved him toward the door. "Come on, then. Best you get to the bank."

Though he encouraged her to remain in the room until he returned with her money, she declined. "I'll follow a ways behind and wait on the bench outside the bank so you can slip me the money on your way out. And don't try to cheat me, either."

Together they departed down the back stairs, although Beatrice waited in the doorway for a short time before following Joshua. After rounding the corner, she strolled along the board sidewalk and settled on a small wooden bench outside the bank. She turned with anticipation each time a customer departed the bank. Why was it taking so long? When Joshua finally reappeared, she heaved a sigh of relief and jumped to her feet. She hurried toward him, her hand extended.

He frowned and gestured with one hand, but she continued forward and grasped his arm. "Get your hand off me." His lips remained in a tight line as he commanded her to release his arm.

She dropped her hold and was prepared to upbraid him but instead, turned and followed his gaze. *Rose!* What was she doing in town? Beatrice had barely formed the thought when Rose was at her side.

Glancing back and forth between them, she arched her brows. "I didn't realize you two had become such good friends."

Joshua shook his head. "We're not friends. I was in the bank and . . ."

When he faltered, Beatrice smiled and completed the explanation. "I sat down out here to rest me feet for a wee bit before doing any more shopping. You know how tired a lady can get trying to find just the right piece of lace or fabric." She dropped to the bench to emphasize her weariness.

"Since I don't see any packages, I'm not sure why you would be so fatigued. Seems you may have had a wasted morning. Except for seeing each other, that is." Rose's lips curved in a smile that didn't reach her eyes. "I'm sure neither of you would consider your chance meeting to be wasted time." She settled her gaze on Joshua's arm for a moment—exactly where Beatrice had been clinging to him.

Beatrice popped to her feet like a jack-in-the-box that had been wound too tight. "Sure, and it was nice to see Mr. Harkness, but if you two will excuse me, I think I'll be on my way. I've a lot of errands to complete before day's end." She gave a slight nod before she hurried down the street, with an empty reticule and a worried mind.

Rose forced a smile as Mrs. Woodfield came to a halt outside the doorway leading into the parlor. How was she going to get Joshua to leave?

The older woman glanced at the threesome—Rose seated between Joshua and Rylan—before she stepped into the room. "I'm surprised to see you, Joshua. Rose didn't mention you were coming to town. What brings you to Grafton?" Before hearing his response, she turned to Rose. "Have you and Rylan completed your work?"

"No. There's much to be done before we're ready."

Grandmother Woodfield was well aware they weren't done with their preparations. She also understood the prior arrangement Rose had made with Joshua.

"Well, then, I'll return to my original question, Joshua. What brings you to Grafton?"

"I know I agreed to give up my Wednesday visits, but then I decided to come to town unannounced and see if I could persuade Rose to spend a little time with me."

Rylan shifted in his chair. "Unless I'm mistaken, you've already been in Rose's company for several hours. Weren't you in the decorating shop with her this afternoon?"

"You can't fault me for wanting to be with her as much as possible while I'm in town." He pinned Rylan with a scathing look.

"I must say I think it's rather odd that you would simply appear and hope that Rose would have time to spend with you." Mrs. Woodfield crossed the room and sat down on the divan. "A reasonable person would have inquired beforehand so he wouldn't waste time. I assume you take time away from your own workday when you come to Grafton, Joshua. Or am I unaware of some business your family owns here in Grafton that requires your attention?"

Joshua glanced at Rose as though he hoped she'd rescue him, but she remained silent. Like Grandmother Woodfield, she wanted to hear why he'd appeared in Grafton today. Even after she'd attempted to dissuade him, he'd come to the pottery and had even managed to finagle a dinner invitation from Ewan. His presence in the decorating shop had been unwelcome and intrusive. He'd peppered her with myriad questions about her contest designs as well as the variety of decorating techniques used in the shop. In the end, his presence had been so distracting Mr. Wheeler had insisted he leave the shop after only an hour.

For the remainder of the afternoon, Rose's thoughts had been a jumble as she'd attempted to recall the numerous events that linked Joshua and Beatrice.

In the past, she had chosen to ignore or accept without question the various explanations given by Beatrice and Joshua. She'd chosen to believe Beatrice when she said the letter from Joshua was merely to help her brother locate employment, and Rose had ignored Rylan's comments about having seen the two of them together. Even after observing Beatrice clutching Joshua's arm earlier that day, Rose's reaction hadn't been one of anger and betrayal, but rather one of surprise.

By afternoon's end, Rose had reached the conclusion she simply didn't care about Joshua as a suitor. She'd inhaled a deep breath as she departed the decorating shop, pleased by the recent revelation. Her relief, however, had been short-lived, for as she rounded the corner of the main building, she'd spied Joshua standing alongside Ewan with a grin on his face.

After several long moments, Joshua cleared his throat. "I don't have any business endeavors here in Grafton, but we weren't particularly busy at the pottery, so I thought it would be a good day to visit Rose." He ended the remark with a weak smile.

"Seems to me you should be exceedingly busy." Mrs. Woodfield met Joshua's gaze. "From what I've heard, you've been quite successful gaining numerous contracts for your pottery." She touched her fingers to the brooch fastened to her lace collar. "I would think your oversight would be much needed in Fairmont. As I recall, your father always maintained close supervision of his businesses. That practice has certainly benefited him. Don't you agree?"

Joshua stretched his neck like a turtle emerging from its shell. "My father and I have very different methods when it comes to the operation of a business. I believe my own success will arrive much earlier in life."

"Do you?" Mrs. Woodfield arched her brows. "Then it seems we all have something to learn from you, young man."

Tessa grasped her mother's hand as she came into the room with Laura. "Tessa has come to say hello before she goes upstairs to enjoy her dinner." The discomfort in the room was palpable, and she glanced among the group. "Are we interrupting something?"

"Of course not, my dear." Mrs. Woodfield extended her arms to the child. "Come give your granny a kiss, Tessa."

Rose met Rylan's inquisitive look with a shrug. She wished she could take him to the library and explain that she wasn't responsible for Joshua's dinner invitation, but she'd have to wait until later. In the meantime, she could only hope that Joshua would leave immediately after dinner.

# Chapter 21

Rylan's confusion heightened when he arrived for dinner and discovered Joshua sitting in the parlor. Though he'd seen him at the pottery earlier in the day, Rylan hadn't expected his presence this evening. Rose had given her word that she would be free every evening until they completed their preparations for the contest. It now appeared her promise would hold true only on the Wednesdays Joshua didn't appear in Grafton.

Throughout dinner Rylan swallowed his rising jealousy and remained silent except when asked a direct question. Mrs. Woodfield sat to his left, and while the dinner conversation continued, she leaned a little closer.

"You need not consider Joshua as competition for Rose's affections, Rylan. I believe she views him as merely an acquaintance." Rylan's mouth dropped open at her remark. "No need to appear so surprised. I see how you look at her. Give her time, and she'll realize, too." That said, Mrs. Woodfield returned to the conversation swirling around the table.

At the conclusion of the meal, Rose shifted in her chair. "Rylan and I are going to be working this evening, Joshua, so—"

"I don't want to keep you two from your plans, but I was hoping I could see what progress you've made thus far. I'd be delighted to give you any insights I might have that could help you, since I have no plans to enter the contest."

Rylan stiffened at the comment. The last thing he wanted or needed was assistance from Joshua. He'd be happy to see the man's back as he left the McKay home. A hint of uncertainty shone in Rose's eyes as she looked to him for guidance, but he didn't respond. The question had been directed to her, so she should be the one to answer.

She gave a slight nod. "I suppose you can join us long enough for a quick view of what we've completed, but then we must continue our work. We haven't time to spare."

"Of course. I understand the urgency." He directed a smug grin in Rylan's direction before stepping around the table and offering his arm to Rose. "Shall we?"

Rose took his arm. After thanking Laura and Ewan for their hospitality, the two of them walked toward the library. Rylan attempted to quell his distaste for Joshua as he followed them down the hallway and into their makeshift workspace but was finding the task nearly impossible.

Though his stomach clenched, he remained at a distance while Rose spread numerous drawings atop the hand-hewn walnut library table. How he wished she'd refused Joshua's request. Yet he could hardly fault her—she'd looked to him for guidance, and he hadn't responded.

"I can see your hand in these, Rose. The drawings are exquisite." He tapped one of the pages. "I particularly like this one. Hands down, I'm sure it would win. Do tell me this one is your favorite."

Rylan leaned to one side to gain a view of the drawing Joshua had chosen. Though it was lovely, it wasn't the one the two of them had favored thus far.

Rose turned her head to the side and looked up at Joshua. "Truly? I'm surprised you chose this one. Rylan and I prefer this one." She shifted the pages and placed another drawing on top.

Joshua nodded. "Perhaps you're right. There's a unique quality to it that I hadn't noticed." Though he didn't examine the drawing for more than a moment, he nodded his head in agreement. "I don't know why you'd create any further designs. This one is perfect—a sure winner."

"Perhaps you're right. If we create too many, we'll never be able to choose which one to enter." Rose glanced over her shoulder at Rylan. "What do you think, Rylan?"

"I think we can discuss it later. We already have an idea we agreed to work on tonight. I believe I'll wait to offer my opinion."

Joshua didn't appear pleased with his answer, but Rylan wasn't certain why Joshua should care. The decision they made would have no bearing on him. Unless he hoped to hurry along their process so he could once again begin seeing Rose on Wednesday evenings.

"Once you complete all of your designs, I'd like to have a look at them. I'm sure I'm not going to change my mind that this one is the best." He tapped the design he'd recently approved.

Rose didn't respond to his request. Instead, she nodded toward the library door. "I don't want to seem an improper hostess, but we must get to work. Why don't I see you out?"

Joshua stepped closer to her side, his movement crushing the skirt of her crimson silk dress into the table. "I have nothing planned for this evening. I promise to be quiet as a mouse if you'll allow me to sit over there and watch you work." He nodded to a chair in a far corner of the room.

Rose shook her head. "Having anyone here while we work would be uncomfortable. I think it's better if we don't have an audience."

Rylan heaved a sigh of relief. The last thing he wanted was an evening of Joshua sitting across the room evaluating their work. He was pleased Rose had exhibited the courage to send Joshua on his way.

Rose walked alongside Joshua toward the door. "I'd like a word with you alone before you go."

Her comment erased Rylan's brief moment of euphoria. Since she wanted to speak with Joshua alone, he could only guess that she wanted to make certain he wasn't unhappy with her or perhaps make arrangements to see him at another time.

Couldn't she see Joshua was up to something? Rylan couldn't be sure, but one thing was certain: Joshua wasn't here because he cared if they won the contest.

Rose led Joshua onto the front porch. The sun had descended and the mountain breeze was surprisingly cool. Though it would have been more comfortable indoors, she wanted to speak to him where they wouldn't be overheard, and where it would be easier for him to depart without embarrassment to either of them.

Though she didn't believe he'd be heartbroken by her decision, having others present might wound his pride. Rose stepped onto the porch, then turned to face him as he pulled the front door closed. Before she could say a word, he closed the distance between them and pulled her into a crushing embrace that left her momentarily speechless. Never before had he behaved in such a forward and ungentlemanly manner.

Placing her palms against his thick wool coat, she pushed against his chest and wriggled free of his hold. "Joshua! What are you doing?" She took several backward steps.

"I'm sorry, but I've missed you so much, and when you said you wanted to be alone, I assumed you had missed me, as well." He took a step toward her, but she held up her hand and stayed him.

"I said I wanted to *speak* with you. You've gotten the wrong idea." His behavior was making this more difficult than she'd anticipated, but she didn't want to prolong the matter. The crisp air filled her lungs like a cooling balm and infused her with the courage to continue. "I asked you to come out here so I could tell you that I don't think there is any future for us as a couple. You should turn your attention to some other young lady. I'm sure there are many who would be happy to have you as a suitor, but I don't believe we're a good match."

He pitched backward as though she'd slapped him but soon regained his composure. "I don't know what's come over you, Rose, but I'm certain you can't be serious. We're perfect for each other." She shook her head and tried to speak, but he touched a finger to her lips. "Let me finish."

She brushed his hand away but remained silent while he continued. He detailed everything from the fact that they both were involved in the pottery business to the longstanding friendship of the Woodfield and Harkness families. She thought to interrupt and tell him she was neither a Woodfield nor a Harkness, but he rushed into a litany of affectionate words that infused her cheeks with disconcerting warmth.

When he once again attempted to draw close, she shook her head. "Though we have some like interests and acquaintances that brought us together, we have nothing more. I believe our goals and beliefs are very different." She expected him to accept and perhaps even be relieved with her decision. Instead, he appeared determined to debate his cause. She sighed and shook her head. "Joshua! There is nothing you can say or do that will change my mind. I believe it would be best if I go inside and you return to the hotel."

He stared at her for a moment. "I know that once I've left, you're going to regret this, Rose. You can contact me at the hotel or write to me once you've had time to think this through. And I won't hold it against you. I know how impetuous women can be."

His disdainful response sent a wave of anger coursing through her and affirmed her conviction that she'd made the right decision. She opened her mouth to tell him as much but changed her mind. With a forced smile, she nodded and bid him good-bye.

After giving a brief nod, he squared his shoulders and descended the porch steps. Rose blew out a long breath and returned inside. Once the latch clicked into place, she leaned against the front door, closed her eyes, and let the tightness in her neck relax. The exchange with Joshua had taken every ounce of courage she could muster, and she needed a moment to gather her thoughts.

She jumped when Mrs. Woodfield stepped around the corner into the hallway. "I'm sorry, my dear. I didn't intend to frighten you." She patted Rose's arm. "You look as though you've done battle. May I ask if you won or lost?" A slight smile played at her lips.

"I suppose it depends upon whom you ask. I've bid Joshua farewell. He isn't the man for me, and there's no sense expending his time or mine on a relationship that will end in naught. Don't you agree?"

"I couldn't have said it better myself." Her smile broadened. "And how did young Mr. Harkness take the news?"

Rose gave a slight shrug. "He believes I've made a terrible mistake and that I'll see the error of my ways in short order. He's willing to take me back once I come to my senses."

"My, but he is full of himself."

Rose chuckled. "Indeed. He said he knows 'how impetuous women can be.'"

"How very insulting. I do believe you've made a wise decision, my dear." Mrs. Woodfield glanced over her shoulder. "As I recall, you have another young man waiting for you in the library, and I'm going upstairs to visit with Laura and Tessa."

Rose strode down the hallway, eager to return to Rylan and their work, but when he looked at the clock with a scowl, her spirits plummeted. "Is there a problem?" She hurried toward the drawings still spread across the library table.

"Do you see how much time has been wasted this evening? We'll never complete the drawing. We were at dinner longer than usual. Then Joshua took up more time with his review of our work—which I did not appreciate or want—and then you left to bid him good-bye and were gone for almost half an hour. I can say good-bye in less than a minute." He folded his arms across his chest and jutted his chin.

"I should have told you it would take me longer than usual. I had an important matter to discuss with Joshua." When his stance didn't soften, she added, "I wanted to tell him that I no longer want him to call on me."

Rylan's eyebrows dipped low at the comment. "You told him you were ending your courtship?"

"Yes." Feeling somewhat self-conscious, she whispered her reply and averted her eyes.

"That is the best news I have heard in a long time." The frown had been replaced by a broad smile, and his eyes seemed to twinkle when she looked up at him.

His response delighted her, yet she hadn't expected him to react with such undeniable happiness. "My decision appears to please you, but I'm not certain why it makes you so happy."

"You're not?"

Did she dare believe it? She wanted to think that during their time together he'd grown to care for her as more than a friend and that he now understood she was not someone who wanted to change things merely for the sake of change. As they'd worked side by side, he'd told her he understood now that the changes she'd instigated had been to make the pottery a safe, pleasant, and profitable company for all of the employees and for her family.

They shared a deep devotion to this contest, but they'd grown beyond that, too. Rylan was one of the most kind, honorable, and true men she'd ever met. And even though he'd most likely not admit it, he was a man of vision, but he needed a little help becoming a man of action. That, she hoped, would be her job.

In the past Rylan had indicated he would court her if it weren't for Joshua. Now she would see if that was really true.

# Chapter 22

Beatrice hadn't expected Joshua to return this evening, but since she had nothing else to occupy the remainder of her day off, she waited in the hallway of the hotel until the young boy who delivered their meals appeared. It had taken only a promise of a tip to convince him to bring her a key to Joshua's room.

Once inside, she returned the key to him—along with her order for dinner and instructions to have the restaurant place the cost on Joshua's bill. He'd likely object, but it was the least he could do for her since he'd gone off to enjoy dinner with Rose and her family.

Hours later, the rattling of the doorknob startled Beatrice awake, and she jumped to her feet as Joshua pushed open the door.

His eyes widened, then flashed with irritation as he stepped inside. "Beatrice! How'd you get in here?" He tossed his hat on the bureau and frowned. "Have you added picking locks to your assortment of abilities?"

The sneer in his tone set her on edge, and she anchored her hands on her hips. "I ain't heard none of your objections to my talents when there's something you want to know about the McKay Pottery. You wouldn't have won all them contracts if it wasn't for me snooping through Ewan's papers late at night." She gave his shoulder a light shove. "In answer to your question, I don't know how to pick locks, but I do know how to convince folks to do my bidding."

"Only some folks, Beatrice, not everyone." He dropped to the side of the bed and loosened his necktie. His gaze settled on the tray of dirty dishes on the floor. "I see you ordered food. Did you put that on my bill?"

"Aye, that I did. Figured you'd want me to have a nice meal since you left me high and dry to fend for meself when I was expecting to have the entire day with you."

"This was my opportunity to learn more about those designs Rose is creating. Did you think I'd pass up that chance?"

She drew herself up to full height. "Nay, but I didn't think you'd expect me to go without me supper, either. And in case it's slipped your mind, ya never did pay me the money you owe me." She grabbed her reticule, opened it, and sat down beside him on the edge of the bed.

He reached into his pocket and tossed the money atop the bed. Without a word, she scooped it up and tucked it inside. "So what did ya find out? Have they decided on a design?"

"They're working on one more drawing tonight. If they don't pick it, I have an idea which one they'll choose. I told them which one was my choice, and I think Rose agreed. Of course, Rylan wasn't committed to the one I liked. My guess is that they'll make a decision by tomorrow or the next day and then produce the one they like." He yanked off his tie. "If they don't like it, then I'm sure they'll create another. I can only hope they'll soon decide."

"No need to look so sad." Beatrice reached for his lips and

attempted to push them into a smile. When he jerked away, she frowned. "Don't take yar anger out on me. I've been doing my best to help ya. I can quit doing me bit if you ain't wanting me around."

"I didn't say I wanted you to leave. I'm going to need your help more than ever." He massaged the back of his neck. "It's been a bad evening."

After a little prodding, Joshua related the evening's events. When he had finished, Beatrice grasped his hand. "Don't ya worry none. I'll do whatever ya tell me. We'll make sure you win that contest." She gave his hand a squeeze. "I'm the kind of woman ya need. Rose would never be able to make ya happy. But me?" She leaned to the side and kissed his neck. "I know how to please ya."

He turned toward her. Placing his fingers beneath her chin, he lifted her head until their eyes met. Her stomach quivered in anticipation, but he didn't lower his head to kiss her. Instead he squeezed her chin between his thumb and index finger. "You know how to please me when I'm putting money in your pocket. Otherwise, I'm not so sure you'd be willing to do anything for me."

Beatrice placed her palm atop her heart. "Now ya've really hurt me feelings, Joshua. Do ya think I care nothing for ya at all?" She lifted her hand and touched her finger to his chest. "I think it's you that has a cold heart. I don't think ya care about Rose McKay or about me. You were courtin' Rose for what you'd gain if you married her, and the only reason you have anything to do with me is because I'll do your bidding, for a price. Once you pay me, you can forget ya ever knew me." She narrowed her eyes. "Tell me I'm wrong."

"You're right. At least about Rose. She would prove to be a proper wife for me." He touched Beatrice's cheek. "But she would never possess your passion. A marriage to Rose would be dull. You, on the other hand, would make my life exciting." He sighed. "But you would never be accepted by my family or by society."

She scooted closer. This might be her only chance to convince him she would be worth the loss of his family and society. "Isn't your happiness worth more than all of those highfalutin folks?" When he opened his mouth to reply, she shushed him. "You could teach me the proper way to behave. Besides, who else is gonna help ya? Ya need me."

"Be patient, Beatrice. We can't do anything that would tip our hand just yet."

Joshua didn't miss the gleam in Beatrice's eyes as she spoke the words "ya need me." The two of them were enough alike that he knew what she was thinking. For the moment, he had to let her believe he would consider introducing her to his parents and making her his wife. If he didn't, she'd refuse to gather more information about Rose's designs.

Beatrice was correct: He did need her. But only for now. Once she was no longer necessary, he would discard her like an old shoe. He lifted her hand to his lips and kissed it before looking into her eyes.

"There's no denying that even though we're of different social classes, we do make a good match." He dazzled her with a bright smile. "I do believe you're right. My parents would accept you in time. My mother would never permit my father to disown me."

She leaned in and gave him a fleeting kiss. "You've made me the happiest woman alive. I can't wait to see a ring on me finger so's I can wave it under the noses of them that said I'd never amount to anything. I'll bet a week's wages that Rose will sit up and take notice. Can I pick it out?"

"Pick out what?" He'd been only half listening while she'd rambled.

She shoved her lower lip into a pout and nudged his arm. "Me ring, silly. I want to show you what kind of ring I want you to buy for me."

He longed to shout that he wouldn't be buying her a ring, but he kept his anger in check. Today's events had been like a never-ending nightmare, but he must remain unruffled. He needed Beatrice to keep his secrets.

Beatrice did her best to convince Joshua he should escort her back to the house, but he finally persuaded her that it wouldn't be wise. Someone might see them, and if word got back to Rose, it could ruin all of their plans.

When they stepped into the hallway, he pressed several coins into her hand and nodded toward the back stairs. "Go down the back way and circle around. You can use this for a cab. There's always one waiting close to the entrance."

"The least ya could do is walk me downstairs and make sure I'm safe until I get to the front street." She tugged on his hand and was pleased when he yielded. It was going to take some strong persuading, but eventually Joshua would realize he was lucky to have her.

When they reached the bottom of the stairway, she stepped outside and pulled him along behind her. Long shadows immersed them in the late-evening darkness. Beatrice clasped her hands behind Joshua's neck and pulled him into a lingering kiss. He might want to forget her, but she was going to do everything in her power to make certain he couldn't.

When she lifted her head, he pulled her back against his chest, but she turned away and avoided his lips. "You should take me shopping for a ring very soon, don't you think?"

"I can't put a ring on your finger until the contest is over. We don't want to draw undue attention or suspicion."

"We both know the McKays will never believe you'd purchase an engagement ring for the likes of me, so I see no reason why I can't tell them I'm engaged to a fellow back home who settled in Bartlett and works in the coal mines. They won't know the difference."

"I suppose that would work. I'll get an inexpensive ring at the general store down the street. Your beau in Bartlett wouldn't be able to afford much more than a trinket. If you're willing to settle for nothing more than a cheap bauble, I'll see to it tomorrow morning. I can leave it with the young boy who delivers our meals."

Beatrice gasped and stomped her foot in the dirt. "I want a real ring. The kind you would buy for Rose McKay."

He cupped her chin in his hand. "Then you'll have to wait. You could use a little more patience, Beatrice. Perhaps waiting on a ring will help you develop that quality."

She pushed aside his hand and stomped down the alleyway. When she reached the corner of the hotel, she glanced over her shoulder. Joshua obviously hadn't been worried about her safety, for he'd already returned inside, but she wasn't much worried, either. Instead of using the extra coins for a cab, she shoved them into her pocket. She'd walk home instead.

Once back home, she circled around to the back door and climbed the porch steps. Before entering, she inhaled a deep breath. No doubt Mrs. McKay would be angry. She should have been back home two hours ago. It had been foolish to take the extra time to walk home, but she enjoyed having a few extra coins in her pocket. Besides, she could make up a story about why she couldn't get back on time, and all would be well.

By entering through the kitchen, she could go up the rear stairway. With any luck at all, Ainslee or Adaira had relieved Mrs. McKay, and there would be few questions to answer, at least until tomorrow.

However, the moment she stepped inside the kitchen, she was greeted with chaos. Catherine all but plowed her over as she rushed down the stairs and into the kitchen. "Get out of the way, Beatrice! I need to get water on to boil. The missus isn't well. You best get upstairs and help with Tessa. Ainslee can't get her to quit crying, and it's making matters worse for the missus."

"So they've been lookin' for me?"

Catherine poured water into two large kettles and set them on the stove to boil. "Mrs. McKay was beside herself when you didn't come back on time. She was set on staying with Tessa, but she couldn't hold out any longer. She's in a terrible condition. Mr. McKay had to carry her to bed and now is off to fetch the doctor." Catherine shook her head. "It's a sad day for sure."

Beatrice stopped and glanced over her shoulder. "Do ya think they'll send me packin' for being late?"

"Quit thinking about yourself." Catherine glared and shooed Beatrice toward the stairs. "Get up to the nursery and take care of Tessa so the missus has one less thing to worry her."

Beatrice tamped down the anger that roiled in her stomach. How dare Catherine speak to her that way! Even if Beatrice had never had any real training, her position as nanny was considered higher ranking than that of a cook.

Once she and Joshua were formally engaged, she'd put that bossy cook in her place for good. She stomped up the stairs, the thought providing her with a smidgeon of fleeting pleasure along the way.

She turned the doorknob and entered the nursery on tiptoe.

Adaira sat in a chair outside Tessa's sleeping room. When she entered, Adaira pushed up from the chair and folded her arms across her waist. Her eyes flashed with anger. "Where have you been, Beatrice? You were supposed to be back hours ago. Laura is terribly ill, and she sat up with Tessa when she should have taken to her bed."

Beatrice clenched her hands into tight fists, willing herself to remain calm and submissive to this girl who had once been no more than a starving urchin in their home country. Now that her brother had married Laura Woodfield, all of them thought they were above her.

"I had a bit of trouble meself, not that you'd care." She lifted her chin in the air and assumed a defiant position. She might have to show respect to the missus, but she'd not kowtow to Adaira or her sisters. Not anymore. Not when her future was secure with Joshua.

"I didn't doubt for a minute you'd have some excuse." Adaira looked her up and down. "You appear just fine to me, but you can save your reasons and apologies for Ewan or Laura. I'm going to see if Ewan has returned with the doctor."

Beatrice stepped to the side and blocked Adaira's path. "What's wrong with the missus? I thought Mrs. Woodfield was taking her to see some doctor in the city."

Adaira paused and pinned her with a hard stare. "I'm not certain, but she's been bleeding something terrible, and it won't stop. She should have been in bed hours ago." Without waiting for a response, Adaira pushed Beatrice aside and strode to the door. "You'll need to be here to care for Tessa until Laura is well. No more excuses, Beatrice."

Beatrice gritted her teeth and stared at the door until her anger at Adaira finally quelled. Thankfully, Adaira hadn't asked Beatrice to expound upon the trouble that had caused her delayed return. Though Beatrice could weave a tale, she needed a bit of time to make certain the details aligned.

A short time later the sound of voices in the lower hallway drifted up the stairs, and Beatrice hurried to crack the door. She turned sideways and pressed against the narrow opening, careful to keep her breathing shallow. The murmur of several voices melded together, making it impossible to gain a clear understanding of what was being said.

Moments later, Mr. McKay's voice could be heard above the others. "I intend to do everything the doctor has asked, but we need to pray for Laura. Rose, make certain you speak to the girls and ask them to pray, as well."

"It would be best if we take turns sitting with Laura so no one becomes exhausted. If she should awaken, we want to be alert and able to assist her." Mrs. Woodfield's voice was clear, but Beatrice didn't miss the slight warble. No doubt the older woman was close to tears.

Careful to stay in the shadows, Beatrice stepped into the upper hallway and peered over the railing. Mrs. Woodfield, Rose, and Ewan stood clustered together. Either Adaira was now in with Laura, or she'd returned to her room.

The three of them continued to talk, but they'd lowered their voices and Beatrice could make out only a word or two. She longed to know exactly what had happened to the missus. News of Laura McKay's medical condition could earn her a tidy sum from Margaret, but she'd want details.

Beatrice plastered her back against the wall as the threesome parted. Ewan returned to the bedroom, Mrs. Woodfield ambled toward the stairway, and Rose stepped down the hallway toward the twins' rooms. Before going more than a few steps, Mrs. Woodfield turned and glanced over her shoulder. "I'll speak to the staff and tell them about Laura's condition. Would you go upstairs and tell Beatrice? She'll need to take full charge of Tessa unless Ainslee and Adaira are willing to step in and help."

The minute both women were out of view, Beatrice slipped into the nursery and ensured Tessa was still asleep, then entered her sleeping room and awaited Rose's visit.

The anticipated knock arrived only a few minutes later. However, it was Ainslee rather than Rose who tapped on her door.

The girl's complexion was rather pasty, and her eyes were rimmed in red. She quickly delivered Rose's message, then added, "Most days I need to spend time at the pottery helping with the school, but I'll do my best to help you. I know Tessa is going to miss having her mother coming in to visit during the day."

Beatrice gestured toward the chair in her room. "Sit down. You don't look so good. I can see ya been cryin'. Is the missus all that bad?"

Ainslee swiped the back of her hand across her eye and nodded. "Aye. The doctor says he thinks she may lose the baby."

"Baby?" Beatrice slapped her palm across her mouth. "Oh! I didn't mean to be so loud, but I didn't know the missus was expectin'. I thought the doctor didn't know what was wrong with her, and she was going to some special doctor or some such."

Ainslee nodded. "Nobody knew for sure what was wrong with her, but now that she's hemorrhaging, the doctor says he's sure that's it. Says it was likely because of the accident she had when she was young. She never was supposed to be able to have a baby, leastwise that's what she told us, but it would be wonderful if Ewan and Laura could have a baby, don't you think?"

Beatrice nodded her agreement, although she was much more interested in passing the news along to Margaret than offering prayers for Laura. She'd prefer delivering the message in person, but unless Laura made a remarkable recovery, getting away for a visit would be impossible. Much as she disliked writing letters, she'd need to pen a note to Margaret this evening and secretly post it in tomorrow's mail.

Ainslee's lip quivered. "I think Tessa would enjoy a baby brother or sister. I do hope God will answer our prayers for the baby and for Laura."

Beatrice offered as much sympathy as she could muster, but her mind raced with the prospect of Margaret's reaction rather than Ainslee's concerns for Laura.

Margaret would be delighted to write and tell her sister, Kathleen, all about Laura's inability to care for Tessa. And what if it turned out that Laura didn't lose the baby? Margaret would surely spin a tale with that bit of information.

Soon after Beatrice bid Ainslee good-night, she sat down at the small writing table and penned a letter to Margaret and then another to Joshua. There would be no need for him to visit next Wednesday. With Rose sitting at Laura's bedside for hours at a time, Beatrice doubted there would be anything to report on the entries for the contest.

When she'd finished the letter to Margaret, Beatrice sealed the envelope and traced her fingers across the address. Knowing Margaret, she'd leave no stone unturned in her efforts to bring Kathleen back to West Virginia. Once here, she'd convince her sister to lay claim to the little girl sleeping in the other room.

For sure it would create quite a donnybrook if that should happen. Beatrice leaned back and reveled in the possibility that the split between the Crotherses and McKays would never be healed.

# Chapter 23

Rose's mind swirled with thoughts of all that must be accomplished before their departure for Pittsburgh. At times, the days seemed to drag at a snail's pace, yet sometimes the hours ticked off at breakneck speed.

Soon Laura would no longer need someone at her bedside every hour of the day and night, and Rose could return to the pottery. Fortunately, she'd been able to rely upon Rylan to bring her daily news of the progress on their entry.

Although Rylan hadn't been particularly pleased by the choice, they'd finally agreed to submit the design both Rose and Joshua had preferred. With Laura's illness, it made sense to move forward rather than spend more time on further designs. Besides, Ewan had urged them to decide upon an entry so there would be time to make changes if they were unhappy once the plate and urn were fired.

With less than two weeks until their design had to be received by the committee in Pittsburgh, she needed to cease making changes. But while she'd been sitting with Laura this morning, she'd decided upon an additional detail she would incorporate when she hand-painted and gilded the urn. Since she'd promised

Ewan she wouldn't make any additional changes, she decided against changing the drawing. While the extra gilding would improve the depth of the piece when painted, it wouldn't prove outstanding in their drawing.

Recently Beatrice had stopped by Laura's room to inquire regarding Laura's health as well as Rose's progress on the designs. Rose had been astonished by the nanny's enthusiastic praise for the drawing they'd chosen. Beatrice's continued interest in the contest seemed a little odd, but Rose was pleased for any bit of conversation during the long days sitting at Laura's bedside. Besides, Beatrice's fervor had eased Rose's concern that they'd rushed to a decision when they made their final choice.

"Making more changes?"

Rose started at Beatrice's question and turned in her chair. "I've just finished, but I won't be able to begin my painting on the urn until it has gone through all of the necessary drying and firing." Laura was asleep, but Tessa managed to peer around Beatrice's skirt and began to cry when she caught a glimpse of her mother.

Still holding the drawing, Rose stepped out of the room and closed the door behind her. She stooped down in front of Tessa. "Good afternoon, sweet girl. Did you have a nice nap?"

Tessa extended her chubby hand toward Rose. After depositing her drawing on a chest in the hallway, she grasped Tessa's hand. "Want to go outside?"

Tessa's curls bobbed as she shook her head and tugged on Rose's hand. As Rose stepped onto the back porch, Beatrice touched her arm. "Would ya be mindin' too much if I took a minute to run back upstairs to me room? I'd like to get a ribbon so I can tie me hair up a wee bit."

"Of course. You go ahead. We'll be fine for a few minutes."

Beatrice glanced over her shoulder to make certain no one was in sight before she picked up Rose's drawing. Her heart pounded as she raced up the stairs to her room. Hands trembling, she knelt down and tucked the sketch beneath her bed, grabbed a frayed ribbon from her bedside table, and hurried back outdoors.

A cool breeze drifted across the porch, and Rose lifted her hand to Tessa's cheek. "I wonder if she should have a sweater and cap. It's cooler than I realized."

"You may be right about that. I'll take her back inside. Ainslee's coming to stay with Tessa as soon as she finishes teaching a class at the pottery school. The weather might be better suited for an outing later this morning."

Rose stood and grasped Tessa's hand. "Ainslee hadn't mentioned she was helping you with Tessa. Will you be gone all day?"

"Aye. It's been some time now since I've been able to see me family, so I'm going to Bartlett for a short visit. I'll be back on the train tomorrow." She didn't miss the cautious look that shone in Rose's eyes. "Ainslee said she didn't mind staying in the nursery tonight. I don't think the missus would object, since I've not had even a minute to meself since the day she had to take to her bed."

They walked at a slow pace, Rose still holding Tessa's hand as they continued toward the stairs. "I know it's been hard on you not having any relief. I'm glad Ainslee agreed to help."

Beatrice offered her thanks, though she wanted to point out that the twins could have helped more in the past, as well. Instead, they continued to go and teach at the school. Both of them appeared pleased when Mr. McKay agreed they could wait until next year to go off to that special boarding school.

Beatrice thought their decision foolish. Unlike her, they were content with their uneventful lives.

She'd packed her traveling case last night, but now she'd need to make adequate space for Rose's drawing. Taking the drawing with her was a daring and frightening decision, but she'd have no opportunity to trace the design before leaving. She couldn't let it be damaged in any way before her return. After carefully tucking it inside, she sat back on her heels, a self-satisfied grin on her lips. Joshua was going to be very pleased with her. In her last note to him, she'd told him to meet her in Bartlett. If he was wise, he'd be there waiting for her.

Beatrice's worries mounted as she paced the length of the nursery while waiting for Ainslee. If the girl didn't arrive soon, she'd miss the train. By the time she opened the nursery door, Beatrice's anxiety had reached fever pitch.

She waved the girl forward. "I was beginning to think you'd forgotten you promised to stay with Tessa. I got to be on my way or I'll miss the train." She grabbed her traveling bag and, after a quick wave, was out the door and down the stairs.

Beatrice was panting for breath when she finally dropped onto her seat in the train, and for the remainder of the journey, she relished the idea of presenting Joshua with the drawing. A visit with Margaret wasn't far from her mind, either. She could give Margaret the latest news concerning Laura's health and entice her with a bit more news regarding the contest, but she'd need to be careful. She didn't want Margaret to discover she was also supplying information to Joshua. That would lessen her chances of a large payday from Margaret. Besides, Margaret would upbraid her for helping a man born into wealth and position. She'd consider Beatrice a fool, and likely tell her so.

When the train hissed to a stop in Bartlett, Beatrice stepped down. With the handles of her traveling bag grasped tight in her hand, she surveyed the group of people waiting on the platform. Joshua was nowhere in sight. Had he discounted the importance of her letter? A thread of anger wound around her heart and squeezed so tight she thought it might cease beating. Lowering her head, she slogged through the mass of people inside the station and pushed open the heavy wooden door. She glanced about, uncertain if she should hail a hansom cab and go directly to Crothers Mansion or stop at the hotel.

She'd not yet come to a decision when a hand squeezed her shoulder and a voice whispered in her ear. "Are you looking for me?"

She blew out a sigh of relief as she turned to face Joshua. "I was beginning to think you weren't here."

"Now, would I let you down? Your letter said it was important." He grasped her arm and turned her toward the hotel. "I have a room for us, but we should probably go in the back way. You know the hotel here in Bartlett is as stuffy and strict with its rules as the one in Grafton."

"I have a special present for you. I think it will occupy most of your afternoon."

He arched his brows. "I thought *you* would occupy my afternoon."

"Just wait. You'll be happy to have time to yourself once you see what I have in my bag."

He winked as he led her up the stairs and opened the door to his room. "Let's go inside and see what you brought."

Beatrice crossed the room and placed her traveling bag atop the bed. She glanced over her shoulder as Joshua stepped behind her and wrapped his arms about her waist. She withdrew the sketch and carefully spread it across the bed. "Feast your eyes on this, and then tell me how lucky you are to have me."

He released his hold on her waist and stepped to her side. He pointed at the drawing. "Is that . . . ?" His mouth gaped open, and he appeared unable to complete his question.

Her red curls danced as she bobbed her head. "Aye, it's the final drawing of the urn they're going to enter in the contest. Rose added the final colors right before I was able to get me hands on it." A jolt of excitement raced through her and she clapped her hands. "Bet ya never thought you'd be marrying anyone as slick as me. We're going to be quite a team."

He inhaled a sharp breath and stared at the drawing. Moments later, he looked up and turned toward her. "How could you be so stupid? Rose will be looking for the drawing, and she's going to realize you took it." He grasped one corner of the page between his thumb and forefinger. "I can't believe you actually brought this with you."

Fury swelled in Beatrice's chest. Of all the scenes she'd pictured in her mind while traveling to Bartlett, this one had not been among them. She'd expected to receive Joshua's unfettered gratitude and amazement. Instead, he was treating her with anger and disdain.

"I brought it because you said you needed to see what they were going to enter in the contest. Ya knew I could na sit down and make a copy, so what did ya think I was gonna do? And ya need not worry about Rose knowing I've had the drawing in me hands. You may think I'm stupid, but I'm far from it. She'll never know it's been in me hands. I'll put it in the library, and she'll think she forgot where she put it earlier today. People forget where they put things all the time."

"That may be true, but I still think it was foolish."

"Was it so foolish ya want me to put it back in me bag and you can forget I ever brought it?"

"Of course not. It's here, and I'll get some tracing paper to make a copy." Joshua grabbed the drawing from atop the bed and carried it to a table near the window. He sat down and examined the sketch. "It's quite beautiful. I'm glad she chose the one that was my favorite." He traced his index finger along the outer edge of the drawing. "Perhaps she does care for me."

Beatrice glared at him. "Don't be thinking about no other lass except the one you're gonna marry." She pointed her finger to her chest. "And that would be me." Still scowling, she dropped into a nearby chair. "They didn't pick that one 'cause she cares about you. They chose it 'cause there wasn't time to work on another drawing. The missus took sick, and Rose has been helping care for her."

"No need to get all riled up. I was only jesting." He chucked her beneath the chin. "Why don't you go down to the general store and see if you can buy some tracing paper for me?"

Beatrice pushed up from the chair. "I'm going to visit Margaret, but I'll be glad to walk downstairs with ya."

"Why are you going to see her?" He arched his brows.

"Nothing that would concern you. I like to keep in contact with all members of me family."

Joshua chuckled. "I'm guessing there's more to your visit than spreading goodwill, but I don't think I want to hear about it."

She curved her lips in a coy smile. Even if he did want to know, she wouldn't have told him.

The minute she stepped inside Crothers Mansion, Margaret came rushing to greet her. "I'm so glad you've finally decided to pay a visit."

Beatrice frowned. "I told ya in me letters that I couldn't leave. You should be thanking me for taking the time to write and tell ya the happenings. Ya know how I dislike writing letters." She glanced toward the hallway. "Are ya not going to offer me a cup of tea and a biscuit? Seems I have to ask every time I come calling."

Margaret rang, and Fia came running. Before Margaret could order the tea, Fia gestured toward the kitchen. "I put the kettle on to boil, and I'll bring yar tea as soon as I can." She shot a smile at Beatrice and scurried away.

There hadn't been time to inquire whether Margaret had increased her wages, but gauging from Fia's smile, Beatrice surmised she'd received a raise.

Margaret scowled in Fia's direction. "I had to raise the wages for the house staff. They threatened to go to work at the hotel in town. 'Tis a sad day when you can't even trust your own relatives."

Beatrice chortled at the comment. "Sure, and you should know about how much confidence you can place in relatives, Margaret."

The older woman harrumphed but didn't disagree. "So what news have you? What about that contest? Have you managed to find some way to make certain Ewan's pottery doesn't win? And what about Laura? Do tell me about her medical condition. Is it worse?" Her eyebrows shot up. "And however did you get away?" She frowned. "Laura must be better. Am I right?"

Beatrice leaned back in the overstuffed chair. "So many questions, Margaret. Before I get to answerin' them, I think maybe we should agree upon a sum of money. What I have to tell you is worth a tidy sum, at least to my way of thinkin'."

Margaret glowered. "But until you've told me, how can I judge the worth of the information?"

"You can't." Beatrice picked up her reticule and savored the moment. "If you're unwilling to pay the price, then I'll be on me way."

Anger smoldered in Margaret's eyes, but they both knew that Beatrice had won this skirmish.

# Chapter 24

*Grafton, West Virginia*

At the sound of footsteps in the hallway, Rose turned toward the door of Laura's room. After spending a few minutes outdoors with Tessa and Beatrice a short time ago, Rose had returned to find Laura awake and eager for company. While Rose was delighted over the improvement in Laura's condition and enjoyed visiting, she was also impatient to meet with Rylan and discuss a few changes to their designs this afternoon. She didn't want to keep him waiting and expelled a sigh of relief when Mrs. Woodfield appeared in the doorway. However, Rose didn't miss the fact that instead of a plain day dress, Mrs. Woodfield had donned a dress of plum silk trimmed with lace at the neckline and several rows of ruffles along the hemline.

The older woman's lips curved in an apologetic smile. "I know I'm supposed to spell you, Rose, but I promised to attend a tea being hosted by the ladies' reading group. We're meeting with possible benefactors who may help in building a library here in Grafton." She stepped a bit closer to Laura's bedside.

"I'm glad to see she's resting. The doctor said she could get up for a little while this afternoon, so I'm sure she'll want to go out on the porch and get a bit of fresh air." She looked at the porcelain clock sitting atop Laura's dressing table. "Sally will be going along with me. I must hurry or I'll be late. Do you mind terribly?"

Rose shook her head. "No. I was supposed to meet with Rylan at the pottery this afternoon, but—"

"Isn't he going to come to dinner, as usual?" Mrs. Woodfield glanced in the mirror and adjusted the silver bar pin fastened to the collar of her dress. "That will permit you time to visit, won't it?"

"Yes, of course. You go on to your meeting. I hope you and the ladies will have success beginning a library. I know it would be helpful to the students at the pottery. Some of the girls have become very interested in poetry and fiction, and the boys have inquired about books that would help them learn more about a variety of trades."

Mrs. Woodfield gestured toward the other room. "Tell Ainslee and Adaira that they are welcome to choose some books from our library and loan them to the girls. I think there are a number of books on brickmaking that belonged to my husband, and there may be some on woodcarving and architecture that he purchased when we were planning to build our house in Bartlett. Perhaps a few of the boys would be interested in those."

"Thank you. I'll be sure to tell the girls. I know their students will be grateful. I'll go up and tell Ainslee after you've left. Perhaps she can bring Tessa down to the library while she chooses a few books."

The older woman stopped at the doorway, turned, and frowned. "Has Beatrice left already?"

"Yes. She wanted to board the noon train today. She'll be back tomorrow. I thought you knew."

"I was aware she was going to Bartlett, but I didn't know when she was departing or that she was staying overnight." Mrs. Woodfield sighed. "I suppose it makes little difference. Either way, someone is needed to look after Tessa."

Rose shifted in her chair. "She won't have all that much time to visit with her relatives once she arrives. It seems it would have been better for her to leave on the early morning train and return this evening, but she mentioned her relatives would be at work during the daytime."

"I do suppose that makes good sense. I hadn't considered the fact that she'd be better able to visit with her family later in the day." Her gaze drifted upwards. "Is Ainslee going to stay overnight in the nursery, or shall I make plans to sleep there?"

Though Mrs. Woodfield's offer was sincere, Rose knew the older woman wouldn't get a wink of sleep in the nursery. "I'm sure Adaira or Ainslee will offer. If not, I'll be happy to sleep in the nursery tonight. You need not give the matter another thought."

"You girls are such a blessing—always so willing to lend a hand." She beamed at Rose. "I'll stop by the pottery and tell Rylan you won't be coming there this afternoon but you still plan to meet with him this evening."

Rose offered a quick thank-you, and once Mrs. Woodfield had departed and Laura had dozed off, Rose leaned back in the overstuffed chair near Laura's bed and closed her eyes. She'd rest for a few minutes and then get back to work on the color changes in her design. If she couldn't work on the plate with Rylan this afternoon, she could at least complete the minor variations for the urn and show them to Rylan this evening. Though she hadn't yet placed it on her sketch, she planned to add the Scripture reference he'd pointed out to her on the frieze in the lobby of the Franklin Hotel.

The chapter in Ephesians had been perfect for the frieze, and it would be perfect on their urn. Perhaps they could add it to their plate, as well. She hoped Rylan would be pleased with her decision. The thought filled her with an unexpected rush of excitement. She'd consistently prayed for God's guidance while she was planning her sketch, and now she wanted to honor Him for answered prayer. So, like the frieze in the hotel, she'd duplicate the Scripture reference and hope that many others would take time to look up the chapter, read it, and give thanks for God's mercy and love.

Sometime later, she was startled awake when Laura touched her hand. Rose straightened in the chair and squeezed Laura's hand. "I'm sorry. I meant to close my eyes for only a few minutes. Have you been awake for long?"

"No, not long at all." Laura's dark auburn curls splayed across the white pillowcase. Her pale blue eyes flickered beneath thick, dark-brown lashes that fanned her porcelain-like complexion. "I was hoping we might sit on the back porch for a short time. What do you think?"

"If you feel up to it." Rose smiled to hide her concern. She had hoped Ewan or Mrs. Woodfield would be here for Laura's first venture out of the house, but she didn't want to deny Laura's request. After all, it was a lovely day.

"I believe I'm strong enough to make it down the hallway, though I don't think I could manage to get dressed."

Rose placed Laura's slippers at the side of the bed. "No one will be able to see us on the back porch, so you need not worry." After Laura had donned her slippers, she slid her arms into her wrapper. Securing one arm around Laura's waist to steady her, Rose fixed her sight on Laura and waited a moment. "Do you feel all right?" She didn't want to release her hold until she was certain of Laura's strength.

"Yes. I'm fine." She gestured to a shawl draped across the back of a chair. "I might want that once we get outdoors."

Rose momentarily released her hold, picked up the shawl, and draped it across Laura's shoulders. As they departed the room, she grasped Laura's arm and continued to hold tight until they reached the porch. Never before had it taken so long to walk the short distance.

Laura slowly lowered herself into one of the padded wrought iron chairs and drew in a deep breath. "I didn't realize how much strength it would take to walk out here." She leaned back in the chair. "The cool air is refreshing, and it's wonderful to feel the sunshine on my face."

The sun danced in zigzag patterns across the porch as Rose sat down in a nearby chair. She removed a small book of poetry from her pocket and leafed through, looking for a poem she might read aloud. Before she could choose a selection, Laura gasped and then shrieked.

Rose's eyes widened in alarm, and her heart pounded. "What is it? What's wrong?" She jumped to her feet, dropping the book of poetry into her chair. Panic seized her as Laura doubled forward.

"Help me back to bed, Rose." She extended her hand. "I won't be able to get up without your help."

Rose leaned over, circled Laura's waist with her arm, and gently helped her to her feet. It was then that Rose's attention settled on a large stain that had transformed the yellow-flowered cushion into an ugly shade of burnt orange. Her stomach knotted as she inhaled a deep breath. She must remain calm, or she'd be no help to Laura.

As they were entering the back door, Laura lurched forward,

nearly toppling both of them to the floor. "Th-the pain—it's unbearable."

"Just a little farther, and I'll have you in bed." Rose sagged under Laura's weight as she continued along the hallway. She silently prayed Ainslee would hear them and come downstairs, but too great a distance separated them from the nursery. She must remain strong.

Laura moaned and her head dropped forward.

"Don't faint on me, Laura. We're almost to your bed." Panting for breath, Rose managed to take the last few steps to the bedside. "Here we are. I'm going to help you into bed."

With a loud groan, Laura dropped onto the bed and drew her legs up in pain. "Send Catherine for help. I need the doctor."

Fear clutched Rose in a viselike grip, her eyes darting from Laura's cramped form on the bed to the vacant hallway. She didn't want to tell Laura that she couldn't send Catherine for help. This was Catherine's afternoon to do the weekly shopping, and she wouldn't be home for at least another hour. And Sally, Mrs. Woodfield's personal maid, had accompanied her mistress to the ladies' reading group. There was no one to send for the doctor.

Ainslee couldn't leave Tessa alone in the nursery, and Rose didn't want the child to see her mother suffering in pain. *What am I to do, Lord?*

She startled when a knock sounded at the front of the house.

With a quick glance over her shoulder, she gestured toward the door. "I'll be right back, Laura." She raced down the hallway and yanked open the heavy door. "Rylan!" Relief washed over her as she shouted his name. "Go and fetch the doctor right away. Laura's in terrible condition. Tell him to hurry!" Rylan remained fixed in place with his mouth gaping. She placed her palms against his chest and gave him a slight push. "Go! I'll explain when you come back with the doctor."

Her command set him in motion. He turned and ran down the front steps as if he'd been struck by lightning. Rose returned inside and stopped only long enough to tell Laura she'd sent for the doctor. "I'm going to put some water on to boil, and then I'll be back in to help you."

She'd done her best to help Laura out of her blood-soaked nightclothes and had placed folded lightweight blankets beneath her before the doctor and Rylan returned to the house. Black leather bag in hand, Dr. Braden stepped into the room and, much to Rose's relief, took charge. With a quiet assurance, he directed Rose as she helped with his ministrations.

A short time later, he shook his head. "I'm afraid you've lost the baby, Laura. Now we must concentrate on getting you well. You've lost a great deal of blood."

"Ewan." Her voice weak, Laura extended a trembling hand toward the doorway.

Rose turned and caught sight of her brother. She stepped to his side and lowered her voice. "How did you know to come home?"

"After he went for the doctor, Rylan came back to the pottery and told me the doctor was with Laura. I came as quickly as I could."

"I'm glad you're here. She needs you." Rose glanced into the bedroom. "I'll go and wait in the parlor."

Ewan's eyes shone with concern as he squeezed Rose's arm and then proceeded into the bedroom. Inhaling a cleansing breath, Rose glanced toward the stairway. She needed to go up to the nursery and tell Ainslee all that had happened in the past hour, but when she spotted Rylan sitting in the parlor, she dismissed the idea.

Rylan stood and strode toward her. "I know I should have asked you before going to get Ewan, but—"

"No need for an apology. I'm pleased you went to the pottery. Ewan wants to be with his wife, especially at a time like this. And thank you for going after the doctor." She took his hand and pulled him toward the divan. "You won't believe what happened." Without giving him an opportunity to guess, she continued. "I had just asked the Lord what I was supposed to do about fetching the doctor for Laura, and a few moments later, you knocked at the door." She looked down at her hand and, embarrassed by her forward behavior, quickly withdrew it from his. "Have you ever had prayer answered so quickly?"

He smiled and nodded. "Once or twice, but usually it takes much longer, and sometimes the answer isn't what I asked for but rather the exact opposite. Still, I trust the Lord knows what I need much better than I do."

"I hope Laura and Ewan will feel the same way. They were so excited about this baby—it seemed like a miracle. Now I'm not sure what they'll think."

Rylan tipped her chin until their eyes met. "I believe they are stronger than you realize. If they grow weary, they will look to the Lord and find rest in Him."

Rose nodded. Although she didn't possess Rylan's assurance, she prayed he was right. "I should go upstairs and tell Ainslee. She doesn't know what's happened."

He nodded but reached for her hand. "You said earlier that you had prayed for help before I came to the door. Why didn't you send Catherine for the doctor?"

Rose detailed Catherine's weekly afternoon of shopping and then added, "Beatrice is off to visit family in Bartlett until tomorrow morning, so Ainslee is looking after Tessa. Didn't Grandmother Woodfield stop by the pottery and tell you I would be busy this afternoon?"

"Nay. I've seen nothing of her. She must have forgotten." He chuckled. "But I'd say it's good that she did. When you didn't arrive at the pottery as we'd planned, I thought I should make certain there wasn't a problem. That's why I appeared at the door." He stood and held out his hand. "I won't keep you any longer. With all that has happened, I don't think we should plan on meeting tonight. I'm sure you're weary, and I doubt we'd get much work done."

Still holding his hand, she stood up and he drew near to her side. "Earlier today I was excited to show you some variations I'd made in the design, but I don't even want to think about them right now. If I don't make it to the pottery tomorrow, perhaps you could stop by in the afternoon, and we can go over the changes. I hope you'll like them."

Together they walked to the front door. "I'm sure I will."

When they neared the front door, he turned toward her and lightly grasped her arms. "I wanted to tell you that I spoke with Ewan earlier today and asked his permission to court you."

"You did?" Rose's exhaustion was replaced by a bubbling exhilaration that left her feeling breathless. "What did he say?"

Rylan's lips curved in a broad smile. "He said that as long as you agreed, he would be happy to give his blessing." He waited a moment and then arched his brows. "So? What do you say, Rose McKay? Are you willing to be courted by a poor Irish potter?"

She grinned up at him. "I would be proud to have you court me!"

He touched his thumb to her lips and then gently pulled her close. "In that case, what would you think if I kissed you?"

She placed her palms against his chest, raised up on tiptoes, tilted her head, and met his gaze. "I think I would like it very much."

# Chapter 25

Rose raced down the back stairway and into the kitchen, her swift approach causing a near collision with Catherine. The cook squealed and sidestepped to protect the luncheon tray in her hands. "You need to watch where you're going, Rose. I don't have time to clean the kitchen floor. I'm already late getting the noonday meal to the missus."

Rose clasped a hand to her bodice and inhaled a breath. "I'm sorry, but I'm looking for my sketch for the contest, and I can't find it anywhere."

Catherine clucked her tongue. "Well, you won't find it out here in the kitchen. Did you look in the library? Isn't that where you do your work?" The cook continued out of the kitchen and proceeded down the hallway, Rose following close on her heels.

"Yes, but I had the final sketch in the bedroom yesterday. I was working on it while Laura slept, before I took her outdoors. I've been attempting to retrace my steps. I recall Beatrice came into the room, and we spoke for several minutes. I thought I had placed it on the small chest in the hallway, but I've already looked, and it isn't there."

The back door banged, and both of them glanced over their

shoulders. Catherine gave a slight nod. "There's Beatrice now. Perhaps she can help." The cook sighed and continued on to Laura's bedroom, obviously pleased she'd be able to deliver Laura's meal without further interruption.

Bag in hand, Beatrice stepped through the kitchen doorway. "Did I hear ya speakin' me name?"

Rose turned and attempted to hide her surprise. Beatrice was wearing a stunning forest-green dress. The bottom edge of the bodice flaunted ivory trim that matched the trim peeping out from beneath the knife pleats at her wrist. A deep green hat with an ivory feather was perched atop her auburn curls.

"You look lovely," Rose said as she walked toward the nanny. "I didn't realize you owned such beautiful clothes."

Beatrice didn't crack a smile or offer a thank-you for the compliment. Instead, she lifted her nose and sniffed. "I work hard for me money and can spend it any way I like. A nice dress is something needed by every woman. It boosts the spirits, is what I say."

Rose merely intended to praise the nanny for her choice of attire, but Beatrice had clearly taken offense. "I wholeheartedly agree." Rose strode toward the kitchen. "I was hoping you might help me recall where I may have placed my contest design. I know I had it in Laura's room when you stopped by yesterday morning, but . . ." She hesitated and clasped a hand to her chest. "I forgot. You don't know."

"Don't know what?" Beatrice appeared wary.

"Laura took a downward turn and lost the baby. It happened shortly after you left for Bartlett. She's still quite weak, but the doctor says she'll be fine once she regains her strength."

Beatrice looked down the hallway toward the closed bedroom door. "Sorry to hear that. I know she's likely disappointed, but I can't say I was lookin' forward to having another wee one in the nursery."

Rose was taken aback by the nanny's callous reply, and an awkward silence fell between them. Turning to walk off, Rose suddenly remembered the lost drawing. "I was telling you about having misplaced my drawing for the contest. I haven't had it since before you departed for Bartlett. Do you happen to recall what I might have done with it?"

Beatrice lifted her bag a few inches. "I need to take this upstairs, but I'll try to recall. I remember you had the drawing, 'cause we talked about it. Give me a wee bit of time to put on me thinkin' cap, and I'll see if I help ya."

After her unsympathetic remarks about Laura, Beatrice's offer of help came as a surprise. Though she didn't want to worry Laura with the unsettling possibility that the design was lost, Rose couldn't tamp down the panic that had been plaguing her since early this morning. While she didn't believe she'd left the drawing in Laura's room, Rose couldn't be positive, but she'd searched the entire house. She stood near the doorway and weighed her decision. Catherine had delivered the noonday meal only minutes ago, and Laura should be awake, yet searching for the design might cause undue worry. Dr. Braden had left orders that she should rest and be protected from any troublesome news.

Perhaps Rose should go in and offer to relieve Mrs. Woodfield. Then again, she wanted to go to the pottery, and such an offer interfered with that idea. Still, she couldn't bear this feeling of dread that had taken hold since she first realized the drawing was missing. After another moment of contemplation, she decided to give her room one more thorough search. If she didn't find the drawing there, she would come back and discreetly search Laura's room.

She kneeled beside her bed and lifted the dust ruffle to make certain the drawing hadn't somehow been pushed underneath. When a knock sounded at the door, she quickly turned.

Beatrice giggled. "That's not the most becoming headpiece I've ever seen," she said, pointing at the dust ruffle that covered Rose's head like a flowing veil.

Rose forced a smile, although she didn't find the incident amusing. Truth be told, she was annoyed Beatrice had bothered her. "I'm rather busy. Did you need something?"

"Nay, but I think you were wantin' this." She pulled her hand from behind her and lifted Rose's drawing in the air.

Rose stared at the sketch, unable to believe her good fortune.

Beatrice sashayed across the room, her hips swaying in an exaggerated motion. "I'm thinkin' ya could offer me a word of thanks, and a little extra in me pay would be appreciated, as well." She tipped her head to the side and winked. "I can always use a few extra coins to help me family with their expenses."

Rose wasn't sure if Beatrice wanted the extra funds to help her family or to put toward another new gown, but she didn't voice her thoughts. Instead, she accepted the drawing and offered her genuine thanks before promising she'd mention the matter to Ewan, who managed the household expenses. "Where did you find it? I've searched everywhere I could think of since I misplaced it."

Beatrice gave a slight shrug. "'Twasn't so difficult. I remembered you'd placed it on the chest in the hallway before we went outdoors with Tessa." She gestured toward the lower hallway. "I moved the chest, and there it was. Had a wee bit of dust on it, but I wiped it off, and it's none the worse for wear."

Thoughts of Rose's earlier search rushed to the forefront of her mind, and she frowned. "I know I looked behind that chest. That's where I thought I'd put it, but when I looked, it wasn't there." She arched her brows, waiting for some further explanation.

The nanny's lips tightened into a thin line, and she glowered at Rose. "If ya want me to put it back where I found it, just be sayin' the word. Instead of being grateful, y'er acting as though ya wish I'd failed."

As Rose shook her head, she attempted to shake away the feelings of doubt that assailed her. Given the importance of the drawing, it was difficult to accept she'd been less than diligent in her search.

"I do appreciate your assistance, Beatrice. I'm sorry my words or actions insulted you. I won't forget to mention your help to Ewan."

Beatrice gave a slight nod and stalked off, clearly not convinced.

Rose hurried downstairs and tapped lightly on Laura's bedroom door. Moments later, Mrs. Woodfield opened the door. "Do come in, Rose. Laura's awake, and I'm sure she'd enjoy visiting with you."

"Has there been any improvement?" Rose glanced into the room.

"Indeed. Her color is much better, and she's feeling stronger this afternoon."

"While I'd like to take time to visit, I was hoping to go to the pottery and show Rylan the changes I've made on my design."

At the mention of Rylan's name, the older woman winced. "I do apologize. I forgot to stop by the pottery and give him your message yesterday." She sighed. "Yet it does seem my poor memory proved advantageous since he appeared when you needed help." She looked over her shoulder toward the bed. "You go on to the pottery. I know you're eager to return to your work, and I'm pleased to keep Laura company."

"Thank you. Tell Laura I'll stop and visit before dinner this evening." Rose hurried out of the house, her excitement mounting at the thought of seeing Rylan. As she entered the building and caught sight of him in the office, she was reminded of the first time she'd seen him. Exactly when had her feelings for Rylan changed? She tried to recall those first moments when she'd thought of him as more than just another employee at the pottery. They'd certainly had their difficulties while visiting the Franklin Hotel, and that hadn't been so long ago.

She smiled at the thought of how drastically her opinion of Rylan had changed in such a short time. While preparing for the contest, she'd observed so much more than a man who disliked change. Hearing stories of his childhood had given her a deeper understanding of why he now longed for consistency in his life, and after sharing his fears with her, he'd embraced small changes, especially once the benefits were made clear to him. His willingness to make those attempts, along with his strong beliefs and his unyielding desire to see the pottery become successful, had melded together and caused her to appreciate him, first as a friend and now as a suitor.

When Rylan glanced out the office door and saw her, he jumped to his feet, his face beaming. His smile warmed her heart, and she grinned in return. She lifted the rolled-up drawing and waved it back and forth. "I'm eager for you to see these changes. At first I thought I'd show them to you this evening, but I couldn't wait any longer." She sighed. "Especially after I thought I'd lost it."

His forehead creased, and his eyes shone with concern. "Lost the drawing? How is that possible?" Lightly grasping Rose's elbow, Rylan led her across the room to a chair near his desk. He sat down opposite her and intently listened while she detailed the incident.

"I'm thankful Beatrice found the sketch. I simply wouldn't have been able to paint the urn with all the details without this drawing."

Rylan leaned back in his chair and nodded. "'Tis a wee bit strange that Beatrice was able to locate it in such a short time after you'd been looking all over the house for hours. And you say you'd already looked in the hallway?"

"Aye, but it may have slipped further down and lodged beneath the chest. In my haste, I may not have looked as well as I thought. Besides, I was so pleased to have it back, I didn't care where she'd found it."

Although Rylan agreed, she didn't miss the shadow of worry in his eyes. She reached out and squeezed his hand, and he smiled. "Sorry, my mind was racing with unpleasant thoughts." He tapped the sketch. "I'm more than eager to see what you've done."

When she revealed the added colors, he agreed they enhanced the drawing, but it was the addition of the Scripture reference that truly pleased him. "It's perfect! Why didn't I think of that?" He chuckled as he spread the drawing on his desk for a better look.

"I wondered if we might be able to include the Bible reference somewhere on the plate, as well. What do you think?"

He massaged his forehead. "I think it would be perfect, but I'm not sure how it would look. The design you're painting on the urn is more intricate, and the reference can be added with a refined touch, much the way it was done in the frieze. Since the design on the plate is rather plain, I think it would overpower the delicate flower and simple strand of ribbon."

His observation was correct. While designing the plate, they had agreed the plate would be centered with one flower that matched the bouquet on the urn and a flowing ribbon that would bear the simple inscription "Franklin Hotels." To add anything further would create an imbalance to the design.

"What if we place it on the back of the plate?"

Rylan shrugged. "We could do that, but who would see it? The guests don't see the underside of their plates."

"I suppose not, but I think we should have it somewhere on the plate to reveal the fact that we thought it important and wanted continuity in the design."

"Then we'll put it on the back of the plate. If we win, maybe Mr. Franklin will prefer it on the front even if it makes the design a bit lopsided."

"Rylan, I get nervous simply thinking about the contest. I don't know how I'll ever be able to wait for the event."

He grinned. "Then I'll have to do my best to distract you."

Beatrice made a hasty retreat to the nursery, smiling as she ran up the flight of stairs. Earlier, her worries had escalated tenfold when she discovered Rose searching for the drawing, but she'd seemingly allayed any mistrust on Rose's part. If all went as planned, the deception would even be rewarded with a few extra coins in her pay next week. While most folks might think her not overly smart, she'd recently been able to fool several people who considered themselves quite shrewd.

There wouldn't be an opportunity to visit Bartlett anytime soon, but she'd pen a letter to Margaret. The older woman would be disappointed to hear that Laura had lost her baby. Not that Margaret cared about the McKays or their feelings. Rather, she would be saddened because Laura's latest medical problems didn't fit into Margaret's scheme. Margaret had hoped the child could be used to drive a wedge between her sister and the McKays. They would doubtless love their own child more than Tessa. Even her foolish sister Kathleen would realize as much. Once she planted the seed in Kathleen's mind, she would convince her sister to assert her claim to Tessa and remove her from the McKay home. Margaret had relished the idea. This act would create pain for Ewan and his family and repay him for a portion of the difficulties she'd suffered after Ewan left her to fend for herself at the brickyard following Hugh's death. Of course, Margaret didn't consider that her own actions had been at the heart of Ewan's departure. Nor did she ponder the impact it would have upon Tessa.

Beatrice had mentioned that fact on one occasion, but her comment had been met with such fury, she'd never again touched upon the subject. Now that idea would have to be laid to rest—and Margaret would not be happy.

Beatrice poised her pen and prepared to write. She wouldn't dwell on Laura's condition; a brief mention would do. The thrust of this letter must dwell upon the contest. After all, if the McKays didn't win the pottery competition, their financial situation would be significantly worsened. That alone should please Margaret. And Beatrice had certainly done her bit to make sure the McKay Pottery wouldn't win.

# Chapter 26

*Pittsburgh, Pennsylvania*
*Late September 1872*

The final days leading up to the contest proved frantic. The entrants had been sent rules that required their drawings arrive at the Franklin Hotel in Pittsburgh one week prior to the event. Ewan declared their submission should be hand delivered to avoid the possibility of damage or late delivery and had sent one of their trusted employees by train with the drawings. All contestants would personally transport their items to the hotel the day before the awards ceremony. The judges would then evaluate the urns and plates, checking for quality, judging how closely the pieces had been balanced in color and design, and determining if the submitted pieces were a true representation of the submitted drawings.

Although the doctor had declared Laura was making fine progress, he refused her request to join the family for the journey to Pittsburgh. Catherine and Sally had agreed they would remain at the house and see to Laura's needs.

They each took their turn bidding Laura good-bye before

departing for the train station. Rose remained along the foot of the bed when Beatrice came into the room, carrying Tessa in her arms. She held the child forward to kiss her mother. After a tight embrace, Laura looked up at Beatrice. "Are you certain you want to make this journey with her? The two of you could stay here. I'm sure Rose will be busy and won't mind if the youngest member of the family isn't present."

"Nay, we don't want to be left at home. We'll have us a good time, won't we, Tessa?" Beatrice chucked the little girl beneath her chin and smiled. Tessa bobbed her head in response. "Wave good-bye so we can be off to the train." Beatrice lifted the child's arm, and Tessa dutifully waved at her mother as she was carried out of the room.

Rose came around to the side of the bed, leaned down, and kissed Laura's cheek. "Do pray for us while we're gone. Rylan and I have worked so hard on these designs." Her smile faded. "If we don't win, I don't know . . ."

Laura grasped her hand. "The Bible teaches we are to cast our worries upon the Lord, for He cares for us. I think you should try to remember that over these next few days. Even if you should lose the contest, I know that God has a plan for our family, and He cares for us much more than we could ever imagine."

Rose squeezed Laura's hand in return. "I know you're right, but I'd still be pleased if you'd pray that we win."

Laura chuckled. "Better yet, why don't I pray for God's will? If you don't win, I'm sure God will provide another way."

Rose nodded, but her level of assurance wasn't firmly set. She and Ewan had gone over the books and cut every available cost. They'd attempted to win contract after contract, all to no avail. Winning this contest would establish their name in the pottery business, and she'd been praying they would win.

Rylan had agreed to meet the McKays at the train station, and when they arrived, he was waiting. Rose didn't miss the glimmer of anticipation that shone in his eyes. Nor did she miss the flicker of displeasure that wiped away his smile when he caught sight of Beatrice carrying Tessa in her arms.

She approached and tucked her hand into the crook of his elbow. "Are you unhappy we've included Tessa in the trip?" She squeezed his arm. "You need not worry about her creating a distraction. Beatrice will attend to Tessa's needs throughout the journey. I promise."

"I'm not worried about Tessa. You know I enjoy time with her. It's Beatrice that causes me concern. Did she ask to come along, or was it your idea?"

Rose shrugged. "I had nothing to do with the arrangements. I didn't find out until the plans were already made. But why does it bother you that Beatrice is with us?"

"I know I probably shouldn't think ill of her, but I don't trust her. Often she seems to be in the middle of things where she doesn't belong, and I question her motives. I don't understand why she wouldn't prefer to stay at home rather than come with your family. Both she and Tessa would be more comfortable at home, aye?"

"I suppose they would, but maybe she just wants to be included and feel that she's a part of the family."

Rylan snorted. "I don't think she wants to be a part of the McKay family. I think she has her sights set on other pursuits."

Before Rose could question him further, Ewan herded the group onto the train. Throughout the journey, Rose did her best to remain calm, but thoughts of losing the contest continued to plague her. How she wished she hadn't pushed Ewan to purchase the pottery. The brickworks would have been less work, they'd not be worrying about future orders or paying bills, and their livelihood wouldn't now depend upon winning a contest. She shivered at the thought of how much would be determined by this competition.

Though Rose thought they should stay in rooms at a less expensive hotel, Mrs. Woodfield had insisted Ewan reserve rooms at the Franklin Hotel. As they entered the hotel, she *tsked* when Rose once again mentioned the expense. "You are entering a competition to win the contracts for Mr. Franklin's hotels. To book our rooms in another hotel would be a discourtesy to him." She patted Rose's arm. "You need not worry. I've told Ewan that I will be pleased to cover the expenses of this journey. It will be well worth the cost to see you and Rylan win first place."

Rose forced a smile. Rather than relieving her anxiety, Mrs. Woodfield's comments created a heavier burden.

Once Ewan had completed the registration, the clerk handed him the room keys. "I have a message for two members of your party." He held an envelope in the air. "It is addressed to Miss Rose McKay and Mr. Rylan Campbell."

A lump the size of a walnut lodged in Rose's throat, and fear cinched a tight hold around her midsection. Surely it was something to do with the contest, but they'd already received the rules and instructions. Nothing related to the competition was to occur until tomorrow.

Rylan stepped forward and retrieved the envelope. He drew close to her side. "Shall I open it?" She nodded. They gathered in a small cluster and waited while he withdrew the piece of stationery and scanned the message. "This says we're to meet with members of the committee this evening for a brief interview."

"This evening? The rules said—"

Rylan passed the message to her. "I know, but it's clear they want us to meet with them this evening."

Rose's fingers trembled as she reread the message. "What can this mean? Do you think our entry wasn't completed properly?"

Beatrice shifted Tessa to her other arm. "How'd they know you was staying at this hotel is what I'm wonderin'."

Mrs. Woodfield turned toward the nanny. "Because they contacted the hotel and asked if we were registered here. Personally, I would think every entrant would be a guest in this hotel during the contest."

"Truly? Well, that's an interestin' bit of news, now ain't it?"

Mrs. Woodfield arched her brows. "I don't know why you'd find it so interesting." She didn't wait for a response. "I think we should all go upstairs and unpack so we'll have time for a leisurely dinner before Rylan and Rose attend their meeting."

The twins wrinkled their noses at the suggestion, and Ewan waved them forward. "You two go and unpack and then come to my room. I'll take you to see a few sights before supper. If you like, we can ride the funicular railway to the top of Coal Hill, where you can look down on the city."

Adaira clapped her hands. "I don't know what a funicular railway is, but I want to go." She grabbed her sister's hand. "Come on, Ainslee. Let's hurry and unpack."

Ewan arched his brows. "Anyone else interested in a ride up the hillside? The view is spectacular."

Mrs. Woodfield shook her head. "As I said, I plan to unpack and rest, and I'm sure Beatrice needs to put Tessa down for a nap before dinner." She glanced at Rose. "I think you and Rylan should go along with Ewan and the twins. Otherwise, you'll do nothing but pace the room and worry. It will be good for both of you." She waved Rose forward. "Come along, now. Our bags have already been delivered to our rooms. You can freshen up and be on your way. You can show me which dress you want to wear this evening, and I'll make certain to have it pressed for you." Rose obediently followed the older woman across the lobby and down the familiar hallway to their room. "It appears we've been assigned to the same room we had on our last visit. I believe that's a good omen."

Rose unpacked and advised Mrs. Woodfield of her selections for tonight as well as for tomorrow. "I think I need only shake out my dresses, and any creases will fall out. Besides, Sally isn't along to press your clothes or mine."

Mrs. Woodfield chuckled as she assessed Rose's choices. "You're right, but I still know how to press a gown, my dear. I didn't always have a maid to take care of my needs. You go along and meet the others." She traced her fingers across her forehead. "And please cease your worrying, Rose. The only thing it does is cause wrinkles."

Rylan was waiting in the lobby when Rose arrived; moments later the twins and Ewan arrived. Any other time, her sisters' excitement would have been contagious, but today she longed for a few moments of peace and quiet.

She tugged on Rylan's arm. "Couldn't we stay here?"

"Why? So you can reexamine the details in the frieze and decide our design is a failure?" He grinned. "Did you think I wouldn't notice you staring at it earlier?"

"I promise I won't look at the frieze or analyze our design, but I'm worried about this meeting with the committee."

"And that's exactly why we need to keep busy outside the hotel. Worrying isn't going to help."

She sighed. "You're the second person who's said that to me within the past half hour."

"Then I'm thinking that means you should heed the advice." He gave her a broad smile as he escorted her out the ornately carved front doors of the hotel.

Along the way, the twins peppered Ewan with questions about

the city. When they arrived at the site of the funicular railway, their mouths dropped open.

Ainslee grasped Ewan's arm, and her eyes opened wide as she peered at the steep track that would carry them up the hillside. "We're going to ride on that? I've never seen such a thing. What if it breaks loose and we fall?"

"It won't fall, Ainslee. Did you see all the people getting off? It has to be safe." Adaira gestured toward the barren hillside. "What happened to all the trees, Ewan?" She leaned closer. "It's quite ugly."

They stepped inside the small station, and Ewan nodded. "This area is known for coal mining, and they've stripped away all of the trees and brush. That's why the area up there is known as Coal Hill." He pointed to the top of the incline.

Adaira stepped inside the small wooden car that would carry them up the six-hundred-foot hillside. "How many people will fit in here?"

"The sign where I paid for our tickets says it holds twenty-three passengers."

Ainslee shivered. "I hope it's just us. If there aren't too many passengers, it will be less likely to break down."

Adaira ignored her sister's remark. "Coal Hill isn't much of a name for a village. You'd think they would have chosen something better than that."

"They've renamed it Mt. Washington, but folks still call it Coal Hill. Many of the people who live up at the top of the hill work for the coal mines." The car slowly began its ascent, and Ewan pointed toward a broken-down switchback stairway that zigzagged up the hillside. "That's how the men who lived in Coal Hill but worked in Pittsburgh used to get down the hillside. Before that, they had to slip and slide down steep, narrow paths, even in the rain and snow."

They peered out the small windows as the cable tugged their car up the mountainside. "Look! There's a car coming toward us." Ainslee clutched Ewan's arm. "It's going to run into us! I can't look." She hid her face in the sleeve of Ewan's jacket.

Ewan placed his hand on her cheek and lifted her head. "There's nothing to fear. That car is on the track coming down. Both cars must run at the same time so that they counterbalance each other, but they can't possibly strike each other." He pointed out the opposite window. "See that other track? That's for the other car. We'll pass close to it, but there won't be a collision."

Ainslee lifted her head but remained close to Ewan. Undaunted by the operation, Adaira moved to the other side of the car. "I want to yell 'hello!' to the people in the other car. Do you think they'll hear me?"

Ainslee glowered at her sister. "I think they'll believe you're daft." She looked at her brother. "How fast do you think we're going?"

Ewan shrugged. "I'm not sure, but it's probably moving as fast as a horse at a good trot. Hard to tell for sure, but we're not going very fast."

"Well, I'll be glad when we get to the top." Ainslee scooted a bit closer.

"Don't forget that we have to come back down, Ainslee. That will be even more fun. Just think about the car going down the hill and if the cable would snap." Adaira swung her arm in a giant sweep. "Whoosh, and we'd be gone."

Rose shook her head. "That's enough, Adaira. You don't need to frighten her any further." She grasped Ainslee's hand. "We're all fine, and this is supposed to be an enjoyable time. When we get to the top, we'll look down, and you'll be able to see all of Pittsburgh and Allegheny City, as well as the point where the Ohio, Monongahela, and Allegheny Rivers converge. It's quite a lovely sight when it's clear."

Rylan nodded. "Aye, but I think we've as much chance of finding a clear day in Pittsburgh as we do of seeing a leprechaun dancing about with a pot of gold."

Rose nudged him and grinned. "No need to dash any hope she has for a wee bit of enjoyment."

When they reached the top, they all proceeded into the station and then to a small overlook, where they could view the city. Ainslee smiled and pointed toward the city. "Look! We did get a clear day. The view is beautiful." She held fast to Ewan's arm as her gaze traveled back toward the tracks and the small car now beginning its descent. "I wish we could walk down that stairway you pointed out on the way up."

Ewan shook his head. "That stairway would be more dangerous than the ride back down."

A short time later, they boarded the car and slowly made their descent down the hillside. They hailed a hansom cab and were only a short distance from the hotel when Rose glanced out the window. Her breath caught, and she grasped Rylan's arm. "Was that Joshua Harkness?"

He leaned toward the cab window to gain a better view, but they'd already passed by. Rylan shook his head. "I didn't see his face, but I doubt it was Joshua. Why would he be in Pittsburgh?"

Ewan leaned back against the cab's leather upholstery. "Because his father's offices are here and his family's home is now in Pittsburgh. I'm sure he's in Pittsburgh quite often."

Rose considered the comment. Perhaps Ewan was right, but she secretly wondered if Joshua had arrived to attend the exhibition that would be held prior to the announcement of the contest winners. He was, after all, the owner of a pottery, and his appearance at the event wouldn't be unexpected by other pottery owners. His father might even have suggested Joshua attend. She hadn't seen him since she called a halt to their courtship. His presence during the competition could prove to be rather distracting and uncomfortable.

# Chapter 27

Dinner had been a waste of time and money, at least as far as Rose was concerned. She'd been somewhat surprised that no one else had been plagued by the same indigestion that had affected her since they'd returned from their outing. With their mysterious meeting so close at hand, she'd expected Rylan to be somewhat afflicted, but he'd eaten dinner as though he didn't have a care in the world. After dinner she returned to her room. The others remained in the lobby while Mrs. Woodfield inquired about tickets for a play or a musical she could attend with the twins.

Rose's palms were perspiring when Rylan arrived at the door to escort her downstairs. "You may have to be the one to answer their questions. I'm certain my voice will tremble."

He grinned and offered her his arm. "I don't think there's any reason to be concerned. They may have asked to meet with all of the contestants this evening. Something unexpected may have caused them to change the rules."

She inhaled a deep breath. "You're probably right." When they arrived in the lobby, she tugged on his arm. "We should stop at the front desk and ask where the meeting room is located."

"I did that after dinner. It's here on the first floor." He nodded toward a hallway that veered off to the left. "We go down the hallway, and the room is the second one from the end on the right side."

Rylan's confidence and the fact that he'd taken time to locate the meeting room in advance helped to ease Rose's jitters. She held tight to his arm as they continued on their way. They'd gone only a short distance when she squinted and stared at a figure sitting in a chair near the end of the hall. She squeezed Rylan's arm and nodded toward the gentleman. "There must be other contestants scheduled to meet with the judges this evening."

"You see? We're not the only ones, so there's no reason to worry."

As they drew closer, she came to an abrupt halt. "That's Joshua sitting outside the doorway. What's he doing here?" Her words hissed in the dimly lit high-ceilinged hallway.

"I have no idea. Suppose we go and ask him." Concern lurked behind Rylan's grin and renewed her apprehension.

Joshua looked up as they approached. "You have a meeting with the judges?"

Rose nodded. "What brings you to Pittsburgh? Are you visiting your family or waiting to go to dinner with one of the judges?"

He snorted. "I don't know the judges. That wouldn't be proper, now would it?"

Her stomach did a flip-flop as his words seeped into her consciousness. "Wouldn't be proper because . . . ?" She let her question hang like laundry swaying in an afternoon breeze.

"Because just like you, I'm a contestant. For me to be acquainted with one of the judges would be highly improper."

Joshua's response and his sly smile both angered and alarmed Rose. Not once had he indicated he planned to enter this contest.

Her thoughts raced back to his visit when they'd revealed their drawings to him. Back then, he'd avowed he wasn't going to participate in the competition. Had he been lying, or was this retaliation because she'd rebuffed him as a suitor?

Rose frowned at him. "You told us you weren't going to enter the competition. When did you change your mind?"

He shrugged and nodded toward the empty chair. "Do sit down, Rose. It may be a while before the judges call us in."

"Us?" She glared at Joshua. "You think they are going to speak to all three of us at one time? Why would they? Do you know why we've been summoned?" Rose dropped into the chair, uncertain her legs would continue to hold her. Joshua's presence and arrogant attitude created a suffocating sensation that left her breathless. "Are all of the contestants meeting with the judges this evening?"

"I'm not privy to that information. Maybe some of us didn't properly fill out our entry forms and they've summoned us to clarify our applications."

Not for a minute did Rose believe his explanation. She'd been exceedingly careful while filling out their paper work. Surely they would have been notified prior to receiving the final rules if their applications had been improperly submitted. She peered down the hallway, hoping to catch sight of other arriving contestants, but there was no one in view.

She startled when the door opened and a white-haired gentleman with a bushy mustache peered at them and then squinted at a paper he held in his hand. "We would first like to visit with Rose McKay and Rylan Campbell."

Legs trembling, Rose walked into the room, Rylan following close on her heels. The man who'd come to the door took his place behind a table with four other men, all dressed in dark suits.

The man sitting in the center of the group motioned to two chairs on the other side of the table. The area had likely been used as a gathering place for gentlemen to meet after dinner, for the smell of stale cigar smoke remained heavy in the room. "Please take a seat.

"I am Mr. Caldwell, the chairman of this group of distinguished judges." His smile appeared more obligatory than genuine, but Rose was certain her own smile probably looked much the same. He settled his gaze on Rose. "I assume you are Miss McKay." When Rose nodded, he looked at Rylan. "And you are Mr. Campbell."

Rylan nodded. "Aye, that I am. May I ask the reason for this meeting, sir? We carefully reviewed the rules, and there was no mention of any private meetings the night before the winners are announced."

"That's true, but it seems there's some irregularity in your submission, or I should say in the submission of McKay Pottery."

"Irregularity? What sort of irregularity are you speaking of?" Rylan's brows drew together. "We were careful to follow all of the rules." He glanced at Rose for affirmation.

"Indeed, we were." She nodded at him.

"Let me get to the heart of the matter. Your submission and the submission made on behalf of Harkness Pottery are very similar. So similar, in fact, that we believe something improper has occurred." He sighed. "While we are quite impressed with your design, we won't award a prize to a dishonest entry. We thought it would be best if we questioned all parties involved. We hope to determine who actually originated the design."

Rose scooted forward in her chair. "If you would be willing to place both designs before me, I believe I can elaborate upon my drawings and how our idea developed. In addition, I am willing to submit to any other evaluation you would like to conduct. Like you, I want the truth to be revealed." Mr. Caldwell unfurled the two submissions, and she gasped when she viewed the fake entry. Rose tapped her finger atop the drawings she and Rylan had submitted. "I assure you, these are the urn and plate designs of McKay Pottery, and the others are an imitation of what we've submitted."

"And how do you think such an imitation could have been created, Miss McKay?" He glanced back and forth between the drawings. "You must admit they are very similar, and for two potteries to submit entries that are so similar seems an impossibility." The other committee members all shook their heads in agreement.

Rose's thoughts whirred. She had no idea how it could have happened. Thankfully, Rylan answered for her. "Unless the design was copied. I can assure you these are the originals, and they were drawn by Miss McKay." Rylan nodded toward the fake drawings. "We've never before seen those, but I would guess they were submitted by Joshua Harkness on behalf of Harkness Pottery."

"Well, yes. I'm sure you met him in the hallway moments ago." Mr. Caldwell glanced down at their application. "And while I appreciate your argument, Mr. Campbell, we need more than your word that these drawings are the originals. I'm sure Mr. Harkness will tell us the same thing. Don't you agree?"

"Aye. If a man would steal someone else's work, I do not think he would hesitate to tell a falsehood." Rylan extended his hand and touched Rose's arm. "Tell them about the design and let them ask Joshua how he decided upon his design."

Rose forced a weak smile and inhaled a deep breath. She leaned forward and pointed to the bouquet of flowers in the center of the design. "As you know, Mr. Franklin requested designs that would be cohesive and also convey the elegance of his hotel. We visited the hotel, and Mr. Campbell was drawn to the beauty and simplicity of the frieze in the lobby, as was I." Rose continued to carefully explain how she and Rylan had developed their design. She touched her finger to the Scripture that was carefully detailed along one edge of the gold ribbon. "You will notice that this is not included on the other drawing. That's because it was a last-minute decision on our part, and no one else knew we had added that Scripture reference except Rylan and me. Perhaps you could ask Mr. Harkness how he happened to decide upon his design. See if he can point out that he intended to incorporate elements of the frieze. And if he claims this to be his work, surely he could draw a quick sketch. I know I would be happy to do so."

"I would also tell ya that Mr. Harkness had a look at our design before it was entirely completed. He visited at the home of Miss McKay and asked to see our designs. At that time there were several sketches, and we had not yet decided which would be our final choice. However, this is the one that he chose as his favorite."

Mr. Caldwell frowned. "Why would you show Mr. Harkness your work when you know that he owns a pottery and would likely submit an entry?"

Rose shook her head. "He said he had no interest in the contest, as his pottery had been inundated with orders." She hesitated and could feel the heat rise in her cheeks. "Mr. Harkness was courting me for a short time, and I didn't want to appear rude."

Mr. Caldwell stroked his chin. "I see. Well this certainly has become a rather complicated matter."

After the men inquired a bit further, Rose and Rylan were asked to wait in the outer hallway. "We'll speak with Mr.

Harkness. Afterward, we'll visit with all of you prior to making our final decision."

If Joshua was nervous, he kept it well hidden. His smug smile as he rose and entered the room was enough to set Rose further on edge. Perhaps Joshua had some other trick up his sleeve he planned to use in an attempt to sway the judges.

Rose glanced at the chairs and with an air of resignation dropped into the one nearest the door. Rylan stepped around her and sat down in the empty chair. "As much as I dislike Joshua Harkness, I didn't think he would do anything as vile as this. He truly has a cold heart and no conscience. I think he had already decided to enter the contest when he asked if he could see the designs."

Rose sighed and nodded. "Given all that we've seen in there, I have to agree. Still, I don't know how he could have drawn such a similar design after seeing ours only one time, and that was a mere sketch before we'd added the colors and final touches." She tipped her head to the side. "Of course, that probably accounts for the fact that some of his coloration is different and the fact that he doesn't have the Scripture included on his."

Rylan shifted in his chair. "I think he intentionally has some differences in his design. He could hardly submit the exact same products. Still, he's brazen enough to offer something so similar that the judges were startled by the resemblance of the two entries."

"So was I!" Rose twisted around to face him. "I know he doesn't have artistic ability. It's something we'd discussed in the past. I do hope they'll ask us to sketch something. At least it would reveal he has no talent."

"That's true, but I'd like to know how he managed to copy the drawing." Rylan slapped his hand to his forehead. "The day you couldn't find it—remember? Was it gone for only a short time before Beatrice returned home and said she discovered it in the hallway?"

Rose scrunched her forehead as she carefully recounted the events of that day. "With all that happened to Laura, I don't recall ever looking for the drawing until the following morning."

Rylan nodded. "So it could have been gone and you wouldn't have known it."

"Gone where?" Her mouth gaped. "You think Beatrice took it and copied it?"

"Nay. I think she took it to Joshua and *he* copied it. The two of them have become very good friends, and I think Beatrice would do anything Joshua asked of her."

Rose's hands trembled and tears blurred her eyes as she thought of Beatrice and Joshua conspiring against her. "How dare they do such a thing!"

Rylan reached out and gently thumbed away a tear that had settled beneath her eye. "I did not want to tell you, but I feel it's best that the whole truth come out. I'm sorry to have made you cry."

"I'm not crying because I'm sad. I'm crying because I feel like such a fool." Her stomach clenched as she remembered introducing Beatrice and Joshua at her party. She'd been trying to extend kindness to Beatrice. To think she would do something that would be so injurious to the McKay family as well as all the workers in the pottery was difficult to comprehend. However, Rose had been surprised at Beatrice's interest in the competition. She'd asked more questions about the contest than she'd ever asked about the pottery, or anything else for that matter. Rose inhaled a deep breath. "Even if I accept the likelihood that Beatrice took the drawing, I don't know how Joshua could have copied it. Beatrice went to Bartlett on her day off. I don't know how she could have traced it while she was there visiting her family."

"You may be right, but who's to say she really went to Bartlett? She could have gone to Fairmont and met Joshua, or he could have traveled to meet her in Bartlett. Either way, I believe the two of them worked together."

Rose considered his comment. "I agree that Joshua couldn't have produced that drawing after merely looking at my sketch for a few minutes. Besides, he looked at several others at the same time. Even I would have had difficulty remembering the details of that one sketch, especially after viewing several completely different drawings. And I don't believe Beatrice is bright enough to contrive this plan on her own. All in all, we may have difficulty proving exactly which one is at fault."

Rylan's features tightened into a deep frown. "They are both at fault. I wouldn't be surprised if he attempts to lay the blame at Beatrice's feet, but he's the one who submitted the entry. If he attempts to say she gave it to him and professed it was her work, we can counter and say he surely must have recognized the design as one he'd seen in your library. After all, he was aware Beatrice works for your family. Besides, you can have her appear and speak to the committee. I'm sure her loyalty to Joshua will falter if she realizes she's been found out."

"Or she'll believe he will give her the sun and the moon if she proves her allegiance to him." Rose removed her handkerchief and blotted the perspiration from her forehead. "I truly can't believe this is happening to us."

Rylan turned and enveloped her hands in his own. "I think we should ask God to protect and guide us during this meeting."

Together they prayed that the truth would shine forth and the committee would absolve them of any wrongdoing. They didn't go so far as to pray Beatrice or Joshua would be punished for their wrongdoing, but Rose fervently hoped the committee members would at least offer a strong censure for their unscrupulous conduct.

The time ticked by, and Rose glanced at the door. "I wonder what Joshua is telling them."

Moments later, the latch clicked open and Rylan clasped her hand. "I think we are about to find out."

# Chapter 28

Though she knew her behavior was inappropriate, Rose clung to Rylan's hand as they entered the room. If she hadn't held on to him, she wouldn't have had the strength to walk the length of the room and stand before the members of the committee. Their dour appearance caused her to squeeze Rylan's hand. What were the judges thinking? Had they already passed judgment in Joshua's favor?

As he'd done before, Mr. Caldwell gestured to the chairs. "Please be seated." He cleared his throat. "We have talked at length with Mr. Harkness, and he avows the drawing he submitted is original and solely his own design."

Rose turned sideways in her chair. "Joshua Harkness! You are as bold as brass. How can you sit in front of these men and tell such untruths? You saw my sketch, you told me you weren't going to enter the contest, and now you present this committee with items so similar in style and design that it casts aspersion on our entry."

Joshua looked at her as though eyeing a pitiful stray cat. "The lady doth protest too much, methinks."

Rose gritted her teeth. "The gentleman doth lack a proper

answer." She glared at him. "I don't need quotes from Shake-speare. I want you to tell the truth, and I believe the truth is that you and Beatrice worked together. She took the drawing from my home, brought it to you, and you traced my original."

Joshua paled at her retort. "W-w-where would you come up with that idea?" He glanced over his shoulder toward the door.

"Don't worry. Beatrice isn't waiting outside in the hallway, but she is upstairs in her room. If need be, I'll go and get her. I'm certain these gentlemen would be more than willing to question one more person. They do, after all, want to get to the truth." Rose turned toward Mr. Caldwell. "Isn't that correct?"

Although Mr. Caldwell appeared somewhat bewildered, he nodded. "Who is this Beatrice?"

"She is a nanny employed by my family to care for my young niece. I believe she's become quite enamored with Mr. Harkness and the two of them have formed a liaison of sorts."

"Perhaps it would be helpful if we spoke to the nanny. Miss McKay, would you do us the favor of asking her to come down-stairs?" He hesitated a moment. "If it would not be inconvenient for the child or your family, of course."

Rose nodded. "I'll see to the arrangements, but it may take a bit of time. I believe my sisters and the baby's grandmother have departed for the theatre, but her father should be in his room. He'll be more than happy to look after her while you speak with Miss Murphy."

"Why don't we adjourn for half an hour? I don't want to rush Miss McKay." Mr. Caldwell clicked open his pocket watch. "Let's all be back here, seated, and ready to begin by eight o'clock. Will that work for you, Miss McKay?"

"Yes. Eight o'clock will be fine." Rose stood, and together she and Rylan departed.

They'd not gone far when she heard the sound of muffled footsteps behind them. Rylan glanced over his shoulder and then came to a halt. Rose turned to see Joshua approaching, his eyes flashing with anger as he drew near. "Don't think I'm going to permit you to speak to Beatrice alone before she goes into that meeting. What's her room number?"

Rose tipped her head to the side. "The fact that you are so interested in speaking to Beatrice only confirms what we already believe: The two of you have joined together and stolen our design."

Joshua glared at her, and Rylan wedged himself between them. His jaw muscles twitched, and Rose squeezed his hand. She didn't want the two of them to end up in a fistfight in the middle of the hotel.

She tugged on his hand. "Rylan, we only have half an hour."

Joshua continued to follow them until they reached the lobby. Still clutching Rylan's hand, Rose stopped near the stairway. "If you don't cease following us, I'm going to go to the front desk and request that you be removed from the hotel until it's time for the meeting, Joshua."

His complexion had turned a deep red, and the vein along the side of his neck bulged. "Just like you, I'm a guest in this hotel, Rose, so I don't think they're going to toss me out on the street."

"Joshua! I've been looking for you." All three of them turned to see Jeremiah Harkness stride toward them with purpose in his step. After a quick greeting to Rose and a nod toward Rylan, Mr. Harkness patted his son on the shoulder and smiled. "Why is it I had to discover you'd entered Harkness Pottery in the contest being sponsored by Franklin Hotels?" Mr. Harkness didn't wait for his son to answer before continuing on. "And why aren't you staying at the house with your mother and me?

I stopped at the front desk and discovered you're registered here at the hotel."

Joshua swallowed hard. "I-I thought I'd surprise you."

"Well, you have! If one of my friends hadn't shown me a list of the entries and wished me good luck last evening, I would never have known. Which one of the designers created our entry? I want to hear all about it."

Rose smiled at Joshua. "Yes, Joshua, do tell your father—and us—who designed your entry."

Joshua glared at her before turning to smile at his father. "We'll talk later, Father. Right now, I have to prepare for a meeting with the committee judges."

Mr. Harkness wrapped his arm around Joshua's shoulder. "You come with me. We'll find a quiet place to sit, and I'll help you prepare. I'm sure you can use some sound advice. Now that you've advanced this far, I don't want you to lose this contest."

Rose and Rylan turned and hurried up the stairs, thankful Mr. Harkness had provided them an escape. When they neared the top of the stairs, Rose gestured toward the hallway leading to Ewan's room. "Please go and tell Ewan we need him to come and care for Tessa. That will give me a little time to talk to Beatrice before we go back to the meeting room."

Rose's heart pounded as she approached the door leading into the suite. There was little doubt Beatrice was shrewd. Rose would need to be careful how she approached the nanny. One misstep and Beatrice would rush to Joshua's aid.

When Rose entered, Beatrice was reclining against the velvet-covered cushions that decorated a pale green chaise in the sitting room. She looked up from an old copy of *Godey's Lady's Book*. "Look what I found in the lobby." Keeping her finger between the pages, she lifted it for Rose to see. "The desk clerk said I could bring it to our room to look at." She hiked a shoulder.

"I don't care if it's old; I like looking at the fashions." Her eyebrows arched a tad. "How come you're here? Mrs. Woodfield said you had a meeting and would be busy this evening." She didn't wait for a response. "If you come to check on Tessa, she's fine. Already asleep for the night, and glad I am for that. Been hard keepin' her entertained in this place."

Rose drew near and sat down opposite Beatrice. "We need to have a brief chat, and then I'd like for you to come downstairs with me. Ewan will sit with Tessa while you're away."

Wariness glimmered in her eyes as she closed the magazine and placed it atop a small table sitting in front of the chaise. "Why you wantin' me to go downstairs?" She glanced at the table. "I'm not lying. The clerk said I could borrow the magazine."

"This has nothing to do with the magazine." Rose smiled and leaned forward. "I need you to speak to the contest judges, Beatrice. There is a question about two of the entries. The one from our pottery and the other from Harkness Pottery."

Beatrice visibly paled. "What's that got to do with me?"

"I understand you and Joshua Harkness have formed a very close, shall we say, friendship. I'm sure it would have been difficult to refuse his request for help. From what I've gathered thus far, it appears you took my drawing to Joshua, and he traced a copy of my design."

"So he's placing the blame on me, is he? Well, he's the one who was set on winning the contest and stealing them bids so he'd make lots of money and his da would be proud of him. I can tell ya it will be freezin' in the middle of summer if he thinks I'm gonna sit back and let him point a finger at me. Sure, and my head was turned by thoughts of marryin' him, but anyone can see that I had nothin' to gain by taking that drawing. 'Twas Joshua who wanted to win that silly contest, not me."

Rose's thoughts reeled upon hearing Joshua had not only convinced Beatrice to steal the drawing but had somehow gained access to their bids so he would be awarded contracts. No wonder he had been so successful while they'd struggled to gain only a few meager deals. His success had nothing to do with hard work or knowledge of the pottery trade. He'd gained his achievements by cheating others. She shivered at the thought that she'd once thought him worthy of courting her.

Careful to use a soft voice and calm demeanor, Rose offered a quick smile. "I think it would be wise for you to meet with the judges and tell the truth, Beatrice. They may chastise you for helping Joshua, but they can do no more than reprimand you."

The nanny's eyes shone with suspicion. "You're sure they won't be calling the constable to haul me away?"

"No. Your actions against me and my family were dishonest, but it was Joshua who submitted work that was not his own." Rose didn't want to say much more. If she told the nanny that some of her actions might indeed be considered criminal, Rose would never get her downstairs.

Moments later Ewan and Rylan arrived. Rylan arched his brows. "We need to get downstairs or we'll be late."

Rose nodded and stood. "Ready, Beatrice?"

"I suppose I'm as ready as I'll ever be." Her lips drooped as she walked toward Ewan. "Sure I am that this will be the end of me job with you."

Ewan returned a sad smile. "We'll talk about your future when you come back from the meeting, Beatrice. I'm sorry to hear that you've been a part of this."

Joshua was waiting near the staircase when the three of them arrived in the lobby. He lost no time rushing to Beatrice's side. Clasping his hand around her wrist, he tugged her close. "We need to talk before the meeting."

Rylan stepped in front of Joshua. "There will be no time for you to speak with her. We're near to late already. You need to release her arm." He pointed to the large clock behind the front desk. "The judges expect us back on time. I don't think they'll be happy if you cause any further delay."

Beatrice tugged her arm free, and Rylan immediately stepped between Joshua and the nanny. Rose took hold of Beatrice's hand and nodded toward the hallway. "Come along. We need to hurry."

Much to Rose's delight and Joshua's obvious dismay, the judges requested a private meeting with Beatrice. "After we've talked to Miss Murphy, we'll have the three of you come in if we have further questions."

Joshua pinned Beatrice with a hard stare. "I'm sure Miss Murphy will confirm everything that I've told you. She knows the design I entered is my own, don't you, Beatrice?"

The nanny's features tightened in confusion as she looked first at Joshua and then at Rose. The look of uncertainty on the girl's face set Rose on edge. "Just tell the truth, Beatrice. That's all that matters right now."

Mr. Caldwell sighed with displeasure. "Please! No more discussion with Miss Murphy."

Joshua moved his chair to the opposite wall, where he could have a clear view of the door when it opened and a clear view of Rylan and Rose. "I plan to tell the judges you influenced Beatrice before she went in there."

"Are you now so worried that you're already making plans for additional deception, Joshua?" Rose shook her head, disgusted by his ongoing deceit.

"There you are, my boy!"

The boisterous greeting caused all three of them to turn and peer down the hallway. Joshua groaned as his father strode toward them, a broad smile on his face. He gestured toward the door as he drew closer. "Why are you sitting out here? Has the meeting not begun?"

Joshua stood and pulled his father aside. Keeping his voice low, he spoke to him for several moments. "There's no need for you to waste your valuable time, Father. I'm sure Mother would prefer to have you at home with her this evening." Joshua grasped his father's elbow and endeavored to propel him toward the lobby, but his father resisted the attempt and sat down.

"I think I'd prefer to wait and experience this with you first-hand, Son. I realize I haven't had enough time with you since you've taken charge of the pottery, but this is an opportunity for us to share an exciting event that will impact the future of the pottery for our family." The older man glanced across the narrow distance and met Rose's steady stare. "Of course, we wish you and your family good luck in your quest to win the contest, as well, Miss McKay." He leaned forward a modicum. "I am truly sorry that you and Joshua decided you wouldn't be a good match. My wife is quite fond of you and had hoped you'd one day become the daughter we never had." He glanced over his shoulder at Joshua. "Of course, I understand that matters of the heart can't be dictated by parents, so we've accepted the decision. But I wanted you to know we're quite fond of you."

"Thank you, Mr. Harkness." She considered adding that she was certain the younger Mr. Harkness didn't share in such fondness for her or in his father's good wishes, but Joshua already appeared so uncomfortable, she decided to keep that thought to herself. Soon enough, Mr. Harkness would discover this wasn't an event that would generate pride in his son.

As they continued to wait, the discomfort became palpable. Rose couldn't imagine why it was taking so long. Then again, Beatrice might be spinning quite a tale for the judges. Her

thoughts raced at the idea, and a sense of panic seized her. She glanced at Rylan who sat beside her, his eyes closed and his demeanor as peaceful as still water. She followed his example and lifted up a silent prayer that God would reveal the truth to the judges and they would make a decision that would reward honesty. As she prayed, her panic was replaced with feelings of peace as well as a measure of sorrow for Joshua and Beatrice.

Her gaze settled on Joshua, who sat rigid in his chair. How had he become so hardened that he would irreparably hurt others in order to get what he wanted? While Beatrice had struggled through years of hardship before coming to this country, Joshua had enjoyed a life of privilege. He'd never wanted for food or shelter, yet something deep inside was longing for more. A vacuum that needed to be filled—perhaps by his father's time and attention, but for sure there was a hole that required filling by the Father above.

The clicking of the door latch interrupted Rose's thoughts, and she turned to see the dull-eyed nanny exiting the door. However, her lackluster appearance was quickly replaced by one of curiosity when she spotted the older man sitting alongside Joshua. "They're waiting inside for the lot of ya." She directed a sorry smile at Joshua. "What I said didn't change things for ya. They knew I'd borrowed the drawing and given it to ya."

He stiffened and leaned close to her ear. "They didn't know for sure. That's why they wanted to speak to you, you idiot. Now you've gone and ruined it for sure."

She stepped away from him, her lips twisted in anger. "Don't be talking to me like I'm some lass you've never courted with sweet words. Is that your da sitting there? Have ya told him about our plans to marry?" She gestured with a flick of her head that sent her red hair bobbing in the older man's direction.

Joshua gaped at his father. "She's daft. Don't believe a word she says."

Rose couldn't believe her ears. Joshua and Beatrice were planning to wed? Was this the man Beatrice had been talking about when she mentioned a wedding veil? Rose's thoughts were cut short when Mr. Caldwell cleared his throat. "Didn't Miss Murphy tell you that I wanted to speak with the three of you?"

"Aye. That she did." Rylan lightly grasped Rose's elbow and nodded to Joshua. "I think we best be going in and see what they have to say."

# Chapter 29

The judges' solemn demeanor remained steadfast as they took their chairs. Mr. Caldwell folded his hands atop the long table and let his gaze travel and briefly rest upon each of them before he spoke. "What began as a simple request to judge entries in a pottery contest has become akin to solving a rather sordid mystery, Mr. Harkness."

Joshua blanched. "I assume that remark is meant for all of us, since I'm not the only party being subjected to this inquiry." He glared at Rose and Rylan. "I can assure you that what I've told you is the truth. Miss McKay had time alone to speak with Miss Murphy prior to escorting her downstairs. I'm certain Miss McKay made promises of financial gain in order to attain the cooperation of her employee."

Rose reeled at the remark. Joshua seemingly had no boundaries. He was intent upon convincing these men that the design was his own. Mr. Caldwell leaned forward and looked up and down the table. The judges all gave a nod.

"After speaking to Miss Murphy, we had our misgivings about whether you would concede, Mr. Harkness. Although we believe the original design was created and submitted on behalf of McKay Pottery, we are willing to give both you and Miss McKay a sketch pad so that you may re-create your designs as submitted to us." Mr. Caldwell leaned back in his chair and arched his brows. "Miss McKay?"

"I'm more than willing to do so."

"Mr. Harkness?"

Joshua's jaw tightened. "What did Miss Murphy tell you? Did she say that I created that design on my own?"

Mr. Caldwell arched his brows. "Before I divulge what Miss Murphy had to say, I'm going to require your answer, Mr. Harkness. Do you want to sketch the design for us, or would you prefer that we make our decision based upon the information we have at hand?"

Joshua hesitated for a moment and then extended his arm. "I injured my hand earlier in the week and haven't recovered full use. I couldn't possibly draw a sketch of the design at this time."

"You are quick with your excuses, Mr. Harkness, but I would point out that you've made no mention of any such problem during our earlier visits, and your handshake was quite strong." Mr. Caldwell looked at the other judges. "Would you agree, gentlemen?"

All of them nodded and murmured their agreement. Joshua's jaw twitched, and his eyes flashed with anger. "It appears you gentlemen have elected to accept Miss McKay's design. Although I disagree with your decision, I am going to withdraw my entry."

Before the judges could make further remarks, Joshua jumped up from his chair and exited the room. Mr. Caldwell shrugged and looked at Rose and Rylan. "That means we have accepted your entry as the original, and it will be placed with the other entries for final judging. I am sorry for this difficulty."

Rose nodded. "I do hope none of this will reflect upon our

entry. I know these meetings have caused undue hardship, and I fear it might influence your decision against us."

"I believe we can be fair, Miss McKay. Thank you for your cooperation." He looked at Rylan. "And you, as well, Mr. Campbell."

As they left the room Rylan looked at her, and love radiated from his eyes to the generous smile that curved his lips. "I'm very proud of you. Never did you let anger or fear take hold of you. I truly believe we will win the contest, and when all of this is over and we have a sizeable contract, we can talk about things that are important to our future—as husband and wife."

Rose met his tender gaze. "I would like that very much. In fact, I can think of nothing I would like more. I know Ewan and Laura will be pleased to know our plans go beyond courtship." She stopped short at the sound of arguing as they neared the lobby. "That's Beatrice. And Joshua."

Rylan nodded. "And Mr. Harkness. We may be able to avoid them if we go directly up the stairs."

Rose agreed, but their plan was foiled when Mr. Harkness spotted them at the end of the hallway. "Both of you! Come here!"

They looked at each other, Rose uncertain whether to flee for the stairway or follow Rylan's lead when he turned toward the older man. He took her elbow. "Come along, Rose. We may as well set things straight before tomorrow. We don't want the contest and Mr. Franklin's award ceremony ruined by a scuffle with Joshua or his father."

As they drew near, Mr. Harkness gestured to a small parlor off the main lobby. Once they were together in a more private setting, Mr. Harkness tugged at his collar and brushed nonexistent lint from his waistcoat. "I apologize for my uncivilized behavior, but after hearing all of these unbelievable tales, I've lost patience. I do hope the two of you can shed some light on this entire matter, because my son and Miss Murphy have somewhat conflicting stories."

Rose couldn't detect who was the angriest: Joshua, Beatrice, or Mr. Harkness. Joshua and Beatrice sat with their arms folded across their chests, their lips sealed tight, and their jaws jutted in defiance. She turned her attention to Mr. Harkness. He was, after all, the one who had initiated this angry gathering. "What is it you wish to know?"

"Would you relate to me exactly what happened regarding your entry in this contest, from the time your design supposedly went missing in your home until now?" He turned a hard stare upon Beatrice and his son. "No interruptions. Let her tell me without either of you interjecting so much as one word. Am I clear?"

They both nodded their heads, and Mr. Harkness motioned for her to begin. Without prolonging the story, Rose quietly detailed the events as they had unfolded. "This evening Beatrice admitted to me that she had taken the drawing to Joshua so that he could copy it. The similarities are too great for the design to have been submitted by two separate entrants, Mr. Harkness, and that design is not your son's work. It is mine. The judges have reached the same conclusion. There was far too much evidence for Joshua to prevail."

"And did you know of his marriage plans with Miss Murphy? She tells me the two of them intend to wed." He sputtered and shook his head. "Not that we would ever give our blessing to such a marriage."

"I didn't know of any marriage plans between them, and I don't believe that has any bearing on this matter, except that I believe Joshua had convinced Beatrice to furnish him with contract bidding information from my brother's desk in our home. That information caused us to lose all but a few small contracts while Harkness Pottery won the bids. I believe he also convinced her to steal the design so that he could win the contest. With the Franklin Hotels contract in hand, he would finally be able to prove to you he was worthy of a position in your Pittsburgh office. Whether he convinced her to help by offering marriage, money, or both, I can't say. Your son would be the one who should answer that question."

Joshua glowered at Beatrice. "Why'd you tell about the bids? There was no need to tell her everything. They would never have found out about the bids, you fool."

Beatrice winced and drew back as though she'd been slapped. "I told her 'cause I knew you'd be lookin' out for yourself instead of me. And I was right, wasn't I? You denied we had plans to marry, and ya would have let me take all the blame for everything whilst you went on with yar fancy life. Well, I ain't gonna sit back and let everyone think y'er such a fine fellow, when all of this was your idea. I had nothing to gain by any of it, now, did I?"

Deep crimson climbed up Joshua's neck and spread across his cheeks. "And did you also tell Rose about how you've been scheming with Margaret Crothers and carrying tales to her, as well?" His eyes flashed with satisfaction as he revealed her secret.

Beatrice squeezed her hands into tight fists. "I'll thank ya to keep your trap shut. You don't know nothin' about me and Margaret Crothers." She whipped around toward Rose. "He's lying to try to turn the attention off himself and onto me. 'Tis an old trick, but it will na work, Joshua. This is about you and how you wanted to become a big shot in your da's company."

Mr. Harkness massaged his forehead. Pain shone in his eyes as he looked at his son. "How did you ever come to believe that underhanded dealings are the path to success?"

Joshua snorted. "You're asking me that? Look at yourself, Father. You and all your successful businessmen friends do whatever it takes to get ahead, and don't tell me you don't. I've overheard too many of those late-night meetings where you schemed and finagled with your cronies."

"I suppose you're right. I've done my share of late-night deals to get ahead of my competitors, but I've never gone to this length, Joshua. While I might not share information that could help a competitor, I would never steal a bid or a design to get ahead."

Rylan shifted on the velvet-upholstered rosewood settee and shook his head. "A man canna blame his father for his own misdeeds." Rylan set his eyes upon Joshua. "You know right from wrong, and it was you who made the choice to gain copies of our bids and our design, not your father. You must answer, not him." He gave a slight shrug. "Of course, I have a feeling your actions will reflect poorly on all of your father's businesses once word gets out, so he will suffer, too."

Joshua flinched at the candid assessment, while Rose continued to maintain a close watch on Beatrice. The girl appeared ready to take flight at the earliest opportunity. Rose doubted Beatrice had the gumption to take off on her own in a large city where she knew no one. Still, the girl was nervous as a feral cat in a cage. If Joshua had spoken the truth, why would Beatrice pay visits to Aunt Margaret? Was there some connection between them other than the fact that Beatrice was a distant relative of Uncle Hugh? Granted, he'd paid for their family's passage, but surely that debt had been paid off by now. She'd never seen Beatrice or any of her family members at Crothers Mansion, and she'd never heard Beatrice mention Margaret's name. Never.

"What's going to happen about all of this?" Joshua's question pulled Rose from her thoughts of Beatrice. Although Rose looked up, Joshua avoided her gaze. "Is anything I've done going to be considered criminal? Should I expect a visit from the police?" He wrung his hands together. "I think we could make amends in some other way, couldn't we, Father? What if our pottery turns over all contracts we've received where I used Mr. McKay's figures to make my bid? That would be fair, wouldn't it?"

Clearly struggling to absorb all that had happened, Mr. Harkness stroked the side of his face. "I suppose that would be a decision for Ewan, as well as for the companies you've contracted with. Even if we close down our pottery, they wouldn't be obligated to switch to McKay Pottery. I think they would simply put out a new request for bids. And then there's the problem of any contracts that have been completed. The compensation for those would need to be repaid."

"That would be easily computed from the ledgers. Most are still open contracts. We haven't fulfilled but a few of them." Joshua brightened at the idea. "You could easily afford to pay off those sums, and this would be settled. As for the contest, there's been no harm done. I've withdrawn my entry, so if their design wins, they'll receive the Franklin Hotels contract."

His father didn't appear as excited with the plan. "This isn't something that can simply be settled by my paying your way out of the situation, Joshua. Indeed, I will do everything in my power to help Ewan McKay recoup the losses caused by your behavior, but this time you will be held accountable to me. It will be a very long time before you have worked off the debt and won back my trust." He gestured to Joshua. "I think we've gone over everything we can for this evening. Tomorrow I'll arrange a meeting with Ewan."

When Joshua turned to leave, Beatrice grabbed his arm. "Don't you be tearing outta here like you never made no promises to me. If you ain't gonna keep your word and marry me, then your da can count on paying me a tidy sum, as well." She pointed her finger at him. "And don't be saying we never spoke about a weddin'."

"*You* talked about marriage. I *never* said there would be a wedding. Maybe you took my silence for agreement, but you'd get going and talk so much, I just ignored whatever you said. Fact is, your jabbering could talk the bark off a tree."

"Is that so? I may talk a lot, but my memory is quite good." Beatrice tapped her finger to the side of her head. "Do you recall all that talk about buying me an engagement ring once this contest was over? You said I should learn to be patient. Well, I've been patient, but now you're trying to escape with your lies."

"Instead of worrying about a ring, you should be thinking about how you're going to explain those visits to Margaret. I'm sure Rose will have a lot of questions for you."

Mr. Harkness pushed to his feet. "Enough! I don't think the matter of a wedding needs any further discussion. We will not be paying you any money, Miss Murphy, and my son will not be marrying anyone in the near future. He'll be too busy paying off his debt to me." He turned to Joshua. "And you need to keep your mouth shut regarding Miss Murphy's problems with the McKays. I don't think they need any further interference from you."

Beatrice curled her lips in an angry snarl. "For sure and that's the truth."

Mr. Harkness gestured for silence and then turned to Rose. "Please tell your brother to leave word at the front desk when he will be available tomorrow. I realize you'll be busy with the contest most of the day."

The streetlamps outside the hotel glimmered through the

windows and reflected off several gilded mirrors aligned on the far wall. "I believe tomorrow morning would be best." Rose closed her eyes, trying to recall the exact schedule of events. "The first gathering scheduled for the contestants is the luncheon and awards ceremony. Then there's a dinner and dance for all of those attending the ceremonies tomorrow evening." She hesitated a moment. "I'll be certain to convey your request to Ewan."

Rose, Rylan, and Beatrice remained in the parlor as Joshua and his father departed. Though Beatrice had earlier given the appearance she might flee, she now seemed docile. "I s'pose I should get upstairs and see to Tessa. I'm guessin' her da would like to get some rest."

Rose led the way upstairs, still pondering tonight's revelation of the nanny's visits with Margaret. "I think Ewan will want to address several matters with you before he retires for the night."

Beatrice shrugged. "Aye, I'm sure all of ya will have a bucketful of questions."

While Rose and Rylan sat quietly, Ewan questioned Beatrice at length regarding her many transgressions. When Rylan had gone to fetch Ewan prior to their second meeting with the judges, he'd detailed some of the unfolding events. But Beatrice's offenses went far beyond the hurried particulars Rylan had specified as he and Ewan had traversed the hallway earlier in the evening.

At length, Ewan leaned into the tufted crimson upholstery of the uncomfortable carved armchair and stared across the short expanse, where Beatrice sat in an identical chair now wringing her hands. Sadness filled his eyes. "I cannot put into words the sorrow you've caused me or the difficulties you've placed at your own doorstep, Beatrice."

Though guilt nagged her, Rose was thankful it was Ewan's task to decide what punishment would be meted out to the nanny. She was certain making such a difficult judgment wouldn't be easy for her brother, but Ewan had far more experience dispensing advice and rendering decisions.

Beatrice shifted in the chair, her discomfort evident. "I've had me share of problems, and I'm seekin' a wee bit of compassion. I need me job here, but if ya decide to send me packin', I'm thinkin' you'd at least give me a good reference letter so's I can find me another job. I am your kin, after all."

Disbelief flashed across Ewan's face. "The fact that we are distant relatives doesn't hold any more meaning to me than it did to you when you were striking deals with Joshua Harkness and Margaret Crothers. It seems to me there's only one thing that holds your loyalty, and that's the person willing to pay you the most money. I fear you've made wealth more important than anything else in your life, but I hope you'll hear me when I say that money is not what you need."

Beatrice curled her lip. "Is that a fact? Easy enough for you to say when you've got everything you need. But for the likes of me, it ain't the same."

"You may have forgotten, but for a great deal of my life I struggled for food and shelter, too. We pay you a fair wage, furnish you with a room in our home and food for your stomach, yet that isn't enough. Rather than helping to plot our ruin, I expected you to treat us with the same kindness we extended to you."

"Aye, I suppose ya did, but I learned a long time ago that a lass needs to look out for herself, else she gets left behind with nothing."

Ewan arched his brows. "And what are you left with right now, Beatrice? Do you think Margaret is going to take you in and provide for you? Now that you can't pass along gossip about my family, will she have any desire to help you?" He shook his head. "I do forgive you for all you've done, but I believe you'll suffer the consequences of your behavior for years to come."

Beatrice jutted her chin. "You say you're a Christian, but you're unwilling to show me even a wee bit of compassion. Is that the way of it, then? You're going to toss me to the wind?"

Rose marveled at her brother's patience. After having listened to Beatrice tell how she'd delivered every jot of news from their household to Margaret's doorstep, she'd expected Ewan to lash out at Beatrice. Instead, he'd remained calm, even when Beatrice detailed Margaret's desire to cause problems with Laura and Ewan's custody of Tessa.

Ewan raked his fingers through his hair, his exasperation obvious. "I am a Christian. That's why I've forgiven you. But that does not mean that you can return to my home as though nothing has happened. My forgiveness does not mean that my trust has been restored or that I would ever again employ you. As for a letter of recommendation, I could not in good conscience write one for you. Such a letter would be unfair to anyone who would hire you based upon my recommendation. Instead, I suggest you return home and begin to seek work in and around Bartlett, where your family is known. I will, of course, pay for your train fare."

"If that's the way you want it, that's fine with me. I'll be wanting me train fare from Pittsburgh to Bartlett right now. I know you wouldn't want someone as untrustworthy as me looking after Tessa any longer." Her lips twisted in a cruel smile as she glanced at Rose. "You best be figuring out how you're gonna attend those fancy parties with no one to watch after Tessa. Seems someone besides me is gonna miss all the fun."

"Tessa's care will present no problem to us, Beatrice," Ewan said. "I do hope you will reflect upon all that has happened. I'll be praying for you."

She pushed up from the chair and extended her hand. "I don't need your prayers, but I'll take the money for me train fare and be on my way."

Rose met her brother's steady gaze. "I'll go up with her."

Beatrice chortled. "Aye. You best make sure I don't make off with some of your belongings."

As Rose followed Beatrice up the stairs, she recalled having invited the nanny to her graduation party, loaning her a gown, and introducing her to Joshua Harkness. Even then, Beatrice had been ungrateful. Still, Rose would not be sorry for extending kindness. She would not permit this mayhem to harden her heart.

She watched the young woman toss her things into a valise and spotted the fancy forest-green dress she'd returned home wearing only a few weeks ago. Like Joshua, Beatrice had an empty place in her life, and she'd been trying to fill it with all sorts of things. Would she ever realize only God could meet her needs?

Despite all the chaos of the evening, Rose smiled. God had met their needs tonight in a most amazing way. With contracts returned, they would soon be in the black, and they didn't need to win the contest to save the pottery.

# Chapter 30

*September 28, 1872*

Rose dressed with particular care for the awards luncheon. She was saving her pale blue silk for the dinner and dance this evening, but for the luncheon something more sedate yet exceptional was needed. At least that's what Mrs. Woodfield had advised as she'd selected the tan and blue brocade polonaise with narrow ruffled trim from Rose's wardrobe. Though Rose had worried it might be a bit elaborate, Laura and her mother had disagreed and declared it perfect for the luncheon.

"You look lovely, Rose. That dress was the correct choice. Neither overstated nor understated—win or lose, it is a flawless selection for the ceremony." She lifted her index finger and motioned for Rose to turn. "I have a strong feeling you and Rylan are going to win today." She glanced in the mirror and patted her hair. "Back when you and I encouraged Ewan to purchase the pottery, you promised me you could make it successful. I believe your promise is going to be fulfilled today."

Rose forced a smile, but the knot in her stomach swelled to the size of a fist. "I hope so, but if we don't win, I still believe the pottery will be a success. Now that we know we lost some of our biggest contracts because Joshua had access to our bids, I don't think we'll have to worry should we lose today."

Mrs. Woodfield pursed her lips and *tsked*. "Of course we would have to worry, my dear. We need an immediate large contract. We can't wait until company contracts expire and they call for new bids. That would take far too long."

Rose rested her hand across her tightening midsection. She was glad she hadn't known this last night. She and Rylan had submitted their entry with pride and confidence, but hearing Grandmother Woodfield verbalize her expectations today caused Rose's assurance to melt like ice on a summer day. Fear continued to follow her out of the room and into the downstairs lobby, where contestants, pottery owners, and a multitude of guests mingled, many of them stepping as close as possible to the corded-off table displaying the urns and plates of the final contenders. Others eagerly waited near the entrance to the large ballroom, where the luncheon was to be hosted.

Mrs. Woodfield spotted Ewan waving at them. Holding fast to Rose's hand, the older woman navigated the crowd like a fearless captain piloting a ship through rough waters. "Why are you waiting back here? With this crowd, we'll be fortunate to find enough seats for all of us at one table." Without taking a breath, she set her gaze upon Adaira. "Where's Ainslee?"

Adaira pointed toward the ceiling. "Upstairs with Tessa. Beatrice has already departed."

"Even if she were still here, I wouldn't have left Tessa in her care," Ewan said. "As for the seating, you need not worry. I understand there are designated tables for the contestants and their guests."

"I do hope they're near the front so we'll be able to see everything." Mrs. Woodfield gestured toward the ballroom. "Come along. It appears they've opened the doors. I can hardly contain my excitement."

Ewan, Mrs. Woodfield, and Adaira took the lead, while Rose and Rylan followed behind. Rose squeezed his arm and nodded toward the older woman. "If we lose, I fear I'm going to have to run away from home."

Rylan chuckled. "I think you may be exaggerating a wee bit."

"I'm not so sure. Grandmother Woodfield has made it exceedingly clear she expects us to win. I was so foolish and naïve to think I could make the pottery into a profitable business with only my talent. I fear I'll now pay the price for my pride as well as for my immature and inexperienced thinking."

Rylan tucked her hand into the crook of his arm. "You need to quit dwelling upon losing and enjoy these moments, Rose. Even if we lose—and I don't think we will—this day is special. We can celebrate that the McKay Pottery is among the finalists."

She forced a smile, but in her heart she didn't agree. Making it this far would likely entitle them to a framed certificate, but without a contract, they wouldn't have a pottery works in which to display the award.

Adaira's eyes shone with excitement as the waiter led them to their table. "Can you believe it? We're right up front." She leaned close to her older sister. "This means you've won, for sure."

Rose quietly explained that all of the finalists were seated at tables near the front of the room. "The person who wins the award will have easier access to the stage."

The gleam in her sister's eyes faded for a moment but quickly brightened as she pointed toward the steps leading onto the platform. "We're closest to the steps, so that must mean something."

Rose chuckled. "It means we have a good view of the stage. Nothing more."

She scarcely touched the chicken in wine sauce, rice pilaf,

or vegetables almandine. With the lump that remained settled in her stomach, eating would do more harm than good. When the waiter later delivered slices of white cake bedecked with an apple-cranberry topping, Rose pushed away the plate.

Adaira leaned toward her. "I'll be happy to eat that if you're not going to."

Rose smiled and retrieved the plate. "Help yourself. I'll do well to keep down the few bites of chicken I consumed."

When at last the luncheon was over and the dishes had been cleared by the waiters, Rose managed a small sip from her water goblet. Win or lose, she wanted this agonizing meal to end so that she could hear the winner announced. She inhaled a deep breath as Mr. Caldwell stepped to the lectern in the middle of the stage.

"I have the distinct honor of announcing the winner of first prize in this prestigious contest, but before I make that announcement, I would ask all of you to join me in a round of applause for our host and the sponsor of this contest, Mr. Richard Franklin, owner of the Franklin Hotels."

Mr. Franklin stood for a moment and waved to the applauding crowd. "Do get on with your announcement, Mr. Caldwell. I'm sure the contestants are eager to hear who has won."

"Yes, of course." Mr. Caldwell tugged at his collar before making a great show as he removed a slip of paper from an envelope. He cleared his throat and held the paper at arm's length. He was making such a production of the announcement that Rose wouldn't have been surprised to hear a drumroll. "The winner of first prize in the Franklin Hotels contest is the Thompson Pottery Company of East Liverpool, Ohio. Please come forward to accept your award."

Rose hadn't expected to gasp, but the sound escaped her lips without warning. She gripped Rylan's hand. "We lost!"

Though she'd contemplated the idea of losing, in her heart she had truly believed they would win. She ventured a quick look at Mrs. Woodfield. Although the older woman appeared utterly composed, Rose didn't miss the sudden droop of her shoulders. Nor did she miss the look of disappointment stamped on Ewan's face.

She forced a smile and stared at the stage, though she didn't hear a word that was now being uttered. Even though she wanted to be happy for the winners, everyone knew the Thompson Company didn't need another big contract. They were already prosperous. Surely the prize should have gone to a pottery that truly needed Mr. Franklin's contract. She silently chided herself for the selfish thought. The contest had been open to all, not just to those who were in need of a contract. In addition to the contract, the prestige of winning this contest would provide years of benefit to the victor. She only wished the victor would have been McKay Pottery.

Rylan nudged her. "Are you listening?"

She shook herself away from thoughts of Thompson Pottery and back to the present. "I heard the announcement. Thompson Pottery won. What else is there to hear?"

Rylan tipped his head toward the stage. "Mr. Caldwell asked the representative from Thompson Pottery to have a seat on the stage while they continue the presentations."

Rose stared at him blankly. "They're likely going to present awards for the runners-up, which will mean nothing more than a certificate."

Mr. Caldwell gestured for quiet as he once again took command of the festivities. "Now, for the announcement we've all been waiting for: Mr. Franklin, will you please come forward and announce the winner of the grand prize?" He turned toward the hotel owner and sidestepped away from the lectern.

Rose's heart hammered a new beat. "Grand prize? What's he talking about? I thought first prize was the highest award. You mean we still have a chance?" She grasped Rylan's hand in a death grip, afraid to let her hopes soar yet unable to suppress her excitement. "Do you think we may have won the contract?"

He grinned at her. "If you keep talking, we won't be able to hear who has won."

She pressed her lips together as the applause ceased and Mr. Franklin greeted the guests. "When we originally announced this contest, we had planned to award only one prize, but once we received so many excellent entries, I soon realized that I wanted to honor more than one entry, as I explained in the note you received upon your arrival."

Rose leaned close to Rylan. "What note? Did you see a note?"

He shook his head. "Nay, but I didn't go through all the papers. I thought you read them."

"I completely forgot about them when all the questions arose about our entry." Her heart continued to pound as she squeezed his hand. "This means we still have a chance."

Mr. Franklin removed an envelope from his jacket pocket. After withdrawing the enclosed paper, he glanced about the audience. "The grand prize winner and pottery that will produce the china for my hotels is The McKay Pottery of Grafton, West Virginia."

Tears gathered in Rose's eyes as the audience erupted in applause. Rylan nodded toward the stage. "Go up there and accept your award."

She rose from her chair, but before she stepped toward the stage, she extended her hand to Rylan. "Not without you."

Rylan stood beside her, his mouth curved in a broad smile. He pressed his lips to her ear. "I hope you plan to repeat those words for the rest of our lives, Rose McKay, because there is nothing I want to do without you by my side."

The color rose in her cheeks as she stepped onto the stage with Rylan. Winning this contest was what she'd set out to accomplish, but she'd gained so much more.

She held tight to his hand while joy filled her heart. Like the clay on a potter's wheel, God had molded and shaped her. She'd believed only Rylan had trouble with change, but it turned out that she did, as well. For her, the change had been needed in her prideful heart.

"Congratulations." Mr. Franklin handed Rose the trophy, then shook Rylan's hand. "We have prepared a contract that awaits the signature of the McKay Pottery owner. Change is coming your way. I hope you're both ready."

Rylan glanced down at her and smiled. "We certainly are, Mr. Franklin."

The changes came almost immediately. They were treated like royalty the rest of the afternoon and evening. Instead of being on the outside as she'd been during her years at design school, the other artists and potters seemed to seek out their company. Still, as the extended celebration of dining and dancing drew on, Rose longed for only one man's companionship.

Rylan walked up behind her and rested his hands on her upper arms. He leaned close. "Come with me." His breath against her neck made gooseflesh rise.

He let his hand slide down her arm until it touched her fingers and then gently pulled her toward a side door.

"Where are we going?" She'd not been down this maze of back hallways. Were they even supposed to be here?

"I want you to see something. Don't you trust me?"

His husky voice made her heart lurch. "Of course I do."

They exited the hallway into the main lobby of the hotel.

Rylan directed her towards the sitting room she'd been so enthralled with when they first visited the hotel. He stopped outside the slightly ajar doors. "Close your eyes."

She complied and he carefully ushered her inside, keeping his hand snaked about her waist. "You can open them now."

The urn the two of them designed sat on an ornate walnut table in the center of the lobby. Gas lamplight glinted off the gilding. The images she'd imagined, mirrored in the tapestries, the massive furniture, and the Minton tile floor seemed to become one with the urn, pulling them all into place.

"I've never seen my work displayed." Tears pricked her eyes.

"It's perfect, Rose. Imagine what the girls back in art school would say now."

Her heart squeezed. She hadn't thought about them in months, partly because they'd been so busy, but mostly because the man beside her had made her forget the aloneness that had plagued her. "I apologize. I called this my work, but it's our work."

"No, Rose. We may have worked on this together, but this urn is the product of your imagination, your talent, and your heart. I'm a simple potter, but you, my love, are an artist."

She tipped her head so she could look into his eyes. "That makes me the potter's lady, doesn't it?"

"That it does." He placed a kiss on the top of her head.

He walked around the table and ran his hands along the curves of the urn. "This may surprise you, but I'd like to suggest a change."

"Really? You'd like to suggest a change?"

"Yes, me." He licked his lips. "I'm thinking you need a permanent name change."

"You don't like the Potter's Lady?"

"I like Mrs. Rylan Campbell much better, don't you?"

"It does have a nice ring to it." Closing the distance between them, Rylan took her hands, lowered his head to hers, and met her lips in a delicious kiss, glazed with promise.

Her heart, already full to the brim, felt as if it might burst. God had blessed her beyond even what she could have imagined.

## Special Thanks to . . .

. . . My editor, Sharon Asmus, for her beautiful spirit and gift of encouragement.

. . . My acquisitions editor, Charlene Patterson, for her enthusiastic encouragement and ideas for this series.

. . . The entire staff of Bethany House Publishers for their devotion to publishing the best product possible. It is a privilege to work with all of you.

. . . The management and staff of the Herman Laughlin China Company for answering my innumerable questions.

. . . The staff of the Museum of Ceramics located in East Liverpool, Ohio, for sharing their knowledge and creating a detailed display of the pottery-making process in their museum.

. . . Mary Greb-Hall, for her ongoing encouragement, expertise, and sharp eye.

. . . Lorna Seilstad, for her honest critiques and steadfast friendship.

. . . Mary Kay Woodford, my sister, my prayer warrior, my friend.

. . . Justin, Jenna, and Jessa, for their support and the joy they bring to me during the writing process and throughout my life.

. . . Above all, thanks and praise to our Lord Jesus Christ for the opportunity to live my dream and share the wonder of His love through story.

**Judith Miller** is an award-winning author whose avid research and love for history are reflected in her bestselling novels. Judy makes her home in Topeka, Kansas.

# More Fiction From Judith Miller

Visit judithmccoymiller.com to learn more about Judith and her books.

Ewan McKay came to West Virginia to help his uncle Hugh start a brickmaking operation. But when Hugh makes an ill-advised deal, the foundation Ewan has built begins to crumble. Can the former owner's beautiful daughter help Ewan save the brickworks—and his future?

*The Brickmaker's Bride*
REFINED BY LOVE

In the Amana Colonies, family secrets, hidden passions, and the bonds of friendship run deeper than outsiders know. Each independent story in Judith Miller's AMANA series describes the journey of a young woman as she comes of age—and finds love—in this historic community.

HOME TO AMANA: *A Hidden Truth, A Simple Change, A Shining Light*

# You May Also Enjoy...

At Irish Meadows horse farm, two sisters struggle to reconcile their dreams with their father's demanding marriage expectations. Brianna longs to attend college, while Colleen is happy to marry, as long as the man meets *her* standards. Will they find the courage to follow their hearts?

*Irish Meadows* by Susan Anne Mason
COURAGE TO DREAM #1
susanannemason.com

*A powerful retelling of the story of Esther!* In 1944, blond-haired and blue-eyed Jewess Hadassah Benjamin will do all she can to save her people—even if she cannot save herself.

*For Such a Time* by Kate Breslin
katebreslin.com

When a family tragedy derails his college studies, Henry Phillips returns home to the family farm feeling lost and abandoned. Can he and local Margaret Hoffman move beyond their first impressions and find a way to help each other?

*Until the Harvest* by Sarah Loudin Thomas
sarahloudinthomas.com

◆ BETHANYHOUSE